PRESUMING *you*

SANA KHATRI

Presuming You
Copyright © 2021 by Sana Khatri
Cover Design by Sana Khatri
PAPERBACK ISBN: 9798711073444

All rights reserved. No part of this publication may be reproduced or transmitted in any form or by any means, including photocopying, recording, information storage and retrieval systems, or other electronic or mechanical methods, without express written permission from the author, except in the case of brief quotation embodied in reviews and certain other noncommercial uses permitted by the Copyright Law

This is a work of fiction. Names, characters, places, events and incidents are the products of the author's imagination. Any resemblance to actual persons, living or dead, events or locales is purely coincidental.

ALSO BY SANA KHATRI

Those Chance Encounters

Can We Pretend?

To the ones who dare to dream, to hope, and to act.
Don't hold back because of your fears; learn to embrace them.
Life is full of chances and unexpected instances, so why not get ahead
in line and grab yours?

Search for 'Presuming You' on Spotify!

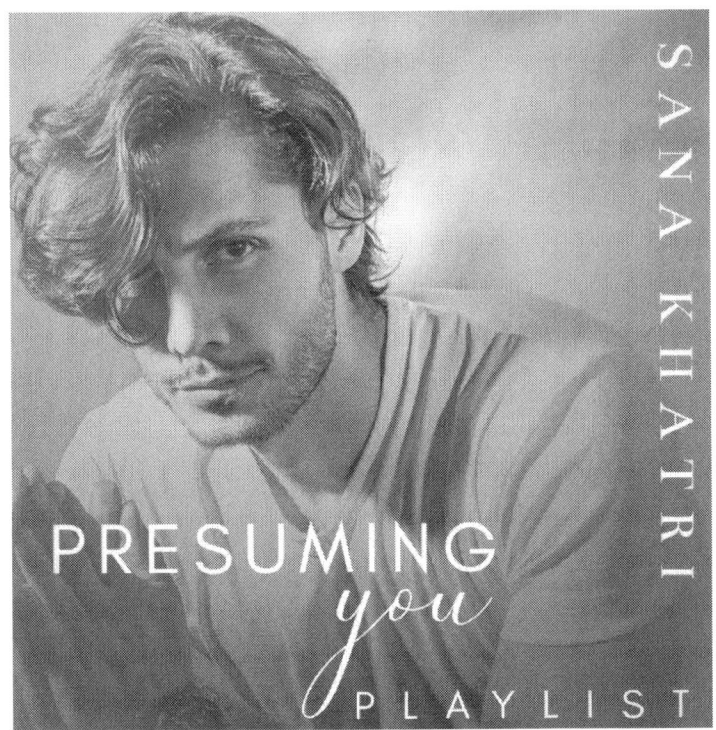

ABOUT THE AUTHOR

Sana Khatri is an International Bestselling author, an IT (Information Technology) graduate, a bunny momma, and a makeup junkie. She resides with her aunts, mother, and her younger brother in Mumbai, India. Because her dad is the one who initially motivated her to keep writing, she makes sure to ask him for book-related opinions and suggestions whenever she needs them. She is an unwavering reader, dreamer, and believer, and prefers to have a speck of reality in her fictitious stories.

Twitter & Instagram:
@isanakhatri

AUTHOR'S NOTE

Hey, you! Yes, YOU! Hello, pretty-face! I can't believe you're reading this; that you've decided to give my story a shot. I'm so thrilled to have you on board. Gallan and Zaira's story is crazy, funny, emotional, steamy, and relatable, and I honestly can't wait for you to go on this ride with them.

Life is busy and hectic as fuck, but I hope I can bring at least a sliver of a smile on your beautiful face through my words and my characters. My #1 goal is to make my readers happy by staying true to myself and writing books that make me feel alive. I really hope Gall and Zaira can do that for you.

Oh, and remember that I love and appreciate you. ALWAYS.

– Love, Sana

A broken door.

A super annoying and adamant rat.

Almost-falls via banana peels.

A destroyed phone.

And a few wild presumptions.

When A-list Hollywood star Gallan Underwood, and graphic novelist Zaira Khan, are trapped inside a trailer, their night turns into a roulette of opportunities, dying dignities, and confessions. Sparks of chemistry allow exploration of a mutual attraction, leading to a bevy of hesitance and truths. Will these two weirdly hilarious souls be able to battle their feelings, their emotions, and everything else that falls face-first into the crazy uptown that is their lives?

PROLOGUE

February 15th, 2020

Captivated – she was absolutely entranced by the closeness of him; by the scent of him, by the lush warmth that coursed through every fiber of her body with him being so near.

The questions in her head were plenty; they were unsteadily audible. She wasn't expecting things to escalate so soon, if to escalate at all, because she was only a spectator, a mere admirer of the illustrious man before her.

She was nothing; he was everything. And together, they made a 'something' that was far beyond her life's normality.

A welcoming chill blanketed her when he slowly, almost tentatively, placed his hands on the small of her back. She shuddered – just a little – and looked up into the eyes of the man who was now holding her. His lips were slightly parted; one of his thighs brushed against hers. She noticed the shift in his pupils, and felt an array of emotions aiding her restless veins.

"But what if I don't wanna let you go? What if I want time to cease – indefinitely?" he whispered, and then bent a little so their gazes met. "Will you stay here – like this – with me, if only for a little longer?"

There was no question about what her answer would be. After all, he ruled her; he was the emperor to the struggling empire that was her stability.

But was she ready for things to change?

Was she ready to dive into something so profound?

Was she ready to experience everything she knew he had to offer?

Maybe.

Hopefully…

"Yes," she said, and then braved placing her hands on his shoulders. "I wanna be *wherever* you are. So I'll stay here with you for as long as you want me to."

His gaze softened, and when he leaned in further, she closed her eyes and accepted her remarkable reality with a smile on her face, and a spark or two of thrill singeing through her skin.

Is this truly happening? she asked herself.

Yes; yes, it is…

1.
zaira

February 07th, 2020 [PRESENT]

"Lights… Camera… ACTION!"

I pushed my glasses up my nose and flinched a little when our director, and the world-renowned asshole, Ross Jonas, yelled the word 'action' with every ounce of energy in his body.

"Ugh, someone please get me a gallon or two of liquid Tylenol," my friend Kenzie murmured from my left.

I chuckled as I adjusted the mouthpiece on my headset. "Go marry a pharmacist. I'm not drugging you anymore."

She scoffed. "You've been doing it for the last seven years, and you'll continue to do it for the rest of your life." When I rolled my eyes at her, she winked and placed an elbow on my shoulder. "Also, pharmacists are bald and overaged perverts. I am so not marrying one."

I looked exaggeratedly at her. "Have I told you that you're an occasional harasser?"

Her brown eyes gleamed as she smirked at me. "Yes, but only a million-and-twenty-three times. That's hardly enough, don't you think?"

"Ugh." I stepped away from her. "We have work to do. Focus."

She shrugged, and then pulled her long black hair in a bun before waking the tablet in her hand.

Work.

Was bringing water and coffee for actors a job?

Was it a job to make sure no one stomped or tripped over the tangled mess of electrical wires surrounding the studio floors?

Well, my mum says no profession is small, and for an Indian Muslim girl like myself, being a part of L.A.'s commercial life is a huge thing. So, getting to work as a crew person for a big budget romance movie was a great opportunity for me...I guess.

I was five when I moved to L.A. with my parents. They're both teachers, and their love for anything and everything book-related inspired me to graduate as an English major.

After working at publishing houses for years, whilst also balancing my degree studies, I felt things starting to get bland for me. So, as soon as I graduated, I decided to start working at movie and television studios for a change. The hustle and adrenaline in those places were crazy, and it was only when I began spending entire days there, did I realize how much I needed that kinda potent thrill in my life.

Kenzie and I became inseparable years ago when I got my first job as an assistant editor at an up-and-coming publishing house. She'd been working there a bit longer than me, and when she saw me almost awestruck by the work environment, and also completely clueless, she showed me the ropes and lifted me up in ways no one ever has.

"Here he comes!" she whispered a little too excitedly in my left ear. "Are you okay? Do you need glucose to manage your BP? Are you breathing? Do you need mouth-to-mouth?"

I whipped my head in her direction and glared at her, but the expression on her face demanded no bullshit, so I just cleared my throat and looked ahead reluctantly.

Life has a bizarre way of working things for you. It's a cunning-minded bitch who cares about nothing but its own entertainment. So, when I got a call about having been accepted to work as a crew member for the movie *Waves That Hold Us*, I wasn't expecting to also be working for the one man I loved and looked up to: Gallan Underwood.

Thirty-three years old. A model. Hollywood's heartthrob. An outstanding and materialistic actor. Entrepreneur.

Yes, *that* Gallan Underwood.

The first time I'd come to know of him was ten years ago. He was one of the leads in this super popular action movie about seven grad students having found out that they possessed supernatural powers which they could use against powerful men and women who were otherwise untouchable by even the law. The movie soon became a fan-favorite franchise, and ever since then, I've been hooked and sailing for Gallan.

"Are you going to give him the book today?" Kenzie asked.

I swallowed and fidgeted with the rim of my glasses, and then opened my mouth to answer her, but my breath caught in my throat when Gallan smiled at his costar and ran a hand over his wavy chocolate-brown hair. His slim-fitted white t-shirt stretched with the movement of his arm, and looked perfectly in sync with his effortlessly faded blue jeans. His 'Ready-to-slice-your-heart-open' jaw, which was peppered with dark stubble, somehow looked sharper than usual in that moment, and his smooth lips glistened when he ran the tip of his tongue over them. His obsidian eyes sparkled against the afternoon light, and when he delivered his line without a single hitch in that husky, flat, and slightly scratchy voice, I almost fell on the ground as a strong wave of internal fangirl seizure took over.

Jesus on a mechanical bull, Gallan was a God-sent miracle on this polluted and overpopulated planet.

We were filming outdoors, so the whole block was closed for the day. The bridge we were set up near, and the welcomingly sunny weather we were graced with – both played as the perfect backdrop for Gallan to shoot a heartfelt scene with his reel-life love interest.

I released a breath – the one I was holding – and relaxed a little when Ross yelled 'CUT', and the actors and stylists scattered around like insects on a tree trunk.

"That's a wrap for today. Rest up, and I'll see you guys tomorrow," he announced.

I pulled the headset off my head and started walking towards the camera guys.

"Wait," Kenzie said, and then grabbed my arm. "You didn't answer my question, Z."

I turned so I could look at her, so I could silently show her my fears and hesitance.

"Hey." She pulled me back, and when I faced her fully, her expression softened, and she placed her hands on my shoulders before giving them a squeeze. "I know you're scared, Zaira, but you have a fair opportunity here, and it kills me that you're not acting on it. After all, how many authors and graphic novelists do you think can say that they've worked for their muses, and have also had a chance to show their work to said muses?"

She was right; Kenzie made a fair point.

I was a self-published graphic novelist, and had spent the last year or so writing and designing my latest comic, *The Ice Bearer*. The book name was inspired by this fantasy book I'd read last year, *A Twisted Belief*, and went really well with my superhero's powers.

Graham Landers, my comic lead, who was inspired by Gallan, controlled ice and frost, and was the leader of a small group of supernatural humans. I'd worked my ass off on the storyline, and designing every single one of the graphics present in the book had taken a lot out of me. I hadn't given up, though, because I wanted my story to be out there in the world, and for people all around the globe to meet Graham Landers and his squad.

I'd dedicated the book to Gallan, because if it wasn't for him and his fantastic work in movies, I wouldn't have been motivated to create an entire story, let alone its vast range of diverse characters.

The Ice Bearer wasn't my first comic; it was my 3rd. But the hard work I'd put into it exceeded that of the other two.

"I can't, Ken," I said, and then shook my head at her. "I know it was my idea to give him a copy of *The Ice Bearer*, but I just…I can't do it. What if he thinks I'm a creep or something? What if he thinks I only got a job here so I could get close to him? The last thing I want is for him to despise me."

My best friend looked at me like I'd just told her that I'd been impregnated by an alien. "Are you for real right now?" She seemed a little too pissed for my comfort.

I shrugged, and shielded my eyes against the glaring afternoon sun. "I'm just not strong enough to do it, Ken, that's all."

"You are," she said. "You're the strongest person I know, Z. You've faced challenges all your life, and you've always excelled over them. You made a place in this society – where some people still see Muslims as enemies – and are thriving so fucking amazingly. If you are determined enough to live your dream and to do what you love to, then giving Gallan a copy of your book – which you basically wrote for him – shouldn't be a hard task. It should be a delicious piece of cake, babe."

I sighed and ran a hand over my wavy brown hair. "You're very bad for my ego."

She chuckled. "Didn't know you even had one."

I rolled my eyes and shook my head. "I'll do it; I'll give him the copy. But I'll do it for you, and you only."

"Right…" she drawled.

"Don't be an ass. I can still change my mind," I told her.

"You wouldn't dare." She then looked over my shoulder. "I mean, it's practically too late for that anyway."

"What?"

She grinned like Joker from Batman, and then turned me around.

I stifled a cough when my saliva got stuck in my throat, and clenched my hands when they began shaking a little.

Gallan – out of his costume – stood only a few feet away from me with his manager, Shane. His blue flannel and dark jeans looked stunning on him, and as he continued to speak animatedly with the guy who managed him, I couldn't help but stare at him. He was a canvas of perfection, and I? Well, I was simply an admirer.

"Here." Kenzie handed the extra copy of my comic to me, which I kept in my purse in case I grew some balls to finally approach my real-life Graham Landers. "Just go for it! I'll be here the whole time, so don't worry."

"How did you get it? It's supposed to be in my locker back at the studio."

She clicked her tongue. "That's where I got it from, silly."

"But–"

"Shh." She glared at me. "You have your copy, and Gallan is here. It's all that matters."

I blinked at her. "I can't do it." My voice was suddenly squeaky, which made me flinch.

"You can! You got this, bish!"

My heart was pounding like crazy, and it was so very hard to focus on one thing, because my mind was thinking of a hundred different things at the same damn time.

What was I gonna say?

What would he say?

How would he react?

Outcomes.

Casualties.

Opinions and–

"Zaira!" Kenzie hissed, and when I glanced at her, I found her scowling at me. "Go! He's going to leave if you don't."

"Uh…"

Oh God, oh God, oh God.

"Just. Fucking. Go." She pushed me in his direction.

I yelped, and then crouched on all fours like a fucking rhinoceros when my left foot came in contact with one of the wires on the ground. My palms hurt, and my dignity poisoned itself, but other than that, I was fine. I think.

I heard Kenzie gasp from behind me, and the conversation Gallan and Shane were in between? Yeah, it stopped the moment I fell face-first to my looming pile of humiliation.

"Ma'am, are you all right?" Shane asked.

I closed my eyes and pressed my lips together before shamefully getting to my feet. Adjusting my crooked glasses, I clutched my comic tighter and released a few long breaths in order to calm myself down.

A deep breath in. A slow one out.

In… Out.

In. Out.

In, and out…

I slowly opened my eyes, and found Gallan looking worriedly at me.

Great.

Just. Fucking. Great.

This is exactly how I'd envisioned meeting my favorite actor for the first time.

"Hey," Gallan said with a smile, and then waved at me. "You alright there?" He looked at me a little sympathetically, which resulted in my entire body to heat in embarrassment.

"Good luck," Kenzie whispered from behind, and I knew she was only teasing me over my predicament.

I smiled awkwardly at the two men before me, and then began walking towards Gallan.

It was too late to back out anyway. I had to do this now. I hadn't taken that animal-like fall for nothing, after all.

Breathe, Zaira, I told myself. *Fucking breathe, or else you'll choke yourself and turn blue in the face like Joffrey Baratheon.*

A deep breath in. A slow one out.

In… Out.

In. Out.

In, and out…

Inevitable collision, here I come…

2.
gallan

February 07th, 2020

"I'm the reason she's hosting the episode anyway. Can't you just ask her to cancel or reschedule it?" I said, and arched a brow at my manager.

Shane narrowed his dark eyes at me. "Careful, G; your asshole side is showing."

I chuckled. "I'm not an asshole."

"Of course." He rolled his eyes. "Fiona agreed to telecast this special edition episode for early promo purposes for *Waves That Hold Us*. Her talk show doesn't even air on Wednesdays, but she's doing it for *you*. It'd be wrong to just cancel on her like this, when all the preparations have already been made."

"I can't skip on the weekly traditions. You've known me for decades, Shane, and you know that my Wednesdays are dedicated to my parents, and my parents *only*. I can't just up and say no to them."

As someone who is always filming, and also managing his own clothing line, I hardly have time for personal stuff. I'd decided years ago that my Wednesdays would be dedicated to my mom and dad, because I loved them with every fiber of my being. They were the reason I was where I was in my life. It's their hard work that has made me a successful actor and businessman. They are my world, and all the fame and money – it doesn't even hold a candle against their importance in my life.

Shane sighed. "I know it's my bad that I booked the interview, but it's the only open spot the production was willing to give us for the movie's pre-promotion." When I raised my arms to my sides in silent question, he ran a hand over his salt-and-pepper beard. "Fine, I'll contact Fiona and ask her to reschedule. I'll tell her that you got double-booked for photoshoots and a press junket. But know that if she ends up biting my ears off or suing me, I'm immediately dropping you as a client."

I grinned. "No wonder that bald head of yours is always glowing. You're full of *bright* ideas, Shane."

He huffed. "Yeah, yeah; go ahead and tease me more. I'm here merely for your entertainment, after all."

I smirked, and then pulled at the collar of my flannel when the air around us warmed further. "You know I love you, man, and I tease only because I care."

The guy had been managing me since my early modeling days, and was a massive part of all my success and career climbs.

Shane opened his mouth to tell me something, but stopped when someone to my right yelped suddenly.

We both looked in the direction of the voice, and I found a figure on the ground, crouched on all fours, with her brown hair covering most of her facial features.

"Ma'am, are you alright?" Shane asked.

The girl didn't answer, and then slowly got to her feet. She was holding something in her hand; I don't know what. And when she opened her eyes, mine landed on her face. I was momentarily left awestruck by her rich caramel skin, and the warmth in her brown eyes – that were barricaded behind a pair of classic black glasses. Her soft, round cheeks seemed flushed, and her slightly pouty lips were pressed together as she looked at me. She had on a pair of grey skintight jeans and a plain pink shirt, and even though her attire was nothing of the extraordinary sort, she somehow looked…*beautiful* in it.

Whoa there, Underwood. Reign your sexual horses in, I internally chastised myself. *You don't even know this girl, so calm the fuck down, dude.*

"Hey," I said with a casual smile, and then waved at her. "You alright there?"

God, she was stunning. With a short form and a full body, the girl standing before me was a delight; she was a sight.

What? I am a hot-blooded man who appreciates the wonders of this world with open arms. *Jeez.*

She gave me a wobbly smile, one that made me grin, and began walking towards me. Her hair was a mess of glossy waves, and she kept fidgeting with it as she got closer to me.

Who are you? I wanted to ask, but couldn't because she'd left me speechless.

Our eyes met when she stopped right in front of me, and I swear on all that's holy in this world that every speck of me came alive with that one look from her.

She shifted on her feet and blinked up at me, and God, the pure innocence that she channeled – it magnetized me; it held me captive.

Fucked – I was completely, utterly, and entirely fucked.

Fantastic.

Fan-fucking-tastic.

3.
zaira

February 07th, 2020

With my legs shaking, I stopped in front of Gallan.

"H…he…hey," I all but whispered, because that was all I was capable of in that moment.

"Hi." He smiled down at me. "Are you hurt?"

I shook my head a little and pushed my glasses up my nose. "No."

"Great, that's good." He flinched a little after saying that, and I realized that he was just as nervous about this impromptu encounter as I was.

Shane cleared his throat a little too theatrically, but Gallan didn't acknowledge him. He instead chose to keep his focus on me.

"Umm, so…uh," I stuttered, and felt beads of sweat running down my spine. "So, uh, I'm a graphic novelist, and…uh, I…" I licked my lips out of extreme anxiety.

He raised a brow as a silent urge for me to continue.

I swallowed and shifted on my feet again. "I'm…I recently published my third comic, and I…" I sighed, completely exasperated with myself, and then decided to just…do it. So, in my haze of determination, I shoved the copy of *The Ice Bearer* at him. Like, I *actually* slapped the book on his chest. I don't know why I did that, but the bird had already left the nest, so all I could do now was watch its demise with horror in my heart.

Gallan looked at his chest, and then slowly clutched the edge of the book. He gently pulled the copy from me, which resulted in our hands to brush ever so slightly. I pressed my teeth over my bottom lip when a strong, unnamable sensation coursed through my body due to that split-second action.

"The book…I mean, the *comic*, is inspired by you, and is also dedicated to you," I said to him, and then wrung my hands together to prevent them from trembling.

He looked at me with a brilliant smile. "Wow, really?" His eyes sparkled beautifully against the afternoon light.

His reaction helped me relax a little, and my lips spread into an easy smile. "Yeah. It took me more than a year to get it ready."

Gallan looked impressed. "That's outstanding, seriously." He glanced at the comic. "I've read loads of these as a kid, but this art, and the vibrant coloration – it's something I've never seen before."

Be still, my drooling heart.

"Thanks." My face and neck flushed at his compliment.

He grinned at me. "No, thank *you* for creating something so unique, and for having me as a muse. It's an honor, truly." He then looked at the book again. "Zaira Khan…" he said my name in that husky baritone of his, which resulted in goosebumps to blanket my entire body. "Did I say it right?" he asked as our gazes met again.

I swallowed and nodded. "Yeah." *Way to sound like a Chihuahua, Zaira.*

But Gallan didn't seem to mind my voice failure. Not one bit. "That's a beautiful name." He then offered a hand for a shake. "It's so nice to meet you, Zaira."

Oh Lord… The way he pronounced my name – it enthralled me; it almost hypnotized me.

I mustered all my strength and shook his hand, only to feel out of breath when the warmth of his skin soothed my otherwise cold palm.

"Thank you for being so kind and supportive about this," I said to him. "I was nervous out of my mind."

He chuckled. "Don't worry about it. I'm still trying to process the fact that someone wrote an entire book inspired by me." He didn't let go of my hand, but instead, squeezed it a little.

I blushed. "You have millions and millions of fans around the world. I'm sure they've done things way better for you than create a comic."

He shook his head and finally let go of my hand. "Maybe, but what you did is very special. I can't wait to read it."

My breath hitched in my throat, and a minor wave of panic took over.

Gallan sensed it, and chuckled before taking half a step towards me. "Hey, relax." He placed a hand on my shoulder. "I'm sure the book is great."

"Uh…"

He laughed. "*Relax*, Zaira."

I released a slow breath and managed to smile at him through my glaring nervousness. "Sorry."

He nodded. "It's fine, and your reaction is understandable. You've worked hard on this book, and expect the best of results. Don't worry, I'll get back to you as soon as I've finished reading it."

My eyes widened. "You will?"

He smirked. "Hell yeah."

"Thanks. My email and social media details are mentioned on the very last page."

He winked at me. "Aye-aye, ma'am."

I grinned. "Thank you once again."

He nodded. "You got it."

"G." Shane placed a hand on his arm. "We gotta go."

Gallan sighed. "Sure." He looked at me with a smile. "I gotta head to a work meeting. I'll be in touch, though. Thanks for making my day with this." He brought the book up to his face and waved it at me.

I chuckled. "I think it's the other way around, but you're welcome." I waved at him and Shane, and swiveled on my feet before walking away.

I had only taken my seventh step, though, when I heard Gallan say something to Shane that pinched at my heart and clogged my throat.

"Take care of this."

"You got it, boss."

My lips parted, and my tears freefell.

Take care of this.

He'd lied.

He'd acted in front of me.

Gallan didn't care about my dedication towards him; he didn't care about my book.

He was already getting rid of it...

Take care of this.

I glanced up, and found Kenzie looking sadly at me. She'd heard, and even *seen* Gallan hand my book over to Shane.

"Oh, Z..." She wrapped her arms around me when I fell against her. "I'm so sorry. I'm sorry I pushed you to approach him."

I sniffed and placed the side of my face on her shoulder. "It's not your fault he's an inconsiderate asshole." A wave of sorrow washed over me after that, and I began crying harder right there and then in my best friend's arms.

"Screw him, babe. You're worth a million Gallan Underwoods," she said.

I closed my eyes and sobbed against her, because truthfully, there was nothing else I could do, nor wanted to...

4.

February 15th, 2020

Adam Lambert's angelic voice blasted through the AirPods in my ears as I sang along to *Superpower* and tapped my feet to the catchy music. I mean, it was 1:57a.m., and there was no one at the studio but me and a couple other crew guys, so who'd witness me going crazy?

We had been setting things up for a filming session that was supposed to start in around 7 hours. Woo, joy.

I bobbed my head to the song and placed the last of the lighting in its place before turning in a circle and shaking my hips to the chorus.

> *"I get back up when I fall*
> *Rip the paint from the wall*
> *When I win, I'mma run and take the money*
> *Try to put me in a box*
> *Make me something I'm not*
> *Don't give a fuck 'cause I'm gonna take back…*
> *My superpower!"*

Mike, one of the crew guys, waved at me, and then gestured behind him with a thumb, letting me know that him and his boyfriend Curt were leaving.

I waved back at him, and then wrapped some of the spare wires neatly before heading towards the locker-room.

The song changed, and as I began singing along, it stopped suddenly, indicating that I had an incoming call.

I looked down at my phone, and smiled big when my mum's face flashed on the screen.

"Hey, gorgeous," I chirped as I received the call, and placed my AirPods in the back pocket of my jeans.

Mum chuckled. "Hey yourself, young lady. How are you?"

I rolled my eyes. "Mum, I'm fine. You asking the same question thirty times each day won't change my answer."

"Well, is your answer an honest one, or is it something you say just to make your old lady feel better?"

I laughed. "I'm being honest; I'm fine."

It'd been a week since I'd given Gallan *The Ice Bearer*. He'd gone back to ignoring me, just like he used to before I'd approached him with my book. I don't know why I thought it'd be a good idea to give him a copy of my work in the first place. I mean, a guy as famous as him must receive presents far more precious than a silly comic book.

I gave him his coffee every morning, as usual, but he didn't spare me a single glance. It shouldn't hurt, but I don't know why it did. It hurt a *lot*. I guess it was because he'd been so incredibly polite and kind to me about the whole thing that seeing the *real* him didn't sit well with my emotions and the thoughts in my head.

"Zaira?" came Mum's voice through the phone.

"Yeah?"

She sighed. "Are you sure you're okay? I know how upset you were just a few days ago when you told me about that as–"

"Mumma! Language!" I pressed my lips together to contain my laughter.

"I didn't even say anything!"

"But you were going to; I know you."

She chuckled. "Yes, well, he hurt my daughter, so he's currently a piece of shit in my eyes."

I tipped my head back and laughed. "Oof, Mother Dear. What's gotten into you tonight?"

She clicked her tongue. "Nothing. I'm just a huge fan of my very talented baby girl."

I grinned. "I love you, Mum."

"I love you too, *meri gudiya*." *Meri gudiya*: my doll. Mum always called me that.

I smiled. "How's Dad?"

"Busy watching those silly crime shows with the neighbors." She sighed again.

I stopped in my tracks when I realized that I'd wandered off to the trailer section while chatting with her. "What is it? What's that sigh for?" I asked.

"He misses you, your dad," she said.

"Mum, I live five blocks away from you."

She giggled, an action that was very unlike her. "I know, but you're either always at work, or busy writing and sketching away on your computer. It's been too long since we've had a family day."

I released a long breath. "I'm sorry."

"Don't be. We're happy that you enjoy what you do."

I smiled again. "This Sunday. You, me, and Dad. We'll have an outdoor day. No work, and no writing or sketching. Just family bonding time. Sound good?"

"Yes!" she said a little too excitedly. "But dinner will be homemade. I'll make your favorite biryani and kheer."

My mouth watered on instant. "Me loves you. SO MUCH."

Mum laughed. "Yes, yes. Of course you do."

I smirked. "Alright, I gotta go. I still have a few things to check on before I head home."

"Okay. Take care, baby. I'll call again later."

I chuckled. "I know you will. Bye, Mum."

"Bye, love."

I disconnected the call and slid my phone into my back pocket. I turned, and was about to head towards the studio when strong noises sounded from the trailer behind me. The hair on the back of my neck stood as fear gripped me immediately.

BANG!

CLACK!

THUD!

I swallowed and braved turning around, and wrapped my arms around myself when the noises grew louder. The trailer's door was slightly ajar, and when I looked to the left – at the name plastered on one of the windows – I cursed and gritted my teeth.

GALLAN UNDERWOOD

Of course it was his trailer. It was the fanciest one among the dozen or so of them that were scattered around the open area.

"Fuck!" someone yelled from inside.

I gasped and placed a hand over my heart. I licked my dry lips and took a step forward, and then two backwards when something crashed inside the trailer. My heart and mind raced simultaneously. Scared – I was absolutely *terrified* for Gallan.

What if someone was attacking him?

Was he being murdered?

"Oh God," I whispered, and then pulled my phone out of my pocket before running towards the trailer. "Don't die, don't die, don't die."

Thank the Lord I'd spoken to my mother a final time. At least now when I get shot or stabbed in the head, I could close my eyes in relief.

Until that very moment, I wasn't aware that I was going to get brutally murdered in Gallan fucking Underwood's posh trailer. Well, life – that bitch – had played me again, and this time, it was *me* who'd galloped straight towards my end.

Quite literally.

5.
gallan

February 15th, 2020

"**F**uck!" I yelled when I tripped over the life-size Twinkie prop on my trailer floor. It was going to be used in *Waves That Hold Us, and* it also looked like a deformed plushy dick. Ross Jonas was one twisted fucker.

I placed my hands on the vanity table to prevent myself from falling, and then groaned when a familiar squeak sounded from behind me.

Rat. There was a freaking *rat* in my trailer. I'd been trying to get ahold of it for the last hour or so, but the pesky little thing kept running away from me. Thank God I'd turned the trailer engine on before getting in, otherwise I'd have to look for the hairy fucker in the dark.

My trailer looked like a crime scene, with things either broken, torn, or violently thrown away. I admit that none of the above actions were performed by the rat; it was all *me*, but the annoying rodent was the reason why I had to reluctantly, and direly, unleash my…uncivil side.

"Choke me with a cucumber," I muttered, and then straightened before flinching at the mess around me. "My bank account is so going to divorce me."

I heard the trailer door open, and immediately turned to see who was outside.

Shit, was it a burglar? I had no weapon to protect myself.

"Jesus fucking Christ…" I heard a familiar voice say in a familiar accent, right before Zaira's face came into view. She stepped inside the trailer, and before I could warn her, her right sneaker came in contact with the banana peel on the floor – curtesy of Mr. Rat – and she went flying forward. Her phone fell over with a sickening *crash*, which made me flinch.

"Ahhhhh!" she screamed, and right before she could fall face-first on the ground, I ran and grabbed her by the arm.

Her foot – the one that'd slipped backwards because of the banana peel – hit harshly against the trailer door, which resulted in said door to shut, and *lock*, with a painful *bang*.

"No…" I said, and then let go of Zaira's arm. "No, no, no!" I tried unlocking the door, tried pulling at the handle, but nothing worked. *Of course it didn't work.*

"Why isn't it opening?" Zaira asked from behind. There was panic in her voice.

I placed my forehead against the door and closed my eyes. "Because it's faulty," I mumbled, and then shook my head. "The repair guy hasn't shown up to fix it yet. It's been broken for days, and only opens from the outside."

"*What?*" she yelled. "You're saying we're stuck here?!"

God, why did her accent turn me on so much? Maybe I had a culture preference, and hadn't realized it until that moment.

I sighed and opened my eyes before turning around and facing her. She looked so adorable with her messy brown hair and those big black glasses. And damn if her wide hourglass figure didn't keep taunting me every time I dragged my gaze over every worship-able inch of it.

Zaira was wearing skintight denim jeans and a loose bubblegum-pink t-shirt with the word '*BUSTY!*' written inside a comic speech bubble, right in the center of the t-shirt.

She sure was busty, that girl. It was hard – pun intended – to stay decent with those perfect tits of hers teasing me from behind that thin layer of clothing.

Focus, Underwood, I internally chastised myself. *Fucking focus.*

"Well, it would seem like we're stuck in here, yes," I told her.

"*Well*," she mocked, and then fixed her glasses before shooting daggers at me, "then call someone to get us out."

Whoa… What was up with her? She was acting like I'd stolen her favorite lingerie or something.

"There's no cell service here, and I don't have a landline in this trailer," I said.

"Are you for real right now?" She stomped over to the only window in the trailer before opening it. "Try now," she all but ordered.

I gritted my teeth at her attitude. This is *not* the version of her I'd seen a week ago.

"You think I haven't attempted that?" I said with an edge in my voice.

"Try again. There's no harm in it, is there?"

"Why don't *you* try it?" I asked, and then clicked my tongue before looking at her broken phone on the floor. "Ah…" I shook my head. "My bad… That option is completely out of the question for you. How insensitive of me."

She was fuming, and for some bizarre reason, I was enjoying every bit of her reaction, even with a hairy crisis on the loose.

"You're an asshole!" she screamed. "I should've known a guy like you would be like…like…" She gestured at me with a hand. "*This*."

"Excuse me?" I stepped forward, and muttered a curse when I half-tripped over a broken piece of wood.

Zaira's lips twitched, but she didn't mock me over my little accident. "I came in here because I thought you were being murdered," she said. "Thought maybe I'd witness it with my own eyes." She had that smug look on her face that Mickey Mouse has when he knows he'll be banging Minnie soon.

"What has gotten into you?" I asked, because I was seriously confused by her behavior. "This is not how you acted a week ago."

She scoffed. "Why do you care?"

She made a fair point, but the thing is, I just couldn't help but care.

"Because much to your dismay, I am *not* an asshole, Zaira."

Something flickered in her eyes at that, but her expression remained stone-cold. "Try making a call again," she said. She averted her gaze from me, and then ran it over my destroyed trailer. "What the fuck happened here? What are you even doing in here at this time of the night?"

I wanted to ask '*Why do you care?*', but refrained myself from doing so.

"I forgot my wallet here after the shoot," I told the truth. "Came here to grab it, and found a rat on my vanity table. Some crew guy must've left the door open, which made it easy for the little dipshit to get in. I've been chasing it ever since, but can't get it to leave."

Zaira placed a hand over her mouth and laughed. Her long nails were painted black, and the immediate thought of her hand wrapped around my cock invaded my head.

Way to stay decent, Underwood.

I swallowed and shifted on my feet when the situation behind my pants got a bit…congested.

"Yeah, yeah. Laugh away at my misery," I said. "Ha-ha-ha, Gallan Underwood chases rats in his trailer. Ha-ha-ha, and he can't even catch them! What a loser."

She rolled her eyes and folded her arms over her chest before narrowing her eyes at me. "You're not funny."

"And ha-ha-ha, he's not even funny!" I said in mock-amusement.

She bit her bottom lip to hide her grin, but I could very easily see the curve of her lips.

"What happened here?" she asked, and walked up to the decimated food/snack area next to the kitchen. She'd completely forgotten about practically ordering me to make a call. I guess I didn't mind that she had.

I slid my hands into the pockets of my jeans before walking over to her. "The rat and some of its friends ate everything. I was able to shoo them all away, but one is still in here," I said, and then stood next to her.

She looked up at me. "How do you know the rest were his friends and not his family members?"

I glanced down at her. "Are you making fun of me, Zaira?"

She shrugged, and via the LED lights above us, I saw a gleam in her eyes that almost set me on fire.

I was so fucked.

"Maybe," she said. "What are you gonna do if I am? Chase me around the ruins that were once your posh trailer?"

I opened my mouth to answer, but nothing came out. Absolutely *nothing*.

What did I tell you? *I was fucked.*

I was *so* fucked, that even the word 'fucked' seemed hesitant to be associated with me.

Now, wasn't that a totally screwed up psychology on my part?

God, I needed alcohol. Alcohol and sleep. Preferably in the same order.

STAT.

6.
Zaira

February 15th, 2020

In a matter of minutes, I'd decided to run to Gallan's trailer in order to save his life, slipped over a banana peel, broken my phone, and almost lost my head in the process of tripping over my ass. During all of this, I'd also learned that Gallan was a funny and decent guy, with an impossibly beautiful face and ridiculously sexy lips. I've been aware of the last two facts for years, but thought I should clarify. Just in case.

But, with all things considered, the guy is an actor, so his behavior towards me could be an act of deceit.

Maybe…

"I don't wanna chase you," he said in response to my question. "I don't have the energy nor the time for it."

Ouch. Why did that hurt so much?

"Wow… And you say you're not an asshole," I mumbled.

He shifted so he could look at me better. "What the fuck's your problem anyway, huh? What have I even done to offend you?"

Was he serious?

"Are you serious?" I turned and glared at him. "You really don't know?" When he widened his arms by his sides with a clueless expression on his face, I ran my fingers through my hair in frustration. "Right after I gave you my comic, you asked your manager to '*take care*' of it. My question to you is: Why accept my book? Why lie about wanting to read it? Why tell me that you're going to give me a feedback on it when you weren't even going to keep it in the first place?"

He narrowed his eyes at me. "That's…three questions. You said 'question', not 'questions'," he said.

What? Was he for real?

I pivoted on my feet, ready to walk away from him, but he grabbed my hand and turned me around. His pull was strong, and took me off balance, because I had to place a palm over his chest to brace myself.

Gallan leaned in a little, which resulted in our eyes to meet. "And what makes you think my statement to Shane meant what *you* think it meant?" he asked.

I swallowed and fisted his grey t-shirt when his warm, minty breaths feathered over my left cheek. "I…I don't know." Jeez, I sounded like a duck in heat.

He shook his head and pulled me closer. "Zaira, I would *never* do that." His expression showed hurt. "The fact that you think I'm a shallow piece of shit – it's shocking and saddening."

I didn't know what to say, so I chose to remain quiet. After all, I'd lost the very last shred of my dignity already.

"When I asked Shane to take care of your book," he continued, knowing that I was too embarrassed by my assumption of him to say anything, "I meant *actually* taking care of it. To keep it safe. I knew that if I kept it with me during the meeting last week, I'd end up losing it. Shane handed it to me later that day, and I've been reading a chapter or two of it every day since then. I'm a slow reader, so it's taking me a while."

Oh. My. God.

Dear Ground,

Could you please open up and swallow me whole, leaving behind no traces of my stupid existence? Thank you very much.

Sincerely

Zaira 'I-Wanna-Die' Khan

"I…I…" I didn't know what to say to him.

He sighed. "You presuming that I'm a complete douchebag is hurtful, but because you're a true fan and have worked so hard on *The Ice Bearer*, I'll forgive you. Just this once, though," he said, and I saw the mirth in his eyes a moment before he grinned down at me.

"Huh, what?" I tilted my head to the side.

He chuckled. "I forgive you, Zaira," he said.

"For what?"

"For seeing me in the wrong light," he answered casually, and then pushed his wavy brown hair to the side.

I raised a brow. "I didn't ask for forgiveness."

"But you were going to." What a cocky ass. Cocky, and unbelievably *handsome*.

"I wasn't going to," I said.

"Hmm… Okay, if you say so."

"You ignored me the whole week. I got you your coffee every morning after giving you the book, and you didn't even acknowledge me. Not once."

Something shifted in his eyes at that. "Do you want me to be honest about it, or do you want me to lie?"

My heart hammered in my chest. "Honest."

He blinked once. "I'm madly attracted to you, Zaira," he said, and those words took the breath right out of me. "I'm so fucking attracted to you that it scares me. I think about you like it's nobody's business, and I've been trying to come up with ways to ask you out on a date ever since you first smiled at me. Shane says what I'm experiencing isn't good for my career, but fuck if I care what he thinks. I want what I want, and what I want is *you*."

I inhaled sharply, and felt heat creep up my body at the sincerity in his words, at the honesty on his face. But above it all, it were his eyes that displayed his truth.

Gallan's eyes were an ocean of stories, of things he didn't say, but preferred only to show.

I wanted to tell him something, but I didn't know what. I'd been attracted to him even before he knew me. I looked up to him; I was inspired by him. And the fact that he felt what he said he did, for someone like *me*, meant the absolute world to me.

Why don't you wanna chase me, then? I wanted to question him. *If you're attracted to me, then why don't you wanna give into the run?*

Gallan let go of my hand and stepped back, and the expression on his face changed from intense to carefree. "So, anyways. Are you hungry?" he asked.

Uh…

Wow, that was a quick shift of behavior.

"Umm…" I glanced at the destroyed food table. "I am, but…"

He chuckled, and then pointed behind me with a finger. "The kitchen cabinets are always locked. With a little help from you, I think we'll be able to clean the countertop and make it accessible again."

He appeared a little too eager to do anything but talk about his confession to me.

Oh well…

I looked at the kitchen. There were wood pieces and torn pillows thrown on the counter, but other than that, everything seemed to be in good shape.

I pushed my glasses up my nose when they slipped down a little. "You really went wild over the rat, huh?" I asked Gallan.

He scratched the back of his head sheepishly. "I may have taken things a little too seriously."

I chuckled. "I don't see it now, the rat. You think it ran away?"

"Doubt it, but I hope it did."

I nodded. "Well, let's get to cleaning, then, because I'm *starving*."

He laughed. "Yeah, of course. Let's do it," he said with a smile.

7.
gallan

February 15th, 2020

"You know, I've always wondered where the name Gallan came from," Zaira said as she continued to sauté oil and cumin seeds in a pan. "The tabloids have never spoken about it. I mean, you're an American – c*learly* – but your name is kinda English. So, what's the story?"

I arched a brow. "Clarify your need for emphasizing the word 'clearly'." I handed her some chopped green chilies, which she added into the pan, resulting in a loud *whoosh* to sound from it.

She clicked her tongue, and then added a couple of curry leaves and a spoonful of chili sauce into the pan. "I didn't mean to emphasize it. It just happened."

I chuckled and shook my head. "Okay…" I began piecing some potatoes. "To answer your question: my mom is Greek, and so is the name Gallan. She came to L.A. years ago from Athens to start her own bakery, and that's when she met my dad. He was her property dealer.

Mom picked the name Gallan for me right after I was born, and I absolutely love it. The tabloids don't talk about it because I don't like mentioning my parents, *or* Mom's origin to them. Her and Dad aren't made for the spotlight, so I don't pressure them to stand under one."

"Ah…" Zaira nodded. "That makes complete sense." She sorted some coriander leaves, which I thankfully had in my fridge, in a small bowl.

"But…" she turned to me suddenly, "you don't have an accent. Like, *at all*. How's that even possible?"

I smiled. "Well, over the years, Mom tried teaching Greek to me, but I refused – *profusely*." I chuckled at the old memories of the two of us arguing about me behaving 'too Americanly'. "She gave up after a while, because she knew I was stubborn – just like my dad. And honestly, I was, *and still am*, very thankful to her for it."

Zaira snickered. "Do you guys visit Athens?"

I grinned. "Oh yeah; every year. We celebrate Mom's birthday there. It makes her feel at home. My family trips are not public knowledge, as you already know that–"

"Your parents prefer to stay away from the spotlight; you told me," Zaira said with a smile.

"Yeah." I smiled back at her.

"Must be nice to just…escape the limelight for a few days. I can only imagine how hectic being so popular must be for you."

I shuddered in response, which made her laugh, and my damn heart swan-dived in my chest upon watching her face light up so beautifully.

After we'd cleaned the kitchen, she'd suggested on cooking *aloo sabjhi*, an Indian dish, for us. It was an overall quick and simple recipe, and sounded pretty delicious for me to say no to. I had some pop tarts that we were going to use as dessert, and because Zaira didn't drink alcohol, I'd decided to stick with diet Coke as our late-night dinner beverage.

She hadn't pushed me to talk to her about the confession I'd made, which was something I was grateful for. I knew she wanted to discuss it, though; I could see it in her body language. But I wasn't sure if I wanted to talk about it. Not yet, at least.

It had shocked me how easily I'd told her what I felt about her. I'd been struggling for days to talk to her, and with Shane looming over me like eminent death, I had no other option but to ignore her. I could've contacted her via email or social media, yes, but where was the authenticity in that? The digital communication method was great, and I truly appreciated it, but not when it came to expressing my feelings for the very first time to a woman I liked.

"So, what's *your* story?" I asked, and gestured for her to step aside so I could take over the cooking. "You're *clearly* not an American."

She rolled her eyes at my use of the word 'clearly', but I saw her lips curving upwards anyway.

"Well, my parents and I moved here from India when I was pretty young," she said. "They're both professors at a university, and…" She shrugged. "And nothing." She giggled, which made me smile. "There's nothing interesting about me. I'm not an A-list Hollywood star or anything. I'm just a girl who works hard, makes mistakes, learns from them, and lives every day as it comes." She then looked up at me. "There; that's my story."

"I love it," I told her. "I love your story. It's genuine and grounding. It's *human*."

Her eyes sparkled against the kitchen lights. "Yeah? You don't find it boring?"

My hands were itching to touch those soft cheeks of hers.

"No, not one bit. I think I like yours more than I like mine."

She blushed and looked away.

She was an Indian…

My hardening-by-every-passing-second dick really appreciated that fact. Like, *really*.

"So, no siblings?" I asked.

She glanced at me again, most definitely surprised by how I'd changed the vibe between us so quickly. "No," she said. "I'm an only child."

"Same. My mom couldn't have kids after me."

She frowned. "That's unfortunate."

"Yeah?" I raised a brow.

She smiled and playfully pushed at my arm. "Don't be a dick."

I chuckled. "I can't help it; it just happens sometimes. Like occasional seizures."

She slapped a palm over her forehead. "*Pagal insaan*," she muttered.

"What was that?"

She blinked at me. "What?"

"You said something. What was it?" I asked.

She smirked smugly. "Curious, aren't you?"

I rolled my eyes and pointed the spoon I was holding, at her. "Tell me."

She grinned. "I said '*pagal insaan*', which is Hindi for 'a crazy/mad human being'."

I tipped my head back and laughed. "Wow, my ego just twerked to Beyoncé at that compliment."

"That's…very specific," she mused.

"I aim to please, Madame," I said.

She chuckled. "Lucky me." She leaned in and added all the potatoes into the pan, and then peppered some salt and oregano over it. "Mix it all in, and then cover it so that it can cook well."

"You got it." I did as she'd asked. "How long do we wait?"

"30 to 35 minutes, depending on the level of heat it gets." She bent to check the electrical stove's temperature. "Make that 40, actually."

"That long, huh?" I cleaned the little mess we'd made on the countertop, and then washed my hands.

"Yeah. Electrical stoves are slow like that." She washed her hands and walked over to the couch beneath the window before settling on it. "Umm, comfy."

I smiled and joined her, taking a seat on the other end of the couch. "I like sleeping on it during breaks. It's just too good to not nap on."

She turned and placed her legs underneath her. "A nap sounds good." She hid a yawn behind a hand and rested the side of her head on the back of the couch.

I mirrored her position, and then pulled my phone out of my back pocket before looking at the time. 2:59a.m.

"Any signal bars yet?" Zaira asked.

I glanced at her, and then at the six signal bars on my phone. I swear there were none a few minutes ago.

"Nope, nothing," I lied. Why? Because I didn't want our time together to end.

Was I greedy?

Yes.

Was I being inconsiderate?

Probably, but I didn't wanna let her go. Not yet.

"Bummer." She sighed and looked around, and her eyes suddenly widened behind her glasses when she saw something over my shoulder. "Is that a real guitar, or a prop?" she asked.

I grinned. "Real."

She looked like a kid in Disneyland. "You play?"

"A little," I said.

"It's a good thing the rat didn't ruin it, then." She looked expectantly at me.

"Yeah, good thing they can't climb on smooth surfaces." I got more comfortable on the couch.

She narrowed her eyes at me. "You're going to make me beg for it, aren't you?"

I pressed my teeth over my bottom lip and shrugged. "Not necessarily, but it's always appreciated."

She grabbed a broken piece of wood from the floor and sent it flying my way.

I got to my feet in order to dodge it, and then laughed when she threw something soft on my face.

"Oh my God! What was that?" she squealed as she stood. "What did I just throw at you?"

I was still cackling as I pulled the article of clothing off my face and looked at her. "It's an underwear," I said between laughter.

The look on her face could spoil a glass of fresh milk. "Why does your underwear smell like flowers?"

"Because it's not my underwear." I sniffed and threw said underwear on the floor.

"What?" She was so confused.

"It's a sample I was sent today by a brand that wants to collaborate with mine. They're working on something new and wanted me to have a look."

She canted her head. "I don't get it."

"This, Zaira," I said, and then pointed at the fallen underwear, "is a sample of a *scented* underwear. It's something the brand is planning on launching in the market soon, and they need my opinion on it."

She opened and closed her mouth a few times. "Scented…scented…" She cleared her throat. "*Scented* underwear? And that's…that's a thing now in this world?"

I laughed again as I pushed my hair back. "Well, apparently it is. I wasn't aware of it until this very morning."

"Wow…" She kept staring at the little red thing next to me on the floor. "It smells exactly like a rose. *Exactly like a rose.*"

I put my tongue to my cheek to stop myself from laughing again. "That's what they're aiming for."

She nodded, deep in thought. "So like…you actually…" She enacted the process of wearing an underwear. You know, lifting each leg and then pulling the garment up to the waist. Yeah, she did all that. "…you're supposed to wear that thing? For real?"

I coughed behind a fist. "I'd like to think so, yes."

She nodded again. "Wow…" She was still staring at the underwear, FYI.

"You okay there, Zaira?" I asked, and then walked over to her before snapping my fingers in front of her shell-shocked face.

"Huh?" She blinked and looked up at me. "What?"

"You alright?"

"Yeah…" She scratched her left lobe. "Yeah, I'm good."

"Great, because I wouldn't want you to look so lost while I'm playing the guitar for you," I said.

Her eyes widened. "Really? You'll play for me?"

Lord, she was so stunning. In that moment, if she'd even asked me to wear that horrific-looking underwear over my head as a fucking tiara, I would've. I'd do just about anything to see that raw excitement and joy on her face.

"Of course." I walked over to the far-left wall in the trailer and grabbed my mahogany guitar. "Sit," I told her.

She did as I'd asked, and when I sat next to her, she smiled timidly and pushed her hair behind her ears.

S-T-U-N-N-I-N-G.

"You ready?" I asked.

"Yes!" She bounced a little, which made me chuckle.

I felt my phone vibrate in my back pocket, but ignored it and kept my focus on Zaira as I began strumming my guitar. "Any song requests?"

She shook her head. "No. Play anything you like."

I winked at her. "You got it."

8.
zaira

February 15th, 2020

"Oh God," I breathed when Gallan began playing the stripped version of *Take It From Me* by Jordan Davis on his guitar. He looked at me and grinned, and a thick strand of his hair fell forward, making him impossibly attractive.

"Know this song?" he asked, knowing full well by my reaction that I did.

"Of course," I managed to say.

"Great; sing it with me, then," he said before winking at me.

I swallowed and fidgeted with the hem of my t-shirt. "I don't think–" I shut my mouth when *he* started singing, and *God*, could that guy sing. His voice had a brush of husk to it; it had a textured grunge that fit so well with the vibe of the song.

Baby, you should stop right now, right here
Right where we wanna be I'll spin you around and let's just see
Where this thing goes, all I know is that I'm all yours, all night
I've got nothing but time

With a smile on my face, I bobbed my head and tapped my feet to his beautiful voice, and when he motioned for me to join him, I did so without hesitation, because why not, right?

Take it from me if you want a t-shirt to sleep in
It's my favorite but you can keep it
Looks good baby you should leave it
Hanging off your shoulders
Now give them bare feet dancing down the hallway

Smiling at me running your finger down the wall
You know what I want, I got what you need
Take it from me...

Gallan grinned, and I realized that we'd unknowingly leaned close to each other while singing.

I looked into those dark eyes of his just as he stopped playing the guitar, and immediately got lost in them. They held me captive; they pulled at every last one of my strings. Gallan's eyes were a vortex of allure. They were irresistible, fatal.

"Hey there," he whispered, and then smiled down at me.

"Hey," I whispered back.

"You can sing," he voiced with surprise on his features. "Like, *really* sing."

"*A little*," I teased. "But your voice…it's breathtaking."

"Nah; it's pretty average."

"Just shut up and take the compliment, Underwood."

He chuckled. "God, you're so beautiful," he said. "So, *so* beautiful."

My breath hitched. "Liar."

He shook his head a little, and then leaned in further. "One thing you should know about me, Zaira, is that I'm a bad liar. A very, *very* bad liar."

I wanted to run my fingers over his stubble, but refrained myself from doing so. "So, you were telling the truth when you said you didn't wanna chase me, huh?"

His brows creased a little. "I don't follow."

"Earlier, you said you didn't wanna chase me. You said you didn't have the energy nor the time for it."

His eyes went to my lips, then came back up. "I lied."

"Well, you're a very convincing liar, then. You hurt me with that statement."

He ran a finger over the side of my face, and with a look of awe on his features, he tucked a piece of hair behind my ear. "Do you wanna be chased, Zaira?" he asked.

I was shivering at the heat of his touch, at the wild hurricane in his eyes. "Gall…"

He smiled. "Gall, huh?"

Shit.

"I'm sorry, I didn't mean–"

"Shh." He placed a thumb over my lips. "I like it. It sounds good when you say it."

Lord, my head was spinning; my heart was beating like crazy. I could hardly breathe; I was barely holding on.

"Where have you been all this time?" His question was a whisper. "Jesus Christ, woman, you're all I need in life." He dropped his hand and shook his head. "You're everything, Zaira."

"You don't even know me," I said.

He smiled softly at me. "So tell me all about you, then. Tell me *everything*."

My cheeks warmed at his request. "Okay, but only if you promise to tell me everything about *you*."

"I promise." He placed his guitar behind him and moved closer to me on the couch. "Go on; I'm listening."

I chuckled. "Okay then, here goes…"

9.
gallan

February 15th, 2020

"What assholes," I said with a shake of my head. "Why does it matter what your cast, color, or sexuality is?"

Zaira shrugged. "Beats me. Throughout my school years, I was looked at like I was a freaking alien or something. I was laughed at over my skin tone, my accent, and even my dressing style.

The guy who was my first, was so sweet and supportive. Until he *wasn't*. Turns out, he only wanted in my pants, and once he'd gotten what he wanted, he didn't hesitate to show his true colors."

The last bit burned a fire in my gut. "Don't Indians have a sex-after-marriage-only kinda policy?" I asked.

She clicked her tongue. "Today's generation doesn't believe in that. I never really liked the idea of 'sex after marriage only' anyway. Life's too short to not live it the way we want to."

I nodded, because she was absolutely right.

The *aloo sabjhi* had cooked faster than we'd thought, but we'd decided to let it sit for a while so that we could talk without food getting in the middle.

As promised, Zaira had told me everything about herself. She loved selective country music, along with Pop, Soul, and R&B. Her favorite dish was her mom's biryani, and she was a huge fan of *Game of Thrones* and *Poldark*.

She preferred TV shows over movies, nights over days, and cherry soda over coke.

She was a Virgo, and liked the color coral just as much as Yin liked Yang. Zaira was perfect – to me, that is.

I shifted on the couch to get more comfortable. "What did little Zaira wear to school anyway?"

She snorted. "I was never *little*," she said, and then pointed at her body. "See? Nothing little about *this*."

I ran my eyes over her full figure, and felt every aspect of me buzzing in appreciation. "Delicious."

She scoffed. "Yeah, no."

I looked at her. "Want me to *show* you, Zaira?"

Her mouth formed an 'O' – in shock, most definitely.

I smirked. "I swear I'd be happy to."

She blinked, and then pushed at my chest. "Asshole."

I chuckled and grabbed her hands before pulling her close. "Tell me what you wore as a kid."

"Why, so you can have dirty dreams about 13-year-old me?"

I rolled my eyes. "No. I'm not a perv, Zaira. I just wanna know because I'm a curious bastard when it comes to you."

She laughed airily. "Full-sleeved t-shirts, flannel jackets, and skintight jeans."

"Mmm." I ran the pad of my thumb over her knuckles. "Hot."

She shook her head. "You're crazy."

"Just honest, babe."

She blushed, and I took the opportunity to finally run a finger over one of her soft cheeks.

I felt her shiver a little, and when our eyes met, I swallowed at the raw, rare beauty on her face.

I never thought I'd feel this way about anyone in my life. I wasn't looking for '*The one*', because I was happy with the way things were in my life.

Until Zaira, I didn't even think about happily ever afters, about the adrenaline that comes with wanting to see, to touch, and to hold someone you were crazy about.

Until her, I didn't know what true attraction felt like, but with her, everything felt amazing; everything felt achievable.

"So, what were you like as a kid?" she asked, and placed her back on the couch's armrest before looking at me.

I blew air through my lips and shrugged. "Usual, but not so much."

She narrowed her eyes. "I don't do riddles, Underwood. Be clear."

I chuckled. "Well, for the most part, I was invisible. I went to all my classes, kept to myself, played basketball for the school's team, and went home to my music and studies. I had no friends, and honestly, I didn't care much for it anyway.

When I started taking drama classes later on, I began meeting people. I had to socialize a lot during that period. At first, I hated it, but when people showed interest in my ideas and my way of performing, I grew more and more confident each day." I hid a yawn behind a fist. "School changed me, and I think it does that for everyone. Good or bad, you learn things from your experiences during those long years. School life sculpts you. I wouldn't wanna change my time as a kid, because then I wouldn't be the man I am today, and to be honest, I like the kinda man I am right now."

She grinned. "I like the man you are, too. A lot."

"Yeah?" I placed a hand over her left thigh, and felt her stiffen, and then relax under my touch.

"Yeah."

I got on my knees and hovered over her. It was a brave move on my part, that's for sure, but when Zaira didn't push me away, it relieved me. It told me that I wasn't crossing the line or being too forward, and that's great because the last thing I wanted to do was make her feel uncomfortable in my presence.

I grinned down at her when she smiled up at me. I grabbed one end of her glasses and slowly pulled them off, and my heart almost leaped out of my chest because...*God*, that girl was unbelievably gorgeous.

"Can you still see me?" I asked.

She placed a hand on my chest. "Yeah. My numbers aren't major, but my optician says if I wear glasses regularly, I won't have to wear them at all after a while."

"That so?"

"Yup," she said.

"You know–" I stopped when loud squeaks sounded from my right.

I groaned and looked in the direction of the noise, and cursed before getting off the couch when that asshole rat looked at me from atop my destroyed bed.

"Finally," Zaira mused. "It's so good to meet you, Mr. Rat." She got off the couch and stood next to me.

"Please don't tell me you're *actually* happy to see this fucker," I said, then handed her glasses to her, which she immediately put back on.

She chuckled at my comment. "He's harmless, Gall."

I looked around at my ruin of a trailer. "Yeah, don't mind if I say that I don't believe you."

"It wasn't the rat who did all this," she countered.

"I'm sorry, are you siding with the rodent?" I asked.

She smirked. "It can't defend itself, so I'm doing that for it."

"You should've pursued law," I mumbled, and huffed when the rat squeaked again.

Zaira laughed. "Aww, it wants to hang out with us."

I gave her an exasperated look. "You're evil."

She flashed her teeth at me, and then whipped her head forward when a crash sounded from the vanity table.

"There goes my favorite cologne," I said in defeat. The rat had knocked it down, and was looking at Zaira and I like *we* were the ones trespassing over his property, and not the other way around.

"Uh, I think we should get that thing outta here," Zaira said with a pout.

"You *think*?"

She rolled her eyes. "The window – let's try to get it out of there."

"Good idea."

We looked at each other, unsure of what to do next.

"Well…?" she said.

"I thought you were going to volunteer this time," I joked.

"But I don't know the first thing about shooing rats," she voiced in all seriousness.

"Yeah, and judging by the mess I've made in here, neither do I."

"But we gotta do what we gotta do," she said.

I sighed and glanced at the rat, who was still looking at us. "True. Let's do this, then."

Zaira swallowed and pushed her glasses up her nose. "Right behind you, Captain."

I chuckled.

It was time for some rat-chasing…

AGAIN.

Lord have mercy.

10.
Zaira

February 15th, 2020

I screamed like a dying hyena and stood on the couch. With bated breaths, I watched as Gallan continued to chase the rat with a wooden shoebox in his hands. The heel of one of his boots hit my broken phone – which was on the floor – resulting in a *CRUNCH!* to sound from the dead device.

R. I. P, my darling...

Getting ahold of the rat was proving to be a challenge; the damn rodent was giving us a run for our money. I can't even begin to count down the number of times Gall almost fell over the broken furniture in his trailer in the process of catching that brown-haired dipshit.

The mission at hand seemed impossible, but him and I were determined. Well, it was mostly *him* who was working on said mission. I was simply... Wait, what was I doing again?

I screamed and stumbled back when the rat jumped over a few fallen pillows and ran straight towards the attached washroom in the trailer.

Yeah, that's what *I* was doing.

It was a purely heroic act on my part...*not*.

"Oh no, you don't," Gall hissed as he ran towards the rat when it began scratching the shut washroom door. "Shit!" he then cursed when he tumbled over something. "Fucking illuminati is conspiring against me tonight," he mumbled.

I placed a hand over my mouth and giggled at his comment, and then screamed bloody murder when the rat sidetracked Gall and jumped on the couch's armrest before making its way to the snack table.

"Why the hell are you screaming?!" Gall yelled, and then placed the shoebox upside down on the snack table, only to miss the rat by a few inches.

"Because I'm scared that thing will murder me in cold blood!" I yelled back.

He groaned. "Weren't you the one who said it was *harmless*?!"

"Are you going to continue to hold it against me now?!"

We were still yelling, by the way.

He scowled, and continued to scan the area for the rat. "Fucking hell, Zaira! No!"

I huffed and stomped my feet on the soft couch, only to trip and fall halfway down.

Bye-bye, dignity.

"Why are we yelling so much anyway?!" I yelled-asked.

Gall sighed and widened his arms at his sides. "I don't know." He looked at me. "We're frustrated, maybe that's why."

My brows creased. He did look pretty tired and upset, and honestly, I felt the exact same way. "Let's just sit–"

Squeak-squeak.

Gall turned at the noise, and then ran towards the rat again. His phone fell from his back pocket in the process, and I immediately jumped down and grabbed it before he could accidentally stomp on it.

As I climbed back up on the couch with the phone in my hand, it vibrated against my palm.

My brows furrowed. I swallowed once, and then pressed the lock key on the iPhone. My heart hammered in my chest when I saw a strong mobile network on the screen, along with 6 call and 2 text message notifications from Shane staring back at me.

No... This can't be right.

Gallan wouldn't lie, would he?

This must be a joke. A bad, *bad* joke. Or a dream; a nightmare.

Maybe I was dead. Maybe the rat bit me and I died of poisoning or something, and was thrown into an alternate universe where things were different from the ones I'd already experienced.

Now, wasn't *that* a new comic plot?

What the fuck, Zaira? Are you out of your Indian mind?

"Watch out!" Gall called, just as the rat jumped on the couch and stood next to me.

I tried to scream, but couldn't.

I tried to move back, but my legs didn't work.

I was dead for sure.

I was reliving the moment of my death.

God, I just hope that it was a quick and painless end. Please, God, I–

"Zaira," came Gall's voice, and when I looked at him, he made a shooing gesture with a hand. "Scare it off so it can go out the open window – just like we'd planned."

What?

"What?" I asked like the moron that I was.

He eyed me suspiciously. "Is there an audio strike in your ears?"

I scowled. "You're acting like a douche."

He shook his head. "Just…" He took a step forward, and the action alerted the rat, because its ears perked, and in a rush, it climbed on one of my sneakers.

"Oh God!" I was ice-cold; I was on the verge of a mental breakdown. "Don't kill me; *please* don't kill me."

"Zaira, it won't–"

"I still have so much to do in life," I said between a dramatic sob. "I wanna be a bestselling author; I wanna have my own publishing house." I sniffed and ran the back of my hand under my nose. "I haven't even tried anal sex! I wanna know what that feels like, especially under the stars.

I wanna take a pregnancy test at least once in my life. I wanna spank a stripper, and I also wanna get mugged in Vegas.

I wanna eat a banana in space, live in the Atlantic and have a pet puffin.

I wanna kidnap a celebrity and go all Kathy Bates Misery on them, and I wanna go to a drag show just so I can scream "YASSSSS, QUEEN," at the top of my lungs. I can't...I can't die before I've done any of that!"

Gall's mouth hung open. "Why are some of your wishes so disturbing?"

I ignored him, and then looked down at the rat. "Be a dear and get off my shoe. Pretty fucking *please*."

It cocked its head and looked up at me. There was some heavy eye contact there, folks; I'm telling you.

It was *intense*.

Like the one between Vin Diesel and Dwayne Johnson. Except, you know, neither I nor the rat were bald.

A loud *CLAP!* sounded from ahead, and just like that, the rat squeaked and ran out the window.

Gall climbed on the couch and slid the window's glass door shut. "Come on; get down," he said, and then offered me a hand before getting off the couch.

I didn't place my hand in his. "Why did you do that? We were having a moment there," I told him after stepping down.

His lips twitched. "You're weirdly adorable, you know that?"

I rolled my eyes. "And you're a great liar; an outstanding actor."

His brows creased a little. "Why do I sense sarcasm in your comments?"

Instead of answering him, I showed him the phone that was in my hand.

He swallowed, and his eyes ping-ponged between me and his iPhone. "Look, Zaira, I can explain." He looked worried.

"You can, can you?" I folded my arms over my chest so I could show him that the ball was in my court.

Wait, is it *ball* or *balls*?

Nevermind.

He sighed and ran his fingers through his hair. "I lied, yeah," he began, and then gazed at me. "I've had signal on my phone all this time, and I lied about not having any. There, you happy?"

I jerked my head back and stared at him. "Are you serious right now?" I felt hurt, betrayed.

He licked his lips and took a step towards me. "I knew I would never be able to gather the guts to ask you out, Zaira, which is why I lied about the cell service when this opportunity landed on my lap. Maybe some deity or god up there was tired of watching me be a miserable piece of shit when it came to asking you a simple question, and decided to do something for me." He scratched the back of his neck and stepped closer to me. "I'm sorry I lied to you, but please know that my intentions weren't bad. All I wanted was to spend as much time with you as I could. I wanted to get to know you better; I didn't want you to leave my sight. I…" He sighed and shrugged.

My heart was beating sporadically; my breathing was uneven.

Why would a guy like *him* want someone like *me*?

After all, he was *the* Gallan Underwood, and I – I was *nothing*.

He was a God; I was a worshipper.

He was a storm, and I was merely a speck of dust against his might.

"Don't". The silk-smooth husk in his voice pulled me out of my thoughts.

I blinked and looked up at him. "Don't what?"

"Don't question things; don't doubt my words."

I searched his all-showing eyes. "How do you know what I'm thinking?"

"I just do," he said, and then erased the little space that separated us by stepping nearer to me. "It's crazy, but it's also true that I can *see* you, Zaira. Like one would a book, I can read you. I can feel you; I can sense every one of your emotions. Your voice calls to me, your eyes grip me, and your presence – it soothes me."

Damn, he was smooth. He left me fucking helpless.

"Gallan..." I released a slow breath and placed a shaky hand over his heart. "We are worlds apart, you and I. We can't possibly be compatible; I am not who the people, the fans, want to see you with."

He shook his head. "I don't care. If the world can't see or understand what I feel for you, then they can go fuck themselves. I want *you*, Zaira; I want an *us*." The sincerity in his eyes was exciting, yet highly terrifying.

I sniffed to get rid of the burn in my nose, and blinked when my eyes stung. "We should...we should call someone to get us out." I looked at the time on my wristwatch – anything to keep my gaze off of the striking man before me. "It's currently 4a.m., so if we leave in the next 30 minutes, we can get some sleep before the 9a.m. shoot."

"Zaira..." He said my name as if he was praying it; like he was holding onto it with everything he had.

I looked at him – tentatively – and braced myself against the whirling emotions on his beautiful face.

"We can't–"

"Zaira, please..." God, he was *pleading*.

"We really should call someone for help, Gall," I managed to say, and took a step back.

I was weak for him, but at least I could try to resist him, if only temporarily.

Something flashed in his eyes at that. Something strong; something...*dangerous*.

Resolution.

Captivated – I was absolutely entranced by the closeness of him; by the scent of him, by the lush warmth that coursed through every fiber of my body with him being so near.

The questions in my head were plenty; they were unsteadily audible. I wasn't expecting things to escalate so soon, if to escalate at all, because I was only a spectator, a mere admirer of the illustrious man in front of me.

I was nothing; he was everything. And together, we made a 'something' that was far beyond my life's normality.

A welcoming chill blanketed me when Gall slowly, almost hesitantly, placed his hands on the small of my back. I shuddered – just a little – and looked up into the eyes of the man who was now holding me. His lips were slightly parted; one of his thighs brushed against mine. I noticed the shift in his pupils, and felt an array of emotions aiding my restless veins.

"But what if I don't wanna let you go? What if I want time to cease – indefinitely?" he whispered, and then bent a little so that our gazes met. "Will you stay here, like this, with me, if only for a little longer?"

After seeing the determination and truth on his features, there was no question what my answer was going to be. After all, he ruled me; he was the Emperor to the struggling empire that was my stability.

But was I ready for things to change?

Was I ready to dive into something so profound?

Was I ready to experience everything I knew Gallan had to offer?

Maybe.

Hopefully…

"Yes," I said, and then placed my hands on his shoulders. "I wanna be *wherever* you are. So yes, Gall, I'll stay here with you for as long as you want me to."

His gaze softened, and when he leaned in further, I closed my eyes and accepted my remarkable reality with a smile on my face, and a spark or two of thrill singeing through my skin.

Is this truly happening? I asked myself.

Yes; yes, it is…a voice said.

11.
gallan

February 15th, 2020

I'd done it; I'd finally told her how I felt. And her response to my request of wanting to stay in the moment a little longer – it'd been perfect.

Zaira felt what I did, and wasn't that the absolute fucking best thing in the world?

I looked down at the gorgeous woman in my arms, and when she smiled at me, I leaned in and took what I wanted: her soft, bow-shaped lips.

Bliss – kissing Zaira was a potion of perfection; a salve of unrivalled remedy.

She whimpered a little when I ran the tip of my tongue over the seam of her bottom lip, and then slowly opened her mouth for me.

I tightened my arms around her waist and kissed her back with everything in me.

"Gallan…" she breathed my name in that accent of hers, and Lord, that one word from her left me painfully hard behind my jeans.

She ran her fingers through the back of my head, and as I placed a hand over her ass, she bunched my hair in a fist and kissed me like she owned me.

I moaned, because the slight burn that coursed through my scalp due to her fingers, and the softness of her mouth on mine – they were both making me crazier by the second.

I was a complete goner for that woman; an entirely lost case.

She gasped when I began tracing my mouth lower so I could taste her the way I'd wanted to ever since she'd stumbled – quite literally – into my life.

"God…" she barely breathed when I nipped at her jaw, and then sucked on the sensitive skin behind her ear. "Gallan." She moved her head to the side to give me better access.

"Mmm." I palmed her full ass and dragged my lips up her throat. "Jesus, Zaira; you smell and taste so fucking good." I kissed her collarbones, and then nuzzled my nose against the side of her neck. "So *good*."

She laughed airily. "Hmm, so it seems that feminine perfumes turn you on."

I moved back and looked down at her. "Is that a good thing?"

Her lips twitched. "Definitely. They are made to attract the male species, after all. As much as the brands out there advertise things otherwise, their fragrances are made with sexual intentions, and sexual intentions only."

I lifted a brow. "And you know that…*how*?"

"Because the perfume I have on right now attracted you. You said I smell good, which indirectly means that the fragrance I'm wearing is working on you."

God, this woman.

"How much time have you spent on this theory of yours?" I asked, and then adjusted her crooked glasses.

She scrunched up her nose. "I don't know, five, or maybe ten seconds?"

I chuckled. "It's a good thing you didn't waste much of your time on it, because I like to think that it's the smell of your pheromones, and not some chemical product that drove me crazy."

She canted her head. "But aren't those available in a strong amount in animals, the pheromones?"

I smirked. "What are we, if not animals?"

Her eyes twinkled. "Kinky."

I laughed and shook my head. "You're something else, aren't you?"

She shrugged. "I guess so."

I bent and kissed her again, and this time when she moaned against my mouth, I lifted her off her feet and walked us to the couch.

She laughed when I placed her on the soft surface and hovered over her, and then fisted my t-shirt when I trailed slow kisses below her ear.

"I was wondering…" she began, and when I looked down at her with a raised brow, she smirked and ran a finger over the side of my neck. "Do you have any weird fetishes or sexual preferences?"

My lips twitched. "I don't. But even if I did, why would I classify them as weird? To me, they'd be completely normal preferences."

She hummed as if seriously contemplating my words. "You make a fair point, but don't most rich people have illegal sexual demands and desires?"

I laughed in amazement. "Where, and *how* do you come up with these questions, Zaira?"

That woman was fucking epic.

She chuckled. "It's all up here." She tapped the center of her forehead. "This is where the magic happens."

I grinned and pressed a kiss on the space between her brows. "*Fascinating.*"

She slapped me playfully. "Don't act sarcastic. It results in you looking bizarrely similar to the Chucky doll."

I tipped my head back and guffawed. "Chucky doll? Seriously?"

She was laughing, too, which made my heart beat like those drumrolls in reality shows.

"I don't know why I even said that!" she sputtered between laughter. "Oh Lord."

I grinned and aligned my face against hers. "You're outstanding, woman," I told her. "Fucking perfect."

She blushed, and I heard her surprised gasp when I splayed a hand on her lower back and pulled her body flush against mine.

Zaira looked up at me with an awestricken expression on her face. "I am *nothing* compared to you." Her brown eyes sparkled against the dimming moonlight.

I shook my head and leaned closer to her. "But you are *everything*, Zaira. To *me*, you're everything."

She trembled a little, and her pupils darkened as she scanned my face. "How did I get so lucky?" she asked. She swallowed once, and then pushed a lock of hair away from my forehead before cupping my face. "How am I here with *you* right now? Just…how?"

I smiled at her, and then kissed the inside of her wrists before gazing at her. "Because a stinky rat decided to wreak havoc in my trailer. And also because you came running to the scene thinking I was getting murdered."

She chuckled. "*So* romantic."

"The epitome of romantic, baby," I mused, which made her laugh.

Timidly, she then leaned forward and kissed me. "I'm so glad I walked into your trailer," she whispered against my lips, and began running the pads of her thumbs over the sides of my mouth. "I'm also very glad that I almost slipped over a banana peel and broke my phone in the process."

I chuckled. "Really? And why's that?"

"Because everything that happened tonight led me to where I am right now. And Gallan?"

"Yeah?"

"Where I am right now is the most beautiful place in the entire world. I mean it." She pressed a chaste kiss on my lips. "Being with you here, like this – it's the only place I wanna be. It's where I feel complete, free, and confident. I know it's too soon to voice this, but it's true when I say that you make me feel like I *belong*, Gallan, and that's something I've been hoping to experience all my life."

My heart soared in my chest at her words. "God, woman." I kissed her once. "You make me feel like I matter; you make me deliriously happy. I'm so glad I got rodent-attacked tonight, because everything I faced led me to *you*, and I'm so fucking grateful for it."

She grinned. "Dramatic baboon."

I snort-laughed. "Did you just call me a baboon?"

She smirked. "Yes. A *dramatic* one."

I grinned, and then tickled her sides, to which she squealed and tried to get away from me. "Nuh uh, Miss Khan. You can't get away. I am *not* letting you go."

She tilted her head to the side. "Yeah?" I noticed that her expression was serious.

I smiled and nodded. "Yes," I said in all honesty. "I'm not letting you go. *Never*, Zaira."

Her chest rose and fell as she breathed shakily. "Okay."

"Okay."

Her eyes glimmered, and when I leaned in and took her lips for a long kiss, she cupped the back of my neck and returned my gesture with a passionate one of her own.

I moaned when she rocked her hips against mine, because her action sent a spark of electrifying thrill zapping through my veins.

Zaira was the excellence I craved; she was the proclivity I yearned for.

She was what I desired, what I needed to make me whole, to let me breathe.

And as she wrapped one of her legs around my waist and kissed me harder, I questioned myself: *Is this really happening?*

Yes; yes, it is...an echo whispered in response, which made me smile.

12. Zaira

February 15th, 2020

"Psst, Zaira. Zaira, hey; wake up, babe."

I groaned and rubbed my shut eyes before blinking them open. "Hmm?"

"Behind you," Gall said, and when I shuffled on the couch, I found him sitting on the floor with a huge grin on his face.

"Here." He handed me my glasses, which I hastily put on before sitting upright.

"What time is it?" I asked, and then hid a yawn behind a hand.

"6:20," he said. "Hey, come here." He patted the clean space next to him. "I wanna show you something."

I got to my feet and ran a hand over my sleepy face. "Did you clear things out?" I sat beside him and stretched my legs out next to his.

"A little, just to make place for us to sit."

I smiled at him. "You're sweet, Gallan Underwood."

He smirked. "Nah, but thanks." He then looked down at me with an expression so profound, that my entire body heated against it.

"What?" I whispered, and then quickly realized that…

"Oh God, my hair!" I began running my fingers through my course locks, and hissed when they (my fingers) came in contact with a stubborn knot.

"I swear I don't have dead Trolls hiding under these," I said to Gallan, and then used all my might in untangling my thick hair.

Curse you, Indian genes.

He laughed. "I'll take you on your word." He then pulled my hands away from my hair before easily unknotting and smoothing my hair out. "There you go."

I stared at him – wide-eyed. "…How? What…?"

"I could see what I was working with, and you couldn't, which is why you were struggling," he stated matter-of-factly.

I rolled my eyes. "Cocky baboon."

He chuckled, and then laughed rhythmically when I playfully pushed him off. "Come here." He wrapped an arm around my waist and pulled me flush against his side before pointing ahead of us. "Look."

I did, and felt an involuntary sigh leave me at the beautiful scene unfolding before me. "Wow…" It was the only word I could think of as I gazed at the sky.

"I absolutely love watching the sun rise. I wake up early every morning just so I can experience this," Gallan said.

The array of colors, the burst of light, the mere serenity of it all – it was beyond beautiful.

"Thank you for showing this to me," I told Gallan, and then placed my head on his shoulder. "It's so calming and energizing at the same time."

He pressed a long kiss on my hairline. "No problem. It's something everyone has the right to witness. And yes, watching the sun rise is a positively surreal experience." He settled a cheek on my head.

We stayed in the moment for a while – basking in the early balmy rays of the climbing sun. Gallan must've shut the ACs and slid the window's glass door open for a clearer view, because warm breezes filtered into the trailer and soothed my slightly sweaty skin.

"I called Shane and told him everything," he said after a while.

My heart raced madly in my chest. Reality – we would soon be heading back to our real lives. This little fantasy bubble we were in – it would burst. Him and I, we–

"You're thinking again," Gallan voiced.

Even through my worries, I managed to smile. "How did you know?"

He shifted a little, and I moved back so I could look at him. "Because I can feel you; because I can read you. You remember me telling you that, don't you?"

I swallowed at the intensity in his eyes. "Yes."

"Good." He then cupped the left side of my face and gently pulled me closer. "Nothing's going to change, Zaira. How I feel about you won't at all change once we leave here. If anything, it'll only grow; it'll deepen. Because, baby, once we leave this trailer, I'll have a chance to make you mine – for good."

I tried to breathe through my emotions as I wrapped my fingers around his wrist. "I still don't understand, Gall. Why me? You keep saying it's because you think I'm amazing and perfect, but it's just…"

"You doubt me? You don't trust what I say?" he asked with a neutral expression on his face.

"No, no." I shook my head. "I believe you; I really do. It's just that…I don't believe in myself. I don't feel like I am what you say I am; that I am deserving of someone like you."

His gaze hardened. "Why would you say something like that?"

I lowered my head a little. "I don't know. Maybe it's because I've spent years of my life listening to people say that I'm worthless, that I'm a burden to the world. It really broke my confidence in myself. It's…it's hard being subjected to such taunts, and somewhere on the inside, it breaks a part of you; it shatters a piece of your imagination and ambitions.

My parents are the best, and have always stood by me. But sometimes…sometimes I don't like pressuring them with my insecurities and…thoughts, so I just keep them all in. That bundled up darkness makes me feel like I'm undeserving of privileges." I sighed and closed my eyes.

I didn't want Gallan to see me like this. I didn't wanna tell him what I had, but it was so easy to open up to him that I just… I couldn't resist.

"Hey." He nudged my face upwards. "Look at me, Zaira." The gentle command in his statement resulted in goosebumps to blanket my entire body.

I opened my eyes and gazed up at him.

"I've said this before, and I'll say it again, only because I want you to know that it's true," he said. "You're phenomenal; you're amazing. You're the most beautiful woman I've seen, Zaira. You're perfect – for me. You're everything, and I pity those who don't see it; who don't see you the way I do. Because what I see is pretty effin fantastic, and I don't wanna lose it."

A tear slid down my cheek at the honesty written on his face. "Thank you," I breathed.

He smiled. "No." He shook his head. "Thank you for being who you are. I'm lucky to have you."

My cheeks warmed at his words. "You know just what to say, don't you?" I scanned his chiseled face; I let my eyes drink in his raw beauty.

He grinned. "I know how to speak the truth."

I chuckled, and then leaned in before pressing my lips to his.

With a soft sigh, he pulled my body closer and kissed me like he wanted to devour me; like he wanted to consume me whole.

"Wait, hold on," I managed to say between kisses.

Gallan moved back and looked questioningly at me. "What?"

"We didn't even get to taste my *aloo sabjhi*." I may or may not have pouted after saying that. "And we can't have it now, because I'm sure the damn rodent has pooped a buffet in it just to spite us."

Gallan chuckled. "I'm sure that's not how things work when it comes to human-and-animal feuds, but okay."

I raised a brow. "Feud? Really?"

He chuckled again. "That damn thing is my arch nemesis, I'm telling you."

I laughed. "I'm sure that's not how things work in general, but okay."

He smirked. "Aren't you a sassy little thing…" His eyes gleamed dangerously.

I stuck my tongue out at him, which made him grin.

God, he was perfect.

Being with Gallan like this – all free and joyous – it was addicting; it was deliriously overwhelming.

I would hold onto it.

I wouldn't lose it.

I wouldn't lose him.

As the sun brightened, and as it bathed us in its warm halo, Gallan and I leaned onto each other for hope, for truth, for comfort, and for our amplifying desires.

For…

For love…

13.
gallan

February 15th, 2020

"Get that smug look off your face, G. It's giving me a major case of acidity," Shane said.

I chuckled and placed my forearms on the trailer's window base. "I'm not being smug; I'm just trying to decipher something."

He arched a brow. "So this is your interpretation face?"

My lips twitched at his question. "I would say so, yes."

Shane rolled his eyes. "What are you trying to decipher anyway?"

"The reason behind you being late in getting here," I said with a smirk. "I called you at 6, and it's 8:15 right now. I don't understand how a 20-minute drive from your place to the studio turned into a 2-hour long one."

He cleared his throat. "Well, something came up – quite literally."

I raised a brow. "Explain."

He ran a hand over his smooth-shaven head. "Uh, you see, Anna wouldn't let me leave…" He shrugged as if to say '*You get the gist, right?*'.

I gagged, just to tease him. "Gross, Shane; I don't need to know about your morning sexual escapades with your wife."

He scowled. "You said 'explain'. So I tried to…"

"Yeah, and what an explaining you've provided in just eight simple words, my friend," I mused.

As Shane wiped his face with a napkin and grumbled something about me being a dickhead, the trailer's washroom door opened behind me.

A smile immediately took over my face when the couch dipped to my right, and a second later, Zaira's face came into view as she knelt next to me and looked out the open window.

"Hey," she said, and then shifted closer to me before pushing her glasses up her nose.

I turned and looked at her. The sunlight hit her features in all the right ways and made her almost seraphic for my eyes.

"Hey, gorgeous." I wrapped an arm around her waist and pulled her close.

She grinned at me, but didn't say anything.

I glanced at her lips, and felt her body tremble a little in my grasp.

I met her eyes, and what I saw there? It was fucking hot.

Desire.

Pure, fiery desire.

While waiting for Shane to come "rescue" us – Zaira's choice of word, not mine – I'd spent every second of the spare time exploring her mouth. We'd made out like teenagers in heat, and with every moan and thrilled shiver she gifted me, my want for her only grew stronger.

That woman fueled a wildfire in my veins with her innocence. She awakened every speck of me with her natural sublimity.

"Ugh," came Shane's voice. "I get it; you two are outrageously adorable, but can you stop eye-fucking each other now?"

Both Zaira and I looked at my manager.

"Don't be a mood killer," I told him.

He rolled his eyes. "There are things we need to discuss before you two start making babies in public, G," he said in his 'I'm-all-business' tone.

Zaira made a noise between a choke and a gasp.

I sighed. "I know that, but we can't do any of it if you don't get us outta this trailer. But if you're hoping for us to jump out this window, then that's a different story."

"If you could, you already would've," he retorted.

"Yeah." I smirked. "But I'm not flexible, you see." I gestured at him with my head. "You flexible, Shane? I never really asked."

"Good God," Zaira whispered, and then slapped my arm. "Gall!"

I laughed and looked at her. "What? I just feel like one of the reasons he looks so fit despite being in his fifties is because of all the Kamasutra him and his wife try."

Zaira palmed her face in white-hot horror, just as Shane yelled, "I do not indulge in Kamasutra!"

A few of the crew members snickered as they passed him, which only made him red in the face.

"I don't know why I even deal with you most of the times," he grumbled, and then headed towards the trailer door. "Fucking Adonis-looking brat."

Zaira laughed at that. "You two are hilarious."

I grinned. "He's the Hardy to my Laurel."

She nodded, still laughing. "I can tell." She wiped at her eyes from behind her glasses and shook her head. "Just...wow."

I chuckled and pulled her closer so I could feel her breaths against my lips. "Hey, Zaira?" I said.

Humor left her features when she looked at my face, and replaced itself with awe. "Yeah?" She held the right side of my face in her hand.

"You ready to face the world with me?" I asked her. "Ready for the world to see you for the wonderful woman you are?"

She parted her lips slightly. "With you by my side? Yes, Gallan; *always*."

Electricity buzzed my veins. "Come here, you." I gently grabbed her jaw and bent so I could taste her.

Zaira fisted my t-shirt and pulled me towards her. "Who knew presuming you the way I did would show me the real you; that it would act as a catalyst for giving you to me," she panted, and then slowly tugged at my bottom lip with her teeth.

I grinned. "If only I'd known, baby. I'd let you presume the fuck out of me just so I could have you the way I've wanted to since the very beginning."

She smiled beautifully. "You have me now," she whispered.

"I do, and I promise to hold onto you for the rest of my life – for better, or for the worse."

Her eyes gleamed brilliantly against the morning light, and when she leaned in and kissed me again, I thanked every holy entity out there, *and* also the bloody rat who'd infiltrated my trailer, for making me the luckiest asshole in the whole damn cosmos.

14.
zaira

February 22nd, 2020

"I think that's illegal, on like, high levels," Kenzie said in all seriousness.

I lowered my glasses and gave her an '*Are you serious?*' look. "How does me not having a mobile phone categorize as illegal? It could easily be a preference of mine."

"But it's *not*," she countered. "And that's the thing, Z; not having a phone on you is *not* a preference of yours. Also, seeing you without one is making me all nauseous and dizzy."

We were at the studio getting things ready for a long-ass day shoot. Not exciting, but hey, good-paying jobs often aren't, right?

"Are you sure you're not pregnant? Because those symptoms point towards that, and not your concern over me not having a phone," I said.

She rolled her eyes. "Don't act sassy with me. Of course I'm not pregnant. Hayden used a condom – *both* the times."

My brows creased in confusion. "Who's Hayden?"

Kenzie stared at me. "The guy I left the club with on Wednesday." She could've just as easily yelled 'DUH' in my face.

"But you said you were leaving with a 'Rob'," I told her. "I remember you saying it *twice*."

"You were drunk when you got in the cab."

"What?" I placed my hands on my hips. "No, I wasn't. I don't even touch alcohol! I wasn't *drunk*, Ken."

She clicked her tongue. "I know for a fact it was a 'Hayden'. He kept asking me to scream and yell and moan his name in bed, so I can't be wrong by any means."

I flinched. "TMI."

She smirked. "He was so freaking hot. And his dick was slightly round in structure; you know, like a crescent or a thick arced banana, and–"

"Oh my God, STOP!" I covered my ears with my hands. "Just…*ewww*, Ken. Gross." I then pulled my hands away when I was sure she wasn't going to attack me with more of her sexual word-vomit. "You ruined the moon and bananas for me. I won't look at them the same way anymore."

She pouted. "But he just–"

"No."

"But at least listen–"

"No!"

"Zaira, I–"

"Shh! No, no, no!"

She opened her mouth, but I made a 'zip it' gesture, to which she huffed and crossed her arms over her chest.

"You're no fun," she muttered.

My lips twitched at that, but I kept my expression neutral. "That's what you get for comparing a random guy's dick to a banana and the moon. Next time you wanna use euphemisms, go for things that are less likely to make a normal human being shudder and beg for a painful death."

She looked at me like I was crazy, and then suddenly glanced behind me, right before…

"Uh…" He cleared his throat, and I closed my eyes in paint-white embarrassment. "Is this not a good time? I can come back later."

I begged the Lord to strike me with lightning, but that didn't happen. *Obviously*. After all, when has he listened to me?

"Hey, Gallan!" Kenzie chirped, and when I opened my eyes and glared at her, she flashed her teeth at me as if to say '*Karma is a bitch, baby.*'

"I'll go and do…just about anything else," she said, and then swiveled on her feet before running away. *Literally*.

Gallan chuckled. "She's a strange one, your friend."

I didn't know how to face him. God, he'd heard me say dick and moon and bananas and–

"Hey, gorgeous." He wrapped an arm around my waist and placed a kiss below my ear. "Umm, you smell *good*." His lips traveled to my neck, my shoulder.

I shuddered in welcoming pleasure when his stubble scraped against my heated skin. "Also, you should wear flannel shirts and skintight jeans more often, because *Jesus*, woman, you look *fine* in them."

I managed to laugh. "That's literally all I wear, Gall."

He chuckled. "I know, but your ass looks especially good today, so I thought I'd plead my wishes to you."

I grinned, and placed my back to his chest. "So crass this morning."

"Mm-hmm, but only when it comes to you."

I sighed when his warmth soothed me, relaxed me; when it grounded me.

"I'm sorry you had to hear me say all that," I told him, and then turned around slowly so I could face him. My body buzzed in appreciation when I saw him – *all* of him. God, that man looked like a *treat* in a simple white t-shirt and faded jeans.

Insert intense fangirl moment here.

Gallan looked down at me with mirth in his eyes. "It was…refreshing to hear what you had to say. A new concept of sorts. I learned a lot from it, I can assure you that."

Aaaaand there goes my fangirling seizure into a pond of many others.

I scowled and lightly pushed at his chest. "You're an ass."

He chuckled. "Nope. Just an admirer of your views towards the male anatomy."

My cheeks heated. "It was *her* who used those…*terms* as descriptive variables, not me."

He grinned and pushed his hair to the side. "But they sounded better when you voiced them."

I rolled my eyes. "Baboon."

He chuckled harder and bent to kiss me, and like the schoolgirl I was turning into when it came to him, my stomach swarmed with giggly butterflies.

We hadn't had the time to go on a date, Gallan and I. The filming schedule was tight, and because I had no phone, the two of us had to stick to talking, and spending whatever free time we could spare at the studio, and at the studio only. Gallan had early promo interviews and photoshoots to tackle, and I was busy plotting another comic when I wasn't at the studio. Things were tough, but we were determined to make things work.

He had wanted to make us official on his social media accounts the moment we'd walked out of the trailer, but Shane was adamant we wait until our first date to do just that. According to him, if we (Gallan and I) were *really* doing this, then we had to do it without 'stepping on cow's shit.' I don't know what that means, and judging by the look of horror I'd seen on Gallan's face right after he'd heard Shane mention cow dung, I can say that he had no clue either.

Over the last few days, I'd come to learn that things not only executed faster in the Holly world, but they also planted themselves into the very heart of the industry like some expensive silicone boob.

All hail the glamour world.

"Oof, that's some heavy thinking going on in that head of yours for you to not answer me at all," Gallan said, which made me smile.

"Sorry." I wrapped my arms around his neck. "So, you were saying?"

"*Asking*, actually. What are you gonna do about the phone situation? My patience is dwindling – *rapidly*. I wanna be able to hear your voice when I'm swamped between interviews and don't have you by my side. After all, a smitten man can only take so much torture."

I chuckled. "When I get the salary check next month, I'll go get a new one, I promise," I told him. "I've been saving up for a while to get a high-end phone, because those have a better performance factor, and it'll be easier for me to sketch some of my comic stuff if I get a device that allows the use of a stylus pen. I don't always have access to my computer when I get an idea I wanna draw or jot down, so yeah, it'll have to be a pricey phone."

"Hmm." Gallan clicked his tongue. "I wonder…however could I speed up the process." His eyes gleamed stunningly under the studio lights.

"What process?" I asked.

"Of you getting a new phone."

I ran a hand over my hair. "I told you I'll–" I stopped midsentence when he brought his right hand between us and wiggled the box he was holding in it.

"What's this?" I asked, and raised my brows at him.

A Cheshire-cat grin took over his face. "My way of speeding up the process."

"Gall…" I looked between him and the beautifully wrapped box in his hand. "If this is what I think it is, then…" I shook my head.

"Then what, Zaira?" he questioned me with challenge in his eyes.

I sighed and shook my head. "You don't have to do these things for me, Gall; I'm not into materialism when it comes to relationships."

"I know that, seriously. But it's *my* fault that you broke your phone, Zaira, so I think it's only right if I take the responsibility of getting you a new one."

I gazed at his hard expression, at his clenched jaw. "You're upset," I said.

He swallowed and wiped a hand over his face.

Oh man, he was frustrated too.

"I just feel like a fool right now for thinking, and *hoping*, that you'd be excited to get your first present from me. I've been working on it for a week now, and you just…" He shook his head and took a step back. "You blew me off by implying that I thought you're a material person, and *that's* why I got you a new phone, which is not at all true."

The hurt on his face shocked me. "Gall, I'm…I…" Shit, what do I say to him that'll make him believe I didn't mean what he thought I did?

"Save it, Zaira," he said. "Once again, your presumption about me turned out to be wrong. I just hope this shows you that I'm not a walking and talking cliché." He turned to leave, but I grabbed his arm and pulled him to me before pressing my lips to his.

"You think you can just walk away after blindly assuming that I thought you were a Hollywood snob? You think I'm so shallow, that I'd look at you in such bad light? Is that what you think, Gall?"

He worked his jaw as he scanned my face. "What else do you want me to think? I didn't bring you a phone because I wanted to gain your affection or attention, Zaira; I did it because I wanna be able to contact you whenever I want. I did so because it's hard for me to function when you're not with me. I don't know what you're doing to me, but whatever it is, I absolutely *love* it. I can't help myself; I act on how I feel. Maybe it's impulsive, but fuck if I give a damn about it."

My lips twitched. "Christ, you're so dramatic, Underwood."

He tried to hold it in, but his smooth laughter slipped through anyway. "It was a little too much, wasn't it?"

"Reminded me of the Snickers candy-bar ad, is all I'm saying."

He laughed harder. "Sorry. I had a lot of work-related pent-up frustration that wanted out."

I smirked. "It's okay. I'm just glad you decided to fall back into rationality."

He rolled his eyes. "Jeez, Zaira, thanks."

I chuckled, and then grabbed the gift box from his hand. "I'm accepting this," I told him, and brought the box up, "but if you buy me any more expensive shit in the future, I'll dick-punch you without a thought. Clear?"

He grinned. "God, why did that threat turn me on so much?"

I laughed and pushed at his chest. "You're a weirdo, Gallan Underwood."

He grinned. "Only for you, though," he said.

"I can't believe you were going to walk out on me just a moment ago," I said.

"I wasn't." He chuckled. "I was going to play hard-to-get for a second, and then I was going to turn around and come back to you anyway."

I laughed and shook my head, and then began unwrapping the colorful paper from the gift box.

Gallan scratched the back of his head and stood next to me in complete silence, almost as if he was nervous.

I placed the paper on the table behind me, and then flipped the phone's box open before pulling the device out.

"Oh my God," I hardly managed to breathe when I turned the phone around and found…

"It's a special edition design. One of its kind – made only for you," Gallan said. "It's inspired by you, of course, and also *The Ice Bearer*."

A tear slid down my cheek. "It's so beautiful…"

The entire back section of the phone was coral in color, with a cartoon illustration on it that looked exactly like me. She had brown hair and eyes, along with adorable and nerdy black glasses. My name was written behind her in a black-and-white comic bubble, and the whole design looked just like a portion or scene from a comic book.

"I'm so glad you think so. Because *The Ice Bearer* is fully coral, with only black-and-white accents for dialogue and characters, I asked one of my fans – who is also a graphic artist – to help me come up with the whole design," he said, and then pressed a kiss on my temple.

I looked up at him. "This was your idea – the illustration and everything?" I asked.

He grinned. "Yeah."

"Gallan…" I shifted and placed a hand on his chest. "Thank you so much." I was awestruck by the man in front of me; by the kindness and interest he showed.

"You don't have to thank me, babe."

I sniffed and shook my head. "I do. Getting me a phone is one thing, but having it customized? That's…that's so thoughtful of you."

He kissed me once. "I'm just happy you like it. Makes everything worth it."

"I *love* it," I said, and then smiled at him. "Who knew you were so perfectly cheesy."

He smirked. "Well, I'm an actor, aren't I?"

I chuckled. "True."

"So, date night tomorrow?" he asked, and then wrapped his arms around my waist.

My heart fluttered. "Hell yes."

As he leaned in and kissed me, I held him closer and just…lived in the moment without giving a damn about the world around us, because really, when it was the two of us, the world didn't even matter.

It never would.

15.
Zaira

February 22ⁿᵈ, 2020

"**H**e wants inside of you – *stat*," Kenzie voiced her 0.02 cents after I showed her my new phone. "Like, he's so ready for you that he has no chance of holding it all in. He's just…" She mimicked – or *tried*, at least – a guy jerking off. She even moaned and everything. "He's ready for a marathon, babe."

I slowly chewed and swallowed a spoonful of my mum's biryani before clearing my throat. "And you know all this…*how*?"

She waved my phone at me. "Duuuuuh."

We were on our lunch break, and because I considered her as my best friend, I'd decided to show her Gallan's present once we'd reached the crew locker room. But, well, Kenzie being Kenzie, she decided to be her usual inappropriate self towards my excitement.

Oh joy.

Lord bless her euphemistic soul.

I rolled my eyes and straightened my glasses. Ugh, I had to get them tightened. They kept slipping down my nose every few minutes.

"Just because he was kind enough to get me a new phone, doesn't mean he's trying to get me in bed, Ken. Him and I discussed it; he understands my policy of no materialism in a relationship," I said.

"So, then what do you call *this*?" She shoved the phone in my face. "What's this? His channeling desire and affection for you? Because *this* very much looks like material to me, Z."

I grabbed my phone from her and shoved it in my jeans pocket. "You're incorrigible," I mumbled.

"Don't use fancy words on me," she said.

I chuckled. "Never change, Ken. Never change."

She smirked. "Oh, I don't intend to."

I grinned and shook my head at her.

"So…" She turned so she could face me fully. "Have you and Gallan…you know, done anything yet?" The curious gleam in her eyes was making me uncomfortable. Just a little.

I drank some of my club soda and shook my head. "Nope. He's being patient, *unlike* your presumptions."

She clicked her tongue. "Maybe it has something to do with the Penis Logic."

I tilted my head to the side. "Penis Logic?"

She waved a hand before her. "Yeah!" She took a final bite of her taco before wiping her hands with a tissue. "Thinking with the dick instead of the brain. Maybe he thinks because he's a celebrity, he should play hard to get. Like, you know, maybe he wants *you* to make the first move."

I looked at her in clear incredulity. "He literally bared his emotions and feelings to me last week in the trailer, Ken. If he's playing hard to get, then I'll say he's pretty shitty at it." I finished my biryani and shut its container before throwing it inside my purse. "I just…I think he's being a gentleman. He's giving me space to breathe."

"To breathe?" She sipped her orange juice. "I don't get it."

I sighed. "He knows how overwhelmed I feel when he's near. He sees it, too. I don't think I'll ever get used to the fact that I get to kiss him every day now. And Gallan actually sees it; he understands how I *see* him." I smiled at my best friend. "He…he knows I lose my ability to function when he's close, so he gives me a chance to let things settle in. He isn't rushing into things because he knows I need the temporary space; he knows I need time to comprehend that him and I – we're *real*, and not just an illusion."

Kenzie looked at me with saucer-like eyes. "Wow, that was some deep shit. Super heavy-duty stuff."

I laughed. "You're crazy."

She shook her head. "No, I'm telling you, that was *intense*. You and Gallan – you're like the modern-day Ross Poldark and Demelza. There's angst between you two, there's honesty, there's obvious attraction, and there's also that craving those two have for each other. It's perfect!"

I blushed at the Poldark comparison. "I don't know... Ross and Demelza are like a power couple, and with Gallan, everything is so new. I'm sort of worried to hope for a lot, or to hope at all."

She placed a hand over mine and gave it a squeeze. "He's smitten, Z; that guy is crazy about you. He's–" She stopped midsentence when loud giggles sounded from outside the closed locker-room door.

Kenzie and I looked at each other, and like the fiends we were, we slowly walked towards the door and put our ears against it.

"But, seriously though. I'd bang him in a *heartbeat*. He's so fucking irresistible," said Aubrey, Gallan's costar. She was a weirdo, FYI, and also Gallan's *ex*. They had dated for a few weeks four years ago, until she'd upped and broken things off with him on Instagram.

But because Gallan was a great guy, he'd agreed to help her out financially with her clothing line a couple years ago. She basically lived off of her sales money, because in terms of acting, she was a total *flop*. The only reason Ross Jonas had hired her for *Waves That Hold Us* was because she was a blonde-hair-and-green-eyed supermodel, and would look good both on the screen, *and* on the movie poster gluing herself to Gallan like a fucking slug.

Calm down, Zaira.

Calm.

Down.

It's *you* who has the guy, not her.

Calm your tits, girl.

"But you broke up with him! And now you wanna bang him?" came a voice I didn't recognize.

Opening the door just a tad bit, Kenzie peeped outside. "It's Aubrey and her crazy friends," she whispered. "Another one of their impromptu visits to the set."

"Her friends come to the set often?" I whisper-asked.

Ken nodded. "Yeah. They ogle Gallan like vultures, and try to get him to go out for drinks with them. He always rejects them, obviously, and it's *so* much fun to watch."

"Why haven't I seen them before?"

She rolled her eyes. "Because you work a lot, and up until last week, whenever you'd see Gallan, you'd scurry in the other direction like a mouse from a cat."

I scowled. "Are you making rodent jokes a norm now? Is this how things are going to be?"

She placed a hand over her mouth to stifle a giggle. "Maybe."

"I mean, you're right," said Aubrey, and Kenzie and I returned our attention to the eavesdropping task at hand. "I *could* get back with him, but he's pretty vanilla compared to what I like."

Three crow-like gasps sounded.

"Are you saying that Gallan isn't good in bed?" Crow #1 asked.

"Good Lord, what a disaster," said Crow #2.

"You told us that he has an 'OMG-me-likey' level cock, so what's the issue?" questioned Crow #3.

Fire burned my gut at that final statement.

Seriously?

Was discussing the length of your partner's dick with your friends a thing now?

"You girls don't get it," Aubrey voiced. "He's just, I don't know… He's sweet in a way that he'll only wanna bang you when he thinks you're comfortable or willing. He won't push your limits or anything, which is a turn off. He's fucking *spectacular* in bed, I can tell you that, but I wanna be treated like a doll, and not glass. I wanna get thrown like a doll; I wanna get mistreated like one. Like, pull my hair and hiss filthy shit to me, dude. Ask me to call you *Daddy*. I want the nasty-nasty."

What the fuck?

"I'm so shocked right now," Kenzie whispered. "That girl has some serious issues."

I pressed a fist over my mouth to hide my laughter. She was right; Aubrey was crazy.

The Crow Squad giggled in a way that made me flinch, and what Aubrey said next – it had me blazing up like the sun on a summer day.

"I'm getting my final rebound with him, that's for sure. I've asked to meet with him at his headquarters next week to *discuss* a new apparel edition for my line, and because he's clueless towards my intentions, he said yes. God, I'm going to have *so* much fun riding that sexy piece of meat."

The four of them chuckled, just as Kenzie whipped her head in my direction and mouthed, *"Over my dead body."*

We heard retreating footsteps, and once Kenzie had made sure the Crows were gone, she opened the door wide and crossed her arms over her chest before looking at me.

"So, what's the plan, Captain?" she asked, all business.

I felt horns forming at the top of my head as I answered her by saying, "I don't know why, but I feel like the bottle of Dexilant in locker 234 is suddenly calling my name. *Incessantly.*"

Her eyes gleamed. "Oh, you evil, *evil* bitch."

I smirked. "No one talks about *my* piece of meat like that." It felt *so* good to call Gallan 'mine'. I was so trilled over the fact that I was ready to run for freaking president, just so I could lose and fall from grace to get myself under control.

"Yasssss, QUEEN. Get!" Kenzie cheered.

I chuckled. "But, however shall we find the one who is well-equipped in getting our significant task executed?"

She gasped as if in serious dismay. "Alas. If only we were aware of the Bad Queen Aubrey's cupbearer." She then placed a hand before her face and looked at her palm as if staring in the mirror. "Oh, I have found her – the chosen one!"

I couldn't hold it in; I started laughing. "God, I feel like I'm Cersei Lannister right now."

Kenzie snort-laughed. "Christ, I can't." She laughed alongside me. "Wait, if you're Cersei, then what does that make *me*?"

I was still laughing when I said, "Qyburn."

She gagged. "Ewww. He's so old and ugly!"

I leaned against the doorframe and pressed a hand over my stomach as I cackled – for real.

She joined me, and then touched the side of her head against mine. "I can't wait to see Aubrey lose all of her dignity in the next few minutes," she said.

I grinned. "Oh yeah, I can't wait, too. And I promise you that whatever happens this time, I won't scurry or look away."

We high-fived, and then headed straight into plan 'Assassinate Aubrey's Dignity'.

Things were about to get really, *really* shitty – quite literally.

16.
gallan

February 22nd, 2020

Aubrey was making these ridiculously horrifying expressions, which were both confusing and funny. I'd wanted to ask her about it when she'd first started making them five minutes ago, but had to refrain myself from doing so in order to not come off as a jerk.

We'd only just begun filming after I'd returned from the lunch break a little late because of the meeting Shane and I had to attend with a potential clothing-line CEO.

When I'd stood in front of Aubrey, ready to say my lines, she'd started acting out of place, which made it hard for me to focus on the scene and the cameras.

"*But you said we weren't meant to be, that you didn't want me, so…so why behave otherwise, huh, Ellie?*" I said my line and attempted at looking heartbroken, even though on the inside, I was very much conflicted and worried.

"I…I…" Aubrey stuttered, and what happened next – it shocked every living soul around us.

Aubrey farted.

Hard.

Like, seriously HARD.

It was like a fucking war horn right before a battle.

And the smell…

God, that stench could put an entire army to sleep. *Permanently.*

"Oh no…" She looked so humiliated and upset. Her face and neck were flushed in embarrassment, which made me frown.

Poor thing.

"Uh…Aubrey, you alright?" I asked tentatively, almost silently, so as to not make her feel any more dejected.

She glared at me. "Alright? ALRIGHT?" She gritted her teeth and shot daggers at me. "I shit my fucking pants, Gallan! I. Pooped. My. Pants! So no, I am NOT alright!" she yelled.

Whoa…

"Sweet mother of the holy Lord, please take me now," Ross said from behind the monitor. "Please go and take care of your…situation, Aubrey. This is very disturbing to watch only a few minutes after lunch."

Aubrey's manager came running to the rescue and dragged her off the set, but not before I got a glimpse of the *situation* behind her pants.

"Jesus Christ." I placed the back of my hand over my mouth to hide a gag, and when I turned around, I found Zaira and Kenzie laughing in a corner like two sneaky conspirators.

The former's eyes met mine when she felt me watching her, and the grin she gave me could only be named 'Evil'.

I shook my head at Shane when he gestured me to join him, and then strode over to the girls before grabbing Zaira's hand and pulling her inside the nearest locker room.

I shut the door and placed her against it, and then pressed my palms next to the sides her head before looking down at her. "What did you do?" I asked.

Those enticing lips of hers curved as she smirked. "Whatever are you talking about, baby?"

I stepped closer to her, and watched as she held her breath. "Spill, Zaira. Now. Tell me what you did." I wasn't angry, no. I was simply curious as to why she'd do something like that, because I knew for sure that it was *her* who was responsible for Aubrey's…well, *situation*.

Her eyes glimmered as she canted her head and gazed up at me. "Well, because you've deciphered me so easily, it is only fitting that I tell you everything, huh?"

And man, did she tell me *everything*.

17.
Zaira

February 22nd, 2020

Gallan tipped his head back and laughed – for the fifth time since he'd pulled me inside the locker room. Yes, I kept count. Screw me.

"I wanna be mad at you – *really* mad – but somehow, I can't find it in me to do that," he said, and then shook his head. "God, Zaira, who knew there was such evil lurking behind that innocent face and those nerdy glasses."

I smirked. "So you're saying that I'm a villain?"

He bopped his nose against mine. "Nah. You're too cute to be a villain."

"For the record, though, let me tell you that I totally felt like one while popping the pills into her coffee mug, so there's that."

He shook his head. "I don't even wanna ask how you know about Dexilant causing a loose bowel. I feel like it'll be beneficial if I stay in the dark about it."

I grinned. "Well, I have my parents to thank for that. As you know, they are professors, so I learned a lot from them growing up."

Gallan chuckled. "I just wish I was present during the time you were formulating the plan in that head of yours." He gently tapped the center of my forehead, and when I winked at him, he bent and kissed my cheek. "Although," he began, and then dragged his lips over my jaw until he'd reached my ear, "knowing that you so easily went all Enchantress on Aubrey, for *me* – it does things to me that I can hardly explain, even to myself." His stubble brushed against my skin, which caused sparks to ignite throughout my body.

"Well." I swallowed once. "I've been known to be very possessive over what's mine."

God, why did I say that?

Shit.

Shit, shit, shit.

Gallan moved back and looked down at me with a raised brow. "Yours, huh?" His expression gave away nothing. Damn it, he really was a great actor.

I pushed my hair behind my ears and hugged myself. "I'm sorry, I shouldn't have said that." I averted my gaze. "You must think I'm such a creep."

There was silence between us for a while, and I was scared I'd ruined everything just by calling him mine.

A silly, stupid mistake.

A word-vomit.

"You know, Zaira, I'm selfish when it comes to you," Gallan said. "I'm so fucking selfish, that I'd have caused harm twice as much impactful to a guy if he'd have said the things Aubrey said about me. I wouldn't have held back – not for anything."

I looked up at him in complete shock. "Gall–"

He silenced me with a chaste kiss. "I crave you, Zaira. Every second of every day since I've seen you, I've wanted you," he voiced against my lips. "When you blinked at me for the very first time, you left me grasping onto the addicting and irresistible fragments of you. And you know what? I absolutely love doing it; I love taking what you give me. I'll accept anything I can have, but I know for a fact that I'll never have enough. And you know why that is, baby?"

I shook my head in response, because in that moment, it was impossible for me to form sentences.

He hummed. "*'Cause I'm selfish. Restless like a river, can't help it. I'm taking what you give me but I still want more. I still want more... 'Cause I'm selfish. Yeah I'm selfish, I'm selfish for you,"* he sang, which put a huge smile on my face.

"I should've known you'd sing Jordan Davis to lure me in," I teased, and then ran a hand over his broad chest.

Gallan grinned and pulled me flush against him. "It was my understanding that you didn't need luring in anymore."

"Well, more is always appreciated, isn't it?"

He chuckled. "Sure is." He then leaned in and kissed me beautifully. "Come on, sing with me, Zaira."

I cupped the back of his head and pulled him close before kissing him. "What are we singing?" I was so lost in his eyes, in his smell, in his taste.

"Anything you want. Just sing with me, because it fucking soothes me," he said with a smile.

And so, that's what we did.

We sang.

Have you seen yourself in a full-length mirror
Spinning around lately
I'd lie, cheat, and steal
Feel the sweet scent overtake me
But the Lord sent an angel to save me
So he can't blame me
When my hands get a mind of their own
Girl, if they get ahold of you, I ain't never letting go
'Cause I'm selfish
Restless like a river, can't help it
I'm taking what you give me but I still want more
I still want more
'Cause I'm selfish
Yeah I'm selfish, I'm selfish for you
Oh, so selfish for you…

18.
gallan

February 23rd, 2020

I laughed out loud and shook my head at another one of Zaira's weird comments. "No, you aren't dead, babe; just keep walking straight." I tightened my right arm around her waist and guided her further ahead.

She looked absolutely ravishing in a white turtleneck, a long brown flannel jacket, and a pair of black skintight jeans.

And God, those legs of hers… I wanted them wrapped around my waist.

Her gloss-coated lips? I wanted them on mine.

Her wavy brown hair… Fuck, don't even get me started on them.

Did I mention I'm a goner for this woman? Because I am – very much so.

"Why else would you blindfold me right after stuffing me with my favorite pastries?" she asked, and then gasped suddenly before stopping in her tracks. "Oh my God, are you sacrificing me to Satan? Are you one of those celebrities who sell their soul to the devil in order to receive fame and money? Is that why you're so popular?"

I couldn't tell whether she was being serious, or whether she was joking. Her tone matched the former, but still, I wasn't sure.

I nudged her a little, and with a huff, she resumed walking.

"No, I'm not sacrificing you. I'd be the biggest idiot the world has ever seen if I even imagined doing such a thing," I told her.

"Awww." She placed her joined hands under her chin. "You can't see it because of the blindfold, but I'm batting my lashes so hard right now."

I chuckled. "You truly are one of a kind."

"So glad you realized my worth and potential," she mused.

I grinned, and once we'd reached where I wanted us to be, I got behind her, grabbed her hands, and placed them atop the marble railing.

Shane had wanted Zaira and I to have an intimate first date rather than an attention-snagging public one. So, in order to make sure my girl had the best time during said date, I'd decided to arrange things at my penthouse.

Zaira had practically hopped and skipped like a schoolgirl during the entire house tour, and when one of my chefs had brought in her favorite pastries – as per my request – she had gotten that adorable anime-like look on her face, which had filled me with joy and pride.

Damn, she was quickly becoming my lifeline – my source for everything livable.

"Oooh, that's some smooth finishing right there," she commented as she ran her fingers over the black marble railing.

I bit my bottom lip and stood next to her. She was the finest type of loony, that woman.

"You like?" I asked, and when she nodded enthusiastically, I chuckled. "I'm glad you do."

"Who knew a dick could be so hard," she said, and then laughed when I made a sound between a choke and a cough.

"What gave you the idea that it's a…dick?" I asked, mildly stunned by what she'd uttered.

She shrugged. "Judging by the boner you get every time you see me, I simply assumed."

Jesus.

I gently took the blindfold off, handed Zaira her glasses, and waited for her to adjust to her surroundings.

"Wow…" she breathed as she looked at the open night sky after wearing her glasses. "Gall, this is…"

"Beautiful?" I asked, and then stepped closer to her.

"Yeah…" She was still looking at the dazzling stars and the ink-blue sky with wide, awestricken eyes. "Just…wow."

Because I had a ridiculously stunning rooftop, I'd arranged for us to dine on it. I knew she would appreciate the sky and nature's serene allure – just like me. One of the many reasons I was crazy about her.

"So, you still think it's my dick you have your hands on?" I questioned, and when she looked up at me, I raised a brow and dipped my chin as a gesture towards the marble railing.

Zaira glanced down, then back up at me. She rubbed her lips together, and then began giggling like a 5-year-old whilst also almost falling against me.

"Oh my God," she sputtered between titters. "I don't know why I even compared your cock to a railing!"

I chuckled. "Because you presumed I was packing a smooth-finished marble behind my pants."

She tipped her head back and laughed. "*Ya Allah…*" she breathed. "I'm so weird."

"Nah…" I pulled her close and turned her so she was facing me fully. "You're perfect, baby. *My* perfect."

She stopped laughing and sniffed as she gazed up at me. "Cheesy baboon," she said.

I grinned and leaned in before kissing her once. "That, I am."

Zaira ran her hands over my black dress shirt. "You're so hot, Underwood," she voiced, and then quickly ran the tip of her tongue over her bottom lip.

I groaned when that action made my cock twitch.

She looked up suddenly, and then tilted her head. "What?"

"You know what, Zaira."

She smirked – just a little. "Do I?"

What a tease.

"Want me to show you?" I asked.

Her pupils gleamed under the moonlight. "Nuh uh; too early for that." She then shifted a little to her right before glancing down. "Damn…" she drawled. "That'll be a long fall."

I chuckled and kissed her left temple. "Why do you think I'll let you fall?"

She looked sideways at me. "Because that's what happens in thriller romance movies."

My lips twitched. "And what gave you the idea that we're the romantic thriller type?"

She clicked her tongue and looked at me, head-on. "Then what category do we fall in?" she asked.

"Hmm…" I made a show of thinking, but only for a second. "Romantic comedy. We definitely are romcom material."

Zaira chuckled. "Well, then my fall would be full of me screaming bizarre obscenities at you, cursing you and your hypnotic dick for luring me in and deceiving me after, and you letting out an evil, cringe-worthy, and sadistic laugh to every word I spit at you whilst falling to my inevitable demise."

For the umpteenth time in just a few minutes, I laughed. "How do you even come up with these things?" I was genuinely curious and surprised.

She pushed her glasses up her nose and tapped her forehead. "It's a writer's brain, babe. That's all it does; it creates stories."

I grinned. "Can't argue with that logic."

A knock sounded on the rooftop door, right before my head chef Mateo poked his head in. "Dinner is ready to be served, señor. Should I ask Eve to set the table for you and Miss Khan?"

I nodded. "Please; and thank you, Mateo."

He inclined his head. "My pleasure, señor." He turned around and left.

With a smile, I looked down at the beautiful woman in my arms. "Ready to get this date started?"

She grinned. "Hell yes, *señor*." She emphasized the last word to tease me, which only made me smile wider.

"You give me life, baby." I kissed her. "Don't you dare change – not ever."

She chuckled. "I promise. Change is overrated anyway." She kissed me back, and Lord, did my heart perform a fucking somersault behind my chest.

Smitten.

I was thoroughly, madly, and *entirely* smitten with Zaira Khan.

19.
Zaira

February 23rd, 2020

"Why a graphic novelist, though?" Gallan asked, and then took a sip of his dragon fruit virgin mojito. "I'm almost done reading *The Ice Bearer*, and I noticed that your dialogue game throughout the book is so much more impactful and descriptive than the usual comic books out there. You could write complete fiction novels, Zaira, instead of limiting your writing potential to just comics."

A blush creeped up my cheeks as I smiled at the honest intrigue on his face. "I'm so glad you think so." I forked some lasagna, and then twirled it around as I looked at him. "I like expressing my stories through art, and with comics, I can do exactly that. If I were to write a fiction novel, more importance would be given to the words, and not to my art – *if* I even decided to add any into my story, that is."

He nodded. "That actually does makes sense. Your art *is* quite crisp and stunning," he said with a smile.

My face flushed at his compliment. "Thank you." I put the fork to my mouth and chewed on the creamy lasagna. "Damn, this is so *good*."

"You said that not two minutes ago," Gallan pointed out.

I clicked my tongue. "Doesn't mean I can't praise Mateo's hard work again."

He smirked. "If he wasn't a 55-year-old guy, I'd think you have a crush on him," he teased.

"And who is to say that I don't have a crush on him anyway?"

He chuckled and shook his head. "Touché."

Gallan's chefs had done an outstanding job of putting together the perfect date night dinner for him and I. They'd created a toasty vibe by burning cinnamon candles, setting up a table with mouth-watering cuisines and beverages, and had also turned on Jordan Davis in the background.

All in all, everything was perfect; the night was the most ideal for Gallan and I's date, thanks to his crew.

I sighed in content and looked around us. "Thank you for doing this, Gallan. All of this is just so beautiful," I said with a smile.

He adjusted my glasses – that were *annoyingly* falling off my face – and winked at me. "You deserve it."

Queue warm fuzzies in my gut.

"You're too kind." I sipped my blueberry mojito. *Virgin*, of course. "I don't think I deserve all of this." I circled a finger to emphasize my point.

Gallan raised a brow. "And why do you say that?" He munched on some Spanish Rice, and then hissed a little before shaking his head. "Damn, Mateo. He took a free reign with this when I told him he could make the food spicy today."

I chuckled. "Well, I love spicy food, so this is heaven for me."

Gallan sniffed and gulped some water. "Yeah, I know. I asked Kenzie what you like, and she said: '*Anything spicy.*' So I had to make sure there was *spice* present in the dinner."

I ate some of the Spanish Rice and leaned back in my seat. "This is *so* freaking delicious. Remind me to thank Mateo later."

Gallan sniffed again and grinned at me. "Will do. But I'm not sure my ass hole is going to forgive me for what it's going to endure come morning."

I pinched my expression and threw an olive at him. "Ewww, Gall. *Gross*."

He chuckled as he dodged it. "Maybe, but it's also true."

I shook my head and laughed. "It is, yes."

He pointed his spoon at me. "So, you said you didn't deserve all of this." He waved the spoon around. "Why did you say that?"

I shrugged and munched on some lasagna. "I've never experienced, or even *seen*, anything like this, Gallan. The guys I was with in the past were total assholes. None of them thought of doing anything of this nature for me, let alone getting me something. It's not like I desired anything of the sort, because you know how I feel about materialism in a relationship. But every once in a while, I would've appreciated if they at least *acknowledged* the fact that I meant something to them. They all behaved as if they were doing me a favor by staying in a relationship with me." I closed my eyes and sighed as I ran my fingers through my hair. "I'm sorry. I didn't mean to dump my bad partner choices on you. It's not something you need to hear."

"Hey." He grabbed my left hand and twined our fingers together. "Hey, Zaira; look at me."

I did, and he brought his lips to the inside of my wrist before placing a lingering kiss there. "I want you to know that *I* appreciate you; I respect you. I want you to know that I desire you, feel lucky to have you. You're special, baby, and I want you to tell me that it's all that matters to you – knowing that you mean everything to me."

"Gallan…" The molten obsidian of his eyes sparked against the nightlight; against the truth in his expression, in his voice.

"Tell me, Zaira." God, I *loved* the way he looked at me, the way he ran his hypnotic gaze over me.

"It's all that matters. Knowing that I mean everything to you – it's all that matters to me. Because you, Gallan Underwood, mean everything to me, too," I said.

He smiled that stunning smile at me, and then gently kissed every one of my knuckles.

How did I get so lucky? I asked myself. *Just…how?*

Only a few weeks ago, I was worried I'd embarrass myself if I came too close to him. That I'd make a fool out of myself if I opened my mouth and word-vomited something weird or unnecessary to him. Because he's *the* Gallan Underwood, and I?

What was I?

His everything, apparently…

Who knew I'd ever say that, ever get to *hear* that?

We spent hours talking about our childhood, about the quirks of being the only children to our parents; about our first wins, our first losses; about love, about friends; about anything and everything; about the silly things that just randomly came out of our mouths, and meant nothing in a literal sense.

Mateo served dessert – a delicious tray of ice cream sandwiches and frosted Nutella-and-strawberries – and as I got to know Gallan even better, I realized that it wasn't just the night that was perfect.

It was *him* that was perfect, too.

20.
gallan

February 23rd, 2020

"No! That's my 'OMG-what-the-hell-is-even-this-face-?' angle. I prefer the left," Zaira said, and then blinked up at me.

I couldn't help but laugh at her comment. "What are you made of, you weird, adorable woman?"

She clicked her tongue. "Flesh and bones. Oh, and gas."

I chuckled. "You weren't meant to answer my question."

"I couldn't leave it hanging in the air, either." Her expression was serious, but her eyes – they were telling me a very different story.

We were sitting on my rooftop couch, ready to take our first official selfie so we could announce ourselves to the world. Weird, I know, but that's Hollywood for you. It's glamorous, sure, but it's also so fucking staged, that all you wanna do is barf in its dazzling, ever-glowing face. But hey, I loved my job, so a little barf every once in a while was doable.

Right?

Right.

"Don't look at me like that," she said, "because when you do, then all I wanna do is pull you by that growing scruff of yours and kiss you until you pass out."

I just could *not* with that woman.

Zaira was a dynamite – ticking and exploding as she went. She just couldn't help being sassy and quirky.

"Come here." I pulled her close and kissed her once. "You're a rare species, you know that?"

The corners of her mouth turned up. "Yes... *I think*."

I grinned and shook my head. "Ready to take that selfie?"

She sighed. "Yeah."

"You'll do great, babe," I told her. "Just be yourself, and I'm sure people will go crazy for you. I know I am."

She laughed airily. "How corny of you."

I winked at her. "Yup."

She placed a hand on the center of my chest and kissed my chin. "Let's do this."

With a smile, I positioned my phone a little above my face angle, and then tapped on the camera app. "Look at me, Zaira."

She did, and when I grinned at her, she did the same.

I snapped a photo, and was about to check if it was good enough, when she leaned in, placed her soft fingers on my jaw, and kissed me.

I accidentally hit the shutter button, and then almost dropped my phone when Zaira opened her mouth and ran the tip of her tongue over the seam of my upper lip.

"Jesus, woman." I grabbed her by the waist and kissed her as hard as I could, because damn, she tasted so good. "You make me hot."

She smiled against my lips and pulled me closer by the collar of my dress shirt. "I know."

I chuckled, and kissed her a final time before moving back. "I hate to say this, but we should wait in on this and post the selfie before Shane goes all John Rambo on us."

She laughed and nodded, and God, the gentle bruises around her mouth – curtesy of my facial hair – made me wanna beat my chest like fucking King Kong.

Call me cliché if you wanna.

She pulled her phone out just as I opened the photos. "I call dibs on this one," she said, and pointed at the accidental yet stunning kiss-selfie. "I want. Gimme, gimme, gimme."

I chuckled. "Fine." I quickly emailed her the photo, and then we both got to posting the selfies on Instagram.

"Okay, here goes everything," Zaira mumbled, and then hit 'post'.

I placed a hand over hers and squeezed, and then made my post, too.

Within seconds, our phones started *pinging* and *dinging* with notifications.

"God, I'm scared," she said as she looked at me. "What did you caption your photo?"

I handed her my phone, and she did the same to me.

therealgallan: *She makes me happy; she completes me. She knows how to put a smile on my face; she's the only one I want. You're my special kinda girl, @i.am.zaira.k, and I'm so glad you chose me.*

That's what mine said, and I watched Zaira's cheeks flush as she read it.

"You really know how to make a girl feel special, huh, Underwood?" she said.

I kissed the top of her head. "Only the one that matters."

I looked down at her phone and read her caption, and it instantly made me laugh.

i.am.zaira.k: *Look what I snagged. Snatched? Scraped? I don't know. Can't believe he's mine. Oh yeah, it sure feels good to say that. Thank you for choosing me, @therealgallan. You're phenomenal, and I am one lucky gal to have you.*

#heismyhottie #bae #tooyummyformytummy

"Too yummy for your tummy, huh?" I said, and then grinned when she chuckled.

"Yup. You taste better than Nutella, and I'll have you know that I *love* Nutella."

I smirked. "I am *very* aware of that."

"You are?" She tilted her head. "But I didn't tell you that."

"Your IG bio did."

She laughed. "Oh well."

I wrapped an arm around her waist. "Stay the night," I requested. "I wanna hold you while I sleep."

Her eyes softened. "Gallan…"

"I'll behave myself; I promise."

She smiled. "I know you will." She turned and faced me fully. "Okay, I'll stay."

I grinned. "Yeah?" That was easy.

She chuckled. "Yup. You don't need a lot of convincing. You're *you*, and I'll always say yes to whatever you ask me for."

I asked my dick and heart to slow the hell down. It wasn't time for them to perform the dance of imminent victory.

"That's good to know," I told her. "Makes my ego go all Beyoncé."

She laughed. "You're crazy."

I pulled her flush against me. "Yes, but only for *you*."

21.
Zaira

February 23rd, 2020

I took my boots off and placed them next to Gallan's near the penthouse entrance once we'd descended the stairs that led us back down from the rooftop. I have to admit, I felt like a literal peacock in her prime time while coming down those spiral, black-metal stairs. I mean…how could I not? I felt fucking fancy as all shit just *being* in the penthouse.

Talk about wealth giving your middleclass anus an itch.

Gallan placed our phones on the coffee table in front of the fireplace, and then grabbed my left hand.

"Come on," he said with a smile, and led me through his lavish abode.

I'd seen almost all of it when I'd first arrived. The warm contrast of the place, the wood-like walls, the plush carpets, the mahogany-and-beige furniture, the golden lights, and the toasty air surrounding the whole house – it all left me speechless and in awe. *A second time.*

Gallan's penthouse felt like *home*, just as *he* did to me.

We'd decided not to use our phones for the rest of the night because we didn't wanna feel overwhelmed by the constantly pouring in Instagram notifications. Whatever the people, the *fans*, had to say about us, could be dealt with tomorrow.

We'd face the world tomorrow.

The night was ours, and we'd live it the way we wanted to.

We reached Gallan's massive bedroom, and he quickly switched the lights on before turning on the air conditioner.

I looked around the clean and mostly open space, and raised a brow at him. "Fancy." I hadn't seen his entire room during the tour he'd given me, but as I continued to glance around, I learned that he was a man of sophistication and simplicity.

To the left was a balcony with closed glass doors. Next to it was a large walk-in closet and a dressing table. To the right was an attached bathroom. Behind me was a king-size bed and an armoire that held all of Gallan's awards, from both his school and college times, and his professional successes from over the years.

The walls of his room were wood-like, just as the rest of the penthouse. Several frames containing pictures of him, his costars, and his parents, were hung throughout the bedroom.

I felt Gallan watching me as I took off my brown flannel jacket and hung it on the back of the dresser chair. I felt the welcoming heat of his dark gaze as I walked up to the armoire and placed a hand on the cool glass.

"Is it crazy that I remember every bit of information from when you walked up those different stages to accept all of these movie awards?" I asked, and smiled as he came to stand behind me and placed a hand on the side of my waist.

"Nothing crazy about that," he said.

Our gazes met through the armoire glass, and every fragment of me buzzed at the gleam in his eyes, which was so beautifully visible, even with the overhead lights haloing our reflections slightly.

"Yeah?" I questioned as I worked on maintaining a steady rhythm for my heart.

Gallan pushed my hair back, pulled the collar of my white turtleneck down, and placed a long kiss over the sensitive spot below my ear.

"Yes, Zaira," he whispered against my skin. "I think it's so fuckin' hot that you remember such small things about me." He slid a hand below my left breast, and I closed my eyes at the way a simple touch from him made me feel.

"You…" I arched my back when he kissed my neck. "Gallan…" I cupped the back of his neck and tilted my head to the side to give him further access. "You… God, you…"

He laughed airily and pulled me to him. "I *what*, Zaira?"

I swallowed and gently pushed him away. Turning around, I worked at calming down, and then folded my arms over my chest when he raised a brow at me.

"You said you'd behave yourself," I told him.

Challenge flashed in his eyes. "That I did, but I just changed my mind, so what're you gonna do about it?" He stepped closer to me.

I pivoted on my feet to get away from him, and that's when my gaze landed on the black acoustic guitar placed on the wall right next to the armoire.

I quickly grabbed it, and placed it in front of me just as Gallan made a move to grab my hand.

"Seriously?" he asked when I practically shoved the guitar at his chest. "You'd rather I play the guitar than kiss you senseless?"

I chuckled. "Yes, because we both know where all the kissing will lead us, and it's too early for *that*."

Gallan huffed. "Fine, you win." He grabbed the guitar, walked over to his massive bed, settled on it with his back to the headboard, and gestured for me to join him.

"So, I don't see *The Ice Bearer* here anywhere," I said as I climbed the bed.

His eyes sparkled. "That's because it's hiding under the massive box of condoms in my nightstand drawer."

I lifted a brow at him as I knelt on the bed. "Gimme an honest reason for cracking that joke, and I promise I'll forgive you."

Gallan tipped his head back and laughed, and my eyes momentarily went to his strong neck; to the glowing skin of his hard chest that was visible from behind his slightly open dress shirt.

"It was an impulsive response; I didn't even think before blurting it out," he said.

I clicked my tongue. "Adonis-lookalike weirdo," I mumbled, and got comfortable between his open legs prior to placing my back against his chest. "Hmmm, this is perfect," I said as I stretched my legs next to his, and grinned when I heard a steady rumble of his husky laughter.

"Glad to know you've settled in well with an *Adonis-lookalike weirdo*, my lady," he mused against my ear, emphasizing the term I'd used for him. "Also, the book is actually in my nightstand drawer, just not *under* the box of condoms, but *above*."

I elbowed him playfully and pushed myself further against him, only to have him groan and hold me tighter.

"Do you want me to die from blue balls or something, Zaira?"

I snickered. "I don't want you to die, period."

He chuckled. "Well, you're making no attempts in that particular direction, so don't mind if I question your intentions a time or two."

God, that man was perfect.

"Just play me a damn song, Underwood," I ordered. *Mildly*, of course.

"So bossy tonight." He placed the guitar in front of us.

I kept my hands on my thighs so as to give him enough room to adjust the guitar.

"Hmm..." he hummed to himself – once – to set the pace, and began strumming the guitar expertly. A couple veins popped on his broad forearms as he tuned things up. Talk about orgasmic arm porn.

Another hum.

A strum.

I was about to ask him what he was planning on playing, when he started strumming one of my favorite Jordan Davis songs, *Dreamed You Did*.

Last night it was so real

I can still feel

You all over me

And I woke up reaching for you
Wanting to hold you
Damn everything felt right
Last night...
When you called me said you want me
Told me you were coming over
Said you're running red lights
At 85 and getting closer
A kiss at the door, ended up on the floor
Ain't too sure what hurts more
That you didn't or that I dreamed you did...

He stopped, and I shifted just a little so I could look at him properly.

"Why'd you stop?" I asked.

Gallan grinned. "Because you didn't join me," he answered easily.

I touched the fingers of my right hand to his jaw before smiling. "I didn't know you wanted me to."

His expression held profound emotions as he continued to look at me. "I'll always want you to join in, baby; there's no question in that."

Be still, my chubby heart.

I leaned in and placed a soft kiss on his lips. "Okay."

He winked. "Okay." He then picked the beat up from where he'd left off, and with smiles on our faces, we began singing together.

Yeah we said everything we didn't say
I ain't saying no word at all
I tried like hell to fall back asleep
Just to see if maybe we
Could pick back up where we left off
When you called me said you want me
Told me you were coming over
Said you're running red lights
At 85 and getting closer

A kiss at the door, ended up on the floor
Ain't too sure what hurts more
That you didn't or that I dreamed you did oh
Is it worse that you're so gone
That I don't even cross your mind
Or that I'll be dreaming that you're coming back again tonight

When you called me said you want me
Told me you were coming over
Said you're running red lights
At 85 and getting closer
A kiss at the door, ended up on the floor
Ain't too sure what hurts more
That you didn't or that I dreamed you did…

I hid a sudden yawn behind a hand, and a final strum echoed against the peaceful silence in the room as Gallan stopped playing the guitar and placed it on the floor next to his bed.

"You need sleep," he stated the obvious.

I raised a brow at him. "How observing of you, *boyfriend*," I teased.

He chuckled. "Come on; get up. Let me find you something to wear."

I clicked my tongue and crawled away from him – because I'm a lazy piece of poop and didn't have the energy to do the sexy 'Getting out of bed' kinda thing those Hollywood actresses did to seduce their wax-like, lollipop-rivaling, cut-to-perfection love interests.

My ass was the Mother of Tardiness, and even though my guy was wax-like, lollipop-rivaling, cut-to-perfection and all that good stuff, I didn't wanna turn into a Hollywood seductress for him.

Because that wasn't me…

Nuh-fucking-uh.

Not that Gallan wanted me to change or anything.

"What makes you think you have something in your closet that'll fit me?" I asked.

He gave me a '*Hush it*' look before opening his walk-in closet.

He rummaged through some piles of clothing, and then turned to me with a smirk. "Take this." He threw a hoodie at me. "You're gonna rock it, I know that for a fact."

I bit my bottom lip and looked at the soft charcoal hoodie in front of me. It had Gallan's clothing-line, *Under the Woods'* logo printed at its center, and when I grabbed it and hugged it to my chest, I could smell his fading cologne on it. I refrained from moaning, and finally got off the bed before walking over to him.

"A little privacy, please?"

He put his tongue to his cheek as he grinned, and grabbed a random pair of sweats and tee from the closet before heading towards the attached bathroom and shutting the door once he was inside.

I placed the hoodie on a hook next to the full-length mirror inside the closet, took off my turtleneck and jeans, and pushed my saggy girls up because…why not, right?

I tightened my bra straps, fixed my underwear, and then finally put on Gallan's hoodie. To my utter surprise, it fit amazingly well; it even complemented my various curves. Its soft sleeves covered most of my hands. I placed one of it under my nose and inhaled, and sighed when Gallan's addicting and heady smell hit my senses.

The hoodie was long enough to skim the top of my knees, but it clearly left my legs open for viewing. I felt vulnerable, if only a little. I didn't have legs-for-days, no; I had short, chubby ones, and I feared how I'd look in Gallan's eyes.

I pushed the hoodie down my knees in an attempt to hide my legs, but of course, it didn't work. With a sigh, I gave up and hooked my t-shirt and jeans next to the mirror, grabbed a rubber band from my jeans pocket, and pulled my hair up in a loose overhead bun. I leaned closer to the mirror and gently rubbed my hands over my face before checking my teeth. Too late for the latter, yes, but the confirmation of them being clean was a welcome relief nonetheless.

Just as I walked out of the closet, the bathroom door opened, and Gallan stepped out of it wearing a bottle-green tank top over ink-black sweats.

"Hey," he said, and then pushed his fallen hair back as he ran his eyes over me. "Damn, babe; you look irresistible." He dimmed the lights in the room, and the muscles on his biceps ping-ponged with each movement of his arm.

Christ, Gallan really was wax-like, lollipop-rivaling, and cut-to-perfection. *Of the best kind.*

I shuffled on my feet and wringed my fingers together as I watched his pupils flare. "It fits perfectly, the hoodie," I managed to say, and then pulled the hem of the hoodie downwards.

It didn't work. *AGAIN.*

He grinned wickedly. "I can see that." He walked over to the bed before settling in. "You wanna use the bathroom?" he asked.

I shook my head.

"You sure?"

I nodded. Yeah, I'd gone mute all of a sudden.

I could hear the smile in Gallan's voice as he said, "Come here, then." He then patted the spot next to him on the bed.

I cleared my throat silently and sat next to him. My hands itched to pull at the hoodie's hem again, but I refrained myself.

When was the last time I'd felt like a potato on a roast – all hot and bothered and ready to burn out of my skin?

Yeah, that's right. *NEVER.*

N-E-V-E-R.

Gallan chuckled. "Jesus. Are you nervous, Zaira?"

I narrowed my eyes at him. He looked highly amused seeing me so flustered. "Don't be an asshole."

"I'm not an asshole."

"You're being one right now."

"Nope, not at all."

When I didn't answer, but just continued to stare at him, he lied down on the bed and pulled me with him. "You can hardly keep your eyes open. Let's sleep," he said.

I rose on my right elbow and looked down at him. "Oh, didn't you know? It's my sizzling-like-a-bacon-in-an-oily-pan desire towards you that's making my eyes go all droopy and drunk-y."

He laughed. "Drunk-y is not a word."

"I know. I just made it up. I'm a novelist, which means I can do that. *Whenever I want.* It's my birthright. It's in my word-spouting, nerdy blood."

He laughed harder. "Get here, you beautifully crazy woman." He pulled me to him.

I chuckled and lied next to him, and then turned so that my back was to his front.

Gallan wrapped an arm around my waist and erased the last bit of space between us. "Ah, heaven." He pressed sound kisses below my ear and pushed his nose against my hair, and our legs brushed when he shifted even closer to me. "Damn, you smell good."

I placed my hands under my chin and closed my eyes. "You say that every time."

"That's because it's true."

I smiled, because I just couldn't help it when it came to him. "Goodnight, you silly, silly baboon."

His chest shook as he chuckled. "Goodnight, baby."

And, as I lay there – wrapped in Gallan's arms – I felt whole; I felt safe.

In his arms, I felt like I could have whatever I wanted. In his arms, I had zero fears or questions about my appearance; about the hesitations related to them.

With Gallan, I felt like I could conquer the world.

I felt appreciated.

I felt respected.

I felt…

I felt *loved*.

And love is exactly what was coursing through me as he pulled me closer and buried his face against the crook of my neck.

Love…

God, what a strong word it was. I hadn't known I'd experience it – ever. Not for anyone but my family and friends. But with Gallan, it was exactly that.

It was love.

I loved him – heart to brain; body to soul.

I was in love with him, and wasn't that the greatest realization in my high-rolling uptown of a life?

22.
gallan

February 23rd, 2020

I was so close to telling her what I felt. I was so close to completely opening up my heart up to her.

I love you, I wanted to say. Because it was true; I was in love with Zaira.

And, when I heard her snoring softly in my arms, with her shoulders rising and falling evenly, the comprehension of how quickly things were changing between us hit me in the most positive ways possible.

Zaira was quickly turning into my world, into my ray of fucking sunshine, and wasn't that the grandest realization in my paparazzi-attracting and camera-crazy uptown of a life?

23.
gallan

February 24th, 2020

I popped a blueberry into my mouth and chewed on it as I continued to slice the bananas on the cutting board. I flipped the pancakes in the pan, and then looked at the time on my kitchen clock.

8:37a.m.

I'd woken up an hour ago with a smile on my face and my arms wrapped around Zaira's luscious body. I'd left her sleeping in my bed as I'd showered, and then come out to the kitchen to make some breakfast for us.

It was too soon for me to feel so at peace and domestic with her, but I couldn't help myself.

I just couldn't.

I shut the stove and pulled two mugs out of the back drawer, just as Zaira walked out of my room. She looked just as stunning as she had the night before. She'd showered, most definitely, because her hair was wet. The smooth skin of her legs enticed me, and the fact that she was barefoot was making me pant a little, just like a happy little puppy.

A smile broke through me when I saw what she was wearing: another one of my *Under the Woods* hoodie. This one was ice-blue, with snowflakes all over it – even the sleeves. It was from last year's winter collection, but Zaira wearing it left me all hot and needy.

There was nothing cold about that woman, after all.

I also relaxed at the fact that she wasn't pulling the hoodie down every two seconds out of shyness, just like she was last night. She seemed a little more confident now; a little more at ease.

"Morning, Sunshine," I practically chirped.

She frowned. "I feel like death." She ran her hands over her face. "Like 'I-will-eat-your-brains-and-walk-with-my-arms-straight-in-front-of-me' dead." She ran her eyes over me. "But you're a divine sight – all shirtless and in just grey sweats – so maybe I'll survive."

I chuckled. "And you call *me* dramatic."

She flashed her teeth at me as she settled on the kitchen counter. "If you don't feed me soon, you'll realize that my condition is in fact true, and not a façade."

I shook my head and walked over to her. "You should try getting into Hollywood. You have a knack for overacting." I spread her legs and stood between them, and then ran my fingers over the insides of her thighs.

"Gallan..." She placed her palms over my pecs.

I looked at her, and relished in her slightly flared pupils; at the rapid movements of her chest. She licked her lips, and I leaned in before pressing mine over hers.

She moaned, and then cupped my face before parting her lips for me. She smelled like my soap and shampoo; she tasted like my toothpaste. Call me a Neanderthal if you wanna, but knowing that she was here with me like *this*, smelling and tasting of the things I used – it made me so fucking hard.

I was about to wrap my arms around her when my doorbell rang.

Once.

Twice.

Three times.

I groaned and stepped back, and grabbed an open box of blueberries before handing it to Zaira. "Have these. I'll get our breakfast ready in a bit."

She took the box and popped a blueberry in her mouth. "Mmm; no wonder you taste like them." She smirked.

I grinned, and gave her two quick pecks on the lips before jogging over to the door.

Ting-tong.

"Coming!" I unlocked and opened the door, and found a scowling Shane on the other end.

"Shane?" I checked the time on the living room clock. "Is everything okay? We don't start shoot until 10, and it's hardly 9."

His scowl deepened. "Have you cared to look outside your balcony this morning, G?" he asked.

My brows knit in confusion. "No… But should I really – look outside, I mean?"

He widened his arms at his sides and entered the house. "Fuck yeah, Gallan. *Yeah.*" He wiped sweat off his head. "Had to battle my way up, even with security shielding me. And this guy here is having a merry time."

I rolled my eyes and scratched at my abs. "Fine, come in, why don't you." I locked the door and walked back into the kitchen.

"What's wrong?" Zaira asked as she looked between me and Shane. She then pulled the hoodie down to her knees and squirmed a little on the kitchen counter.

"Apparently, it's a third-degree crime that I haven't looked outside my balcony this morning," I said to her, and then came to stand next to her.

Her expression pinched. "Huh?"

Shane clicked his tongue and stepped into the kitchen before facing Zaira. "Your *darling* boyfriend and *you*, dear Zaira, are the talk of the town. You two have gone viral."

"What?!" Zaira and I said in unison.

Shane rolled his eyes and pointed a finger at me. "Don't look so surprised; you're always in the headlines."

"Yeah well, but it's for things I am *aware* of. I don't know what I did this time. Did I accidently share a dick pic in my sleep?" I looked at Zaira after that, and found that the color had drained from her face.

"Hey…" I wrapped an arm around her. "Baby, you okay?"

She gazed at me with big, fearful eyes. "I think it's about the selfies we posted last night."

I whipped my head towards Shane, who nodded at her guess.

"Don't keep me in suspense, you bald bastard. Just tell me what happened."

Zaira laughed a little at my choice of words, which made me smile.

"I think you two should check your phones first," Shane said.

My smile immediately vanished, and my heart started beating faster than a kick drum.

Good fucking morning to me.

24.
gallan

February 24th, 2020

"Nineteen million..." Zaira said for the fourteenth time. Yes, I've kept count. "Nineteen. Fucking. Million."

"Zaira..." I said her name with caution.

She looked at me. "Nineteen million, Gall – that's how many people liked the selfie. Nineteen *million*!" I didn't tell her that twenty-five mil liked *mine*. She'd throw a fit.

Our "making ourselves official" selfies had gone viral, which is why Shane had come banging on my door with a Max-Schreck-rivaling scowl on his face. Paps were circling my penthouse like hungry vultures – ready to snatch at anything they could get their hands on.

Oh, the joy of being an A-list Hollywood star.

I put my tongue to my cheek to hide my grin over Zaira's astonishment. "Yeah, and that's a good thing, isn't it? It just shows that *millions* of people like you."

She shook her head. "There are some pretty mean comments in there." She looked crestfallen. "Someone called me a Hispanic elephant."

My jaw and fists clenched at that. "What's their IG handle?" I asked.

"Gallan..." Shane's voice held warning.

I glared at him. "That person deserves a piece of my mind."

"I have a social media team working tirelessly on those haters. They are being reported, and the social experts are personally contacting Instagram to take down the negative comments and accounts."

"But isn't that wrong?" Zaira said. "These people are only stating their honest opinions, so why report them?" A tear slipped down her left cheek, but she quickly wiped it away.

Shane gave me a look.

I sighed and cupped Zaira's face. Her eyes were misty; her expression showed sadness.

I didn't wanna see her so distressed.

It was breaking me.

I placed a soft kiss on her lips. "Those people are bullies, baby," I told her. "They do these things out of infatuated spite. They don't mean it; they just wanna hurt you with their baseless words. I know you're not used to all this, but trust me when I say that Shane knows what he's doing. You're nothing what those bullies are calling you. You're amazing; you're stunning. You're *mine*, and I'll be damned if I let some pathetic bully hurt you or dampen your spirits."

She sniffed. "Why are people so mean on social media, Gall? Don't they have a heart? Don't they have empathy?"

"They just are who they are, babe." I pushed some of her hair behind her ears. "They think what they're doing is right. They don't care about feelings, about another's emotions. They spread lies and negativity because they think it's fun. Hurting people brings them joy."

Zaira cried, and fuck, my heart ached so bad for her.

"Come here." I pulled her in for a hug, and her body succumbed to mine in an instant.

"97% of the negative comments and accounts are off," Shane announced. "Once the team is done getting rid of the rest, I want you both to turn off comments for the selfie posts."

I nodded, just as Shane's phone pinged with a text.

He looked down, and then sighed in relief. "A 100%. All gone. Do it now." He gestured at Zaira and I's phones that were on the kitchen counter.

I turned off the comments on her, and then my post, and then placed our phones inside the cutlery drawer before looking down at her. "Problem solved."

She wiped her nose with the hoodie's sleeve and gazed up at me. "But what if they start commenting on my other posts?"

"They can't. Selective commenting has been activated on your account, and the ones who spoke negatively in the posts have been removed from Instagram altogether. So, unless they wanna get permanently banned or fined for harassment and bullying, I don't think they'll create new accounts and try to comment on your posts again."

She blinked at him. "Thank you, Shane." She then looked at me in surprise. "Wow…"

I smiled. "I told you he knows what he's doing."

She smiled a brilliant smile. "Yeah, you did. And yes, he does."

"You're welcome, kid. So…" Shane started. "Now that you know I've saved the day, it's time to address the paps and scheduled interviews."

I groaned and pulled away from Zaira before going back to the stove. "Can't you work your magic on both of those as well?" I pouted a little and wiggled my fingers at him, which made Zaira laugh.

Shane rolled his eyes. "Can't. The paps want to know more about you and Zaira, and all the big talk shows have lined up for interviews."

"When?" I asked, and then threw the cold pancakes in the trash before grabbing the pancake mix from the back counter.

"Today. Ross cancelled shoot for the day. He wants you to "figure your shit out" before the media comes knocking on his door. Zaira works for him, and if *you* don't deal with the press, *he* will have to, and we both know how impulsive and weird he is in that department."

"This is ridiculous," I mumbled, and looked at Zaira, who was watching Shane and I with a neutral expression on her face.

"It *is* ridiculous, but the media wants a story, G," Shane said, and I turned my attention to him. "They need an official statement; an assurance of sorts."

A statement? I'll show them *statement*.

I placed the pancake mix box on the counter, opened my cutlery drawer, pulled out my phone, opened the IG app, and then clicked on the camera icon on the top left.

I walked over to Zaira, placed the phone at an appropriate angle, and pressed and held onto the record button.

She made a sound, but quickly relaxed when I wrapped an arm around her just as the IG story video started recording.

"*Hey, guys,*" I began with a smile. "*Thank you so much for all your love and support in last night's post. Zaira and I are ecstatic to see your enthusiasm. I hope you keep the positivity flowing, and also respect our wishes by giving us some privacy. It's very new for the both of us, and we'd like to cherish and develop what we share. I love you all from the bottom of my heart, and I appreciate you being here, rooting for us. Stay safe and healthy. Ciao.*" I signed off with a wink, and then threw my phone back inside the drawer before raising a brow at my manager. "Well, was that *statement* enough for you?" I asked.

He shook his head and walked over to the balcony before peering down. He quickly turned, and then smirked as he came to stand in front of me. "Well, it certainly worked because the paps are leaving, so I'll say yes. Yes, it was statement enough."

I grinned. "Wanna stay over for breakfast?"

He waved a hand before him. "Nah. You kids have fun. I'm gonna spend time with my wife today." He gave me a wink, and I faked a gag just to tease him.

"What about the interviews?" Zaira asked me. "Don't you wanna do those?"

I shrugged. "I do them plenty. I'd rather spend time with you," I said.

She blushed, and this time, *Shane* faked a gag to tease *me*.

Asshole.

"I'm gonna cancel the interviews," he said, "but just this once. I can't keep denying the big names all the time."

I gave him a three-finger salute. "Aye-aye, Captain."

He rolled his eyes again as he headed for the front door. "Have fun, and don't care about the media," he told me, his expression kind. He was a great guy, my manager, and I was a lucky fucker to have him, that was for sure.

I smiled at him. "Thanks, Shane. You're the best."

He winked. "That, I am." He then patted my shoulder once. "Have a good day, son."

"You too, Shane."

With a smile and a nod, he walked over to the elevator.

I shut the door and headed to the kitchen, where Zaira was waiting for me, still munching on the blueberries I'd given her.

"Hey, gorgeous," I said as I came to a stop in front of her.

"Hey." She smiled.

I pushed the hem of her hoodie upwards, and felt my entire body buzz when I saw her exposed skin.

"Are you gonna feed me, or what?" she asked.

I chuckled and leaned against her. "Stay with me today," I commanded gently.

She raised her brows. "Will you stuff my tummy whenever I'm hungry?"

I laughed. "Of course."

"Do I get to keep this hoodie?" She hugged herself.

I smiled. "Yes. This, and a few more."

She narrowed her eyes. "No materialism, Underwood."

"Seriously? But you just *asked* to keep the one you're wearing."

"Yeah, and I'll pay you for it with cuddles and kisses. I like this one, so I only want this one."

"And how do you know you won't like the others?" I questioned.

She shrugged, but said nothing.

I arched a brow. "I have a coral one that I know you'll look stellar in."

She tilted her head to the side. "Do I wanna know why you have a *coral* hoodie? Should I be worried?"

I laughed. "It's a sample for this year's Fall Collection edition. Haven't you seen those?"

"I saw them on your website. They are pretty pricey for a broke ass like me."

I shook my head at her sharp humor. "The one that I have is yours, then."

She looked conflicted. "No." She bit her bottom lip. "I only want this." She tapped her chest. "You can wear the coral one for me."

I smirked. "And here I thought you needed more excuses to gimme cuddles and kisses. 2 hoodies account for 2 days of make-outs. And you get to experience my impressive cooking skills. It's a great deal."

She rolled her eyes. "Fine, but let me text my mum and Kenzie to let them know where I'm gonna be today."

"*And* tomorrow," I corrected her.

"We have shoot tomorrow."

I pulled our phones out and sent a quick text to Ross from mine, and within seconds, he replied back.

"We *don't* have shoot tomorrow," I said to Zaira, and then showed her Ross's reply.

"'*I need more time to figure my shit out, dickhead.*' That's what you wrote?" She looked so shocked.

I chuckled. "Yup. Ross doesn't mind being called one, because he knows he *is* one." His reply to my message was: "*You do you, asswipe.*"

Zaira shook her head. "Hollywood people are crazy."

I laughed, and watched as she texted her mom and Kenzie.

"Here." She gave me back her phone. "I am officially yours. So, what are we gonna do today and tomorrow?"

I liked the sound of her being officially mine. *A lot.*

"I was thinking you could pay me for the hoodies," I said with a smirk.

"Our lips will fall out of our faces if kissing is all we do for 48 hours."

I laughed again. "Well, there's always Netflix & chill."

"I can't believe you just said that. What are we, sixteen?" She pursed her lips.

I gave her a chaste kiss. "Fine. Let me get some food in you so that you start looking like less of a zombie and more of a human, and *then* we'll decide what to do with our free time."

She gasped and threw a blueberry at me. "Did you just call me a zombie?!"

I winked and stepped away from her. "Yup."

She got off the counter and began stomping over to me, but I turned around and started running.

"Come back!" She ran after me. "You shall face my wrath for your insolence."

I laughed as I dodged my living-room couch. "How dramatic of you, babe."

She huffed and continued chasing me. "Stop. Running!"

I waited until she was close, and then turned before grabbing her. "Gotcha."

She squealed and tried to run away, but I lifted her in my arms and walked us to the kitchen. Settling her on a stool, I got to work on making us fresh pancakes.

She watched me while I worked, and then cleared her throat. "So, you won that chase by foul. I get an extra pancake for it."

I grinned. "You got it."

"And another for calling me a zombie."

"Mm-hmm," I said around a smile.

"And I deserve a kiss for being so patient with your pompous ass."

I lifted my brows at her. "I am *not* pompous, but okay." I leaned in and pressed a kiss on her blueberry-tasting lips. "There. Happy?"

She hummed as she nodded. "More."

"Didn't you *just* tell me that our lips would fall off of our faces if we kissed too much?"

She clicked her tongue. "They're gonna fall off in the future anyway because of the eminent apocalypse that'll hit us, so why not have mine fall off now?"

I laughed and shook my head. "God, what have I done to deserve you?"

"Oh, a great many things," she said with excitement. "For example, being hot and sexy; being kind to people; having a husky voice and a too-good-to-be-true smile that gives me mini orgasms *all the time*. Being extremely talented, funny, and–"

I shut her up with a kiss. I cupped her face and moved back before looking down at her. "I love you, Zaira Khan," I said as I looked into her eyes. "*I love you*."

My heart soared at my confession. That blood-pumping sucker was proud of me, just as I was of myself.

Zaira's eyes misted as she held my wrists and smiled up at me. "I love you too," she whispered. "So much."

I grinned. "Yeah?"

She nodded. "I do. I think I have been in love with you even before we started dating." She swallowed once. "But I'm scared, too, Gallan. *So scared*. It's too early, and–"

"We'll figure things out as they come to us," I told her. "One day at a time, baby. We got this. I know we do."

Her smile widened. "Okay then. One day at a time – we'll face everything that comes at us one day at a time."

25.
gallan

February 25th, 2020

"Nooooo." Zaira hugged my waist and buried her face against my chest. "No, please."

I chuckled as I pushed my hair back. "But you said you wanted to go real bad."

"I can't." She shivered a little. "I can't, I can't, I can't."

I swallowed to hide my laughter. "So what, are you planning on peeing all over my living-room carpet?"

She looked up at me with big, pleading eyes. "Please, can I?"

I grinned. "That's unhygienic, and you know it, babe."

She pouted. "But I don't wanna go to the bathroom." She blinked repeatedly, with fear written clearly on her face.

I finally let go of my laughter. "It isn't my fault you wanted to watch the movie at 12a.m. I told you not to, but you were too stubborn and didn't listen to me."

"But how could I not watch it, though?" She stomped her right feet. "James freaking McAvoy is in it, so I *had* to! I've been putting it off for far too long. Kenzie didn't wanna watch it, and when you agreed to, I decided to just…watch it."

When Zaira had seen *IT: Chapter 2* streaming on Netflix, she'd all but pleaded with me to watch it with her. She hadn't seen the first, and only wanted to see the second because James McAvoy was one of its cast members. I couldn't say no to her, so I'd indulged her wish. Little did I know that my girlfriend would turn into a screaming, sobbing, and trembling mess every time Pennywise made an appearance.

She was scared of clowns, and by the time the movie credits had rolled, she'd been fearful out of her skin to even move from the couch, let alone go to the bathroom.

The entire day with her had been heavenly, though. Binging on movies and TV shows, eating food like there was no tomorrow, and kissing at every open chance – that was all we'd been doing.

The last seventeen or so hours with Zaira had been some of the most beautiful hours of my life. I mean it.

"I wanna pee," she whined. "I can't hold it in any longer. The dam is about to break! The walls are about to collapse!"

I couldn't help but laugh, *again*. "Then let's just go to the bathroom. It's only a few steps away, Zaira."

"No!" She hugged me tighter. "Don't make me!"

I clicked my tongue and slowly dragged her over to the living-room bathroom.

"Gallan, no! He's in there! I know he's in there!!!" She tried to stand her ground, but I continued to bring her closer to the bathroom.

Once we were in, I gently took her arms off of my waist and made her stand in front of the toilet. She turned and faced me, and then began scanning the room to see if she could find Pennywise somewhere.

"Just sit on the damn toilet and pee, Zaira," I said with a chuckle, but my voice, *and* my words, startled her, because she screamed and covered her eyes.

Jesus, that woman really was a character.

"Zaira…"

She whimpered a little. "You sound like him," she mumbled.

I put a fist to my mouth to contain my growing amusement. "Sound like who?"

She abruptly took her hands off of her eyes and glared at me. "You know who!"

"Baby, there's no one here. Just sit and pee."

She sniffed and lifted her hoodie a little.

I turned my back to her and waited for her to get the job done.

"What if it comes out of the toilet and bites my vagina off?"

I tipped my head back and laughed. "Seriously?"

She didn't reply, and I heard her *getting the job done*.

I faced her just as she turned on the faucet to wash her hands. "See? You're all good, and so is your…*vagina*."

She huffed and walked over to me before hugging my waist again. "Get me outta here."

"You could simply walk out yourself," I retorted.

"But then I wouldn't be able to cope a thorough feel of your biscuit-like abs."

I grinned. "If you wanted to touch them, all you had to do was ask."

"No fun in that," she mumbled, and placed a kiss on my right pec. "You saved me from Pennywise. My *hero*."

Now I knew she was only teasing me.

"Were you even scared to begin with?"

She pulled back and nodded. "I still am. His creepy laugh is continually buzzing in my ears. I'm waiting for him to pop out of nowhere and eat me alive." She shuddered. "The next time I try to watch a horror movie, shake me out of that decision…for as long as you have to."

I hummed around a chuckle. "Okay."

"And remind me to also not fall so easily for that walking and talking Scottish orgasm-inducer's charm. That man is sexy and talented as fuck, but he acts in some of the most twisted fucking movies."

"Should I be concerned about the fact that James is an orgasm-inducer to you? Should I be heartbroken, sad, or angry over it?"

Zaira snickered and placed a chaste kiss on my lips. "No, because you're the only one I want. Everyone fades in comparison to you; in comparison to what I feel for you."

I kissed her once, and then another time. "You should be scared more often if *these* are the things you're capable of saying. My ego really appreciates it."

She playfully pushed at my chest with a smile on her lips. "You're an asshole."

I winked. "Nope, I am not."

She rolled her eyes. "Take me to bed; I'm sleepy."

"But what if Pennywise is there, waiting for you?"

She gasped and pushed me away, which made me guffaw. "Asshole!"

I laughed and walked backwards, and she began following me.

"Get that smug look off your face, Underwood."

I smirked, and then stopped when I reached the bedroom. I looked back for a second, and then placed a finger over my lips in a "shh" gesture. "Keep quiet; he's in there sleeping."

With a groan, Zaira grabbed a cushion off the couch and charged at me.

I ducked just as she threw it my way, and then lifted her up when she was close enough.

She squealed, and then started laughing when I peppered kisses over the space between her breasts.

"Now there's the Zaira I love," I said, and then placed a knee on the bed before settling her on the navy sheets.

She smiled at me, and I hovered over her before pressing a long kiss on her lips.

"I love you, baby," I said after breaking the kiss. "I love you even more than Pennywise does red balloons."

She laughed and slapped me playfully. "You're an ass," she voiced, but when I shook my head 'no', she did the same and cupped my face. "But I love you too, you annoying tease. I love you so much."

Take that, James freaking McAvoy.

26.
Zaira

February 25th, 2020

"Yeah no. That's a '*Don't let the door hit ya where the good Lord split ya*' for me," I said to Kenzie. We were on the phone talking about some weird sexual experience she'd had with a guy the night before, and as per usual, her experience was one I could hardly wrap my head around.

"I don't even know what that means, but let's forget about *me* and my Daddy-calling hook-up, and talk about *you*."

"What about me?" I asked, and got more comfortable on Gallan's living-room couch. He'd gone to his bedroom to order us some takeout.

I still couldn't believe he'd told me he loved me. It was surreal, that moment. I had never even dreamed of him ever saying those words to me, let alone him kissing me the way he did every single day.

I was one lucky pumpkin, that's for sure.

"Don't act nonchalant," Kenzie said through the line. "What happened after he said those three orgasmic words?"

I'd made a massive mistake of telling my nosy best friend about Gallan and I's confession to each other. And now, because she was an unavoidable force, I had to deal with her 20-questions.

"Nothing happened, Ken," I told her. "We're taking things slow; he's giving me space, and I respect him for it."

I could feel her rolling her eyes as she said, "Yeah, like everything that has happened in your relationship with him so far has been *slow*."

I chuckled. "I know you're upset. You want the gory details, but I can't give you any because nothing has happened."

"Then *make* something happen!" she practically yelled through the line. "Give him some accidental stripteases."

I had to laugh at that suggestion. "You know that's not how Gallan is, right?"

"He's a *man*, Z, and men are all the same."

I rolled my eyes. "Not him."

She sighed. "Whatever. If you wanna be one of *those* couples, then so be it. I'm just being a good friend and assisting you in getting rid of the cobwebs that I know are surrounding your mitten-kitten."

I laughed – hard. "Mitten-kitten? Seriously, Ken?" God, she was weird.

"What? It's a term I made up for your vagina. Don't you like it?"

"I'm not even going to comment on that."

She chuckled. "But you gotta admit it's a cute term."

"Uh…" Before I could say anything, Gallan's bedroom door opened, and he strode out – shirtless – looking all hot and yummy.

"Took you long," I said to him.

"What?" Kenzie asked.

"Not you; I was talking to Gallan," I told her.

"Oh, so he's back from ordering your *takeout*." She emphasized the last word just because. "I'll let you two have fun. And do *not* forget about the accidental stripteases. They *always* work."

I shook my head. "Alright, you crazy lady, I'll text you later. Bye."

"Bye!" She disconnected the call, and I placed my phone on the coffee table just as Gallan came to sit at the edge of the couch I was lying on.

Things on Instagram had calmed down after Shane had worked his magic. When Gallan and I had finally decided to check the app, we'd found thousands of supportive messages from not only his fans, but also from his Hollywood buddies and their families. It was so positively strange to see all the big names – whom I'd been watching and adoring for years – follow me on social media and boost Gallan and I's relationship. I was scared shitless of all the attention I was getting, because it was something I wasn't used to. Hell, it was something I had never even *dreamed* of experiencing. But with Gallan by my side, I was almost fully sure I could settle into the Hollywood vibe just fine.

Fingers crossed.

Our two-day agreement was over, and after having dinner with him, I was to leave for my apartment. I didn't want to, obviously, but I *had* to.

Who knew time could go by so fast when you were busy watching Netflix movies, eating popcorn and ice cream, and kissing your boyfriend like he was a Jolly Rancher candy?

Well, certainly not *me*, until I finally did realize that everything comes to an end, and so did our little getaway from the outside world.

Boo.

"Forty minutes until food arrives," Gallan said, and then scratched at his left armpit. "Jesus, I hate when things get all itchy a few days after shave."

"Aww. Did you use a rash cream or something on it?"

He shook his head. "No. I've been using the products I use on a daily. Things just start to get scratchy a week after I shave." He huffed. "Fucking body hair. Annoying pieces of shit."

I chuckled. "Look at us, talking about armpits and unwanted hair. That's *such* a healthy conversation to have."

He grinned. "Yeah well, we have forty minutes to kill before the takeout guy shows up, so…" He shrugged.

"Oh, but I can think of something that is far more important than body-hair talk," I said.

His eyes gleamed a little under the ceiling lights. "Can you?"

"Mm-hmm."

"And pray tell, what might that thing be?" He canted his head and quirked a brow.

I bit my bottom lip. "Come here and I'll show you."

With a grin, Gallan hovered over me and easily settled between my open legs. He placed his forearms next to the sides of my head and touched our foreheads together.

I loved it when he was so close. This way, I could very clearly see the vibrant spark in his dark eyes – one that he seemed to have almost always.

Gallan was divine perfection; he was my source for pure inebriation.

He awakened me like the moon did the stars; he grounded me like the sky did the storm.

I placed my fingers on his jaw and pressed my lips to his. He responded in kind and parted mine with his tongue. I moaned, because I couldn't help it. He tasted like the blueberry Pop Tarts we'd had a few minutes ago, and somehow, it just made me kiss him harder.

I shuddered, just a little, when he ran a hand below my breast, on my stomach, and then lower – to the outside of my left thigh. So much – he made me feel so much, *too* much…

His calloused touch soothed me; our lips merging, colliding – it set me ablaze.

His hand traced over the goosebumps on the back of my thigh, and I let go of an uneven breath because I wanted more, because I craved more of what he was giving me.

"Gallan…" I whispered after breaking the kiss. "Gallan, I…"

His hand reached my knee, which sent pinpricks all over my body. "Yes, Zaira."

"More…" the word was barely audible as I uttered it. "Gimme more."

His gaze darkened. "What do you want, baby? Tell me, and I'll give it to you."

God, he really was perfect.

I grabbed his hand – the one that was on my knee – and brought it right over to where the hoodie was covering my sex. "More," I said against his glistening lips.

He took a raspy breath and swallowed. "You sure?"

"Yes, Gallan. *Please*."

"Fuck." He looked down, and his chest moved at an erratic rhythm.

"Gallan..." His name was a plea coming from my lips.

Without a word, he pushed the hem of my hoodie upwards, and muttered a string of curses before looking at me with wide eyes. "You have no underwear on?" he asked.

I grinned. "Nope. Haven't been wearing any since yesterday."

"The fuck?" He looked so confused that it made me laugh.

"The ones I wore on date night are in your washer. Didn't you notice?"

He shook his head, and then looked between my legs. "Jesus, woman, you're so hot."

My heart thumped at his compliment; my pussy ached to feel his touch.

"Gallan..." I whispered again.

He smirked slightly at the urgency in my voice, and just when I thought he was going to call me out on being desperate, he gently flicked a finger over my throbbing clit.

My body arched on its own accord, and I held onto the couch's armrest when a too-strong sensation coursed through my body.

Gallan leaned in and brought his face close to mine before massaging me with deep strokes. "So wet; so hot..." He nuzzled his nose against mine. "Zaira, you're everything, baby."

I cried out when he slowly pushed one, and then a second finger inside me. "God, yes, Gallan."

I looked down, and felt a rush pass over me when I saw his fingers working me. He looked stunning atop me, with his chiseled body flexing with every movement of his hand; with his glossy hair curtaining his right temple.

My gaze landed on the bulge in his pants, and I clenched around his fingers.

He hissed, and his cock twitched behind his sweats as he continued to pleasure me.

I leaned in and brushed my lips over his, and then slowly – with my heart beating in my throat – I ran the back of my hand over his bulge.

Gallan moaned, and his balance slipped a little, which resulted in his face to fall next to mine. He moved his fingers faster when I began stroking him through his sweats, and his shoulders stiffened as he continued to breathe heavily against my neck.

"You don't have to do–" He halted midsentence when I worked him harder.

He moved back and looked down at me. "Zaira…baby…" His pupils were flared. His cheeks were a little flushed, and so was his broad, smooth chest.

He twisted his fingers inside me, and I arched my back. "Come for me, Zaira."

Those words… They were a command rather than a request.

I pulled his sweats down with both hands, which made him stop what he was doing. My mouth quite literally watered as I saw the patch of brown hair on his hipbone, and the length of his cock. I wrapped my fingers around the base, just as he dripped a little on my inner thigh.

I began working him again, and his fingers resumed their job of fucking me. The moment we were sharing? It was filthy; it was hot. What Gallan and I were doing was euphoric; it was provocative.

"Fuck my fist, Gallan," I whispered against his lips. "Fuck my fist."

"Jesus, woman." His eyes met mine, and he began thrusting his hips faster against my hand. He used his thumb to circle my clit in sync with his fingers.

My gut warmed, my entire body buzzed and shook, just a second or two before my orgasm hit me – hard.

I cupped the back of Gallan's neck and kissed him, and moaned against him when he groaned and came all over my thigh.

His powerful body shuddered as he went through his release with me; as we both whispered each other's names while pleasure coursed through us. And once we were spent, Gallan slumped against me and nuzzled his nose into the crook of my neck. I let go of my hold on him and placed my hand on the side of his hip.

"That was the most teenager-ish thing I've done in my life so far," he mumbled, and then wrapped his arms around me.

I chuckled and dug the fingers of my other hand into his soft hair before massaging his scalp. "And that was the hottest, most beautiful sexual encounter I've had in my life so far."

He pulled back and looked down at me. "Yeah?"

I nodded, because what I'd said was a 100% true. "Yeah."

Gallan smiled and peppered a few kisses on my jaw before settling his face against the side of my neck again. "I know I have to clean you up for the mess I've made, but I'm still reeling from that orgasm, so gimme two minutes, tops, to recover."

I closed my eyes as I laughed, and kissed the top of his head as I continued to massage his scalp. "Okay," I said with a smile. "We'll sober up after two minutes."

27.
Zaira

February 27th, 2020

"**M**ay the devil take her and rot her in the deepest depths of stinky Hell," Kenzie muttered from my left.

I chuckled as I added a cube of sugar to Gallan's coffee, and then stirred it with a spoon. "You do realize that your job's in jeopardy, right?" I told her, and when she gave me an '*I don't give a fuck*' look, I rolled my eyes at her. "You're lucky Aubrey's manager didn't ask Ross to fire you after that loose-bowel incident. But you may not be so fortunate this time if she finds you cursing at her."

It was just another day at shoot, or rather, it *wasn't*. Things had been quite different for me, I had to admit. Everyone at the studio kept looking at me like I'd just dropped onto the phase of the Earth from planet Venus or something. There was judgement in their gazes; there was question, confusion, anger, humor, and worst of it all – there was disgust. Most of them thought I didn't deserve Gallan, that I'd trapped him into a pretense relationship. It was too much to cope with, because the impact of their thoughts and behavior towards me was heartbreaking.

But in truth, I also couldn't blame them. It was only natural for them to have such reactions, because Gallan was one of the most good-looking, talented, and successful actors in Hollywood. He was big in the industry, and for someone like *him* to pick someone like *me* – it was sure to start a scandal.

Paps had been harassing me for the last two days, but I wouldn't tell that to Shane or Gallan. They'd followed me everywhere I'd went with their cameras at the ready, and had even crowded my car on the way to the studio. It was too much, but it wasn't anything I couldn't handle. I'd been dealing with bullies most of my life, and the only way to shoo them away was to keep on living my life and pretending they didn't exist. *At all.*

But anyways, the reason why Kenzie was upset was because ever since I'd arrived at the studio, Aubrey had been giving me the stink-eye. She was acting as if I'd snatched the very last piece of a limited edition Chanel handbag before she could buy it. Not that I could afford said handbag, but it's just a hypothetical explanation to her behavior towards me.

It's funny she even noticed me, because up until a couple or so days ago, I was nonexistent to her, and at least 79.69% of the cast and crew involved in *Waves That Hold Us*. Funny…

Kenzie huffed. "I wanna pull chunks of hair off of that skinny skull of hers and stick it on her jaw to give her an early-Endgame Thor look."

I stared at her in confusion. "That makes no sense, Ken."

She waved her arms at her sides like a frustrated pigeon. "It does!"

I shook my head. "She's missing the belly," I told my friend. "Also, overweight or not, Thor/Chris Hemsworth is too hot and too perfect to be replicated by someone as mean and weird as Aubrey."

Kenzie giggled. "True," she agreed.

The two of us then high-fived, just as my phone *pinged* with a new text.

I pulled it out of my back pocket, and smiled big when Gallan's name flashed across the screen.

Gallan: *Where are you?*

I chuckled at his message. He'd asked me the same question not 20 minutes ago.

Me: *Red Room.*

Gallan: ………………….

Gallan: *I don't know what that is. Is it a secret sexual innuendo that I should be aware of, or have you finally been asked to join the Marvel Universe?*

I grinned and shook my head. I knew Kenzie was watching me.

Me: *Not the latter, unfortunately. The Red Room I'm referring to has the plushiest red pillows, the silkiest of red bed sheets, and a shit ton of sex toys.*

Gallan: *Ha-ha. Funny. Like you'd ever go to such a place without inviting your ready-to-please-24/7 boyfriend.*

I laughed, and Kenzie began furiously stirring Aubrey's coffee – making all sorts of *clicking* and *clacking* noises – to get my attention. I didn't indulge her, of course, because I was a tease like that.

Me: *I didn't have to. Alejandro here is treating me just fine.*

Gallan: ………………

Me: *??????????*

Gallan: *Who, in the name of Yoda, is Alejandro?*

I imagined steam coming outta his ears and nose as he must've typed that message.

Me: *My Dom, of course.*

Gallan: *Jesus fuck, Zaira. You're into BDSM?*

I placed a hand over my mouth and laughed.

Me: *Only the type that leaves bruises and some ongoing pain.*

Gallan: *Fuck me 12 ways to Easter…*

Me: *I'm sure Alejandro can do that.*

Gallan: *Why don't I trust a word you're saying right now?*

I bit my bottom lip.

Me: *Because you know me well. Because you can read me like a book.*

Gallan: *Exactly. Now, tell me where you are.*

I chuckled, and Kenzie banged the spoon she was holding, on the wooden table. I made a '*Gimme 5*' gesture with my hand and got back to texting Gallan.

Me: *At the studio kitchen.*

Gallan: *Come to me, then.*

Those four words elicited something welcoming in my chest.

Me: *I'll be there in 10.*

Gallan: *Make it 3.2. It's been an hour since I've kissed you. I need my fill.*

Me: *But how can I leave Alejandro like that?*

Gallan: *I'm going to kill that imaginary Alejandro of yours with my bare hands.*

Once again, I found myself laughing.

Me: *You wouldn't dare. He's so sweet and caring and attentive.*

Gallan: *Zaira...*

He was annoyed, I could tell.

Me: *Gallan...*

Gallan: *Why are you torturing me like this?*

Me: *Lol.*

Gallan: *Come. To. Me. NOW.*

Me: ....*Lol.*

Gallan: *I don't even know what to say to that.*

Me: :–)

Gallan: :–/

Me: :–*

Gallan: *Stop doing that.*

Me: *Lol!*

Gallan: *Stop that, too!*

Me: *Lmao? Rofl?*

Gallan: *Zaira, seriously...*

I chuckled.

Me: *Fine, I'll be there in 5. I'll apologize to Alejandro for my abrupt departure.*

Gallan: *I'm not even going to acknowledge that. At all.*

Me: *Hahaha! Baboon. See you in a few. Love you* :')

Gallan: :–D *Love you too.*

With a smile, I showed Kenzie the text conversation, who then laughed after having read it.

"You two are weirdly adorable," she said with a shake of her head.

"I know," I replied with a smirk.

"So…" She handed my phone to me with a glint in her eyes that could rival the one The Mask has when he's about to beat someone's ass. "Did you take my advice after all?"

I quirked a brow as I pocketed my phone. "What advice?"

She gave me a *'Really?'* look, to which I simply shrugged in nonchalance.

"The one about accidental stripteases!" she said with a huff.

I chuckled. "I kinda did, but not really."

She began rubbing at her temples like I was being an inconvenience and pain in the ass to her. "I don't know what to do with you."

I chuckled harder. "If you really must know, Gallan and I had a nice and steamy moment after your advice practically glued itself into my head."

Her entire demeanor changed. "Yeah?" She looked so proud of herself.

"Yeah," I said. "I think what you said kinda stuck with me, and it made me brave enough to initiate a move."

"Oh, I *like* that!" She bounced on her feet. "What was his reaction when he *saw* you?"

"When he saw me?" I was confused. "He sees me every day."

"Oh my God, no!" She placed her hands on my shoulders. "When he *saw* you, Zaira."

Ah… I see what she meant.

"I mean, it's just my vagina, and not freakin' Madonna. He didn't pass out or anything after looking at it," I said.

Kenzie laughed and walked back to the table to grab Aubrey's coffee. "Only you can say something like that," she mused with a shake of her head.

I chuckled and grabbed Gallan's coffee. "I mean, it's true, isn't it?"

"Sure is."

Ping.

I pulled my phone out of my pocket and looked at it.

Gallan: *I'm about to send a search party for you, and Shane with a loaded pistol for Alejandro. You better come to me if you want your Dom alive.*

I cackled.

"I gotta go, Ken. Things are getting serious here; he's texting life-threats now."

My best friend laughed. "Well, you better shoo away, then. The last thing we need is the heartthrob Gallan Underwood throwing a hissy fit because his girlfriend was busy shacking up with an imaginary sex God. Now, wouldn't that be a smashing headline of this up-and-coming decade?"

I shook my head around a grin. "Alright, weirdo, I'm out. You good with delivering the coffee to Aubrey without me?"

She waved a hand before her. "I'm cool; you go please your Hollywood hottie. I've got Aubrey."

We hugged once, and I then headed straight for Gallan's new trailer, with chubby hippos wearing sparkly-pink tutus performing a well-orchestrated ballet in my stomach.

All those romance novels and movies that tell you how "butterflies" flutter in the heroine's belly as she's about to meet her guy? Yeah, that's total BS. It's the hippos, I'm telling you.

It's always them.

Chubby, cute, willing to dance 24/7.

It's them hippos.

Always.

28.
gallan

February 27th, 2020

"You know you don't have to knock, right?" I said with my eyes on my laptop screen as I continued to scroll through the pictures on it.

In my peripheral view, I saw Zaira poking her head in through the slightly open trailer door. "I can't know for sure what you must be doing in here all alone, so it's better to announce myself rather than accidentally witness something that might scar me for the rest of my nerdy life."

I rolled my eyes as I faced her. "Come here." I patted my left thigh with a smile, and then shifted a little in my chair.

She walked in, shut the trailer door, placed the coffee mug she was holding on the worktable in front of me, and then sat on my lap.

She looked irresistible in her long red flannel shirt and skintight jeans. Her hair was a mess above her head, and her glasses, as usual, were falling down her nose. She was cute, my girlfriend.

Zaira looked around the trailer for a minute or two, and then brought those hazel eyes to me before giving me a complacent smirk.

"What?" I asked. I wrapped an arm around her waist and pushed her glasses up her nose.

"This," she responded as she circled a finger in the air. "This is a neat trailer. Better than the previous one."

"Yeah?" The layout for the new one was way simpler and elegant than the one I'd destroyed during my rat chase. But the new trailer was also slightly more expensive, as it had a lot of comfort and preference adjustments done to it.

Zaira ran her fingers over the back of my head. "Yeah." She then clicked her tongue. "But I'll have you know that the people you'd hired for the lighting job yesterday were total and utter asshats. It's a miracle Ken and I were able to get them to work according to our instructions."

I chuckled. "I'm sorry." I pressed a kiss on her chin. "Thank you for helping them out, though," I said. "I wish I'd been there to guide the workers with you instead of Ken."

Zaira smiled. "It's no problem, Gall. I know your Wednesdays are meant for your parents, and your parents only. It's one of the reasons why I adore you so much. You put family first, and that's such a beautiful trait."

"Thanks." I tightened my arm around her. "But I feel kinda bad because you gave up your day off in favor of assisting the electricians."

Her eyes gleamed behind her glasses as she canted her head. "I'm sure you'll make it up to me in that regard."

My lips twitched at the mischief in her voice. "I will, will I?"

She bit her bottom lip and leaned in slowly. "Yes," she whispered, and then glanced at my mouth.

With a smile, I touched my lips to hers, and in an instant, she opened hers and kissed me back.

I swallowed a moan and held her face with my free hand before feathering my tongue against hers.

It was heaven when we kissed.

It was fire when her breaths hitched against me.

It was divine when our bodies intertwined the way they did as we lost ourselves into the sea of our wants, of our lust.

Of our love.

Zaira pulled back and placed the tips of her soft fingers over my mouth. "We can continue this later. Drink your coffee before it goes cold."

I relished the redness around her lips for a moment, and then grabbed the coffee mug off the table when she gave me a '*Do as I say*' look.

As I took a sip of it, though, a thought, or a feeling, perhaps, nagged at me. I looked at Zaira. "Will you think it's weird if I say that I don't like you working as a crew member anymore?" I gulped some more of the coffee as I waited for her to say something, because damn, caffeine was what I needed – in plenty – after kissing the woman in my arm.

Zaira shook her head. "Not weird, no."

I placed the mug on the table and used my hand to cup the side of her left thigh. "Then don't work here. My assistant at *Under the Woods* wants to retire early and spend time with her husband and kid, so her position will be up for grabs soon. I can't think of a better person for the job than you."

Zaira sighed. "I've signed a contract with Ross, Gall."

"Fuck the contract; I'll talk to him about it."

She shook her head. "What's the rush? Shoot ends in a few weeks; I'll come see your office after."

I huffed. I'm aware that I was being a brat, but that attitude fell under the territorial category, so that should be explanation enough.

"Why don't I take you to the office with me this weekend? You can see how things work, from both my side and my assistant's. After all, she is the one who handles everything when I'm on set. It's not a hectic position, I promise. It's just a lot of calls and boring meetings and flashy presentations."

"Wow…" Zaira placed a hand over her heart. "That's such an adventurous job; I'm practically preening at the opportunity," she deadpanned.

I rolled my eyes and bopped her nose with a knuckle. "Smartass."

She chuckled, and then bent to press a quick kiss on my forehead. "But in all honesty, it sounds great. I would love to be your assistant."

I grinned. "Yeah? So does that mean you–"

"Nope," she cut me off with a smirk. "I am *not* leaving here until the movie wraps up."

I huffed. *Again.* "Name your price?"

She tipped her head back and laughed. "All I want is your patience. It's just a few weeks, Gallan. They'll go by quicker than you think."

"Hopefully. I pray that they do."

She shook her head at me. "Baboon."

I smiled at her use of term, which made her chuckle again.

"I just want to make sure you have a proper job," I said to her. "You're talented and amazing, and I'll be honored to have you."

Her eyes softened. "You're phenomenal, Gallan Underwood." She brushed my hair away from my eye. "Fucking outstanding. And I'm so lucky to be the receiver of your kindness."

I swallowed at her words. "You really know how to make a guy blush, don't you?"

She smiled. "Only a certain actor who I'm madly in love with."

I grinned and leaned in so I could kiss her, but stopped when I realized…

"Photos…"

"Huh?" Zaira looked at me in confusion. "What?"

I quickly finished my coffee and turned my laptop around before waking its screen. "Help me pick one," I said to Zaira, and then waved a hand over the dozen or so photos of me. "It's a photoshoot I did at the beginning of the month for a new hoodie edition for March. My assistant, Sage, suggested I go with the pastel theme because it's in trend, so that's what my designers did. I have these photos for advertisements, promos, and for my website, but *People*'s mag wants to do a feature, and they asked me to choose a shot for their March front cover. I don't know which one to pick, because honestly, they all look the same to me, so I'll leave the decision up to you." I cleared my throat a little after I was done.

Zaira patted my shoulder. "Breathe, Gall. *Breathe.*"

I ran a hand over the back of my neck. "I really went all freight-train on it, didn't I?" I asked as I laughed.

She chuckled. "You did, yes. For a second there I was worried you might need CPR if you maintained that speed and octave."

I gave her a *look*, which only made her chuckle more.

"Photo, babe – pick one." I tilted my head towards my laptop.

With an arm draped around my neck, she shifted on my lap and leaned forward. She adjusted her glasses, moved the cursor around as she browsed the photos, and once she was done, she sat back and looked at me.

"Damn, that was *hard*." She released a long breath. "My nipples and I – we are on the brink of explosion. Seriously. We really, *really* love seeing you in hoodies, especially ones that are pastel in color and have cute quotes on them. Queue bodily volcanoes."

I was so confused.

"I'm so confused right now," I said with a shake of my head. "I literally don't know what to say to you, or how to react to your bizarre comments. I'm just…"

Did I also mention that I was speechless?

Because I was.

Zaira looked at me like I'd just informed her that the Earth was asymmetrical. "Please don't tell me you're unaware of a nipple explosion." Her voice and expression were so serious, that I began questioning every bit of my existence.

"Uh…" I managed to shrug, which made her frown.

"It's a thing in Kingdom Fangirl," she began. "Nipple explosion is the same as ovary explosion. It's *BOOM-BOOM* in both situations, the destruction of body cells; the death of souls, and the insistent quivering of the affected person's body – hence the bodily volcanoes. It's legitimate; it's a trigger for true, dedicated fangirls."

"I… Umm…"

Wow.

Just…what the fuck?

Zaira gazed at me with big brown eyes, and when she knew I wasn't going to say anything – because I really didn't know what to – she opened her mouth as if to say something, but then shut it before dissolving into a fit of giggles that began so suddenly, that it startled me a little. Dumbfounded, I sat there with my tongue between my teeth for a good few minutes and watched her come down from her wave of shocking amusement.

"Oh God," she sputtered between fading giggles. "Gallan, your face!" She began laughing.

My own laughter joined hers. "In my defense, you left me horrified and tongue-tied."

She bent and tittered harder, and then sniffed a couple times before wiping tears from her cheeks. "I can't believe you took me seriously."

"Well, after the rat stampede, I've planned on taking everything seriously," I told her, and then grinned when she ruffled my hair.

"But..." She finally stopped laughing, and with a smile on her face, began fixing my hair. "On a serious note, I really love all your photos from the shoot." She moved back just a little, and then finger-combed my hair for extra measure. "However, I absolutely *love* this one." She tapped a peach-colored nail over one of my photos. "I think you look positively irresistible in it."

It was a shot in which I had on a pastel pink hoodie with the words '***Pink Until You Sink***' at its center. With one hand in the pocket of my dark jeans, and the other cupping the back of my neck, I had a cheeky smirk on my face which was meant only to attract the customers.

"Yeah?" I looked between her and the photo. "You think this is front cover material?"

She ran a knuckle over my jaw. "*You*, my dear boyfriend, are front cover material, which naturally means so are your photos," she said.

I smiled. "Can you hear the rustling of my feathers? Because I'm practically preening like a peacock right now."

She chuckled. "Baboon."

I let go of an airy laughter. "I'm serious; your compliments really make me wanna dance in the rain with my arms open wide."

Her lips twitched. "I think peacocks dance in the rain to attract mates, and not because they're happy or ego-satiated."

I pressed my teeth to my bottom lip. "That so?"

She smirked. "Uh huh."

"Wanna see my moves? I've been told I'm a lady-killer when it comes to Squash The Bug and The Chicken."

She placed a hand over her mouth and laughed. "The dance moves?" she asked.

"Yeah." I chuckled when she playfully pushed at my chest. "I promise I'm a mean hip-shaker."

Zaira cackled and shook her head at me. "God, Underwood, you're a miracle. A crazy, beautiful, empathetic, and silly miracle."

I grinned and pressed a long kiss on her cheek. "And you wouldn't have me any other way, right?"

She cupped my face and smiled. "No, I wouldn't." She touched our foreheads together. "I love you just the way you are, and there's nothing about you that I wanna change; nothing about how I feel about you that I wanna alter. You're my kinda weird; my kinda normal. Never forget that, Gallan."

My heart damn near burst out of my chest at her words. "I won't," I told her, and then kissed her. "I promise I'll never forget that."

29.
gallan

February 28th, 2020

"Curse your fame-drenched, well-hung donkey-nut!" Zaira yelled out of nowhere when I maneuvered the motorcycle we were both on to the left side of the empty area provided by the set crew.

It was next to impossible for me to keep a hold on my laughter *and* to properly guide the vehicle I was controlling with her spewing such unworldly comments while sitting in front of me.

"Need I remind you that it was *you* who wanted a ride on this thing?" I told her, and then placed my chin on her left shoulder before guiding us further ahead at a reasonable speed. Man, I fucking *loved* the feeling of the wind in my hair. It was relaxing and fulfilling – just like being with Zaira was.

She was simply *gorgeous* in a purple turtleneck and white jeans. She was a treat for my damn eyes.

She huffed as she fixed her glasses. "But when the impulsive idea struck, I wasn't aware that my excruciating and unglamorous death would flash before my eyes as soon as I sat on this murderous junk of metal!"

I chuckled and rode a little faster. "This motorcycle is one of the most lavish ones out there, and you just called it a piece of junk." I placed a gentle kiss on her earlobe. "Also, you're not gonna die, babe. I won't let anything happen to you."

She rested her back against my front, and I could feel her warmth through my thin Henley. "My eyes are twerking, which means something is going to happen."

I pressed my lips together. "They are, are they?"

"Yeah." She sighed. "It's a superstition we Indians have. If your eyes twerk, either something bad, or something good is going to happen to you. Depends on which eye it is, though, but both of mine are twerking so I'm not sure what to think of it."

I hummed. "Fascinating. But I think the superstition has something to do with eye *twitching*, and not *twerking*."

"You're being very sassy this morning, Underwood. Stop now or else your tonsils will show."

I laughed and swerved to the right. "I don't even know what that means, but okay."

She shoulders shook as she chuckled. "I don't know what that meant, either! I just said it because I'm scared and am spewing shit outta my mouth. It's like…" She waved her left hand before her face. "It's like: You Can't See Me! My death is a stealthy bitch, that one. I know she'll pop out of nowhere – when I'm least expecting it to."

"Did you just reference *and* do a John Cena impersonation?" I asked.

"Yes! Love the guy." She straightened a little in excitement. "Hot, yummy, straight-to-the-point when it comes to certain things, and so funny!"

I raised a brow at that, and when I realized she wasn't going to be able to see it, I cleared my throat. "Ahem…"

Zaira looked at the motorcycle's side mirror and gave me a coy smile. "But no one compares to my outstanding, loving, caring, magnificent, alluring, and delicious boyfriend!" she chirped.

I scoffed in a teasing manner. "Yeah, no one except for *John Cena*."

She laughed a little. "Aww, babe; you are my #1. You always will be."

My lips *twerked* at her words. "I better be, or else I'll have to find a way to gain all those muscly pounds if I am to compete with a pro wrestler. Because I *will* compete for ya, Zaira – however I can."

Through the mirror, I watched as a blush creeped up her soft cheeks. "Cheesy baboon," she said, which made me grin.

I was about to take another turn when, in my peripheral view, I found someone waving at me. I turned, just as a crew guy hollered, "They're here, Gallan!"

I nodded and smiled. "Thanks, George. I'll head back in a few."

He gave me a thumbs up and jogged towards the studio.

I placed a foot on the ground and shut the motorcycle's engine before slowly getting off of it.

"Who's here?" Zaira asked.

I winked at her. "You'll see." I offered her a hand. "Come on; get down."

She pursed her lips and shook her head. "No." She hugged the motorcycle's front. "I'll fall and crack my skull open. Then all my dirty, kinky fantasies will flow out and seep through the muddy ground and you'll *see* them; you'll know how weird I really am."

I scratched the side of my neck as I laughed. "I already know you're weird. *Adorably* weird." I tilted my head to the right. "Hop off, beautiful."

She watched me with narrowed eyes for a few seconds, and when I gave her a smile, she rose slowly, took my outstretched hand, and squealed as she got off the vehicle. "Wow…I'm…*alive?*"

I chuckled. "Of course you are." I pushed some of her wavy hair behind her ears. "Let's head in, hmm?"

She shook her head. "I have an entire bottle of Bisleri worth of piss I need to get out. That ride horrified my very soul."

"Who is being dramatic now, huh?"

She flashed her teeth at me, which made me shake my head at her.

I leaned in and pressed a quick kiss on her cheek. "You go empty up that bottle of Bisleri of yours, then. I'll be in the studio. Meet me at stage 20 when you're done, okay?"

She nodded with a grin on her face, but didn't move.

I smirked and kissed her once more, and then another time when she moaned. "Enough for now?" I asked.

She kissed my chin. "Never, but the dam is about to break here," she patted her pelvis, "so I'm going to have to let you go."

I couldn't help but chuckle again. "Alright. I'll see you in a bit."

"You will." She skipped over to my trailer – because I'd told her she could use it whenever – but stopped just shy from the door and turned around. "I love you, Gall," she said.

My heart drummed in my chest. "I love you too, baby."

She blew me a kiss, faced the trailer, unlocked its door with the spare key I'd given her, and then headed in.

With a schoolboy smile on my face, and a bit of a pep in my steps, I headed towards the studio.

Man, I was one lucky baboon, wasn't I?

30.
Zaira

February 28th, 2020

"I finally have a celebrity crush!" Kenzie yelled as soon as I answered her call. "For the first time in monumental history, I have a celebrity crush!"

I rolled my eyes as I zipped and buttoned up my jeans. "I haven't seen you today. Where in Satan's name are you?"

She grumbled something incoherent, and then said, "You're getting off topic."

I grinned. "Fine, fine. So, who is this *crush* of yours?" I walked over to Gallan's vanity table and sat in a chair in front of the mirror.

"Tom Hiddleston!" Kenzie almost damaged my eardrum as she yelled the name.

Oh dear...

"Uh..." I sanitized my hands and put the phone on speaker before placing it on the black-marble table in front of me.

"What? What's the 'uh' for?"

"Umm..."

"Zaira!"

I chuckled and grabbed a spare hairbrush that was on the vanity table. "I don't know what to say to your choice of celebrity, that's all."

She made a sound. "But why?"

I sighed and began brushing my hair. "I mean, Tom's a good-looking and talented guy. And that accent – *oh la la*... But I've never seen him as an attractive person." I placed the brush on the table and grabbed a tube of cherry

Chapstick from my jeans pocket. "I mean, if you have a secret alien fetish or whatever, then I would say he's the right choice of crush for ya." I pushed my glasses up my nose when they fell forward.

There was a pause on the other side.

"Hello?" I said. "Ken, you there?"

"Are you on something, Z? Cocaine, heroin, ecstasy?"

I laughed. "You know I don't do any of that."

"Then why the hell would you compare my sexy Loki to aliens?!?!?!?!!" she yelled.

"Because he just...looks like an alien to me." I slipped the Chapstick in my pocket. "His facial structure and eyes are so...alien-y."

"I'm going to ignore the vile words that just left your mouth."

I chuckled. "Aww, Ken, I–" I stopped when the trailer door opened and Gallan walked in.

"Zaira? Hello... Still alive and breathing?" Ken said.

I grabbed my phone as I got to my feet, and then turned before walking over to Gallan.

"I'm here," I told Kenzie. "Gallan just showed up while I was talking, so I got distracted." I winked at him, and he smiled and shook his head at me.

"Hey, sexy asshole who my best friend is smitten over," Kenzie sassed, which made Gallan laugh.

"Hey, best friend to my girlfriend who likes men who look like aliens," he sassed back.

Kenzie gasped. "Tom. Does. NOT. Look. Like. An. Alien!"

I chuckled. "Sure."

"Ugh, you two are so mean!!!"

Gallan stepped closer to me. "No, we aren't. We just love teasing you," he told Kenzie.

She huffed. "You guys are like those suffocatingly annoying couples who have the same opinion on everything. Doesn't mean you're right." She clicked her tongue. "I can't wait for the time when you two start looking alike. That's what happens to couples like you. That's what you *deserve*. Muahahahaha!"

I looked at Gallan, whose brows were furrowed in utter confusion. When our eyes met, his widened like saucers.

"Where did you find this creature?" he asked me.

I laughed. "I think she'd just escaped an amusement park after working there as a mascot for 3 years when I found her."

Gallan bit the inside of his cheek. "The costume, and the sweat it absorbs – they've really done a number on her, it seems."

"Don't forget farts and burps," I said to him. "The costume also absorbs the smell of those two."

Gallan laughed airily. "Can't forget that, obviously."

"Uh, EX-SQUEEZE ME?!?! I can hear you two, remember?!" Kenzie yelled. "Also, I've never worked as a mascot at an amusement park! Or a mascot *anywhere*, for that matter. I'm not even mascot material!"

Gallan chuckled as he shook his head. "Okay, okay; I get it. Will you kindly relax a little and not scream your lungs out?"

Kenzie made an undecipherable noise. "Whatevs. I gotta go. I have to get ready for a hot date tonight. I'll see you assholes tomorrow."

"You ditched work to get ready for a *date*?" I asked her. "Why do you need an entire day for that? Also, who is your date? Where and when did you meet him?"

"Calm down, *Mom*," she mused. "I have a salon appointment before the date that I couldn't miss. My date is the same guy I told you about a few days ago. His name's Hayden, and I met him at the club. You were there, don't you remember?"

"I thought it was some guy named Rob you left the club with."

"For the last time, Z: it was HAYDEN, not ROB. I don't know why you keep thinking there's a Rob. There's *no* Rob, just like there's no Alejandro."

I tilted my head to the side. "Whose Alejandro?" I asked.

"Oh-my-God, seriously?"

Next to me, Gallan chuckled.

"What?" I told him.

He put his tongue to his cheek. "Alejandro is your imaginary Dom, babe. You forgot him already? He'll be so damn heartbroken to know that."

I scowled at him. "Careful, Gall; your dickhead side is showing."

Kenzie laughed. "How does that feel, Z? Don't like it when the tables turn, do you?"

I rolled my eyes. "Have fun on your date. I'll talk to you later."

She laughed harder at that.

With another roll of my eyes, I ended the call and slid my phone into my back pocket.

"You're all pouty and cute right now," Gallan said.

I flipped him off, which made him laugh. "And you say you aren't an asshole."

He winked. "I'm not."

I shook my head. "What're you doing here? Didn't you say you were gonna be at Stage 20?"

He smiled, and then revealed a sleek black package from behind him. I hadn't seen it on him when he'd walked in. But I guess when you're busy trying to tell your best friend that her celebrity crush looks like an alien, you don't bother much about anything else.

"What's this?" I asked Gallan.

He handed the package to me with a broad grin. "Look for yourself."

I raised a brow and took it from him. I untied the silver ribbon on it, and then carefully opened the neatly folded black flaps.

"Whoa…" My eyes widened when I saw the copy of *People's* magazine in my hands. "This is just…*wow*." I ran my fingers over Gallan's photo on the cover – the one I'd helped him pick only yesterday. "I'm so proud of you." I looked up at him. "This is beautiful. Congratulations, babe."

He leaned in and pressed a kiss on my lips. "Thank you. I'm very happy with how it turned out. Your choice of photo really did make an impact."

I smiled. "I'm glad." I squeezed his hand once. "It was fast, though, the printing process. Doesn't it take days for the copies to be ready?"

He shook his head. "Once I finalized the cover photo and did a short phone interview with them yesterday, they got to the whole printing process fairly quickly. The issue is set to release on March 1st, so there's hardly any time left. This," he pointed at the copy in my hands, "is one of the advanced copies they sent me for early promo and sharing purposes. The final ones come out on Sunday."

"Does that mean we get to keep this copy?" I asked him.

He chuckled. "Yeah. I have a few more that came in. I got this one for you."

"Yay, thank you!" I hugged the magazine to my chest. "I love it so much, and I haven't even read your article yet."

"Pages 11 and 12," he said with a smile.

"I'm so ready!"

He laughed and wrapped his arms around my waist. "Why do you have to be so damn adorable all the time?"

I used my right hand to cup his face. "Because I have to keep up with the aesthetics of a chubby and nerdy novelist, that's why."

He grinned, and then bent to kiss me. "How do you say I love you in Hindi?" he asked against my lips.

I nuzzled my nose against his. "Well, if *I* were to say it, then it'd go like: *main tumse pyaar karti hoon*. If you were to say it, then the *karti* would turn to *karta*. Simple."

"Uh…" Gallan shook his head a little. "This is way outta my league."

I laughed. "You asked, didn't you?"

He chuckled. "I sure did." His prismatic eyes searched my face, and in that moment, I saw how Gallan *truly* looked at me. How he reacted with me so close to him.

He looked at me with love in his gaze.

He looked at me with awe on his face.

And when he leaned in and claimed my lips again, I realized that he kissed me like I held significance; like I was the ink and he the page.

"I-love-you-in-Hindi, Zaira," he said with a smile.

I chuckled. "I-love-you-in-Hindi, too, Gallan. So, *so* much."

31.
gallan

February 28th, 2020

"Are you, you know… Are you, like, *real?*" Zaira asked, her eyes wide enough to most probably fit the entire peninsula in them.

I ran a hand over my jaw. "Of course he's real, babe."

She fidgeted with her glasses and looked at me. "I didn't ask you." She hugged the magazine tighter to her chest.

I put my tongue to my cheek at the sass in her voice, and raised my hands in surrender. "Okay, okay…"

Kenneth, who was in front of me, laughed at Zaira and I's little exchange. "Yes, Zaira; I'm very much real," he answered her question – which was meant for *him*, not *me*. Just clarifying.

She returned her gaze to him. "Can I, uh, touch you a little bit?"

Amara, Kenneth's wife – who was next to him – chuckled. "Aww, you're just like me when I'd first met him. All I wanted to do then was touch him to make sure he was actually real." She looped her arms around Kenneth's. "But he's kind of a weirdo, so you better be careful."

Kenneth rolled his eyes, whereas Zaira and I chuckled at Amara's 'warning'.

"My wife here loves pulling my leg," Kenneth began, and then pressed a kiss on the top of Amara's head. "But don't worry, this is just her way of pissing on what's hers."

She gasped and elbowed him in the ribs, which only made him laugh.

"Untimely pissing is our son Isaac's department, not mine," she said to him.

Kenneth clicked his tongue. "And who taught him to do that?"

Amara glared at him. "He's naturally talented at it, just like his dad."

I hid my grin behind a fist. Their son was only a few months old, and also the cutest little thing I'd seen in my entire life.

"Well, if that's the case, then should I, too, piss on what's mine?" Zaira asked, and then glanced sideways at me.

I wrapped an arm around her waist and bent to press a kiss on her temple. "You don't have to, because I just did that for you."

She blushed as she looked at me. "Charmer," she whispered, which made me grin.

"Oh God," Amara said, and Zaira and I looked at her again. "There's *two* of you now!" She pointed between me and Kenneth. "Why are the men of Hollywood always so ridiculously cheesy?"

Kenneth and I high-fived, and the girls rolled their eyes at us.

"Hell-O, you good-looking lot!" Dylan chirped as he walked over to us.

Zaira gasped. "OH-MY-GOD-YOU'RE-DYLAN-ROWE!" she said in a rush, and then cleared her throat. "Uh…I'm sorry." She flinched a little.

Dylan chuckled. "Why, hello, Zaira."

She was about ready to melt in a puddle, judging by the expression on her face. "You know who I am?!"

"Sure do. I've seen both yours and Gallan's IG posts from a few days ago," he said. "Also, this guy," he pointed at me, "talks about you nonstop whenever we chat." He winked at me, and then looked down at Zaira. "I think you two look very beautiful together. I'm really happy for you and him."

Zaira shifted on her feet. "Thank you. That means a lot, really. I look up to you, you know? I'm inspired by your drive and passion. You single-handedly ruined Rachel Jonas after what she did to Kenneth. You're so fierce, Dylan. I really need some of your adrenaline and dedication to keep me going." She shook her head around a sigh. "Lord knows I need it after being exposed to the whole public side of Hollywood."

His eyes gleamed as he grinned at her. "I would love to help you out!" He grabbed one of her hands. "How about you and I go on a shopping spree tomorrow? We can talk all about Hollywood, clothes, fashion, boys, and everything else that interests you."

"Really?" She looked like a kid whose parents had just told her that they were taking her to the *Louvre*.

Dylan chuckled. "Yes, really."

"Uh, excuse me, but that is *not* going to happen," Amara interrupted.

Dylan looked at her. "Why not?" he asked.

"Because for going on a shopping spree with you, one needs to have great amount of patience and resilience," Kenneth said. "You aren't a normal human being, D; you turn into Donatella Versace when you shop. You don't stop until you quite literally *drop*, and make the person who tags along with you regret and question their decision of joining you."

Dylan scowled at his best friend and client. "Fuck you, K." He looked at Amara. "I promise I won't break her." He then glanced between me and Zaira. "I promise."

I chuckled, and so did Zaira. "I trust you," she told him.

Kenneth laughed, and Amara sighed.

"If you weren't married to my brother," the latter said to Dylan, "I would have drugged you with eyeshadow fumes the moment you suggested the shopping spree idea. But because I don't want Conner questioning me about why his husband isn't acting like a human being, I'll entertain this notion once, and once *only*." She pointed a finger at him. "Don't break the poor girl."

He rolled his eyes. "Aye-aye, Captain." He faced Zaira again. "Let's discuss some of the places we should go tomorrow."

Amara huffed. "Absolutely *not*. Let her breathe for a few–"

I laughed and shook my head as the two began bickering. Zaira kept glancing between them with wide, amusement-filled eyes.

I looked at Kenneth and jerked my head to the right. With a nod, he followed me to the other side of the set.

"Thanks once again for doing this, man," I told him, and then crossed my arms over my chest. "I know this is gonna be a bit weird for you – you know, with Ross being Rachel's dad and all. I just…" I sighed and pushed my hair to the side. "You're fine with it, right? You're okay with working with Ross on another project?"

Kenneth leaned his shoulder against the wall to his left and slid a hand into the front pocket of his jeans. "I'm here, aren't I?"

I smirked at him. "That, you are." I scratched my jaw. "I seriously can't thank you enough for doing this. When Ross said he wanted to hold an audition to select someone who would be my brother in the movie – because the actor he had initially approached for the role cancelled at the last minute – I knew I didn't want that. Auditions put a stop to filming, and I'm not a fan of such interruptions. I've known you for years, and I love working with you, so your name was the first that came to my mind when Ross told me about the kind of person he wanted for the role."

He inclined his head a little. "I appreciate it." He ran a hand through his perfectly styled hair. I swear I've never seen him with disheveled hair – *ever*.

"As for Ross," he then continued, "he has paid the penalty for trying to break into my house when the whole Rachel scandal went live, so I guess that's forgivable. And, when he called me last week to tell me about the movie and role, he also said that he has zero contact with his daughter anymore, and doesn't even know where she currently is. That's bullshit, of course, but as long as things stay professional between him and I, I don't see why I can't work with him again."

I shook my head a little. "If only I had the kind of resolve you do, man."

Kenneth chuckled. "You do, actually. You've supported me since day one of the scandal, and even before that whenever I've needed help. But you signed this movie with him just months after the whole drama flared on the news channels. This shows that you know the correct professional approach needed to survive in this industry, and I admire that."

"Always here for you, brother," I told him.

He smiled, and then pointed over his shoulder at Dylan, Amara, and Zaira – who were laughing and talking animatedly with each other.

"So, about Zaira…"

I raised a brow at him. "What about her?"

"How serious are you about her?"

"I love her, dude," I told him almost immediately; without any hesitation. "I fucking love her."

Something profound flashed in Kenneth's eyes as he smiled at me. "Don't screw things over, then, you hear me? Don't make the same mistakes I made with my Amara. Hold onto Zaira; don't fucking let her go. If she's your *it*, then make sure you treat her that way."

Him and Amara had gone through hell before getting their happily ever after. Rachel Jonas had kept Kenneth on a leash; she'd forced him into a fake relationship to boost their careers and promote their movie. But she'd later taken things too far. She'd recorded him and Amara during an intimate date; she'd threatened to make their photos and videos public if Kenneth didn't continue to stay in a media relationship with her. Her husband and manager had encouraged her to do most of those deeds, and when things had seemed impossible to tackle, Dylan had pulled Kenneth out of it all and exposed Rachel to the media. He'd saved his best friend; he'd given Rachel a massive piece of sizzling karma.

Life wasn't an easy game to play, but if one had true friends by their side, then even the darkest specks of it could be handled with a smile; with a scorching torch of confidence held in a fist.

My eyes went to Zaira, and I grinned when she laughed at something Dylan whispered to her.

"You know," Kenneth said, and I looked at him again, "when I see you, it's like I'm staring in a mirror or something. The way you look at Zaira is exactly how I feel about Amara. The emotions you have for Zaira – they replicate the ones I have for my wife. This is proof enough that you're walking in the right direction. Now, as long as you don't trip and fall on your dick, you should be perfectly fine."

I chuckled. "Solid advice, K; keep up the good work."

He grinned. "I do what I can."

With another chuckle, I looked at Zaira again, and my heart – that smitten fucker – began fox-trotting in my chest when her eyes met mine and she waved at me.

She was a remedy I didn't know I needed; a cure I didn't know I was searching for.

She was firelight – so blissfully blinding; so fucking all-consuming. And I'll be damned if I ever let her go; if I ever hurt her or her beautiful soul.

32.
Zaira

February 29th, 2020

"You lured me in with a promise of feeding me homemade Indian food," Gallan said from behind me. "That's the only reason my '*patience is wearing thin*', as you so nicely put it."

I chuckled, and finally managed to open my apartment door. "You're being sassy again, Underwood. Is this part of your midnight hunger crisis?"

He huffed but said nothing.

With a grin on my face, I pushed open my apartment door and stepped inside. I placed the keys in the black glass bowl on the table next to the door, and then looked at the time on the living room clock.

1:27a.m.

The shoot had run late, and when I'd asked Gallan to come over to my place around thirty minutes ago after things had packed up on set, he'd said yes.

Throughout the 18-hour shoot session, it had been a treat to watch Kenneth and Gallan work together. It was as if they knew how the other worked; their synchronization with each other was awe-inspiring. Their dialogue delivery, their body language during each scene, and the teasing way in which they corrected each other over minor slipups – it was all so impressive to be an audience of.

Amara was a dream. She'd worked seamlessly on Kenneth's makeup and touchups, whereas Dylan – well, him and I had had some really good laughs while mocking Aubrey when she'd miss her lines or get frustrated over them.

I smiled as I fixed my glasses, and then turned to face my very surprised boyfriend.

Gallan's eyes were wide as he looked around my small apartment. I knew he liked what he saw. How could he not? The place quite literally SCREAMED my name in every literal way, after all.

"Damn, babe. These walls are so fucking cool," he said, and then looked around the area again. "All of this is so *you*."

My smile broadened. My parents' neighbor was big on renovations and interior designing. I'd seen catalogs upon catalogs of his work in the past, and it was all pretty damn impressive. So, when my dad had suggested I ask Frank, his neighbor, to renovate my place, I'd said yes in a heartbeat.

From the newspaper-print walls to the white accent furniture; from the small yet comfortable living room to the black-and-grey combo kitchen; from the spacious bedroom with an attached bathroom and a cozy balcony, to the black marbled floors – my place looked stunning, classic, and super sleek.

"I'm glad you like it," I told Gallan.

He walked over to me. "I'm impressed," he said.

I grinned. "Good to know." I grabbed his right hand and tugged him towards the kitchen. "Come on; let me feed you. I promised you homemade food, after all." I winked at him from over my shoulder.

He chuckled. "Homemade *Indian* food, to be exact," he said.

I shook my head a little. "Yes, that." I let go of his hand and opened the refrigerator once we were in the kitchen. I pulled out a container full of *Chicken Yakhni Pulao* that I'd made the day before, and then popped it into the microwave before turning it on and setting the time.

"Okay, so now we wait," I announced, and then walked over to Gallan, who was sitting on my kitchen counter with a smug look on his face.

"What?" I asked as I stood before him.

He smirked. "I like the idea of you working in the kitchen, and of you cooking for me."

I rolled my eyes. "Did a Neanderthal bite you in the neck on a full moon or something?"

He chuckled. "I'm sure it doesn't work like that."

"With you, it's really hard to tell sometimes."

He grinned, and then slowly ran a knuckle over my left cheek. "Come here."

Goosebumps erupted throughout my body at the slight gruffness in his voice; at his short yet impactful command. I took one step forward and stood between his legs, and when he leaned in and kissed me, I closed my eyes and moaned against him, against his irresistible taste.

"Hey, Gall," I whispered over his lips, and then placed my hands on his thighs.

"Yeah?" he responded.

"What do skinny jeans and dusty, someone-definitely-got-murdered-here attics have in common?" I asked.

He looked so freaking puzzled as he blinked at me. "*What?*"

I clicked my tongue. "I said: what do skinny jeans and–"

"No, I got that," he cut me off. "I'm just a little confused as to why you'd ask me something like this while we're *kissing*, Zaira."

I chuckled and pressed a quick peck on his lips. "Just answer the question."

He scratched the side of his neck. "Uh…" He shook his head. "I don't know, seriously. I'm still reeling from the abrupt change of your behavior."

"Do you want three guesses?"

He pressed his teeth to his bottom lip. "No?"

I winked at him. "Too bad, Mister Spoilsport. The answer is ballroom. What skinny jeans and dusty, someone-definitely-got-murdered-here attics have in common is a *ballroom*. Get it? *Ball* room. *Ball*…room."

"Good Lord," he muttered. "You aren't human, are you? You're from planet Jupiter or something, isn't it?" he asked, and then shook his head.

"Because humans can't say shit like this. It's physically impossible for them to."

I laughed. "Well technically, it's Kenzie's joke. She's the one who came up with it. I was just passing it along as a promotion."

Gallan shook his head – *again*. "What *are* you?"

I laughed harder. "Someone who is going to feed you yummy food and kiss you until your lips fall off."

He grinned and adjusted my glasses. "Promises, promises."

The microwave *dinged*.

I smirked at him. "It isn't a promise if I intend to deliver." I stepped away from him and walked over to the microwave.

"What have I done to deserve you, you unique woman?" he asked.

I looked at him over my shoulder. "A great many things, actually – one of those being that you wear jeans that have enough room for your *balls*."

He leaned back and laughed, and damn if that action didn't fill me with warmth.

Gallan was my palette of colors; he was a stroke of brightness in my otherwise dull canvas of a life.

He was starlight – so stunningly overpowering; so fucking hypnotizing. And I'll be damned if I ever walk away from him; if I ever let anything or anyone get in the way of what we shared.

Of what I knew we both deserved to *have*.

33.
Zaira

February 29th, 2020

"Alright, alright; I give up," Gallan said as him and I entered my bedroom. He'd been trying to pronounce the word *Yakhni* for about an hour, but couldn't even come close to saying it correctly.

After a yummy dinner, him and I had spent a couple or so hours watching a Netflix movie with a big-ass bowl of popcorn and a large container of caramel ice cream as our delicious company. What can I say? We were trash for carbs and didn't shy away from admitting it.

Gallan looked at the balcony's closed glass doors, the bathroom, my queen-sized bed, the dressing table next to it, and then finally, he turned and raised a brow at me. "Aesthetics on point, huh?"

I winked at him. "Always."

He grinned, and then grabbed the hem of his white t-shirt before pulling it up and over his head. With his forearms still in it, he began turning it upside down, and something about the way he looked down at the piece of clothing as he worked on it, about the way his hair fell forward and framed his side profile, about the way he looked so calm and candid in that moment, made me grab my phone from the back pocket of my jeans and take a photo of him.

He looked up, and I smiled as I walked over to him.

"I couldn't help it," I told him, and then stopped right in front of him. "You seemed so…at peace that I had to take a photo." I glanced at said photo. "Also, with the newspaper wall in the background, you look super fucking hot, boyfriend."

He chuckled and let his t-shirt fall on the floor, and then wrapped his arms around my waist. "I noticed that these walls look way different than the ones in the rest of the apartment." He grabbed my phone from my hand, gently took off my glasses, and then placed them both on the nightstand to his left.

I ran my fingers over the smattering of dark hair on his chest and smiled up at him. "Yup. The wall print in here has a lot of comic features from past newspapers and magazines. I spend most of my time in this room, so I wanted to surround myself with inspirational vibes."

Gallan grinned. "You continue to surprise me."

I wrapped my arms around his neck. "And why's that?"

He grabbed my ass and pulled me flush against him. "I don't know; I'm just constantly in awe of you, and I like it – a *lot*."

I bit my bottom lip. "You're something else, aren't you?"

He smirked. "Do I feel another presumption coming?"

I rolled my eyes and leaned in to press a long kiss on his jaw. "Baboon."

As usual, he smiled at my use of term, and when I faced him again, he took my mouth in a hard, almost bruising kiss. "Ross was staring at you a lot during shoot today," he said against my lips.

I moved back and looked at him. "What do you mean?"

He sighed and pulled me even closer to his chest. It was as if he was scared I'd walk away or disappear if he let me go.

"He just…" He sighed and blinked at me. "He was staring at your ass and tits and it riled me the fuck up."

I cupped the back of his head. "He's a known perv in the industry, Gall. Anyone and everyone in Hollywood knows that. He can't help it; it's just who he is." I brushed my nose against his. "He can look all he wants, baby, but you're the only one who'll ever get to have me."

Gallan's eyes shone beautifully against my bedroom lights. "I know, but…" He swallowed. "Kenneth said that the old bastard used to eye Amara the same way he did you, but after the whole Rachel thing, he stopped. He doesn't even *dare* to glance at her during the award shows or movie premieres they cross paths at. What if…" He let go of a long breath and shook his head. "What if he's targeting *you* now?"

"And why would he do that?" I asked.

"Because…" He trailed, and then scowled. "Because you're mine, and that sick psycho loves going after women who are taken."

I sucked in a breath, and my heart began thudding madly at the first three words he'd uttered.

Because you're mine.

Because you're mine.

Because you're mine.

"Say it again," I told him.

Gallan bent so that our faces were only a feather's breadth apart. "Say what?"

"You know what."

He smiled. "You're mine, Zaira," he said. "Every inch of you is mine – mine to taste, mine to touch; mine to worship and love, and mine to fuck. *Always*." He erased the dwindling space between us and kissed me.

I moaned, and when he splayed his hands over the back of my thighs before lifting me up, I wrapped my legs around his waist and bunched his hair in a fist.

"Fuck, baby," he groaned, and then began walking us to my bed.

"I want you, Gallan," I said almost breathlessly. "God, I want you inside me so bad." My vision was glazed over by my need for him; my mind felt drugged with the way he kissed me.

He nuzzled his nose against mine. "I love it when you talk dirty to me."

I laughed. "Of course you do."

He placed me on my bed, and then sat back on his knees as he ran those dark eyes of his over my body.

"Take off your shirt," he commanded.

I let go of a short breath, and then pulled my purple turtleneck over my head before throwing it on the floor.

"Pants – off," he said next.

My fingers were trembling in impatience as I unbuttoned my white jeans and pushed them down my thighs. Gallan slid them off me completely and let them join my shirt on the floor.

"Spread your legs for me, Zaira," he ordered, and Christ, his voice held a hunger just as wild as the one I was feeling.

I widened my legs.

"Touch yourself," he said, "but only over your underwear."

I cupped one of my breasts, and used my other hand to rub myself over my black panties.

"Jesus," he hissed, and began unzipping his jeans. "Don't stop."

My lips parted in a silent cry as I continued to stroke myself. I felt beads of sweat running down the back of my ears and onto my neck.

Gallan got off the bed and pulled his jeans and underwear down, and then fisted his cock as he came to kneel to my left. "Bra, underwear – off now, Zaira." There was a husk in his voice that made me ache for him further.

I quickly did as he'd asked, and once every piece of my clothing was on the floor, I watched as he propped himself on an elbow and lied next to me. I exhaled shakily when he ran a calloused hand over my quivering thigh and leaned in to kiss me. "You okay with this?" he asked sweetly – his tone a vivid contrast to his flared pupils and rapidly moving chest.

"More than," I answered.

He grinned, and then his fingers were on my folds. He parted them, and slowly, he pushed one, and then a second finger inside me.

My back and head bowed off the mattress, and when he began circling his thumb over my clit and finger-fucking me in earnest, I cried out his name and fisted his cock.

"No, don't," he said against my lips. "I don't wanna come like this, this time. I want to be inside you; I want to feel your walls pulsing around me when I let go. I want to feel *your* pleasure as I give into mine."

God, his words... They burned every single vein in my body. They made me feel powerful and wanted. They made me feel sinful and desired.

With a nod, I let go of him, and when he kissed me again and pushed his fingers inside me, I moaned as my orgasm crashed against me, made me see stars. I bunched my bedsheet in a fist and bit Gallan's bottom lip when he circled his fingers inside me a time or two, and then slowed them down before running them up and down my folds.

"Mmm." I smiled when he moved back and gazed at me.

He brought his fingers to his mouth, and then began sucking on them with his eyes closed. "So good," he groaned. "So fucking *good*."

I pressed my thighs together when a throbbing sensation built between them again. "Gallan..."

He looked at me then, and I swear I'd never seen such intensity in his eyes before.

He pulled his fingers out of his mouth, shifted so he could straddle me – which resulted in his hair to fall forward – and placed his forearms next to the sides of my face before hovering over me. "Hands above your head, Zaira," he said against my lips.

I placed the back of my hands over the pillow that was above my head.

Gallan smiled, grabbed himself, and started circling his wide head over my still-sensitive clit.

"Oh my God," I rasped. "You fucking tease."

He chuckled. "I like you like this – all flushed and naked; all sweaty and greedy." He ran his tongue over the side of my neck. "I love it when your heart beats this fast." He pressed a kiss over my heart, and then took my left nipple in his mouth before sucking on it. "And I love how responsive you are to each and every one of my touches." He looked at me again. "And I sure as hell love seeing your pupils flare and darken for me." He dragged his crown over my clit once more, and then slowly, oh so slowly, pushed himself inside me.

"Fuck!" I cried out when he filled me; when he thrust himself inside me fully.

"God, Zaira…" he breathed, and then twined his fingers with mine before squeezing my hands. "You feel *perfect*."

I rocked my hips against his. "Don't hold back, Gallan," I said to him. "Take me the way you want to take me; take me without restraint, without hesitation."

He swallowed. "Baby…"

I brushed my lips against his. "I love you," I breathed. "I love you so much, and I want to feel every inch of you claim every inch of me."

He let go of a breath and touched his forehead to mine. "Every part of me is yours already," he said. "All of me belongs to you. You own me, Zaira – heart and soul; body and mind."

My eyes stung at his words. "Gallan…"

He smiled and kissed me, and when I opened my mouth for his, he began moving inside of me in deep, thorough thrusts. He pulled out, and then slammed into me again, which made my breaths hitch. His hold on my hands tightened, and I widened my legs when he started taking me harder.

"Moan my name," he all but growled.

"Gallan…"

"Again." He thrust into me faster, and I clenched around him when my orgasm drew nearer at his commands.

"Gallan…"

He groaned and jerked inside me. "Jesus fuck; I'm close."

I arched my hips and met his movements with ones of my own, and when he moaned my name as he came inside me, I screamed his as my orgasm finally caught up to me. I closed my eyes when my mind buzzed, when my throat and gut tightened at the height of my pleasure.

I had never felt this pieced-together while falling apart in someone's arms like I did with Gallan.

I'd never felt a desire this strong and honest with anyone but him. Because with him, things were always true; always real.

Because with Gallan, I was safe; I was whole.

I was *me*.

I sighed, and smiled when he started running his tongue lazily over the back of my ear, down to my shoulder, and then to the sides of my breasts. He peppered them with sound, open-mouthed kisses, and then sucked on each nipple at an agonizingly beautiful pace. "I don't know how the fuck did I even get this lucky," he said against my skin. "But I'm grateful to whatever force that is out there that gave you to me." He looked down at me with a grin. "I don't think I even like the version of myself from before you anymore. I like me like this – with *you* in my life."

I squeezed his hands. "I like you like this, too – with me letting you have movie-like sex with me and letting you order me around like I'm the elf to your Santa."

He laughed as he shook his head. "Never change, babe. Never change."

I chuckled. "Oh, I don't intend to."

"Good." Something flashed in his eyes.

I raised a brow at him, but before I could ask what he was up to, I ended up squealing instead when he flipped us to the side and started kissing me.

God, I fucking *loved* my life.

34.
gallan

March 1st, 2020

Zaira continued to drum her chilly fingers over my chest. The room was extremely cold due to the air conditioner, and when I'd asked her if she wanted me to change its temperature, she'd said she loved it the way it was. I didn't mind the cold, not really – not when Zaira was by my side.

I felt complete with her so close to me; I felt like I was home. With her head rested on my chest, my fingers in her hair, her breaths breezing against my skin, and her naked body tangled with mine – she was my slice of heaven, my comfort, and my solace.

My safe place.

"Babe?" I said softly.

She pushed herself further against me and hummed. "Yeah?"

"So, I was checking you out on Amazon the other day, and I realized that you have two other comics that you released before *The Ice Bearer*." I'd actually looked her up the day she'd given me the copy of *The Ice Bearer*. It wasn't because I didn't trust her, but because I'd turned into a curious creep ever since the moment our eyes had met.

Joe Goldberg from '*You*' would be so damn proud of me.

Zaira circled her long nails around one of my nipples and sighed. "Yeah, I did. It's a duet, actually, but I don't talk about it because it didn't really do well. I can't afford to hire a fancy PR company to help with promo, so that's a downside, too." She sighed again. "Also, many people refused to read both books because they didn't like my heroine. They said they couldn't relate to a chubby superhero who could read minds. As if comic books are ever relatable. They are written for the thrill and adventure. If people want relativity, they should read fiction and nonfiction novels."

I let go of a slow breath and shook my head. I'd seen that she barely had reviews on any of her books. Even *The Ice Bearer* had only a dozen reviews on Amazon. She was so talented, and it *killed* me to see that she wasn't getting the recognition she truly deserved.

"Gimme a sec, will ya?" I told her.

She looked at me with confusion on her face, but nodded and moved back without saying anything.

I rose and got off her bed, walked over to my discarded jeans, and grabbed my phone from its back pocket. When I turned around, I found Zaira looking at my naked ass with a grin on her face.

"Stop that," I said as I got back into bed.

She raised a brow at me. "Stop what?"

I wiggled my fingers at her mouth. "This."

She rolled her eyes. "I'm not doing anything."

"You're distracting me."

She lied back down, and the white blanket we were snuggled under only a moment ago slipped down one of her breasts. My dick hardened when I saw her peaked nipple, and her soft, smooth skin that was waiting to be tasted once again.

"Ahem…"

I glanced to the left, and found Zaira giving me a smug look. "Stop that."

It was *my* turn to roll my eyes. "Ha-ha, very funny."

She chuckled. "Why do you need your phone at 5a.m. in the morning anyway?" she asked.

I smirked at her. "You'll see." She opened her mouth to say something, but I cut her off with a question. "You got a copy of *The Ice Bearer* with you?"

She nodded. "In the nightstand drawer behind you." I knew she was very confused, but there was a hint or two of curiosity in her eyes that kinda excited me.

I shifted and opened the drawer, pulled the copy out, shut the drawer, and then covered the lower half of my body with the blanket after turning back around again. I opened the Instagram app and angled my phone in front of my face. *"Hey, guys,"* I greeted as I started filming the video. *"I hope all you lovely people are doing well. I know it's a bit early in the morning, but I have a little something-something for you, so just hear me out."* I brought the copy of The Ice Bearer close to the side of my face. *"See this gorgeous book right here? Yeah, this is my baby Zaira's latest release. It's a comic she wrote dedicated to me, and it also has a character in it that is inspired by me. How freakin' cool is that?! So, what I want you all to do is: go and grab yourself a copy of this book – it's available with every online retailer – read it, post your pictures with it, and tag me and Zaira in said pictures for a chance to win a signed* Under the Woods *limited edition hoodie from me."* From my peripheral view, I saw Zaira snaking her hand over to me, and before I knew it, she'd bunched the blanket in a fist and was sliding it down my thighs. That woman was a fucking tease. Good thing the camera was focused on my upper body only.

I quickly put aside the comic I was holding, and then grabbed Zaira's hand as I continued to film the video. *"We will be picking 25 winners, and this contest is international. So, wherever you may be in this world, you are free to enter."*

Zaira began twisting her hand in my grasp, which made my lips twitch.

"The contest ends on the 6th of March, so hurry up, guys!" I winked for good measure. *"May the best of you win. Ciao!"* I ended the video with a grin. I hit post on it, and then locked my phone before placing it on the nightstand. "What do you think you were doing?" I said to my sassy girlfriend.

She huffed and tried to pull her hand away from mine, but I didn't budge.

"Zaira…"

She scowled. "What?"

I sighed when I deduced her mood. "You're upset. Why?"

She swallowed and looked away from me. "Why did you do that?"

"Do what?"

"You know what, Gall."

I brought her hand to my lips and pressed a few kisses on the inside of her wrist. "I wanted to help."

She finally freed herself from my hold, and sat up straight before pulling her hair up in a messy knot. "You didn't have to." She looked at me again. "Your fans are going to think I'm using you to get book sales and fame. This is wrong, Gallan." She shook her head. "Do I want to reach heights of success and have my name up there with the bigger ones? *Yes*. But I don't want to do that by taking a shortcut. That's not the right thing to do."

I flinched a little, because her words kinda hurt me. "Is that what you think I am, then – a shortcut?" I asked. "Does my support not come into play in this? Does my wish of wanting to see your talent get noticed and praised not mean anything?"

Her eyes widened a little, and she sucked in a breath as she reached for me. "Gall, no…" She shook her head again and knelt in front of me. "Baby, that's not what I meant. It's just that…" she swallowed. "It's just that your fans already think that I've trapped you in a relationship you don't want to be in, and with what you just put up on IG, it'll only make them think that I'm with you for all the wrong reasons. Their opinion of me will only solidify with this promo contest that you just announced."

I tugged her to me as I lied back down on the bed. I let the blanket fall on the floor and pulled her body close to mine. "Why does it matter what the others think about you?"

She rose on an elbow and looked down at me. "I'm worried about *you*, Gallan, not *me*." She ran her fingers over my jaw. "You've worked hard for *years* to get to where you are today. Your fans adore you for your talent and kindness; for your drive and uniqueness. They're inspired by you – just like I am. I don't want them to turn on you or lose their belief in you because of me."

I kissed her fingertips when she slowly dragged them over my mouth. "If they support me, then they know the kinda guy I am. If they support me, then they know what I believe in, and what I love. If they truly are my fans, then they should know that what I did just now came from my heart, and not from a place of force or reluctance. If my fans really know me, then they shouldn't have a doubt about my intentions pertaining the contest; pertaining *you*. At least by doing this, I'll now get an idea of the number of real and fake fans I have. This benefits the both of us; it's a win-win situation."

She clicked her tongue. "If I get tagged in comments and posts where people ask me to choke on my own shit and die, I'm blaming *you* for it."

I shook my head a little. "Stop. No negative expectations are allowed here." When she pressed one of her nails against my right cheekbone, I chuckled and grabbed her hand. "Let's talk about something else."

She raised a brow. "Don't you wanna get some sleep? It's 5a.m."

"Do *you*?" I asked with a smirk.

She rolled her eyes. "I always think about burping on your face whenever you're right about something, but then I don't do it."

I laughed and squeezed her hand – the one I was holding. "What have I done to deserve you?"

She opened her mouth to answer, but I cut her off. "Don't answer that."

She scrunched up her nose a little. "But you asked."

"Shh." I rose a little and gave her a quick kiss. "I can't handle your sass right now." I placed my head on the pillow again. "Be your non-sassy self."

Her lips twitched. "Have you ever thought about farting in the middle of having sex? Or farting while you're getting head? Or your *partner* farting in your face when you're between her legs?"

Good Lord Almighty…

"Do you have an off button?"

She giggled – something she hardly did. "I'm just trying to *talk about something else*. You wanted that, didn't you?"

"I meant that as an actual conversation, woman," I told her. "*An actual conversation*."

She pursed her lips. "Fart is serious business. Like, *very* serious."

I sighed and began running the pad of my thumb over the back of her fingers. "Let's just sleep."

She leaned in and laughed, which made me grin. "The fact that you're denying talking about it means you've experienced either one, or all three of the situations I asked you about."

I chuckled and shook my head. "I refuse to indulge in your scary curiosity."

She pouted. "*Baby…*" she sang.

"What?" I asked around a laugh. That woman made me so damn happy.

"Did you fart while *we* were having sex?" she asked.

I could *not* with her.

"Aaaaand that's my cue to stop answering you and go to sleep." I let go of her hand, grabbed the blanket from the floor, and draped it over our bodies. I then shifted to my left so I was facing her fully. "Lie down, come on. It's time to get some shut-eye."

With a huff, she did as I'd asked, and then wrapped an arm around my waist before snuggling close to my chest. "You smell nice," she mumbled.

I grinned. "So do you." I pressed a kiss on the top of her head. "Night, baby."

"But it's the morning."

I laughed. "Alright, then; *morning, baby*."

I heard the smile in her voice as she said, "Morning."

Man, I fucking *loved* my life.

35.
gallan

March 3rd, 2020

"I just feel like this isn't on the same tangent as our characters' rapport," Kenneth said as he scratched his jaw, and then glanced down at the script pages in his hand.

I pushed my hair back and rolled the pages I was holding, and then slid them in the back pocket of my jeans. "Yup. I think this should be more of a tough love kinda situation."

When Kenneth and I had seen the scene changes in our script for the day, we'd raised our concerns and questions about it to Ross. Because he knew he couldn't argue with *both* Kenneth and I, Director Dearest had given us a free reign to do a little improv while we performed the scenes, which, to be honest, was pretty cool.

Kenneth and I were busy throwing ideas at each other with respect to the vibe we wanted to create for the audience, and I was very happy and relieved that I had such a talented and experienced actor like him by my side for a project this tangible and challenging.

He was about to respond to my suggestion, but stopped and looked to his right when Amara stomped over to him with a scowl on her face.

"Why are you touching your face?" she asked, and then crossed her arms over her chest.

Kenneth swallowed. "Uh…"

"You were scratching your jaw right now, Kenneth!" she chastised. "I just finished doing your makeup, so can you *not*?!"

He raised his hands in surrender. "Sorry, sorry."

Her scowled deepened. "You're doing the next touchup by yourself. I'm not fixing what you so carelessly scraped off."

He frowned. "Seriously?"

"Very."

"But I don't know how," he said in defeat.

She lifted a shoulder. "Should've thought about that before *scratching your fucking jaw!*" She said the last four words a little too loudly, which made a few crew members snicker.

Kenneth pursed his lips. "Fine, but if I look like a deranged clown during the takes, I'll just put the blame on you."

Amara turned and looked at me. "Talk some sense into him." She pointed a finger at Kenneth's face. "Do the bro-talk or whatever."

"What's bro-talk, baby?" Kenneth asked her, which made me chuckle.

She whipped her head at him. "Do. Not."

He looked at me and mouthed, "*Help*," but before I could say anything, someone grabbed my bicep, turned me around, and threw their arms over my shoulders before pulling me flush against them.

I smiled as I placed a hand on her waist, but my joy faded almost immediately when I realized…

"Baby, you're crying…" I cupped the back of Zaira's head as she continued to sob against my chest. "Babe, hey; talk to me." The first thought that came to my mind was: Ross must've done something. That old bastard must've made an uninviting move on her.

Kenneth and Amara stopped their argument and looked at me, and I knew by the expressions on their faces that they, too, were thinking what I was.

Anger flared throughout my body as I clenched my jaw. I saw red. Fucking *red*.

If Ross had touched her, or even made an attempt at it, then he'd lose his fucking hands.

If he'd looked at her the wrong way, he'd regret the day he was born.

I'd make that motherfucker pay, no matter the consequences.

Kenzie marched over to us, with Dylan and Shane right behind her. She, too, was crying, which both confused and scared me further.

"Will someone please tell me what's wrong?" I asked as I looked between Dylan, Shane, and Kenzie.

My manager shrugged. "I don't know, really. She was crying on her way here," he gestured at Kenzie, "so D and I followed her to make sure everything was okay."

I looked down at Zaira again. "Baby?" I placed my hands on her shoulders and nudged her gently. "I'm really starting to worry here, so could you *please* tell me what's wrong?"

She moved back and gazed up at me, and God, the way her eyes shone in that moment – they made me catch my breath just so I could look at her without interruption.

She sniffed and stepped back, pulled her glasses out of the side pocket of her white hoodie, and put them on. She then swiped at her phone – which was in her hand – and then turned it around so I could see the screen. "I will never be able to thank you enough," she said a little shakily. "Words can't express my gratitude, Gallan. You made this happen for me, and I don't know if I'll ever be able to pay you back for your generosity and kindness."

I blinked and swallowed at her words, and then glanced down at her phone. I kept staring at it for a while, because I didn't know what I was looking for, but when it finally registered to me, I brought my eyes back to hers and grinned at her.

"Holy shit, baby; congratulations!" I cupped her face and kissed her wet lips. Various thoughts of murdering Ross in cold blood left my mind, and I felt nothing but pure joy and pride as I looked at the gorgeous woman in front of me.

She hitched out a little sob and smiled at me. "*You* made this happen for me, so thank you, Gall."

I shook my head and stepped closer to her. "It's your determination that got you here. I just gave you a little push, Zaira, that's all. It's your passion and talent that have risen you to this accomplishment, and damn, sweetheart, I'm so fucking proud of you."

The Ice Bearer had reached the #1 spot in the *New York Times Bestselling List* under the Graphic Book and Manga category. The early responses I'd received on my contest had been *crazy* good, but I wasn't aware that my little act to help my girl out would turn into something this big. The happiness and excitement on her face were infectious, to say the least, and the awe she held in her eyes as she looked at me – man, that made me wanna spread my arms wide and dance like a fucking peacock.

Zaira held my wrists. "The sales keep increasing every few minutes. Kenzie and I were tracking them all day, but we lost count a couple hours ago. Then, someone messaged me on IG and asked me to check the *NYT* list, and I just..." Her chin trembled. "Up until the day before yesterday, I didn't even have a single sale to my name, and now..." She shook her head and let go of my wrists. "Now I can't even keep track of them. It's not about the money for me – it never will be. I'm just so incredibly happy that people are giving my book a chance; that they'll hold my hard work, my blood and sweat and tears, in their hands. That they'll go on the adventure *I* wrote; meet the characters *I* created. I'm both ecstatic and scared shitless, but I'm even more curious to see how they'll react to the story."

I kissed her once, twice, and then pulled a napkin out of my jeans pocket before wiping her tears and snot with it. "I know you care about getting your story out there to the right audience, and not about the money. And I also know that once people start reading your book, they're going to lose their marbles over Graham and his squad. You're incredible, Zaira, and so is *The Ice Bearer*. I can't wait for readers to fall in love with you, your energy, and your book."

"Amen to that!" Amara said, and then grinned at Zaira. "Kenneth and I've ordered more than 50 copies of your book, and we can't wait to give them out to our families, friends, and my makeup team."

Kenneth chuckled as he looked at me. "Yup. We practically spammed the online retailers after I saw your contest video. They probably think we're either nuts, or bots making a bulk purchase, but as far as the copies get delivered to us, I don't really care."

I laughed. "Thanks for the support."

He nodded. "Of course."

Zaira sniffed. "I'm speechless," she said. "I don't know if I even deserve all of this. I just–"

"Of course you deserve it!" Dylan cut her off as he came to stand next to her. "I can't wait to take all sorts of awesome pictures with my copy when it arrives! I'm going to promote the literal shit out of your book, babe. I'm going to promote it so hard, that Graham will start *quaking* in his skintight jeans."

Zaira's lips twitched. "He doesn't wear skintight jeans," she told Dylan. "He wears *only* jeans – ones that have enough room for his *balls*." She looked sideways at me.

I put my tongue to my cheek, and slightly nudged one of her sneakers with my left boot.

Dylan gave Zaira an incredulous look. "Huh?"

Shane placed a hand on his shoulder. "Trust me, D, you don't wanna know whatever it is that she meant by that. These two," he pointed between me and Zaira, "are A-grade basketcases. They've already drained half of my brain in the short time they've been together. You're better off, I promise."

Everyone laughed at that, whereas I flipped my manager off for his snarky remarks. In turn, he smirked and gave me a two-finger salute.

Asshole.

Kenzie hugged Zaira from behind. "Aww, you used my skinny-jeans-and-dusty-attic joke, didn't you?" she said to her.

Zaira chuckled. "You bet your silly ass I did."

"Hey!" Kenzie slapped her arm in a playful manner. "My ass is plump and posh, and so very ready to be manhandled by Robert Pattinson."

"Wait," Zaira and I said together, and then laughed before high-fiving each other.

"Wasn't Tom Hiddleston your celebrity crush just the other day?" my girlfriend asked her best friend.

Kenzie stepped back and shrugged. "I changed my mind."

"I wish I could do that so easily," Amara mused, and then teasingly elbowed Kenneth in the stomach.

"Show mercy," he said to her, which made us all laugh.

I held Zaira's hand and twined our fingers together. "Hey, you."

She looked up at me. "Yeah?"

I bent and kissed her, and she smiled against my lips before sliding her fingers through my hair. "It's been a hot minute, so I just thought I'd remind you that I'm really fucking proud of you," I said to her.

She cupped the side of my face and placed her thumb over my chin. "Whatever happened today wouldn't have been possible without you. My book would've remained unknown and unread had it not been because of–"

"Shh." I kissed her again. "If I hear you singing my praises one more time, I'll take you to my trailer and make you scream so hard that you won't be able to sing for a while. Accept the reality and let me keep reminding you of how goddamn sexy, delicious, and talented you are."

Her breath hitched against my lips. "My, my, Underwood. You're being quite sure of yourself today."

I smirked. "Oh, babe, I am *more* than sure when it comes to you and your body." I dragged my hands down her waist and to her full ass. "I–"

"Excuse me?!" Dylan said a little too loudly.

Zaira and I moved back and looked at him. His arms were folded across his chest, and he was looking between us with amusement in his ice-blue eyes.

"Sorry," I told him, and then chuckled.

"Apology accepted. But please keep it in your pants the next time we're around." He gestured at himself, and then at the others – who all seemed *really* busy admiring the Stage 35 construction with intrigue on their faces.

Zaira grimaced and punched me in the arm. "Yeah, Gall; conceal your carnal urges while we're in public," she sassed.

I rolled my eyes. "Carnal urges? Seriously? What are we, characters of an erotic novel or something?"

"Actually, you two were very close to putting those characters to shame with the way you were looking at each other," Dylan said.

"Alright, that's enough." Kenneth turned, and jerked his head to the right when our eyes met. "Come on; practice time. We need to get the improv scene perfected before filming resumes."

I gave him a nod, and then looked at Zaira. "Stage 6 in the next thirty minutes?"

She smiled. "I'll meet you there."

I grinned. "Can't wait."

She shook her head around a laugh. "Go, practice." She shoved me a little. "Ace the heck out of this scene."

I gave her a wink. "Will do."

She smiled again, and just like that, she enlightened my world for the millionth time since she'd walked into it; since she'd dazzled it with her addicting personality and silk-like voice.

Why yes, I was a smitten mother-trucker when it came to my girlfriend, thank you very much.

36.
Zaira

March 3rd, 2020

I wiggled my toes under Gallan's chin again, and stretched my arms above my head as I yawned. We were relaxing on my living room couch after he'd fucked the literal daylight out of me around an hour ago, and even though I was sore, I was so ready to have him inside me again.

He was sitting on my couch – shirtless – with his jeans hung low on his hips, his glossy hair curtaining his right temple, a couple pillows on his lap, and my legs propped on top of said pillows.

It was almost 9p.m., and I was hungry beyond belief, but because I was lazy and didn't feel like getting up and making us dinner, I pushed myself further against the couch and wiggled my toes over Gallan's scruff with my eyes closed.

After shoot had wrapped up a couple hours ago, he'd said that he wanted to take me out on a lavish date to celebrate my book success. I had, of course, refused, because I was in no mood to be out and about with my eye candy and have the paparazzi circle us like foxes, when him and I could very easily have an intimate and cozy time in my apartment with homemade food and ice cream instead. And when I'd told Gallan exactly that, he'd tried to persuade me, but had given up when I'd threatened to kick him in the nuts.

I was a phenomenal girlfriend, wasn't I? A complete role model.

I shifted and looked at him when he didn't tickle my feet like he'd been doing for the past few minutes whenever I'd tease him with my toes, and my brows furrowed when I noticed the expression on his face. He was staring at his phone with his jaw clenched tight, and his nostrils a little flared.

I sat up straight and pulled my legs back. "Gallan?"

He whipped his head in my direction. "*What?*" he almost barked the word in my face.

My breath hitched in surprise, and my stomach knotted when I saw the anger in his eyes. "What…what happened?" I managed to ask through my shock.

His eyes narrowed. "What are you talking about?" His tone was accusatory and rude, which didn't sit well with me.

"Why are you acting like this all of a sudden, Gallan?" I questioned.

He exhaled roughly. "Like *what*, Zaira? *Like an actual fucking human being?*"

I clenched my hands into fists. "Don't use that tone with me."

He scoffed. "What, am I not sweet enough for you anymore? Not cheesy and romantic enough to fit your preference? Is that the only way you like me? Huh, Zaira?"

I couldn't help the tears that fell down my cheeks upon seeing this…side of him.

This wasn't my Gallan.

This wasn't the man who held my heart.

This wasn't the man I'd fallen in love with.

I got to my feet and pushed my oversized t-shirt down to my thighs as more tears painted my cheeks. "I'm not doing this with you right now," I said to him. "Something has happened, I know that, because this isn't you. And, because you aren't ready to tell me what it is that has caused this sudden change in your behavior, I'll just leave it be and let you decide what to say or do next." I turned around and headed for the kitchen. "I'm making dinner; join me if you want to."

"I'm not hungry," he voiced blandly.

"Fine." I swiped at my eyes from under my glasses and focused on evening out my breathing. I pushed a fallen strand of hair behind my ear as I opened my refrigerator and pulled out the items I'd need to make *Chicken*

Korma. When I began placing the veggies and chicken on the kitchen counter, I realized that my hands were shaking. I swallowed as I tried to steady them, but when I failed, I gave up with a sigh and moved to the drawers and cabinets behind me so I could grab the needed spices and herbs.

Things had been just fine when Gallan and I had stumbled into my apartment with our lips locked in a relentless kiss. When he'd stripped me out of my clothes and placed me on the couch. When he'd unzipped and unbuttoned his jeans before pushing himself inside me. When he'd taken me in a way I knew he wanted to take me. When he'd kissed me breathless after and said that he loved me.

When I'd said I loved him too…

Things had been absolutely *fine*, until they weren't. I didn't know what had caused him to behave the way he had with me, but I wasn't one to get in his space and force him to tell me something, so the next move would be *his*, not mine. If he wanted to talk, he could. If he was willing to answer my questions without spitting words at me like I was the cause of his distress, then, and only then, would I listen.

I swallowed again when a lump formed in my throat, right before another wave of tears obscured my vision. It was hard for me to get a grasp on Gallan and I's little argument – if I could even call what had just happened between us an argument. I guess it's because I so easily lose myself in him that I don't exactly spare a thought to the other side of the coin – to the flip side of *him*. It's really easy to live and enjoy the positive notions of a relationship, but when the negative ones appear, they make us realize that we are, after all, only humans. That we have both good and bad days; that we are allowed to crash against the wave of emotions, and bounce back to sanity when our minds desire.

I slammed the bottles of herbs and spices on the kitchen counter and grabbed a knife from its wooden holder to my left. I slid out a cutting board from next to it, placed it before me, and then grabbed a tomato. I saw a flash of movement, and a moment later, Gallan sat on the stool that was right in front of me on the other side of the counter.

"Baby." His voice held caution, hesitance. *Regret.*

I dropped the knife on the board and looked at him. I didn't say anything, because it wasn't *me* who needed to do the explaining. It was *him*.

He swallowed and placed his elbows on the kitchen counter. "Someone I know – a girl named Bailey – got married today," he said, and then blinked at me. "I've known her since the beginning of my career. We met during my first modelling gig; we started things off together, in a way. But…" he sighed and dragged his fingers through his hair. "But then things changed and we got into this…this fluctuating relationship that didn't last long, and even after I decided to end things, I told her that she could reach out to me whenever she needed to. We started texting on and off after that, but nothing crazy-deep or anything." He ran his hands over his face and looked at me. "She'd text me whenever she'd need me to bail her out of a bad relationship, or if she ever needed money. She wasn't really doing well professionally, and usually ended up being with guys just for their wealth and status." He closed his eyes and clenched his jaw before releasing a slow breath.

"Hey." I reached out and gently grabbed his right wrist. "It's okay; take your time."

He gazed at me with pain on his face. "I just saw her latest post. She's put up a photo of her and her husband. She's married, Zaira. *Married.* And when I asked her about it, she blocked my number *and* my social media accounts." He shook his head. "The guy she's married to is old, too. Fucking perv. I know why she's with him, and I don't like it. I care about her, and what she's done is not something that I will be able to get her out of if she ever needs me to."

I let go of his wrist, placed a small towel over the cutting board, and walked around the counter to where he was sitting.

He looked up at me with a vulnerability that pinched at my heart, and when I placed my forearms on his shoulders before running my fingers through the back of his head, his eyelids fluttered as he leaned into my touch.

"It's not about her not telling me about any of this, or even about her blocking me," he began. "It's about her safety and happiness. Am I angry she hid so much from me? Yes. But it's not my place to demand she tell me why. She isn't obligated to share everything with me, but marriage is a serious thing, and I can't help but feel like a stupid piece of shit for always being there for her and caring for her, when in the end, all she did was stomp on my belief. And I don't know how I'll even react if she ever contacts me again and asks for my help. I just…I don't know."

"Gall…" I straddled him, which resulted in our faces to align. "When was the last time you spoke to her – text or otherwise?"

He exhaled against my cheek and circled his arms around my waist. "A few weeks ago, maybe. Come to think of it, she hasn't been responding to my messages for a while. I just assumed she must be busy with a gig or something, so I didn't try calling her. Then I got occupied with *Waves That Hold Us* and everything else that came with it. I haven't really contacted her much."

I gave him a small smile and placed a hand on his bare chest. "Maybe she found someone else who worries about her just as much as you do, and that's why she let you go. I know that the whole idea of it sounds a little hard to believe, but it could be because you're used to her coming to you for aid, and now that you know she might not anymore, a part of you is a little unsure and worried about letting her go." I placed a soft kiss on his lips. "Not everyone we meet during the course of our lives is supposed to be a constant variable. Some remain a part of our existence, while others don't. Some want to stay with us, and some decide to walk away. It's easy for some to move on and find a different purpose, while for the rest – it's not as fluent. You're strong, passionate, and caring, Gallan, and if Bailey has decided to move on, it may not be because she doesn't want you in her life anymore, but maybe because she, too, cares about you and wants you to live your life without her problems getting in the way every so often. Maybe this is her way of saying that she has someone now; that she's found what she was looking for. Not everyone expresses things the same way, baby. Some like to hurt you just so they can save you from themselves."

He swallowed. "And what if she's suffering and needs me?" he asked. "What if she's hiding something from me?"

I cupped his face between my hands. "But what if she doesn't? What if she's not?"

He shook his head. "I can't help but think that–"

"If she ever reaches out to you again, I promise you that we'll be there for her in a heartbeat," I said to him. "If she needs help, we'll give her that. But until and unless it's *her* making the first move, you won't do anything. Promise me that you'll trust her decision and let things be, instead of doing something that might make her hesitant to reach out to you in the future."

He searched my face for a while, and then, with a sigh, he gave me a nod. "I promise."

"Good." I wrapped my arms around his neck and kissed him again.

"I don't deserve you, Zaira," he whispered against my lips. "In every life that I'll ever live, I will not deserve you – ever. You're too fucking good for an asshole like me, but damn if I can't help but take everything you have and *are*. I'm selfish; I'm greedy. I'm hungry for you. I always will be."

Warmth filled every part of me at his words. "You're not an asshole, Gallan."

He pressed his forehead to mine. "I am; I did act like one with you, even though you didn't deserve it. You support me and look after me, and I – I disrespected you by raising my voice at you. I'm sorry. So damn sorry."

"Shh." I brushed his hair away from his eye. "You're allowed to have these days. You're only human, after all. Just…" I swallowed. "Just don't push me away like you did earlier. Don't keep things in and let them consume you. I'm here for you, Gall; I'm here for anything you need.

I know it's not easy living the life you live; doing what you do. But please know that I'll forever be by your side; that I'll forever want what's best for you."

"I really don't deserve you," he said again. "But I want you; I *need* you like one would their heartbeats. Thank you for being you, and for loving me the way you do."

I smiled and pulled him closer to me. "I wouldn't know how else to behave with you," I told him. "And even if my life depended on it, I wouldn't know how *not* to love you."

He grinned, and the pain, the anger, the confusion – they began fading from his dark eyes.

"You know your compliments make my ego twerk to Beyoncé, right?" he said.

I chuckled and shook my head at him. "Baboon." I took his smiling lips in a sound kiss. "I'm starving. Help me make dinner, come on."

His grin broadened, and goosebumps enveloped my entire body when he said, "Anything you need, baby – I'm here. *Always*."

And just like that, everything was fine between us.

Abso-fucking-lutely *fine*.

37.
gallan

March 5th, 2020

I thanked the hairstylist who'd been working on me, and then looked at myself in the green room mirror. I fixed the sleeves of my crimson blazer, made sure my white V-neck t-shirt was neatly tucked inside my black jeans, and adjusted the dark leather watch on my right wrist.

One of my favorite talk show hosts, Randall Casey, had asked me to come on his show for a quick interview. He'd said he wanted me to talk about my latest *People's* mag feature, and also a little about *Waves That Hold Us*. I was onboard, of course, because I loved interacting with him whenever I was a guest on his show.

But – yeah, there was a *but* – he also wanted me to bring Zaira along with me this time. He wanted us to shine some light on our relationship, give the audience a glimpse of our chemistry, and talk a little about *The Ice Bearer's* overnight success. Shane thought it was safe for Zaira and I to make a public appearance of this caliber, but my girlfriend… Well, let's just say that she'd come close to erupting out of her skin when I'd told her about the interview. It had been a literal task to get her stubborn ass out of her apartment, but with the help of my manager, Kenneth, Amara, Dylan, and his husband Conner, I'd been able to put – yes, *put* – her in my car and lock her in before driving her to the studio.

"It would be just one snort, Shane!" I heard Zaira yell from outside the green room. A moment later, she marched in with a scowl on her face, with my very sweaty and frustrated manager trailing her. "Just *one* snort, that's it!"

I let go of a hiccupped breath when I ran my eyes over her. It's the first I'd seen her ever since the crew had whisked her away to the vanity room to get her ready about an hour or so ago.

She was wearing a long, full-sleeved, pink-laced evening dress that caressed and embraced her full body perfectly, and drove me fucking *mad* with want. Her hair was pulled up in a confusing-looking yet beautiful updo. She had makeup on her face, which was something I hadn't seen her in up until that moment. She had eyeliner on, along with blush and eyeshadow and all that other shit I didn't know the names of. But God, it was her lips that made me swallow the tightness in my throat; that made me so fucking hard behind my fitted jeans that the room started closing in on me.

Pink – her lips were painted a subtle and dewy shade of pink. Pink – that I wanted to run my fingers over; pink – that would be my fucking demise.

My Zaira was a queen of her own making. She was royalty and allure; power and grace.

A force so brilliant that you couldn't help but get drawn to.

"But I don't have any drugs! I don't even use them, Zaira! Where the fuck do I even bring them from?!" Shane said.

Lord have mercy.

I cleared my throat to rid myself of my lust-fest. "What's going on here?" I asked.

Zaira turned to me, and then sucked in a breath before dragging her eyes over my form. She took her time in assessing me, and then tilted her head to the side as she looked between my legs. "I can see your hog," she said, and pointed right at my dick.

"My *what*?" I tried not to laugh at her choice of word.

She brought her gaze to my face again. "Your hog."

"Jesus, please take me now," Shane muttered as he began wiping his sweat-slicked head with a napkin. "This was so not a good idea."

I ran a hand over my slicked back hair. "I don't know what's happening here, guys. I'm very confused right now."

"This…this *creature*," Shane began, and pointed a finger at Zaira, "has been forcing me to drug her for the past hour and a half. I don't know why she thinks I would have some, but she's convinced on giving me hell TODAY OF ALL DAYS!"

I wanted the ground to open up and chew me off.

I looked at Zaira. "Why do you wanna be drugged?"

She pursed her lips. Those dewy fucking pink lips. "I didn't say *drugged*. I asked him to *roofie* me."

"It's the same damn thing!" Shane said in exasperation.

I bit the inside of my cheek to hide my amusement as I walked over to Zaira and cupped her face between my hands. "Why do you wanna be roofied?"

"Because I'm scared," she said softly. Her eyes misted over, and her chin trembled a little. "I don't wanna do this interview."

"Why not?" I asked.

"Because I'll screw things over if I say something wrong or inappropriate. We'll be on live television, and I can't cope with the thought of thousands of people watching me, judging me, and most definitely mocking me."

"It's millions of people, actually, not thousands," Shane added from behind, but raised his hands in surrender when I glared at him.

"Baby, you look so fucking beautiful," I said to Zaira, and bent so that our noses brushed. "I've never seen anyone look this perfect. You're funny, sweet, and smart. You'll ace this interview and inspire people who might need a voice like yours to stand up for them. You'll rule this thing, Zaira, and I'm sure of it. Just believe in yourself a little, will you? Because I believe a shit ton in you, and I know you've got this in the bag."

She blinked at me as she shifted on her feet. "Can you still roofie me, though?"

Shane groaned. "Jesus, are you up there, or what? Fucking take me already!"

I chuckled and shook my head at Zaira. "Nope. I know you can do this sober."

"But what if I can't?" She ran her fingers over the lapels of my blazer. "God, just look at you; you're fucking gorgeous and Adonis-looking. I don't even com–"

"Shh." I ran a knuckle over her flushed cheek. "I can't kiss you right now because of your damn lipstick, but if I could, then I'd show you just how fucking stunning I think you look." I leaned in further. "Wasn't my *hog* indication enough?"

She glanced at me for a second or three, and then burst into an elegant laughter. "Stop it." She playfully slapped my jaw. "Baboon. I just said that because I'm a chubby bundle of nerves right now."

A couple knocks sounded on the door, right before Randall waltzed into the green room with a camera-worthy smile on his face. He looked polished and sophisticated in his usual three-piece, with his grey hair combed back to showcase his facial features. I had to admit, though, that for a guy his age, he looked pretty damn charismatic and upbeat.

"Is everything alright here?" he asked. "Some of the crew said they heard a lot of yelling, so I thought I'd just check in on you guys myself."

"The screaming was all Shane," Zaira stated, just as I said, "That would be my manager, Shane."

The manager under accusation shot daggers at us from where he was standing next to the mirror.

Zaira pressed her lips together to hide her smile, whereas I wiped a hand over my mouth to do the same.

Randall chuckled as he looked at Shane. "It's understandable. I called you guys in last-minute, so you mustn't have had enough time to prepare yourselves. My apologies." He then turned to Zaira. "How are we feeling about our first television appearance?"

She rocked on her feet and looked up at him. "Like I'm about to jump off a cliff and fall face-first into a bunch of very pointy boulders."

I sighed, Shane shook his head, whereas Randall simply chuckled again. "Nervousness is one of the feelings that shows us that we're truly alive, Zaira," he said. "It's a feeling that may not be a pleasant one, but it sure as hell is a lively one." He brought his right hand before him and jerked his head at it. "See this?" he asked Zaira. "Happens to me before every show. It makes me feel alive, even though I don't necessarily enjoy its presence."

I looked at his hand, and found that it was trembling. Confused – because I'd never seen him anxious even once during my encounters with him – I looked at his face again, and the subtle wink he gave me told me enough. He wasn't exactly nervous; he was just pretending to be so, so that he could put Zaira at ease and show her that she wasn't alone in feeling what she was.

And, his idea worked like a charm, because I watched as she relaxed her shoulders after looking at Randall's hand.

"Wow," she breathed. "Didn't know someone as confident as you felt this way."

Randall smiled. "I'm only human, aren't I?"

She grinned up at him. "Yeah, you are."

He nodded. "You've got this, Zaira. Just try to relax, be honest but smartly vague, and remember to always keep a smile on your face." He gently squeezed one of her shoulders. "And leave the rest of it up to me. I promise you that we'll have a blast."

"You're right." She sighed. "Okay, I can do this." She swallowed. "I got this."

I grinned, and Randall did the same. He then walked over to Shane and patted his arm. "Come with me, will you? I think you are in dire need of a napkin change, because the one you're currently trying to work with is awfully done for, my friend, and the last thing we need is a pool of your sweat drowning us all. There are better ways to go, after all."

Zaira and I laughed at that.

Shane grumbled something I couldn't understand, and then said, "Yes, that would be great, thank you. I am very much in need of a new one."

Randall stepped outside the green room. "I'll have someone come get you two in a few minutes," he called out to Zaira and I, and then headed towards his personal green room with Shane by his side.

Once alone, I ran my fingers over the long frills of Zaira's dress before stepping closer to her. "Will I sound crazy if I say that I wanna quite literally rip your dress to shreds and fuck you against the wall until the both of us can't stay standing anymore?"

She turned and looked up at me. "I would say that your wish makes you come across as deranged, yes," she said matter-of-factly, which made me grin.

"And what if I said that I wanted to lift your dress up and taste you until you were falling apart on my lips?"

Her eyes darkened; her mouth parted as she sucked in a breath. Her cheeks flushed; her chest rose and fell rapidly.

"Speechless?" I asked.

She exhaled slowly as she nodded.

"How badly do you want my mouth on you, Zaira?"

I watched as she bunched her dress in a fist. "So bad," she whispered.

"And how badly do you want me buried inside you? How badly do you want my cock?"

Her eyelids fluttered. "Gallan…" She stepped closer to me, and I snaked my arms around her waist.

"You want me, don't you, baby?" I questioned against her lips.

She nodded again as she looked unblinkingly at me.

"Good, because I want you too – so fucking badly that I can't think of anything but your body on mine, under mine," I said.

She ran the back of her fingers over my scruff. "Randall did say we have a few more minutes before we're needed on stage," she whispered.

I chuckled. "With the way you look right now, Zaira, a few minutes with you won't be enough." I gently ran the tip of my nose over her jaw. "With you, sweetheart, minutes don't mean shit. With you, it's always forever – time with no boundaries or limits or exceptions."

"You can't get me all hot and bothered like a volcano about to erupt, and then do absolutely nothing about it," she said.

I faced her again. "Oh, babe, I *will* do something about it, but just not right now," I told her. "I want you in my bed tonight, and once I know I can take you without interruptions, it'll be game on."

She grabbed the lapels of my blazer and brought her enticing body impossibly close to mine. "Gallan fucking Underwood, you better live up to your promises, or else–"

"Don't you trust me?"

"Do I get brownie points if I say that I do?"

I slowly, just barely ran my lips over hers. "You get everything I have and everything I am, but not just for answering my question, but for who you are and what you mean to me."

She cupped the back of my neck and touched her forehead to mine. "Corny bastard," she said. "You know just what to say to make me putty in your hands. This is so unfair."

I pressed a quick kiss on her cheek. "It helps that I have someone like you as inspiration and motivation. I don't even think; I just say things out loud and hope that you'll like them."

She moved back a little and raised a brow at me. "Are you being sarcastic right now? Because I can't tell if you are."

I lifted a shoulder. "I don't know, am I?"

She rolled her eyes. "Smooth, Gall. *Smooth*."

I winked at her. "Told you you're a great inspiration and motivation."

She chuckled and shook her head. "Baboon."

I grinned. "Hell yeah, I am. But only for you, and you *only*."

A knock sounded on the door, followed by, "Hey, guys?"

Zaira and I pulled away from each other and looked at the crew member who was standing in the doorway. She – Mona, according to her nametag – smiled at us, and then pointed a thumb over her shoulder. "Randall wants you guys on stage in less than 2."

Zaira tensed at that, whereas I nodded and grinned at Mona. "We'll be there in just a second," I told her.

"Sounds good." She turned and headed towards the stage.

I held Zaira's hands in mine and smiled down at her. "You ready to ace this shit, babe?"

She puffed out air through her mouth and looked at me. "Heck yeah, I am. Let's go and rock the fuck out of this interview."

And rock, we did. I don't think I've ever had this much fun during a talk show appearance as I did with Zaira by my side. She was a dream – seamless and perfect. She spread joy and inspired people. She earned respect and won hearts. And later, when I took her to my penthouse and claimed her the way she deserved to be claimed, she stole a fragment of my soul and made me whole for the first time in my life. By unpiecing who I am, she completed me; made me see myself again.

And by giving everything that she is – to me – she satiated me in ways far unimaginably beautiful; too ineffably fulfilling.

38.
gallan

August 26th, 2020

"You slimy tumor of a woman!" Zaira yelled as she struggled against my hold.

I groaned behind my mask as I held onto her waist tighter, and helplessly lifted a shoulder at the bookstore attendant when she glared at me.

Corona virus. COVID-fucking-19. The life-threatening pandemic had hit the world all of a sudden, had disrupted our regular lives and turned us into very different versions of ourselves. It had put a stop to so many things, to almost every essence of our normalcies.

The last few months had been a task, to be honest. The changes that the virus had brought in my lifestyle – they weren't something I was ready for, or had even dreamed of experiencing. Shoot for *Waves That Hold Us* had been temporarily called off, and every single one of my TV appearances and interviews for the movie's pre-promo had been cancelled as well. I had to shut down my *Under the Woods* HQ and office, and the only way I had been able to keep my employees paid was through my own pocket, and the decent online sale I'd been able to make.

My parents were constantly on edge about my health, whilst also worrying about theirs, and even though I had more time to spend with them due to the lockdown, the fear of accidental close contact or anything else that might cause harm to them – it heightened my precaution radar by a solid one-thousand.

The beginning of August, though, had brought in a lot of changes – for the better, thankfully. Things were opening back up, and I was to go back to filming in the next few days. I'd planned on reopening my HQ soon, but I had to make sure I had the right safety facilities available for my employees before I called them back into work.

Zaira and I had gotten a lot closer during the quarantine period. We alternated between spending at-home time in my penthouse for a week, and her apartment the next. My parents were smitten with her, and even though the situation we were dealing with didn't allow for them to have a lot of in-person meetings with her, they still made sure to video call her every chance they got.

I'd tried my hardest to grasp onto every little thing Zaira did and said during our candid, one-on-one moments, and learning her every move, the various shifts in her behavior, the way she reacted and responded to certain things – it had all been a privilege, in a way. She had so many layers to her being, and I'd felt nothing but satisfaction and awe while unwrapping and learning every curve of them.

"I'm going to kick you in the cunt so fucking hard, that you'll end up flying to the Caribbean with a palm tree up your ass!" Zaira yelled.

Fuck me six ways to Tartarus.

The small number of customers in the store all turned and gave us a weird look.

Zaira and I had had a lovely brunch with Kenzie, Shane, his wife Anna, Kenneth, Amara, her best friend Sloane, Jake (Sloane's husband), Dylan, and Conner. It's the first we'd met in person since the pandemic had hit. We'd stuck to video calls and texting during quarantine, but it was Kenneth's birthday, so Amara had ordered us all to gather at *Jacque's Cuisines* for a quick celebration.

I'd noticed the changes in Zaira's behavior a few minutes after she'd had her mojito, and because I knew she didn't exactly consume alcohol, and also that it was *Dylan* who'd given her the mojito in the first place, I was damn sure it was him who'd done something to her drink.

When Zaira had seen a bookstore on our way to my place, she'd asked if we could go in for a quick browse. She wanted to see if they had some collectable toy she was looking for, and because I couldn't say no to her, I'd indulged her wish.

Big. Fucking. Mistake.

The store didn't have what she wanted, and when one of the employees had apologized for being out of stock in that respect, she had simply…erupted.

I shouldn't have listened to her in the first place, so her outburst was partially my fault. I should have taken her straight home the moment she'd began giggling and hiccupping out of the blue after we'd left the restaurant. I should have stirred her away from other humans the moment she'd started talking like a valley girl on a Saturday night. Man, I should've just said no to her request when she'd looked up at me with her big, pleading eyes.

"You bit–" I covered her mouth from over her mask before she could curse at the bookstore employee again, and just when I thought I'd have to drag her out of the store kicking and screaming, Shane and Anna came rushing in.

"What did she do now?" the former questioned as he looked from me to Zaira. I'd managed to text him in between my attempts of taming my girlfriend, and I was so damn glad he'd perfectly understood the meaning behind my fractured plea for help.

"Isn't the situation self-explanatory?" I told him as I struggled to hold a stubborn Zaira.

He glanced between the arm I had around her waist, to the hand I had over her mouth, and then at the fuming employee in front of us. "Do I wanna know the gory details?" he asked me.

I tried not to laugh as I said, "Nope."

He ran a hand over his bald head and looked at his wife. "Deal with the people here while I work on the exit?"

She nodded. "You got it." She threw a wide smile at the customers and bookstore workers. "How about we have a little chat, why don't we?"

"Come on, move it," Shane told me.

I turned Zaira around in my arm so I could look at her. "I'm going to move my hand away from your mouth, and you and I – we're going to quietly leave here and go home, okay?"

She blinked up at me.

"Zaira? Do you understand?"

She sighed against my hand, and then gave me a slow nod.

"Alright, I'm doing it." I slowly pulled my hand back, and watched with bated breaths and a pounding heart as she kept looking at me.

"You good?" I asked her.

She nodded again.

"Perfect. Just don't talk – *at all* – and we'll be golden, huh, babe?"

Another nod.

I exhaled in relief and turned to Shane. "Let's go."

He moved to the door, and shielded me and Zaira from a few paps that began surrounding the area as we left the store.

I kept one arm around Zaira's waist, and the other at the ready for when/if she decided to suddenly start cursing again.

"Step back, please," Shane told one of the paps. "Back, I said. *Back.*"

I swallowed as I glanced sideways at Zaira. She had no expression on her face, which was scaring the shit out of me. If she began screaming again, the media hawks would have a fieldtrip with the footage and photos. I didn't want her to be a subject of amusement for them – or *anyone*, for that matter. And, God forbid, if that happened, then it'd upset and stress her, and I wouldn't be able to take that.

"Go straight home, you understand me?" Shane said with warning in his eyes when the three of us stopped in front of my Porsche.

"I've learned my lesson," I mumbled as I opened the passenger side door for Zaira.

She got in without a word, and didn't even look at me when I shut the door.

I faced Shane. "Thanks for helping us," I said to him. "I didn't even know what to do in there. I was clueless and scared."

He clicked his tongue. "It's part of my job to keep your ass safe, so you don't have to thank me for anything I did just now. Just..." he gestured towards Zaira with humor on his face. "Keep this creature out of trouble."

I chuckled. "Stop calling her a creature, and maybe I will."

He rolled his eyes. "She's not a normal human being, I'm telling you."

I shook my head as I grinned. "Yeah, and neither are you. I'm surrounded by aliens, but what can I do about it?"

He rolled his eyes. "Yeah, yeah. I'm an alien 'cause I'm bald. I get it."

I shrugged. "Your words, not mine."

"Just go home before I lose my shit on you, G."

I laughed. "Graphic." I winked at him as I opened my car door. "Thanks again for the assist, man. I mean it," I told him.

His eyes softened, and he smiled at me. "You got it, kid. Drive safe, and text me when you're home."

I gave him a two-finger salute. "Will do. You and Anna good with all this?" I jerked my head towards the lingering paps.

Shane smirked. "We got this, don't worry."

With a smile, I got in my car and shut the door. I looked to my right, and found Zaira sound asleep. Her head was rested against the closed window, and she had her arms wrapped around herself.

I sighed as I ran my fingers through my hair. I started the car, pulled my phone out of my pocket, and dialed his number. I put the phone to my ear and waited for him to pick up, and when he did, I scowled when I heard the smile in his voice.

"Hey-hey, pretty face."

"My girlfriend is broken. What did you do, Dylan?"

There was a pause, and then, "What are you talking about?"

"You know damn well what I'm talking about."

He chuckled, the asshole. "How bad was it?"

"Let's just say that it could've been worse and leave it at that."

"Yikes." He chuckled again. "I'm sorry?"

"What makes you think I'll forgive you after what you did?" I asked.

"The fact that you found it cute, and *enjoyed* watching the inebriated side of Zaira? That you were the first one to witness it?"

Well…

"She turns into a blend of Khal Drogo and Arya Stark, man," I said to him. "It's fucking scary."

Dylan laughed. "Good Lord. That bad?"

I glanced at a sleeping Zaira. "Yup. Almost ripped a bookstore employee apart because the store didn't have what she was looking for."

"Fuck, man." I knew he was trying not to laugh harder. I could feel his struggle.

I scratched the side of my neck. "What did you give her anyway?"

"I asked the waiter to add a teeny tiny bit of vodka in her mojito."

Jesus fuck.

"And how much, exactly, is 'teeny tiny bit'?" I asked.

"Uh…" Dylan cleared his throat. "One shot worth of it, at least."

He's gotta be shitting me.

"*At least?* Are you fucking kidding me right now, D? You know she's never had alcohol before, right? She doesn't drink."

He sighed. "I know, I know. But when we were out shopping a few months ago, she'd told me she wanted to try drinking. She didn't want to do anything crazy, but she said she wanted to give it a go."

"And you thought vodka was the way to go, today of all days? You remembered her wish from all those months ago *today?*"

He huffed. "We didn't exactly hang out after that because of COVID. Today was the first time we all met in a long while, and when you excused yourself to go to the bathroom, I quickly asked the waiter to slip some vodka in Z's drink. I didn't know things would go wrong."

I leaned back in my seat. "And Zaira didn't hear you?"

"No. Her and Kenzie were busy discussing who had better abs: you, or Chris Hemsworth."

I couldn't help but chuckle. "That sounds like them."

"Yeah. You won, by the way. They compared photos and came to a unanimous decision that you have better abs. They also asked me, and I voted *you*, so there's that."

I shook my head. "Am I supposed to thank you for that?"

"I mean, if you want to…"

I rolled my eyes. "You lost that chance when you slipped alcohol in my girlfriend's drink."

"Technically, it was the waiter who did it. I simply asked him to carry out the deed."

I put my tongue to my cheek. "Fuck you, D."

He chuckled. "In the next life, maybe. I already have a husband now, so you're out of luck."

I laughed airily. "You're an asshole, you know that?"

I heard the amusement in his voice as he said, "Yes, I'm well aware of that, thank you very much." There was some noise in the background, and then he asked, "So, what are you going to do now?"

I exhaled and placed a hand on the wheel. "Go home and hope Zaira doesn't have a hangover when she wakes up. She's definitely a light drinker, but I don't know how that'll affect her once she's up. I'll see, though."

"She's sleeping?"

"Yeah."

"I'm really sorry, G," Dylan said. "It was immature of me to spike her drink. I did it because I wasn't expecting you two to leave the restaurant so early. I thought you'd stay longer and I'd be able to break the news of having put alcohol in her drink to the both of you. If I'd known you weren't going to stay, I wouldn't have done it. I thought it'd be safe and fun to do it when she was surrounded by all of us. I didn't think rationally, and I'm sorry for that." The regret in his voice was clear as day, which made me sigh.

"It's fine, D. It's done; she'll be okay," I said to him.

"If she's upset when she wakes up, will you tell me? I'll apologize to her personally."

I smiled. "I will, I promise."

"Okay." He cleared his throat again. "She's a stellar fucking human being, G. She's amazing, and I'm so glad I'm friends with her."

My smile turned into a grin. "She's pretty darn epic, isn't she?"

Dylan chuckled. "Sure is."

I bit the inside of my cheek. "Don't worry about anything, alright? I'll talk to her about the drink thing. I'm pretty confident she won't be upset or angry when she learns it's you who did it."

"Who did what?" Zaira asked groggily.

I turned and looked at her. "Hey, you're up." I ran a knuckle over her chin when she sat up straighter and looked at me.

She leaned into my touch. "I don't know what happened. Everything is kind of slurry," she said.

I chuckled and put my phone on speaker. "Well, I got to see a *very* different side of you today, thanks to Dylan," I told her.

"Tell Zaira I'm sorry!" Dylan hollered.

Zaira glanced between me and my phone with confusion on her face.

"Tell her yourself; you're on speaker," I said to Dylan.

"Zaira, babe, I'M SO SORRY! I didn't mean to spike your drink, but–"

"You did *what*?!" Zaira cut him off.

"Uh..." There was a pause. "Sorry?"

"You know I don't drink, Dylan!"

"But you said you wanted to try!"

"Not like this, I didn't!"

He groaned. "Sorry..."

Zaira sighed and looked at me. "I really said those things to the bookstore lady, didn't I? I wasn't dreaming; it was real."

I nodded. "It was, yes."

"Oh God." She ran her hands over her face, and then fisted her hair. "My head hurts."

"You need rest, Zaira," Dylan said. "You gotta sleep it off."

She scowled. "No shit, Sherlock," she grumbled.

"So, umm, I'll call you later to check in, okay? Don't ignore my call."

"Yeah, okay," she told him.

"Talk to you later, D," I said to him, and then disconnected the call before placing my phone on the console. I then looked at Zaira and placed a hand over her thigh. "You gotta forgive him, babe. He only wanted to have a little fun. He didn't mean to hurt you in any way."

She let go of her hair and lifted a shoulder. "Who says I'm upset with him?" Her eyes gleamed as she raised a brow at me.

A surprised laughter left me at that. "Seriously?"

She smirked. "Hell yeah. If he can have fun, then so can I."

I shook my head and grinned at her. "You're one in a fucking million, you know that?"

She chuckled. "Oh, I know," she said. "I know."

39.
Zaira

September 15th, 2020

I ran a hand over my pin-straight hair and practically skipped over to my apartment door. He rang the bell again – this time in a rush. I fixed my dress and gently rubbed my eyes to make sure my contact lenses were okay, because I'd opted not to wear my glasses. I swiped a finger over my upper lip, and then finally unlocked and opened the door.

"Why, hello there, mister," I sang as I rested my hip against the knob.

His eyes traveled over my body – over the *Under the Woods* orange Halloween edition t-shirt dress I was wearing – and then came up to my face again. He placed an elbow on the doorframe and leaned against it, which resulted in his slim-fitted white dress-shirt to rise just a little. His forearms flexed on their own accord when he shifted on his feet and bent so that his face was close to mine. "Hey, you."

I took a step closer to him, gently tugged on his black tie, and pressed a soft kiss on his smiling lips. "Happy birthday, baby."

Gallan grinned. "Thank you." He kissed me once. "God, I missed you today."

I chuckled. "How was the meeting?" I grabbed his left hand and walked him into the apartment with me. "Wait." I stopped and looked at him. "Why aren't you wearing your mask and gloves?"

He pulled his tie off and threw it on the coffee table, kicked the door shut as he unbuttoned his shirt from the top, and folded his shirt sleeves up to his elbows. "I *was* wearing them, but took them off before coming up here," he said. "And, to answer your initial question: the meeting went way better than I was expecting it to." He smiled and tugged me closer. "None of them decided to leave."

I pulled my hand from his, fixed his shirt's collar, and cupped the side of his face. "I told you so, didn't I?"

He laughed airily. "You did, yeah."

He had his very first employee meeting since the pandemic at the *Under the Woods* HQ earlier. He'd been stressing over it for days, and for some reason, he was under the impression that his employees didn't want to work for him anymore. That was ridiculous, of course, and I'd told him exactly that, but my stubborn guy had still decided to worry over the "logicalities" of our current situation until he'd quite literally dozed off in my bed the night before.

Being able to spend every literal second of every day with Gallan since the pandemic hit had been a blessing. The lockdown and quarantine conditions we faced had shown me a side of him that I hadn't seen before. We'd had our fair share of arguments over small, domestic things, of course, because we weren't a reality show couple but a *real* one. But the moments where we spent hours upon hours cleaning and cooking and laughing over ridiculous things – those were the treasures I'd stamped and glued onto the scrapbook that was my heart. The candid days I spent with Gallan were invaluable, irreplaceable. They were the essence of a magic not rare, but priceless and precious nonetheless.

"Hey, no; wait." I grabbed Gallan's forearm when he started walking towards my kitchen.

He turned and looked down at me. "What's wrong?"

I pushed some of my hair behind my left ear. "You can't go into the kitchen yet."

He raised a brow and tilted his head a little. "What are you up to now?"

I lifted a shoulder. "I may or may not have baked you a birthday cake," I told him.

The afternoon light pouring in through my open living-room window reflected against his side profile as he scanned my face. "Zaira..." He swallowed. "You didn't have to."

I sighed and placed a hand on his chest. "Of course I had to. I spoke with your mum earlier, and she said you were adamant on not celebrating your birthday with her, your dad, and everyone else this year because of the social distancing rule, and even though you've already told me that a hundred different times, I couldn't just not celebrate the day you were born." I ran the pad of my thumb over his bottom lip. "I've set up a quick zoom call with the others while you cut the cake, and said cake is big enough that we can pack it into containers and send it to everyone tomorrow. Sound good?"

He blinked at me. "I don't deserve you," he all but whispered.

"You very much do." I once again grabbed his hand. "Close your eyes."

He chuckled. "Okay..." He did as I'd asked with a beautiful smile on his face.

"Perfect. Come on; cake time." I led him into the kitchen, and then let go of his hand once we were standing in front of the counter.

"Are you leading me into your kitchen, or a sacrifice pentagram?" he mused.

"You're funny when you want to be, Underwood."

He smirked. "I know."

I clicked my tongue. "Open your eyes."

He did, and then looked down at the cake I'd made him. "Whoa..." His eyes widened a little as he glanced between me and it. "You made that?" The awe on his features made me blush.

"I did," I said as I rocked on my feet.

I'd spent a total of six hours making the massive red velvet cake. It had been a tough task to get it to look perfectly round, and then for it to bake exactly how I wanted it to be baked.

Making it presentable had been an intricate kind of torture. The fear of screwing things up was paralyzing, and I'd only released an air of relief after

I'd written **Happy Birthday, Gallan** on the cake's big-ass forehead around thirty minutes ago. Whoever says baking and icing a cake is easy is a liar and deserves to live seven days in burning, scorching hell with Ramsay Bolton.

Gallan bent and pressed a long kiss on my lips. "This cake is beautiful, and I love you so much more for doing something like this for me. I'm humbled," he said.

I nuzzled my nose against his. "I love you, too. And, I did it because you deserve to be celebrated, Gall. You're fucking amazing, and seeing the happiness on your face over my small gesture means the world to me."

He clicked his tongue. "Nothing about you is small, baby. You're grand, extravagant, and so is everything you do. You're perfect."

My silly heart marched to the beat of my racing pulse. "Cheesy baboon."

Gallan grinned. "Ay, but only for you."

I smiled and shook my head at him. "So, you ready to taste what's yours, or what?"

He arched a brow, and I realized what I'd accidentally said, and what he'd taken for it to mean.

"It's not what I–"

"Too late," he cut me off, and then wrapped his arms around my waist before pulling me against his body. "My mind has already taken residence in the gutter." He leaned in and took my mouth in a back-arching kiss.

"Everyone must be waiting for the zoom call," I said breathlessly against his lips.

"Don't care," he almost growled, and then bit my bottom lip before kissing me again.

I moaned against him as I bunched his hair in a fist and kissed him back. "You're bad, Gall," I whispered between kisses. "So, so bad."

"I like being bad with you." He lifted me off my feet, and I wrapped my legs around his waist. "And right now, Zaira, I can't think of anything but having your pussy wrapped around my cock."

"Jesus fuck, Gall," I said in a rush. "You on a pill or something?"

He chuckled. "Nope. I'm just drugged on *you*." He settled on the living room couch, and I shifted so I could straddle him.

"You're incredibly horny, that's what it is," I told him.

He laughed, and then rocked his hip against mine. "Maybe, but you want me inside you just as bad as I want you pulsing and clenching around me."

Holy. Hannah. Hold. My. Hand.

Gallan and his dirty mouth would be the end of my pour vagina. The sensory overload was too much for her soul.

He grinned when I didn't say anything, and then jerked his head at me. "Push your panties aside and finger yourself."

My cheeks flushed at his command. I swallowed, and then lifted my t-shirt dress a little before sliding my underwear to the side. I then pushed two fingers inside myself and began moving them in and out at a slow pace.

Gallan's chest rose and fell unsteadily, and as he licked his lips and watched me work myself, he began unbuttoning his shirt with one hand, and unbuckling his belt with the other.

"Push all the way in, Zaira," he ordered. "Faster, come on."

A whimper left my lips as I did what he wanted me to. "God," I breathed.

Gallan's eyes gleamed as they met mine. He smirked, and then unzipped his pants before pulling himself out. With his hair slicked back, his shirt open and showcasing his beautiful body, his hand wrapped around his cock, and his throat bobbing as he gazed at me – Gallan looked ready to own every last piece of me. The desire in his eyes was undeniable; the grin that he gave me was fatal for the growing fire in my veins. And the way he seemed so confident in the way he held me captive under his presence – it was achingly beautiful.

"Pull your fingers out and give me a taste," he commanded as he stroked himself.

My heart was beating so fucking wildly as I stopped working myself and brought my fingers to his lips. I let go of an uneven breath when he sucked on my digits, and the warmth of his mouth caused goosebumps to prick my skin.

"Take me in," he said, just as I moved my hand back.

I rose a little, and he began rubbing his crown over my throbbing clit. "Gallan," I whispered against his lips.

"Take me in," he repeated, but this time in a tone that set me afire – completely.

I pushed myself down, and the both of us moaned out loud when he filled me; when my walls began pulsing around him.

"Christ, Zaira," he hissed. "So tight; so hot." He grabbed my ass in a slightly painful grip and began thrusting inside of me at an unrelenting pace.

I placed my hands on the back of the couch and started rocking my hips to match his movements. "Just like that, Gallan," I hitched out, and then crashed my mouth against his. "Take me just like that."

It was filthy – the way we fucked.

It was greedy – the way our tongues clashed and our lips moved against the other's.

It was enrapturing – the way we fisted each other's hair and moved to the rhythm of our eager bodies.

Gallan dragged his nose over the side of my neck, and then gently pressed his teeth on the sensitive skin below my ear. "I'm close," he said.

I moved back and rode him faster, and when our eyes met, I tipped my head back and screamed his name when my orgasm took over me.

He spat a curse, and then gripped the sides of my waist before practically pounding into me as he, too, gave into his orgasm. His gaze remained fixed on my face, on my expression. On how I took everything he gave me; on how freeing it felt being bound to him – body and soul.

I grinned, and began running my hands up and down his abs when he placed the back of his head on the couch and gazed up at the ceiling. "Wow," he said, and then whistled.

I chuckled. "Wow is right."

He looked at me. "You're so hot, babe." He bit his bottom lip as he ran his eyes over my body. "Especially when you wear *Under the Woods* stuff."

I leaned against him and kissed him softly. "Gotta support my amazing boyfriend whenever I can."

He grinned. "I appreciate you and your support like I do every breath that I take."

I exhaled as I ran my fingers over his cheek. "You know just what to say to make me fall even more in love with you, don't you?" I said.

He gave me a crooked smile. "Yup. Master manipulator of words – that's me."

I playfully slapped his chest. "You're a baboon is what you are."

He laughed and pulled me closer. "How about a round two?" He wiggled his brows at me.

"I don't want your dick falling off on your birthday, Gall."

He rolled his eyes. "You're just waiting for it to happen, aren't you?"

I chuckled and kissed him once, twice. "Bingo."

He began pressing sound pecks on my jaw, neck, and throat. "I want you again," he mumbled in between kisses.

I giggled and pushed at his shoulders. "Not now. Cut the cake first, and then I'll think about it." I squealed when he tickled my sides. "Stop," I said between laughter. "Gallan, no."

He moved back and frowned. "Cake can wait."

I shook my head. "Nope. Your dick can wait."

"It really can't, Zaira."

My lips twitched at his stubbornness. "Then *make* it wait."

He put his tongue to his cheek. "You don't play fair."

"Didn't know we were playing a game," I told him.

He huffed. "Fine. Cake first, and then sex."

I grinned. "Good boy."

He shook his head around a smile. "I'm only doing it because I am a hog for everything you cook."

I chuckled. "Got it." I swiped a bead of sweat from his temple. "Oh hey, and Gallan?"

He looked at me. "Yeah?"

"The next time we fuck like this, I want you to give me a hickey to remember it by," I said to him.

His dark eyes shone at that. "You got it."

I clenched around him at the promise in his voice, which made him hiss.

With another chuckle, I moved back and got to my feet. "Let's clean up so we can get that call in order."

He pulled up his underwear and pants before joining me. "You're very excited about this call, aren't you?"

I smiled and wrapped my arms around his neck. "I am, and so are our families and friends."

He looked a bit sheepish as he held me to him. "I'm feeling really special today, and it's giving me a major case of acidity," he said.

I laughed, and so did he, and when he kissed me and told me that he loved me, I once again thanked every single star up there that had a hand in bringing us together.

Having Gallan was not only fulfilling, but it was also a medium of happiness I didn't know I could have – not until it quite literally changed the very facet of my life and made me see a side of myself that I most probably would never have if it weren't for him and his trust in me.

"Gallan?" I said.

He touched his forehead to mine and smiled at me. "Hmm?"

"Aren't you glad where my presumptions about you have gotten us today?" I asked.

His shoulders shook as he laughed silently. "Fuck yeah, I am. More than words can express."

"Not a master manipulator of words now, huh?"

He grinned. "Nah, not this time. You've left me speechless, just like you did the very first time I looked at you."

"That so?" I blinked up at him.

"Uh huh."

And just like that, he claimed another piece of me for himself, and in doing so, he made me feel whole in ways I knew no one else could make me feel.

40.
gallan

September 16th, 2020

"Gaaaallannn," she sang my name in my ear.

I groaned against the pillow and pulled the blanket up higher.

She placed a hand on my shoulder and shook me gently, which woke me up.

"Gaaaallannn," she sang again, and then dragged her nails down the side of my neck.

I opened my eyes and looked at the time on the digital watch on the nightstand.

2:37a.m.

I turned on the bedside lamp, pushed some of my hair away from my eyes, and shifted on my back so that I could look at her. "What's wrong? You okay?"

Zaira, propped on an elbow with her hair in a messy updo, smiled down at me. "I have a question," she said.

Good Lord, have mercy.

"At 2:30 in the morning?"

She placed a hand on my naked chest. "Yup," she answered with a *pop*. The expression on her face wasn't giving me much to go with, but I was curious as to why she was thinking what she was, so late in the night.

After I'd cut my birthday cake yesterday, had had a long and emotional video call with our friends and families, and fucked her senseless on her kitchen counter, Zaira and I had spent hours piecing and packing a large portion of the cake for said friends and families.

It was honestly an aspect of consideration how even the smallest of things – like having the people you love and care about wish you on your birthday through a laptop screen – could bring you the biggest of joys. The pandemic has taught a lot of us a lot of things, and has not only given us the time and sense of fear to keep our priorities first, but also to realize that our parents and friends and colleagues are the ones who complete us and make us who we are. I'd be a mere leaf on the ground – aimless and immobile – if it wasn't for my mom and dad, who made me the man I am. If it wasn't for Shane or Kenneth or Dylan, and their continuous encouragement, then I wouldn't have had the drive and determination to keep hustling every single day without giving up. And, if it wasn't for my Zaira, then I wouldn't have learned to appreciate the little things in life that I had, up until her, never given a single thought to.

It's strange yet fascinating how we evolve for the better when reality knocks sense into our ignorant and snobby brains. Even though the times with COVID are devastatingly hard on a majority of people, I've seen them fight the odds and stand their ground against everything thrown their way. I've been counting my blessings, too, because those are the things that have kept me and everyone I care about, safe.

"Gall." Zaira nudged my feet with hers under the blanket. "Listen."

I yawned as I scratched my head. "I *am* listening, Zaira."

She huffed. "You looked lost in your own head."

I grinned. "I'm here now, and I promise you that I'm listening."

She smiled again. "Okay, I have a question."

I chuckled. "You said that already," I told her. "And even though I'm terrified of your question, I'll let you ask it because you won't let me go back to sleep otherwise."

She smirked. "You're getting smarter."

I rolled my eyes. "Ask the question, babe."

She shifted a little in excitement, and then leaned in. "Why do you think dogs lick our skin?"

…What?!

I groaned. "I have a feeling that one of these days I'm going to regret giving you the liberty of asking me these inhuman and bizarre questions."

She rolled her eyes. "That doesn't exactly answer my question, Gall."

I clicked my tongue. "I don't know the answer, Zaira. I can't believe you woke me up in the middle of the night to ask me why dogs lick our skin." I laughed when she scowled at me.

"You're an asshole," she mumbled.

I rose a bit and pressed a kiss on her cheek. "Tell me the answer," I whispered.

She smiled a little as she looked at me. "It's simple. Dogs lick our skin because they know there are bones underneath it."

Jesus. Fucking. Christ.

I was shocked. Slightly numb, too, if I were being honest.

"Is this another one of Kenzie's jokes?" I asked her.

Her lips twitched. "Nope. Original. All *mine*," she said proudly.

"Fuck, Zaira. When the hell did you get so dark?"

She let go of a long breath. "I'm just being logical. Dogs love bones. We have bones. Hence, they lick us. Beneath those innocent eyes of theirs are tiny little hungry demons."

"You're being scary is what it is, not logical," I told her. "Please, never, *ever* repeat that again."

Her eyes gleamed in amusement. "I can't promise that, but I'll try."

I chuckled. "I'll take it. With you, I guess that's the best I'll get."

She raised a brow. "You're getting better at negotiation. I like that."

"Just adjusting to my niche, that's all," I said.

"What are you, an Okapi?"

I laughed. "What the hell is even an Okapi?" I asked.

"It's an animal that comes from the giraffe family but looks kinda like a zebra," she replied matter-of-factly.

"And you think I'm a zebra-like giraffe?"

She slapped my chest playfully. "You said you were adjusting to your niche, so that's the first thing that came to my mind."

I bit my bottom lip. "Zaira?"

She blinked at me.

"Why are you like this?" I asked her.

She stared at me for a long moment, and then suddenly burst into laughter. "I don't know," she said. "I seriously don't know." She laughed harder.

I joined her, and then shook my head when she began dragging a finger over my nose. "You're madly flawless, you know that?" I told her.

She smiled and bent to kiss me. "Oh, I know, babe. *I know*."

As I laughed and kissed her again, I once again counted my blessings, because it's always a sensible idea to show appreciation towards what you've been so generously gifted, isn't it?

And Zaira – she was the perfect kind of present. She was the only thing I would never give up on.

Not for anything.

41.
zaira

September 18th, 2020

For most probably the *billionth* time in the last few minutes, Kenzie shifted on her feet in a way so awkward and weird that it irked the fuck out of me.

It was the first day back on set for everyone since the pandemic. The studio's been following rules and keeping things clean, and every few minutes, the entire area underwent sanitization for the safety of both the crew and the cast members.

Only a week or two worth of filming remained, and then, *Waves That Hold Us* would finally wrap up, and I would *finally* be able to join *Under the Woods* as Gallan's assistant. His excitement over the same has been far more supreme than mine, and even though I know that working for him will bring a massive shift in our relationship both personally and in the public eye, I was eagerly looking forward to the change of pace that would follow after the end of the movie's shoot.

A flash of movement from over Kenzie's shoulder caught my attention, and when I looked at it, I found Aubrey – dressed in her costume – smirking at me from where she was standing next to her manager a few feet away from me.

The vibes she gave off were unsettling, to say the least. I honestly didn't understand what her problem was with me. It wasn't like I came anywhere close to comparison to the kind of life she led, or *how* she led it. I wasn't rich like her, and neither was I a supermodel with looks that people got jealous over. I was simply *me*, and the fact that she despised my presence made absolutely no sense to me. But, because I didn't care about her or her thoughts and opinions of me, I decided to do what I've been doing ever since my first day on set: ignore her.

Kenzie shifted on her feet – again.

I averted my gaze from Aubrey and looked at my friend. Because I could only hold my tongue for so long, and also because my patience was on the brink of falling over the edge, I leaned in and whispered to her, "What the fuck is wrong with you, Ken?"

Gallan was currently in the middle of filming an emotional segment with Kenneth, so the only sounds surrounding the studio were their voices, and their voices *only*. Everyone else was quiet and focusing on their jobs, and because *my* job at the moment was to hold onto Gallan's water bottle and coffee and do absolutely *nothing* else, I was getting fidgety and bored.

And awfully annoyed by Kenzie's movements.

She swallowed and shifted on her feet. AGAIN.

"If I answer you, do you promise to not go ballistic on me?"

I narrowed my eyes at her. "I will make no such promise."

She sighed. "Fine, but just don't…just don't get all Mom-ish with me."

I scowled. "Just tell me what's wrong with you before I lose it, Ken."

She pushed some hair behind her ears and shifted on her left foot.

Lord, please give me the strength to not push her to the ground, I prayed. *Just keep me sane for a few more hours, that's all I'm asking.*

"So, uh, I met this guy last night…" She let the words hang in the sanitizer-cloaked air.

Insert intense eye roll here. That girl was never going to learn to stay in her lane when it came to the XY chromosome.

"It's always a guy with you, isn't it?" I clicked my tongue.

Kenzie pursed her lips. "Yeah, yeah…whatevs. Will you listen to the whole story?"

I widened my eyes. "There's more?" I mused.

This time, it was *her* who scowled at me. "You're being a bitch, Z."

I bit the inside of my cheek as I chuckled. "Sorry. Go ahead; recite your story."

Larry, one of the tech guys, turned from where he was standing behind a camera, and when our eyes met, he made a 'zip it' gesture at me before going back to whatever it is that he was doing.

I looked at Kenzie, who waved a dismissive hand in the air and stepped closer to me. "He's an asshole; don't bother yourself with him."

I huffed. "He's right, though." I quickly glanced at Gallan and Kenneth, who were fully engrossed in their scene. "We might cause unnecessary distraction."

She rolled her eyes. "So, as I was saying, I met this guy last night, and we sort of hit it off pretty fast. As it is the case with me, one thing led to another, and we ended up in his apartment." She ran a hand over her face. "Now, I thought things would go as they always do: sex, a little chat, and then we'd go to sleep. But that's not what happened, because the moment we stepped inside his bedroom, he started acting…differently."

A tendril of worry crawled up my spine. "What do you mean 'differently'?" I asked her.

She chuckled and squeezed one of my hands in assurance. "Relax; it's nothing bad, I promise. He just…" She cleared her throat. "Well, he wanted to roleplay."

…Oh.

"Oh…"

Kenzie grinned. "Yup. He wanted me to be the Anastasia Steele to his Christian Grey."

I raised a brow. "Okay, I get that, but that doesn't explain your need to shift on your feet in the most irritating way known to the human species," I told her. "I'm so fucking close to shoving you on the ground, Ken. Like, *very* close."

She bit her bottom lip. "Well, as of now, I'm still his Anastasia, and until he tells me that the roleplay is over, I can't go back to being myself fully."

I was so confused.

"I seriously can't understand this," I said to her. "What does you continually shifting on your feet have anything to do with you roleplaying a fictitious character? As far as I know, Anastasia didn't have a foot crisis, so your action can't be a part of the role you're playing."

She sighed and looked at me as if I was an inconvenience to her. "What's one of the things Christian Grey did to Anastasia?"

"Do you seriously want me to list them or even surf through them and come up with an answer?"

She chuckled. "Point."

"Just tell me, Ken," I said. "I'm already in the mood to cause you physical harm. Don't make things worse."

She leaned in further. "I'm currently trying really hard to keep the two Ben Wa Balls that I have inside me from falling off. He said I can't take them out until he says I can. So, you know, every time I get the urge to orgasm, I move back and forth to keep things...*in*."

Oh-my-innocent-baby-Jesus.

When I said nothing and kept staring at her, Kenzie shrugged a little and whispered, "I have two more in my pocket if you wanna try. They're fun, but also tough to hold onto."

I wasn't sure whether or not she was being serious. Her expression, though, gave me vibes of the former.

"Kenzie?"

"Yeah?"

"I'd rather carve a thousand bananas with my teeth in the shape of dicks – *without stopping* – than try shoving Ben Wa Balls up my vagina."

She looked at me with wide eyes, and then, all of a sudden, burst into laughter.

Her action turned heads, of course, but it wasn't until what happened next that I felt my face heat like a sweet potato on a stove, and my spine grow cold to the point of numbness. Kenzie's balls – the ones she had inside her, of course – slipped out of her and fell on the studio's floor with two massive clinks. To make matters worse for my dwindling existence, I was wearing a denim skirt. And, to make matters extremely deadly for my dignity, said balls rolled to a stop right in front of my feet. And, to make things impossibly lethal for my sanity, the moment those stupid fucking steel balls took residence next to my sneakers, is the exact moment when Gallan, Kenneth, Amara, Dylan, and Shane turned to look at me.

As if my life wasn't giving me enough reasons to turn blue in the face every so often.

Amara stared at me with big, saucer-like eyes. Kenneth raised his brows at me, and then at the object of mass destruction at my feet. Shane hid his face behind his napkin, whereas Dylan smirked at me like a cat after winning a fight. And Gallan…

Well, let's just say that I'd never seen him look at me the way he was in that moment. His dark eyes gleamed almost unnaturally as they ping-ponged between me and the balls. The grin he gave me could only qualify as dangerous. And, the way he ran his tongue over his bottom lip before giving me a thorough once-over – yeah, that did *nothing* to calm my already stumbling heart.

"I'm so sorry, Z," Kenzie breathed. "I didn't mean for them to just…fall off like that."

Right… She was sorry. *Fucking sorry!*

God, I just wanted the floor to open up and consume me whole. There were so many eyes on me, and I was scared to move even a centimeter, let alone a step.

Wasn't it the most appropriate time for the apocalypse to hit? Maybe not a full-on swipe of the universe, but just a small portion of it – including the studio.

Maybe.

Hopefully.

Quite possibly.

"Ross, let's roll from the top. I didn't like the way I delivered some of the lines in between the segment," Gallan's voice cut through the otherwise gastric-worthy silence.

Ross, who was sitting behind a bunch of monitors, gave Gallan a thumbs up and made a rolling gesture with his arm.

I sighed when everyone started preparing for the scene's refilm.

Phew. Attention averted.

Right before the cameras started rolling, Gallan glanced at me and gave me a wink so subtle yet impactful, that it not only warmed me all over, but also made me shamelessly wet behind my sorry excuse of an underwear.

I was one lucky bitch when it came to my guy, wasn't I?

Yes, I fucking was.

42.
Zaira

September 18th, 2020

"I can't believe how smoothly Gallan moved all attention from you to himself," Kenzie said as we entered the locker room. "Awesome rescue tactic."

When Kenneth and Gallan had finished refilming their segment to save me from melting in embarrassment after the ball-dropping accident, Ross had given everyone a timeout for lunch. All of my stuff was in Gallan's trailer, so I'd decided to tag along with Kenzie to the locker room so she could grab her bag.

Gallan had proposed for our squad to have lunch with him and I in his trailer, and had already texted me a total of eleven times in the last few minutes to come to him before he came and got me himself.

I chuckled at Kenzie. "I mean, he did use a very reasonable excuse to pull me out of–" I stopped when my phone *pinged* with a new message.

"Gallan needs to get a life," Kenzie mused as she glanced between me and my phone. "You've only been separated for what, five minutes?"

I laughed and read his newest message to her. "*Zaira, where the heck are you? It's been exactly seven minutes and thirty-three seconds since I kissed you. Not that I'm keeping track of time or anything…*"

She began cackling as she moved to her locker. "That dude is really something else. You know I–" she stopped, and when I looked at her, I found her staring at something to her right. I couldn't see what it was because her body was blocking my view.

"Ken, you okay?" I said.

She didn't seem to have heard me, so I called out again. "Ken, babe. You all right?"

She turned slowly, and swallowed when our eyes met.

"Hey, what's wrong?" I asked as I walked over to her.

She looked a little pale, and even a little angry.

"Ken, you're scaring me."

She let go of a breath and moved to the side.

I looked to where she was looking, and my entire body instantly went numb when I saw the words written in bright red lipstick at the very center of my locker room door.

ATTENTION-HUNGRY WHORE

"Zaira..." Kenzie's voice sounded like an echo in a cave, because in that moment, it felt like I was far, far away from everything.

From reality.

I wasn't expecting the tears to fall, but when they did, I didn't even have the drive to wipe them away. I was too shocked; too stunned. I was hurt; I was just...sad.

So *this* is why Aubrey had been smirking at me earlier...

I watched as Kenzie pulled a pile of wet wipes out of her purse and began cleaning the stained words off my locker door. And, even though they disappeared almost immediately when she swiped at them, they remained inked into my brain; they were on the forefront of my mind.

ATTENTION-HUNGRY WHORE

Was I really?

Was I a whore for falling in love with Gallan for absolutely no other reason but because of my heart and my feelings for him?

Was I a whore because *he* chose me to be his?

Was I a whore for loving a man who was selfless and beautiful, and loved me for exactly who I am and how I make him feel?

Kenzie threw the wet wipes in the bin and walked over to me. She held my hands in hers and gave them a squeeze.

I braved looking into her eyes, and swallowed when my emotions thickened at the understanding I saw there. "He can't know about—"

"He won't," she said.

I sniffed. "Nor can Shane or the others."

She nodded. "No one will know, I promise. But, if that bitch does something like this again, I won't stay silent."

We both knew who she was talking about.

We both knew who had pulled this little stunt.

"Am I really a whore, Ken?" I asked, right before my breath hitched and a sob left me.

"Oh, Z…" Kenzie hugged me to her, and I buried my face in her hair. "You're the sweetest and nicest person I know. You're always so happy and cheerful and encouraging. You're the most amazing and perfect best friend I could've asked for. You are *not* what that blonde-haired cunt thinks you are. You're my bestie; you're the life of our squad. And, most importantly, you're the woman Gallan loves and respects. You're important to us all, babe."

"Why is she so mean to me?" I asked between tears and held Kenzie tighter. "I haven't done anything to her, so why, Ken? Fucking *why?*"

Kenzie sighed. "Because you have what she doesn't. Because she's petty and disgusting and a worthless brat who gets upset when everything doesn't revolve around her."

I pulled back and looked at her. "But that's wrong. I have what I have because I deserve it."

My best friend grinned. "Exactly."

I swallowed and gave her a small smile. "I'm so lucky to have you, Ken."

Her eyes misted over. "Me too."

Ping.

I glanced at my phone in my hand, and Kenzie wiped my tears with her fingers.

"Gall?" she asked.

My smile broadened. "Yeah."

She chuckled. "Go wash your face so we can get going. The last thing we need is your possessive boyfriend marching in here thinking you're getting banged by an imaginary Dom."

Despite my tears and snot, I laughed. "You're ridiculous."

She winked at me. "I know."

I sighed and grabbed her right hand. "Hey, Ken."

She smiled at me. "Yeah?"

"Thank you for *always* being there. You mean so damn much to me."

She blinked a few times, and I knew she was trying not to cry. "No need. You deserve all the love and support. I'm just happy that I'm one of the people who gets to give you that." She leaned in and touched her forehead to mine. "Just promise me something."

"Anything," I said to her.

She squeezed my hand. "Promise me that you'll never let Aubrey get the best of you. Promise me that you'll let her bark all she wants, and never give her the satisfaction of having hurt you. Even though the things she does may pain you, promise me that you'll fight them, and promise me that you'll involve all of us in it so that we can fight alongside you. Promise me, Z."

I exhaled as I mulled over her words, and then, while looking into her eyes, I gave her a nod. "I promise."

She flashed her teeth at me. "Good, because she isn't worth even getting a whiff of your shit. Even your poop is far more precious than her stupid fucking face."

I laughed and shook my head at her. "Never change, Ken."

She chuckled. "I won't, don't worry." She winked at me then. "You ready to see your hottie?" she asked.

I grinned. "So damn ready."

43.
Zaira

September 21st, 2020

With a look that, according to me, had the power of getting even Geralt of Rivia's attention, I glanced between Kenzie and her annoyingly loud TV. And, when she refused to acknowledge me or my expression, I sighed and began pulling at the lint on my Marvel onesie pajamas.

I'd been spending the last couple of days with Kenzie in her studio apartment while she overcame her breakup with Mr. Roleplaying Christian Grey. I still didn't know what his real name was, and Kenzie hadn't bothered to tell me the same – not after he'd broken things with her over her failure of keeping her...balls inside herself.

The literal ones that he'd given her, of course.

I wasn't aware that the male species could get so sensitive over sexual objects of bizarre nature, but Mr. Roleplayer had changed my view of seeing him and at least 53.69% of the guys this world was filled with.

What an accurate percentage. Someone please get me a life-size glass of chocolate frappuccino as a reward.

Gallan had been understanding over the fact that I needed to be there for my best friend, even though the guy she was trying to get over was one she knew next to nothing about.

Him and I had been texting and calling whenever we could during his breaks on set, and as much as I didn't like working there, I also couldn't help but feel a little hollow being cooped up in Kenzie's house and not being able to see my boyfriend dazzle the cameras with his pure talent and charisma.

With another sigh, I closed the Gwenpool comic I was trying to read and looked at my best friend again.

"Ken..." I said her name with a pinch of exasperation. "Can you *please* turn down the TV volume a little?"

Kenzie, who was watching "hardcore" porn at an insane amount of volume, with a bucket of ice cream on her lap, her face streaked with tears, and her hair tied in a funny bun, finally glanced at me. "No."

I put my tongue to my cheek. "Just a little bit, please? Like, a tiny bit only so that I can re–" I stopped when my phone rang. With a huff, I grabbed it from the coffee table in front of me and looked at it. Gallan's name flashed on the screen, which put a huge smile on my face. And so, in my haze of wanting to hear his voice and talk to him, I hurriedly received the call. I had only just opened my mouth to say 'hey' when the pornstars fucking ruthlessly on the TV screen beat me to it with their...comments.

"Yes, James. Yes! Fuck me just like that. Fuck my tight, wet pussy with that big cock. Oh, yes! Fuck yeah, James. Call me a slut and spank my tits. Tear me apart with that thick, hard cock."

To say that I was mortified would be an understatement. I was *so* close to drowning myself into the pool of my own embarrassment, and the urge kept growing as I kept listening to the two unashamed performers spit unimaginable things at each other.

"Uh, babe?" I heard Gallan say after a while. "What's...uh, what's..." He cleared his throat. "Am I interrupting something?"

Body, meet demise.

Brain, meet doom.

I was dead.

I had officially, fully, with a 100% guarantee, DIED.

Goodbye, world. Peace out.

"Zaira?" came Gallan's voice.

I let go of a breath and glared at Kenzie. "If you don't mute that volume right fucking now, I'm going to kick *that*," I pointed at her TV when she looked at me, "so hard that the only moans you'll be hearing will be the ones coming from its shattered glass and broken plastic."

She scowled, and then pressed the mute button on her remote which, thankfully, quieted James and his...partner-with-a-tight-pussy.

"Thank you," I said to Kenzie, and then got to my feet before walking over to her living room window. I slid its glass door open and leaned against the wall to my left. "Hey," I told Gallan. "Sorry you had to hear all that. Kenzie said porn helps her heal after a breakup. And, before you ask, *no*, I didn't ask her why, and *no*, I have no desire of knowing why."

Gallan laughed. "I wasn't going to ask you anything. I just wanted to say that I miss you. It's been two days since I've touched or kissed you. It's unacceptable and needs to be fixed."

I chuckled. "Well, I don't know how much longer Ken is going to heal for, and until she's done, I can't leave her side."

"But you've known her for years. Has she never told you about this...process? About how long it lasts?"

My lips twitched at the amusement and confusion in his voice. "No, she hasn't. Actually, this is the first time she's acted this way since I've known her. Usually, she's pretty chill and understanding, even directly after a breakup. I guess this guy really affected her in a way others didn't."

Gallan sighed. "Did you ask her why? I mean, did he do anything that–"

"No, no," I cut him off. "It's nothing like that. I've interrogated her at least two hundred times in the last 48 hours. If there was something serious, she'd have spit it out – either in annoyance, or by accident."

"You're a good friend," Gallan said, which made me smile.

"Thank you."

"You got it. So..." There was a noise, and then, "Whoops, hold on, babe."

I laughed. "What are you doing?"

"Trying to open my salad container with one hand and failing marvelously."

I grinned. "I thought you'd have already had your lunch by now."

Gallan huffed, and then sighed. "Finally," he mumbled. "Uh, what did you say, Zaira?"

I chuckled. "I said: I thought you'd have already had your lunch by now."

"No, I didn't. A scene ran longer than we'd thought it would, and I've only just now sat down in my trailer to relax."

"Ross works you hard, huh?"

He groaned a little. "I just wanna snuggle with you in bed. I'm tired."

I pushed some hair behind my ear. "Didn't take you as one who got tired over a scene, babe."

Gallan sighed again, and I don't know what it was about that action, but I sensed something pressing in it. Strained even.

"Gall?"

There was a pause. I heard him chewing on his salad, and waited patiently until he said, "Yeah?"

"Something's wrong." A statement.

He was quiet for a while, and it made me restless; it made me shift on my feet.

"Gall..." I voiced a little urgently. "Tell me."

He let go of a long breath. "It's nothing, Zaira."

"Bullshit."

Another pause.

"It's nothing concrete. It's just... I could be wrong about it."

"About what?" I asked in agitation.

"I wanted to tell you this in person. I wasn't going to keep this from you. I just feel like now is not the time to–"

"Fucking tell me already, Gall."

He muttered a curse. "Promise me you won't think much of it? Promise me that you'll not act on it?"

I dug my fingers into my hair. "I won't promise you shit until you tell me what you're talking about." God, who knew Gallan could be this frustrating.

"Zaira..." His voice held firmness. A bit of warning.

I rolled my eyes. "Fine, I promise. Just spit it out now."

There was a sound of something clicking shut. "I heard Aubrey say something earlier, and it kind of unsettled me."

My heart began beating a little faster. "What did you hear?" Just the mention of her name was enough to make me nauseous, but the fact that Gallan had heard her say something – most probably something about *me* – it just…

"I heard her when she was on the phone," Gallan began. "I don't know who it was, of course, but it's what she was telling them that…" he trailed.

"What did she tell them?"

He exhaled. "Zaira…"

"Stop saying my name, damn it!" I all but barked. "Tell me what she said!"

"Everything all right, Z?" Kenzie hollered.

"I don't know; I'll keep you posted," I answered without looking at her.

"Okay…"

"Babe, come on; calm down," Gallan said.

"You either tell me what she said, or I disconnect the call," I told him. "The choice is yours."

"Jeez, woman. Fine." He huffed. "She said, and I quote: *'I'll teach that obese, glasses-wearing cunt a lesson she'll never, in her entire worthless life, forget.'* Now, I'm pretty sure I'm wrong in assuming that she said those things in reference to you, and for that reason, and that reason alone, I didn't wanna bring this topic up until we met in person."

I was numb, shocked.

I didn't know what to think, or to even think in the first place.

"Of course she was talking about me, Gallan. She used the words 'obese' and 'glasses-wearing cunt' in a single sentence. It's sweet of you to think that maybe she wasn't referring to me, but in truth, she *was*." My throat felt tight, and so did my chest.

"Baby…" I could hear the pain in Gallan's voice. "You're none of those things, and you know that. *I* know that."

"But I am," I said a little shakily. "And I can confirm that she was talking about me."

The silence on the other end was deafening.

With a hand on the windowsill, and my forehead resting against the wall, I told Gallan about the locker room stunt Aubrey had pulled a couple days ago. He didn't interrupt me, and as I finished relaying everything to him, my voice hitched, and I stopped right before telling him that I was a little scared of what Aubrey was doing. I wasn't ashamed to admit it, because what was happening – it was terrifying me. I wasn't used to this lifestyle or its various bumps and curves. I didn't know things could be this way, and that I'd have someone who didn't even know me personally come at me like this or think so negatively of me.

About me.

And why? Because Gallan chose me and didn't give her unnecessary attention?

It was so damn confusing.

"I'll talk to Shane. He'll know exactly how to handle this," Gallan said. "If I confront her personally, which I *really* fucking want to, she'll turn things around and make you come across as a liar, and that'll only blow my lid in the most unacceptable of ways." Pause. "Am I right to assume that you didn't take a picture of your locker before wiping it?"

I sniffed. "I was too hurt and shocked to do anything, and Kenzie was too upset to keep those words up on my locker any longer than I wanted them on there."

"I'm so sorry, baby. You don't deserve this, and even though I should be asking you why you didn't tell me about it immediately after seeing it, I also understand how much something so despicable must have affected you. You had every right to let it sink in and get over it, and I respect that."

I swallowed my tears and closed my eyes. "I'm scared, Gall," I whispered. "Why is she doing this? Why is she like this?"

"She has a history of being a grade A bitch. She lucked out with this role in *Waves That Hold Us*. Before this movie, she hardly had any gigs, let alone a project in a different field. She sort of has a reputation, and doing what she did to you – it's a norm for her. It's sad, I know, but she thinks what she's doing is right. Not this time, though." Anger was clear in his tone. "Because this time, she messed with the wrong person. She hurt *you*, and I'll make sure she understands that if it happens again, the consequences will be crucial."

I shook my head a little. "Gallan…"

"I know, Zaira. *I know*. I promise that I won't do anything myself. I'll let Shane handle her, but warning her to stay out of your way is necessary."

"Shane is perfectly capable of doing that, too, Gall," I said to him, and then opened my eyes. "You won't engage in a conversation with her unless it's related to filming. Promise me."

"You can't–"

"Promise. Me."

He groaned. "Fine. But if she tries something else even after Shane has worked his magic, you'll tell me about it immediately. Swear it."

I ran a hand under my nose. "I swear it."

"Good."

A distant knock sounded through the line, followed by Gallan saying, "Yeah, I'll be there in five."

"You have to go back so soon?" I asked him.

"Yup. Fuck Ross. He won't rest until we drop dead at his feet."

I chuckled. "You're getting grumpier by the day."

He laughed. "There's my Zaira."

His words warmed me to the very core.

"She never left in the first place."

"Please don't talk about yourself in third person," Gallan mused, and I was relieved to hear his voice return to its usual carefree and upbeat tone. I was also relieved that the Aubrey matter was getting sidelined, because I didn't wanna end Gallan and I's call with her being the final topic of discussion.

"Okay, but if I stop talking about myself in third person, you'll have to answer my question," I said to my boyfriend.

"Nooooo," he said dramatically. "Fuck, babe. *Why?* Do I get other options?"

I laughed. "Nope. It's either a question, or you'll have to hear me refer to myself in third person." I laughed more when he groaned. "Oh, and I won't stop there. I'll spam you with third person messages until you give in."

"So, death by question is eminent, no matter what I choose now?"

I pressed my lips together. "Mm-hmm."

Aubrey could try to break me with her disgusting tactics, but she could *never* take away what Gallan and I had. Because what the two of us shared – it was much stronger than anything she was, and anything she did.

"Fine, then. Go ahead, butcher me," Gallan said.

I chuckled. "Yay! Okay, so which one out of the two is faster – hot or cold?"

Silence.

"Gall?"

"No."

I laughed. "What?"

"I'm not answering that," he said.

"Why?"

"Because I'm terrified that my answer will encourage you to ask more of these questions."

"You always say that," I told him. "Also, does this mean that you know the answer to my question?"

Pause.

"Yes, unfortunately."

I giggled. "Then answer it!"

"No."

"Gallan?"

"…Yeah?" he answered a bit hesitantly.

"If you don't answer, you're going to get spanked in the dick the moment I see you in person."

I heard him suck in a breath. "Jesus fuck, woman. *Graphic*."

I grinned. "Answer."

He sighed as if I'd asked him to hand over the reins of his life to me, and not answer a simple question.

"Hot," he said finally, almost begrudgingly. "The answer is 'hot'. Because you can CATCH a cold but you can't catch hot, so it's faster than cold. There, happy?"

I smirked. "Yes, very. Thank you."

"Good. I'll just go and scrub my face with liquid detergent so that I can wash away the trauma this question of yours has caused me."

"Where the heck are you even going to find liquid detergent on set?" I asked him.

"I'll make do, don't you worry."

I bit my bottom lip. "Call me later?"

I heard the smile in his voice as he said, "You know I will."

"*I love you…*" I sang.

Gallan chuckled. "I love you too, Zaira."

44.
gallan

September 26th, 2020

I gave Ross another nod which, instead of making him leave, made him stay and ramble on some more. I wasn't at all interested in listening to him, but the guy was incapable of understanding indirect and subtle hints.

Oh well…

"I very much like the way you approach this particular scene," he said, and then pointed at a paragraph on the page he was holding. "However, I think Kenneth's way of performing this…" More pointing. "…is not as commendable as yours. I also think that you should…"

I tuned him out, and my eyes – like they always do – went to Zaira. She was sitting in a chair on the far-left corner, with Kenzie next to her. The latter was busy on her phone, while my girl…

Well, she looked…distressed. Her eyes were unfocused behind her glasses; the mask covering the lower half of her face made it hard to witness her expression. Her shoulders were slumped, whereas her gloved hands were close to ripping apart my copy of the day's script.

"Gallan, are you lis–"

"Yes, Ross. *Yes*," I cut him off as I glanced at him. "I'm listening, and I'll talk to Kenneth about your vision of seeing this scene executed in a specific way. Now, will you please excuse me?"

His lips moved, but no words came out.

Hallelujah.

I flashed my teeth at him. "Thank you." I swiveled on my feet and made my way over to Zaira.

She'd been acting this way ever since I'd told her about overhearing Aubrey on the phone. I think it's more about me knowing of Aubrey's intentions of wanting to bother her that has had Zaira this stressed. She's worried it'll affect me in some way, which is why I've found her to be always on edge or easily spooked while on set since filming started back up.

Things haven't been as smooth at home as well. I think we've spent a total of three hours together in the last few days. Zaira has been keeping me away, and I know it's because she thinks it'll keep me safe from a scandal or unnecessary trouble, but what she doesn't understand is that her change of behavior is affecting me more than any of Aubrey's cheap stunts ever would.

"Hey." I knelt in front of her, which brought us face-to-face. "Babe?" I placed my hands on her wrists.

She gasped and made to pull her arms back, but stopped and relaxed when our eyes met.

"Hey." She gave me a faint smile.

God, I absolutely *hated* seeing her so on edge.

I rose a little on my knees so that I was closer to her, and then pushed her mask down to her chin. "What're you thinking?" I asked, and when she opened her mouth to respond, I gently cut her off. "Don't even try to say 'nothing', because I know you're thinking of something."

"If you're already so sure, then why ask?"

"Because you're clawing at my script pages as if you were born to do it, and I wanna know what in particular is causing that reaction," I told her.

She looked down at said script, and then at me. With a sigh, she loosened her hold on the pages, closed her eyes, and shook her head. "I'm sorry."

"Why are you sorry?" I took the script from her and handed it to Kenzie, who grabbed it, got to her feet, gave me an understanding nod, and headed towards the locker room.

"Because I haven't been myself for the past few days," Zaira answered.

I pushed her glasses up her nose. "You haven't, yes, and I'm scared about it," I said honestly. "I don't like watching you like this, Zaira. It fucking *kills* me to see you this lost. This isn't you; you're not weak. If anything, you've given me the strength to move forward whenever I've fallen back or doubted myself. Where's that woman now, huh? Where's my pillar, my sole source of untimely amusement?"

She opened her eyes and searched my face. "My humor isn't untimely. If anything, I like to think that my comedic timing is on point almost every time I crack a joke." There was no mirth in her voice as she said those words. She was only trying to convince me that she was doing fine. She wasn't, of course, and the dimness in her eyes, her slightly pale complexion, and her stiffened posture were all proof of that.

"Don't pretend with me, Zaira," I told her.

"I'm not," she countered a little too quickly, which confirmed that she was in fact pretending.

"Don't lie to me either," I said.

She swallowed. "I'm not…" She exhaled slowly. "I just…" She licked her lips and shook her head again.

"I can read you, remember?" I whispered.

She looked into my eyes. "I know," she breathed.

I leaned in and pressed a kiss on her lips. "Then you shouldn't keep your thoughts to yourself, babe. You shouldn't worry about Aubrey."

Ever since Shane had had a meeting with her and her manager five days ago, Aubrey hadn't so much as spared a glance in Zaira's direction. The only time she even gave me the time of day was when we were filming, because I was unavoidable in her uptight life when we were in front of the cameras.

Shane had once again done what he did best: protect Zaira and I and keep us away from unnecessary drama. For that reason, and for that reason alone, I wanted Zaira to not stress about anything and keep her focus on the *present*.

She flinched a little at my mention of Aubrey's name.

With a sigh, I rose a little on my knees and touched our foreheads together. "*We don't need no map; we know what turn to take. Roll on by, everyone inside, we don't hesitate...*" I began singing, because I knew for a fact that the two things out there in the disastrous excuse of our world that were bound to make my girl smile and pull her out of a bad funk were:

1) A Jordan Davis song.

2) My voice, of course.

Totally egotistical about the second one, but hey, it is what it is, right?

Zaira sniffed a little as she looked at me. Her soft lips slowly spread into a smile, and when she gently touched my jaw with her gloved fingertips, I grinned and continued singing.

See that hotel sign
Flickering vacancy
Ain't nobody else around
Just population you and me
Trouble town
Hand 'round the wheel of my heart, girl
And the pedal down
Fast lane to a disaster
Where you light me up, take me high
Kill me with a kiss
And baby, you're dangerous
Better buckle up
'Bout to take a little trip
To trouble town
Yeah, trouble town...

She took a shaky breath and blinked at me. "You don't play fair, Underwood," she whispered, and then gave me a long kiss. "You always do this to me."

I nuzzled my nose against hers. "So what, you don't want me to get all down and dirty for you?" I asked.

She chuckled. "I'd hardly call your singing dirty. If anything, it's soulful and soothing. It relaxes me and helps me stay sane, in a way."

Mission accomplished.

"Good," I said to her. "Because that's exactly what I was aiming for."

She exhaled as if tired. "I know I'm making this into something huge in my head, but I just…I don't know." She swallowed and looked at me. "I get this really bad vibe when Aubrey is near. Does that make sense?"

I nodded. "It does, but that's only because you know who she is and how low she's capable of stooping. You need to try to forget about her and her petty personality. I know it's easier said than done, but I know you can do it." I ran a knuckle over her cheek. "You're a badass, babe; you're inspirational. Think of this whole ordeal as an obstacle you've overcome and won't have to look back at again. After all, what are our lives if not a maze of disgustingly hard-to-establish goals and hurdles?"

"You sound like Kenneth," she mused.

I chuckled. "I do, don't I? Maybe I should stay away from him and his melodramatic ass."

She rolled her eyes. "As if you could ever do that. You two turn into smitten puppies whenever you look at each other."

I couldn't help but laugh. "There's my Zaira."

She smiled sheepishly, and then cupped my jaw with one of her hands. "Thank you for doing this. Thank you for making me see, Gall."

I shook my head a little. "You don't–"

"I do," she cut me off, and then kissed me once.

I smirked. "You can't shut me up with just a single kiss," I told her.

Something flashed in her eyes as she raised a brow at me. "That so?"

"Uh huh." I ran my hands up her thighs and grabbed her waist, which made her shift in her chair.

"There are people around, Gall," she whispered.

"So?"

She huffed. "*So*, you can't touch me like that in public."

I tilted my head to the right. "Says who?"

"Me." She grabbed my wrists and tried to pull them back, but I held onto her tighter. "Gall, people are watching."

"Let them. You're mine, and I have every right to touch you and taste you wherever and whenever I want to." I parted my lips and kissed her.

She whimpered and opened her mouth for me, which made me smile.

"I have to speak to Kenneth about the scene we're about to film, so I gotta go. But Zaira…" I said her name with a bit of command, which made her blink at me.

"Yeah?" she all but breathed.

I ran my eyes over her sinful body, and then glanced at her face. "If I don't see you in my trailer in the next thirty minutes with your underwear and jeans on the floor, your legs spread wide, and your wet pussy on display for me to devour, then we'll have a problem. You hear me?"

Her chest rose and fell rapidly as she looked at me with wide eyes. "Christ Almighty…"

I grazed my teeth over my bottom lip. "Was that a yes, Zaira?" I snaked my hands higher and let my fingers brush over the sides of her breasts.

"I…" She swallowed. "Uh…"

"Aren't you wet for me, babe? Because I'm sure as fuck hard for you," I said to her. "So hard that it's taking all my willpower to keep things under control; to not unzip both our pants and fuck you senseless right here, right now."

She licked her lips. "Can't this scene of yours with Kenneth be filmed later, then?" she asked.

I chuckled and got to my feet. "It can't, unfortunately. Ross really wants it done before the lunch break." I gave her a wink when she gazed up at me. "Just thirty more minutes. I'm sure they'll go by fast."

"Now that you've got me all hot and bothered, they won't, you asshole," she mumbled at me.

I put my tongue to my cheek. "Try, babe, because that's what I'll be doing, too." To emphasize my point, I briefly adjusted myself in front of her, which made her eyes darken.

"You're a merciless prick," she told me.

I laughed and began walking backwards. "Thirty minutes, Zaira," I said to her. "Thirty." I grinned when she scowled at me, and with another wink at her, I turned around and headed towards the vanity area in search of Kenneth.

45.
gallan

October 1st, 2020

I almost slammed the landline receiver on its base, and scrubbed both of my hands over my face as I took a calming breath.

Three meetings with potential partners for three very different collaboration chances.

Three presentations from those very partners for a chance for each of them to prove how and why their products and ideas would match that of my brand.

And lastly, three demo trials that would help me decide *if* I wanna shake hands with these TBD partners and spice up *Under the Woods* a little.

No pressure or anything, right?

…Right.

The idea of wanting to give my fans something new from my clothing line was a thought I'd had in my mind for months. Shane was totally on board with it, and so were Zaira and the others. Once my assistant had spread word of me wanting to temporarily partner up with other clothing lines, the calls, emails, and letters we'd been receiving had been endless. With the help of my employees, Shane, and my friends, I'd been able to narrow down my choices to two, and because I'd already made a promise to Mr. Henley, owner of a brand that sold…uh, *scented underwear*, I had to keep him on my very short list of potential partners.

Ross had been feeling a little under the weather for the past few days, which is why shoot had been called off. He'd thankfully tested negative for COVID-19, and according to Dylan, it was Ross's heart that was causing him issues. He apparently had some blockage that needed to be fixed through either a bypass or an angioplasty, but the stubborn fucker refused to do anything until *Waves That Hold Us* was fully wrapped up.

That guy really put his work before his health.

My landline rang for what was probably the sixty-ninth time. I made no move to pick up the receiver, and only kept staring at the damn thing until it stopped ringing.

Thank fuck.

Mr. Henley was very passionate about his underwear idea. He'd been continually sending me physical samples of various designs his company was working on, and when I'd booked a meeting with him yesterday, his secretary had started blowing up my landline with updates of his whereabouts.

"Mr. Henley has left his cabin, Mr. Underwood."

"Mr. Henley is in his car, Mr. Underwood."

"Mr. Henley is twenty minutes and fifteen seconds away from your HQ, Mr. Underwood."

"Mr. Henley just farted a buffet in his car and rendered most of us unconscious, Mr. Underwood."

Okay so the last one's a joke, but I swear the other three aren't. I honestly can't come to terms with the fact that people like Mr. Henley and his secretary even exist in our world. But then again, it's 2020, so nothing should shock or surprise me anymore. There might as well be an alien invasion at this point. Or a leaked Bigfoot sex tape. Or a scientific research that shows why Vin Diesel still looks like he's 25 while the rest of us continue to age like there's no tomorrow.

A knock sounded on my office door, which made me jump to my feet.

I fixed the lapels of my navy-blue Armani suit, and put on a professional smile just as the door began opening. "Mr. Henley! It's such an honor to have you he–" I shut my mouth and almost choked on my saliva when Zaira, dressed in a white pencil skirt and a pink blouse, stepped into my office and looked at me like I'd lost my marbles.

All of them.

Her hair was open and pin-straight. Her pink, glossy lips formed an 'O' as she kept staring at me. The nude pumps she was wearing, along with her glasses, only added to her sexy-as-all-fuck look. And her legs…

God, her legs were made to be wrapped around my waist. Her golden skin was flat-out begging to be tasted, and so were her bow-shaped lips.

"Is this a sexual fetish of yours that I'm just now discovering? Do you like calling your partners 'Mr. Henley'?" She asked with a tilt of her head.

I gave her another once-over before smirking at her. "Lock the door, Zaira."

She sucked in a breath, but immediately did what I'd asked her to.

With a grin, I sat back down in my chair and watched – with a dick that was most definitely going to pop out of my pants at any given moment because it was so damn hard – as Zaira made her way over to my table.

She placed a large paper bag on it. It's the first I'd seen it, because I was too busy devouring her with my eyes to have noticed anything else.

I jerked my head towards the bag. "What's this?" I asked her.

She slowly, almost frustratingly, squirted some hand sanitizer onto her palm from the bottle on my table. "*Reshmi Chicken*, freshly baked naan, and homemade *Gulab Jamun*." She rubbed her hands together as she winked at me. "I was getting bored so decided to make you a good meal."

Jesus Christ, that woman.

I squeezed myself from over my pants, and her eyes instantly followed my action. "You look so fucking hot, Zaira," I told her. "And when you bring me homemade food at work – it sparks my sleeping Neanderthal to life." I wiggled my brows at her.

She laughed. "Aww, my sweet, sweet caveman." She laughed some more. "Also, I'm glad you approve of my attire. Kenzie and I went shopping yesterday, and I decided to get some clothes befitting that of an office environment. I mean, I can't exactly wear jeans and flannel shirts when I start working as your assistant in the next couple of days, now can I?"

I got to my feet and walked around the table until I reached her.

She shifted a little, and kept her gaze on me as I placed my hands on either side of the table to trap her in.

"Why didn't I get pictures of you trying out the outfits that you purchased yesterday?" I said against her lips.

She lifted a shoulder. "Because I wanted to surprise you." She bit her bottom lip and smirked at me. "How else would I have seen your live reaction towards me if I'd sent you pictures yesterday?"

I chuckled. "Touché." I leaned in further and began dragging the tip of my nose over her cheek. Once I was close to her ear, I brushed my lips over her lobe before whispering, "And for the record, I wouldn't have minded if you'd decided to wear your regular clothes to the HQ. Though, I will say that seeing you in a fuck-me blouse and a skintight skirt – it makes me crazy in a way nothing else ever has. I'm one lucky fucker to have a girlfriend and assistant like you." I moved back and looked at her.

Zaira's cheeks were flushed, and her eyes had darkened to the point where they looked more black than hazel.

"Soon-to-be-assistant," she rasped. "Sage hasn't left yet."

I shrugged. "But she will in just two days. She's sick and tired of me as it is, and I know for a fact that as soon as her time is up, she'll bolt outta here and never look back."

Zaira placed a hand on my chest. "She adores you, Gall."

I straightened her slightly crooked glasses. "She told you that?"

"Uh huh." She ran her eyes over me. "God, you look so fucking sexy with slicked-back hair."

I couldn't help but chuckle. "And here I thought you'd notice my new three-piece."

She grabbed the lapels of my jacket and pulled me closer. "I love it, but I like you more when you aren't wearing anything at all."

"That so?"

"Yeah…" she breathed.

I smirked at her flustered expression, and erased the final bit of space between us by pressing my lips to hers.

The sound that Zaira made was enough to drive me nuts, and when she arched against me and opened her mouth for me, I let go of my control and pushed myself against her. I bunched her hair in a fist, and let my free hand explore her beautiful curves.

"Turn around," I ordered between kisses.

She didn't hesitate, and quickly faced the shut glass windows behind my chair.

I looked at her tight ass, and spat a curse before rubbing myself against it. "Fuck, babe."

She let go of a shaky breath, and then began moving her ass up and down to match my friction.

"Bend over," I commanded, and grinned when she placed her elbows on the table, pressed her tits against the pile of papers on it, and lifted her hips for my viewing.

"Pull up your skirt," I told her as I took half a step back.

She did, and I almost came in my pants when I saw the pink lacy underwear barely covering her full ass.

"You really went all out for me, didn't you?" I asked, and then grabbed her cheeks before kneading them between my palms.

"Nothing but the best for you," she said around a smile.

I chuckled, and then reeled one of my hands back before spanking her hard against her left ass cheek.

Zaira cried out, and her body pushed forward at the intensity of my action.

I froze when I realized what I'd done in the heat of the moment. "Shit, babe; I'm sorry," I said to her.

What the hell was I even thinking?

Shit.

Zaira turned her head and looked at me with a raised brow. "Why are you apologizing?" she asked, confusion clear on her face.

I scratched my jaw. "Your reaction…" I shook my head a little. "I thought I hurt you when I–"

"What, when you *spanked* me?" she said with a smirk.

I put my tongue to my cheek. "Well, yeah."

She grinned. "You think I'm that weak?"

"It's about comfort, babe, not strength," I countered.

She shrugged. "I'm never in discomfort when I'm with you. Everything you do turns me on, and I trust you to do the right thing at all times. And if, God forbid, you ever did something in the future that made me uncomfortable, I'll simply chop your dick off and feed it to my alley dog, Jacob."

I choked on a laugh. "You named your alley dog?"

She rolled her eyes. "It was a Twilight referenced joke, Gall," she said.

"Ah, I see." I chuckled and moved a little to the left when she tried to back-kick me. "How violent of you, girlfriend."

She clicked her tongue. "Says the guy who just slapped my ass like it was a fresh slice of beef."

I scrunched up my nose. "Please don't *ever* say that again."

Zaira laughed. "Are you going to fuck me, or are you just going to stand here and chit-chat?" She gave me a challenging look.

In response, I unbuckled my belt and unzipped my pants before lowering them to my knees. "Face forward."

She quickly obeyed, and gasped when I roughly pulled her underwear down her legs.

"I can smell you, Zaira," I said as I ran my hands over her thighs. "I can smell how much you want me."

She hummed as she kicked her underwear off, and murmured a chorus of yeses when I slipped a hand between her wet folds.

"Spread your legs for me, baby," I told her.

She did.

"More."

She obliged.

"So compliant," I muttered, and then pushed my underwear down before grabbing myself.

"Gallan…" Zaira rasped when I ran the head of my cock over her entrance, and then screamed my name when I thrust inside her in one go.

"Yes…" she hissed, and then rose on her elbows. "Gall, faster."

I grunted as I pumped into her hot pussy. "I'm going to fuck you so hard, Zaira, that you won't know what's left and what's right." With my heart beating a little unevenly, I began pounding into her. Each time I pulled, and then pushed out of her, her body rocked forward and bumped against the table.

I grabbed her waist and fucked her harder, and tipped my head back as I groaned when the sound of our slick skin slapping together met my ears.

Zaira made me wild. She turned me into a version of myself that was unexpectedly new, yet thankfully embraceable.

That woman didn't just make my dick hard, but she also made my heart soar and my soul do a fucking ballet whenever she was near. The kind of effect she had on me was one I thought I'd honestly never get to experience, but now that I had her and had had the honor of knowing her, falling for her, I didn't know how else to live my life.

"Up, come on," I said to her.

She lifted herself, and yelped when I pulled her flush against my chest. "Fuck yeah, babe," she moaned when I pushed myself deeper inside her. "God, don't stop." She placed the back of her head on my left shoulder.

I gently wrapped the fingers of my right hand around her throat. "How badly do you wanna come, Zaira?" I asked against her ear as I continued to fuck her.

She whimpered. "So bad," she breathed.

I could feel her pulse against the pad of my thumb, and for some reason, it turned me on even more.

"Show me how desperately you wanna come all over my cock," I said to her.

"Asshole," she spat, and then started rocking her hips in time with my movements.

I chuckled and ever so slightly tightened my hold on her throat. "I love how your pussy wraps around me, baby." I nipped at her lobe. "And I fucking love how you taste on my tongue." I sucked on the skin below her ear, which made her hiss.

"So you remembered the hickey thing, huh?" she questioned breathlessly. She cupped the back of my head with one hand, and bunched the hem of my jacket with the other.

I licked her now-bruised skin. "Of course I did."

She shifted her head so that our lips were merely an inch from the other's. "Make me come, Underwood," she said when our eyes met.

I grinned. "You got it." I took her lips in a kiss, and used my free hand to stroke her swollen clit.

Zaira moaned against my mouth, and I felt her clenching around me a second before she orgasmed. She broke the kiss and groaned my name as she continued to rock against my cock and my hand.

I pressed my forehead to hers just as my spine numbed and my gut clenched. My thrusts turned rough, and as I roared her name and came inside her, I swear on my balls I saw stars.

Zaira smiled lazily at me. "That was hot," she slurred.

"That's one word for it." I gave her a long kiss. "*You're* hot."

She laughed. "You know I–"

The loud ringing of my landline stopped her.

I huffed and pulled out of Zaira before carefully leaning forward and pressing the speaker button. "Yes."

"Hey, boss," came Sage's smug voice. "I'm sorry to burst your hyperactive sexual bubble, but Mr. Henley is here. I've asked him to sit in the waiting room for now, but I'm not sure that'll work for long. He isn't one to '*be a part of a queue*', he told me. So you better hurry up if you wanna secure that deal with him." The line went dead.

"Wow." Zaira placed a hand over her mouth and laughed.

I scratched the side of my neck. "This Mr. Henley guy and his scented underwear are going to be the death of me," I grumbled.

She laughed more. "This is absolute gold."

I rolled my eyes. "Yeah, yeah; make fun of my misery."

She pouted. "Aww." She gave me a sound kiss. "Let's clean up so that you can go have your meeting."

I smiled. "Okay." I shifted and bent to pull my underwear and pants up, but stopped midway and whipped my head at Zaira when she slapped my...ass.

"What was that for?"

She grinned wickedly as she pushed her skirt down her thighs. "You get what you give, my love. You get what you give."

My lips twitched. "Fair enough." I pulled up my underwear and pants but kept the latter unzipped. My eyes then landed on Zaira's panty on the floor. With a smirk, I quickly snatched it and brought it to my nose. "Mm, I'm keeping this." I pocketed the lacy little thing and winked at her.

She pushed back her glasses as she rocked on her feet. "You know what, Gallan?" she asked.

I took a step towards her and leaned in so that our lips brushed. "What?"

Zaira slowly bit down at my bottom lip. "You're a dirty mother-trucker," she whispered. "And a dangerous one, too."

I grinned against her mouth. "Oh, babe; I know." I kissed her. "*I know.*"

46.
gallan

October 2nd, 2020

"The pressure of looking good for the cameras at all times," Kenneth said.

I clicked my tongue. "The pressure of trying to act as if we aren't frustrated," I countered.

"Crazy traveling schedules."

"Having to watch the movie over and over during premieres."

"Hmm." Kenneth nodded. "Swarming paparazzi that just won't back up."

I pointed a finger at him. "Get ready; I've got the worst one coming," I told him.

He grimaced. "Give it to me."

I shuddered a little. "Two words: Repetitive. Questions."

Dylan, who was with us, groaned in agreement as he continued to eat greasy French fries from the paper bag in his hand.

Because it was the second to last day of filming, Kenneth and I were discussing the hell we would soon be going through in order to promote and make *Waves That Hold Us* a hit: press junkets.

As artists, we lived for the cameras and spotlight and the attention, but we had our limits, too. There was only so much a person could take, and when it came to a movie's promotion, the "so much" and "too much" factors didn't exist. Bleary eyes, lack of sleep, fatigue, headaches, mental distraction – these were things Kenneth and I were used to, but that didn't mean we welcomed them all the time. It wouldn't hurt if Ross went around beating the drum of his upcoming release for once rather than kick me and the others in the cast into the promo-hole.

Due to COVID, our appearances had been minimized, but still, Kenneth and I were scheduled to travel to a few cities in the US, and a few in the UK as well, to promote *Waves That Hold Us*.

We had virtual interviews and signings, social media live coverages and sessions to execute, and even a few magazine photoshoots and one-on-ones to go through.

Yeah, our lives weren't as smooth-flowing and glamorous as a lot of people assumed them to be.

"How do you keep eating these," Kenneth said to Dylan as he gestured at his oily fry bag, "and still look fit and healthy?"

Amara walked over to us and stood next to her husband.

Dylan shrugged at Kenneth. "I don't know."

Kenneth rolled his eyes at him and looked at me. "I agree with your last one. Repetitive questions are the worst." He shook his head. "I mean, how many times will we have to answer why we decided to do this movie until the two of us lose our shit and punch an interviewer in the throat?"

I chuckled. "If only we could get that satisfaction."

He laughed. "Man, I hate press junkets."

Amara turned to look up at him. "You hate a lot of things," she stated matter-of-factly.

Kenneth grinned. "Yup, but I don't hate *you*." He bumped his shoulder against hers.

She gave him an incredulous look, and then snatched Dylan's paper bag from him. She flipped it upside down – which resulted in a few fries to fall on the floor – and then put the bag over Kenneth's head. When it didn't go all the way down to his neck, she applied pressure, which worked, yes, but it also ended up tearing the sides of the greasy bag.

I glanced at Dylan, and he glanced at me. Together, we began laughing, and Kenneth soon joined us.

"How do I look?" he asked. He placed both hands on his hips and posed for us.

"HAWT," Dylan said between laughter.

"That's not even a word," Amara told him.

"Motherhood has changed you drastically, babe," Kenneth said from behind the paper bag.

She scowled at him even though he couldn't see it, and then flattened the bag on his head by pressing it down with her palm. With a victorious smile, she then skipped away from us and into the vanity area.

"Is she gone?" Kenneth asked.

I quickly grabbed my phone and took a picture of him, and then sent it to Zaira. She wasn't on set but with her parents for a family-only day. Sucked for me, but she was excited to finally spend some time with her mom and dad as the lockdown thing had cooled down a bit.

"Yeah, she left," Dylan told Kenneth, who pulled the bag off of his head and threw it in the bin behind him.

"Phew. Well, that was an experience." He swiped his fingers over his now-oily face and scrunched up his nose.

My phone dinged with a new message. I looked down at it, and chuckled as I read Zaira's response to Kenneth's photo.

Zaira: *Tell him that I dig the new look. Total serial killer vibes.*

I showed the message to Kenneth, who laughed and gave me a two-finger salute.

"Dude, you're...greasy," Dylan said to Kenneth, and grabbed a box of tissues from the nearby snack table before helping him clean up.

Ding.

I looked at my phone.

Zaira: *Will you wear a paper bag for me, and also roam around your house naked while you're at it?*

I grinned and shook my head at the screen.

Me: *Do you want me to fall and crack my skull open?*

Zaira: *No. I want you to fall and crack your dick open.*

I coughed to hide my surprised laughter.

Me: *You're crazy, babe.*

Zaira: *I know, but that's one of the reasons why you love me.*

I smiled.

Me: *True that.*

She sent me a picture.

I tapped on it, and almost groaned when I saw her *very* teasing selfie.

She'd opened the top buttons of her red flannel shirt, which gave me a full view of her bomb-ass tits. She'd tilted her head to the side, which clearly showed me the hickey I'd given her yesterday. Her glasses were lowered to the tip of her nose; her lips were painted cherry-red. And the smile she gave the camera – it was all sorts of sinful and tantalizing. And of course, my dick very much appreciated every part of it.

God damnit, that woman was a glass of Macallan on a winter evening. She tasted like luxury; she felt like the best fucking sensation to have ever been experienced.

After giving her selfie another thorough assessment, I clicked on the message bar and began typing.

Me: *Is that a new tattoo on your neck, or do you have a very passionate and thirsty-for-you boyfriend?*

Zaira: *Oh-my-God, seriously???!!!*

I laughed. Kenneth and Dylan gave me knowing smirks, but I flipped them off and got back to texting.

Me: *What?*

Zaira: *I'm disowning you, Gallan Underwood. RIGHT FUCKING NOW.*

Me: *Unfortunately, I do not come with a return policy. I'm a one-time purchase only.*

She sent me the eye-roll emoji at least a dozen times.

Zaira: *I wanna see your policy papers.*

I chuckled.

Me: *The paper mites got to them.*

Zaira: *How ancient are you, exactly?*

Me: *I had an on-and-off affair with Susan B. Anthony. That's all I'm saying. Go figure.*

She didn't respond immediately, but when she did, it was with another picture. Not *hers* this time, to my dismay. It was a picture of a dining table full of Indian food. Gravies, rice, desserts, beverages – you name it, and they were all present.

Zaira: *If I look like Tweedledee after today, you can blame it on this monstrosity of a feast, and on my mum's obsession for cooking.*

Me: *I'm sure you'd make a very sexy Tweedledee, babe. My inner Mad Hatter appreciates all your curves. Every single one of them.*

Zaira: *Aww, I love it when you talk* Alice in Wonderland *to me.*

I couldn't help but laugh again.

Me: *I can even dress like him if you want me to.*

Zaira: *You were going in the right direction just two seconds ago, but you screwed it all up by suggesting roleplay. You ruined my favorite childhood story for me, Underwood. How can I ever forgive you?*

I put my tongue to my cheek.

Me: *I meant for Halloween.*

Zaira: *Sure you did.*

I chuckled.

Zaira: *I have to go...*

She followed that text with a series of crying-face emojis.

Me: *Go have fun. Text me when you're home.*

Zaira: *Mum's gonna gimme a truckload of leftovers when I leave.*

Me: *I'll need some extra pounds on me if I'm gonna survive the upcoming press junkets without falling into a coma, so bring in all the leftovers you can.*

Zaira: *Lol, you got it.*

Zaira: *Gotta go for real! Byeee! I love you, and I hope you have a kickass day on set.*

I smiled.

Me: *Thanks, babe. I love you too. See you tonight.*

Zaira: *Oh, you can count on it* ;–)

47.
zaira

October 4th, 2020

I furrowed my brows and pushed my phone a little closer to my ear. "What did you say?"

Gallan's words, hard to understand because of the shitty network on set, continued to sound confusing. "I – you – *crack* – and – *crack* –"

I sighed and moved to Stage 32. "Gall? Babe, I can't hear you well."

Click.

Clack.

Buzz.

"Can you – *crack* – now?"

I frowned. "Not fully, no." I crossed Stage 32, 20, and then walked out of the studio and into the open air. "Okay, now I've left the haunted house. Speak away."

Gallan chuckled. "I was saying: you should've let me stay with you at the studio if you were gonna work this late. I don't like the idea of you in there by yourself."

When Ross had yelled "*And that's a wrap for* Waves That Hold Us*!*" a few hours ago, I'd never been more relieved. Even though I had an overall good experience working as a crew member, I also couldn't be more thankful to have been done with the task. It'd been hard to enjoy working on set during the last few months, especially after Gallan and I had made ourselves official to the public. Being the constant topic of judgement and gossip among coworkers is never a rewarding feeling, and now that the movie had finally wrapped up, I could breathe easy knowing I wouldn't have to walk into a room and get looked at by people like I was a fucking ball they could toss around for their amusement.

With a slight shake of my head, I smiled at Gallan's concern towards me. "I'm not alone, Gall. A couple guys are here somewhere. We haven't locked up yet. It was the last day of shoot, so it makes sense that us crew members have to stay back and make sure everything is packed and kept in order. I just have a couple more things to do and then I'll be home."

He exhaled. "You should've joined the cast and me for the celebratory dinner."

I grinned. "I'm not part of that world. It was *your* hard work that needed celebration, not mine."

"Don't fucking say that," he said, which made me laugh.

"You're whining," I mused.

"I'm upset with myself for leaving you behind."

A door opened and closed somewhere in the studio.

"You didn't leave me behind. I'm here doing my *job*," I told him. "Also, it's not like it's the first time I've stayed back to help out. I've been working here for months, and during most nights, it's me and a few others who close things down. How else would we have gotten stuck in your trailer all those months ago if I hadn't been here while you were trying to catch yourself a sneaky rat?"

He laughed airily. "True. But I have every right to worry. You can't ask me not to."

"You do have that right, yes, but I'm a grown-ass woman who is fully capable of taking care of herself."

"I know, I know." Pause. "But Zaira…"

I ran a hand over my messy bun. "But what, Gall?"

"It's 2-fucking-a.m., babe."

I clicked my tongue. "And why does it matter?"

"Because I miss you and need you in bed with me? Because I wanna feel your body against mine as I go to sleep?"

I chuckled. "I'll be home soon, I promise. Watch a movie until then. Rest a little, Gall; you deserve it. You've been stressing about the upcoming promos and interviews like crazy. Use this time to do nothing but relax."

"But I wanna relax with *you*," he all but whined, which made me laugh.

"Yo, Zaira!" came a voice from behind me.

I turned, and smiled when Martin, one of our supervisors, waved at me.

"Hey, so I know it's last minute," he began, "but can you lock up tonight? Make sure things at 20 are all set, too." He glanced at his watch and began fidgeting with its band as he faced me again.

"Uh…" I straightened my glasses. "Can you gimme a minute?" I pointed at my phone.

He gave me a grin that was very unlike him. It was wide and toothy and a little wobbly. It confused me.

"Hey, uh, babe?" I said to Gallan. "I gotta go. Martin wants me to lock up tonight, so I'll have to get to work now if I wanna make it to you in an hour. I'll call you as soon as I'm done here, okay?"

Gallan sighed. "You sure you don't want me to come over? I'll be there in twenty."

I smiled. "Nope, I'm good. You get some rest. I'll call you once I've finished locking up."

"Okay." Pause. "Be careful, alright?"

"I will."

"I love you, Zaira."

"And I love you." I disconnected the call and slid my phone into the back pocket of my jeans before making my way over to Martin, who was still acting a little out of context to his personality.

"Hey." I crossed my arms over my chest. "Where's Larry?" I asked.

Martin gestured behind him with a thumb. "He left out the back door. Said he had some work to do at home."

I tilted my head to the side. "But I thought you and him were going to lock up tonight, especially after Ross's strict instructions of getting everything done perfectly. I didn't peg you one for leaving such a responsibility to one of the juniors."

He pushed his *Lakers* cap further down his forehead. "Umm, well Larry isn't here anymore, and I can't stay long because my girlfriend isn't feeling too well. She's having these contractions that are scaring her."

"She's due in January, though, isn't she?"

He nodded. "Yeah, but she's been having issues lately. I'll have to take her to the doctor's."

Well, that explained his agitated behavior.

"Okay, I'll lock up. You go take care of your girlfriend."

Martin looked at me with an expression that made me *really* look at him. Like, stare at him for a solid minute or so.

Was it regret in his eyes, or was it hesitation on his face? I honestly couldn't tell. All I knew was that it didn't sit well with me.

"Thanks, Zaira; you're the best," he said, and then jogged past me and towards the exit.

"Martin?"

He stopped and looked at me. "Yeah?"

"Do let me know what the doctor says about the contractions," I said to him.

He nodded, and with another stiff wave, walked out and headed for the crew parking lot.

I turned and looked around the equipment-filled, wire-flowing room. "Oh boy…" I muttered, and then, with a scowl on my face, I spat a few curses into the air and got to work.

48.
Zaira

October 4th, 2020

I had only just wheeled the last of the massive crate carts towards the end of the room when I heard a *swish*, followed by loud, consistent rattling. I whipped my head towards the studio entrance just in time to see Aubrey, flanked by four of her friends and Martin, grinning at me like she'd won an Olympic gold medal as the wide shutter-door continued to roll down before my eyes.

It took me a moment to realize what was happening, and when my brain finally registered the act, I stumbled a little as I began running towards the shutter.

Aubrey wiggled her fingers at me. "Ta-ta, *bitch*," she spat.

I ignored her words and continued to run.

I ignored the giggles and snickers of her friends as they mocked me.

I ignored the look of guilt on Martin's face as he kept his eyes on the ground, most definitely too ashamed to look at me.

What the fuck was Aubrey even thinking?

God, I knew she was demented, but I hadn't at all comprehended that she'd be this disgusting.

I'd only just reached the entrance when the shutter slammed shut completely, caging me in.

I stopped right in front of it, and began banging my fist on it. "Open the fucking door, Aubrey!" I banged the shutter some more, but pulled away when the force I'd used ricocheted against my wrists.

I hissed and shook my hands, and then kicked the bottom of the shutter. "Open the door!" I didn't want the tears to fall, but they did anyway. I didn't want fear to tighten my chest, but it didn't listen. I didn't want goosebumps to mar my scalp, my arms, my entire fucking body, but they started pricking my skin anyway.

And I didn't want my breathing to turn shallow, but my lungs didn't obey me at all.

"Aubrey..." I sucked in a bout of air as I tried to hold back my tears. "Open up!" I slapped the shutter. "Open! Open! Open!" I was so scared. I didn't know what to do. I felt trapped, and rightfully so.

I tumbled back and sped through every room, but even as I kept opening and shutting doors throughout the massive studio, I knew there wasn't anything I could do on my own unless Aubrey or someone else decided to open the shutter from the outside.

My suspicion was quickly confirmed when I reached the studio's rear exit and found it to be locked, too.

"Fuck!" I kicked at the metal door, and cried out when pain shot through my right leg at my stupid, impulsive action.

I muffled a sob behind my hand, and with the help of a supply cart, I dragged myself back toward the entrance.

I wiped my nose with the sleeve of my black hoodie. "What do you want?" I whispered as I placed my forehead against the shutter. "*What do you fucking want?*" I screamed, and began banging my fists on the door again.

"For you to suffer," came Aubrey's voice from outside. "You thought you'd won when Shane held a meeting with me and my manager and practically insulted me in front of him, didn't you? You thought you'd taught me a lesson and driven me away, huh?" When I didn't answer, she laughed hysterically. "My manager almost dropped me as a client after everything Shane told him, you know that?" She hit the shutter, which made me gasp and move away from it. "You tried to ruin my career, you cunt, and for that, you're going to pay. *You're going to fucking pay!*"

I did *what*?

Oh, that bitch wasn't serious.

"You know what, Aubrey?!" I yelled. "I didn't even care that you existed before you started making yourself known to me after Gallan and I posted those pictures of us on Instagram. I didn't care about who you were and what you did; I only cared about Gallan. I always have."

"You aren't anything, Zaira. I'm *Aubrey* – a rising star; a fashion icon. An up-and-coming entrepreneur. And what are *you*? ABSOLUTELY *NOTHING*. You're a *nobody*."

Her friends laughed. Fucking crows, all of them.

I scoffed. "You didn't even have a career before Gallan, *Aubrey*. Everything you are, and everything you have, is because he took pity on you and helped you stand back on your feet. He helped you with your clothing line, with your modelling career. He helped you get in the spotlight by staying in a fake relationship with you, and he helped you get back in the media's eyes by agreeing to do *Waves That Hold Us*, despite knowing that you would be his costar. So the next time you decide to beat your own drum, know that it was *my* boyfriend who saved you from getting kicked to the curb by not only your manager, but also by Hollywood." I was panting and sweating, and my vision was slightly blurry due to the heaviness in my head.

"*You don't deserve him!*" Aubrey screamed. "You don't deserve *anything*."

I had to laugh at that. "And you *do*?"

"Of course I fucking do," she hissed, and I could tell that she'd gotten closer to the shutter. "I thought sending the Instagram trolls your way would make you run for the hills, but that didn't work." She threw something at the gate, which shook it wildly and made me suck in a sharp breath. "I tried to overwhelm you with paparazzi, tried to scare you off with that locker room stunt, but you just wouldn't leave." Three consecutive pounds on the shutter. "*Why won't you fucking leave?!*"

She was the one behind those fake Instagram accounts?

She was the one who'd asked the paps to swarm my car every morning?

I don't know why I was surprised, but I was.

"Because I love Gallan, that's why," I said easily. I shifted on my feet, and bit back a curse when a new wave of pain shot through my right leg. "I don't want him because he's someone unattainable, or someone who is successful and rich and handsome. I want him for him; because I truly love *him*. I see parts of him that you would never even think of searching for. All you care about is wealth and spotlight, but Gallan and I – we see the good in each other; we complement each other. We *fit* together."

"Bullshit," Aubrey spat, just as one of her friends said, "Aubs, you're gonna get wrinkles all over your face if you get any angrier."

Aubs?

…Just…wow.

"You don't love Gallan, Zaira; you're only with him for his money and fame," Aubrey sneered. "When he realizes what you really are, he'll dump your down-market ass and come back to me. *I know it*." She giggled.

I swiped my hands over my eyes from under my glasses. "Don't be ridiculous, Aubrey. You really think you can get away with this?" I told her. "You really think your stupid bout of spite is worth everything you've earned? Are you really ready to lose it all in the name of unwarranted pettiness?"

"As long as you learn your lesson, yes."

I snorted. "Are you being serious right now?"

"As a heart attack," she almost sang the words. "Anyways…I'm done talking. I gotta head home and get my beauty sleep. I hope you feel perfectly accommodated in there." She cackled, that hyena. "Until then, bitch. Good-fucking-bye!"

I heard sharp *clacks* of heels against the ground, followed by receding snickers.

Fear gripped me further, and beads of sweat began running down my face, neck, arms, and back.

"Aubrey!" I once again slammed my palms against the gate. "Stop being stupid and open the fucking door!"

There was no response, and a few seconds later, the lights in the entire studio went off, in turn bathing me in greying darkness.

With my heart in my throat, I looked to my left, and found a touchpad on the wall next to the shutter. My breathing quickened. "Martin?" I asked, and when no one replied, I screamed, "*Martin!*"

"What?" came his voice. Regret and shame were crystal-clear in his tone.

"So what, you're gonna stand guard outside for the rest of the night? You really think I can escape?"

He was silent for a while.

"I couldn't leave before I apologized," he said so slowly that I hardly caught it.

"You're *sorry*?" I asked, and then laughed humorlessly. "I trusted you, and you played me. *You fucking lied to me!* You're just as much a part of this as Aubrey and her girl-gang."

"I know, okay? I know." He cursed. "She offered good money, Zaira, and I know that's no excuse for what I've done, but it was something I couldn't let slip from my hands. I need the cash, especially now that Kira is expecting and filming is done. I don't know if Ross will hire me for his next project, so until then, I'll have this money to keep me and my girl going."

I closed my eyes and cried. I couldn't help it; it just happened. I've never felt more helpless and weaker than I did in that moment.

"I'm sorry, Zaira," Martin said. "You've always been kind to me; you've always been eager to help. I just...I guess my greed blinded me. I'm sorry."

"What's the passcode to unlock the gate, Martin?" I asked as I opened my eyes.

"Wh-what?"

"The passcode – what is it? Only the supervisors and Ross have it, so I'm sure you know the numbers that open this gate. I've seen you enter them in the past, so don't even try to deny it." I punched said gate for emphasis. "Tell me what it is. Aubrey isn't smart enough to know that you gave it to me. We'll be even, I promise. Just…just please…" My voice cracked a little, so I cleared my throat and swallowed. "Just tell me the code, Martin."

"I can't." He sounded helpless, which was laughable because it was *me* who was in a bad situation, not him.

"Can't, or won't?"

He released a frustrated sound. "She's shut down the power, Zaira. The touchpad won't work. It's wired in with the main line."

"Well, then turn the power back on and gimme the damn code!"

"Don't make this harder for me," Martin almost begged.

"Harder for *you*? Are you shitting me?" When he didn't say anything, I gritted my teeth. "*Fuck you!*" I screamed. "Fuck. You. Martin!"

"I gotta go. Once again, I'm sorry. I know I've gotten myself in trouble for this, but at least the money will help Kira. I…" Silence. "I'm so sorry, Zaira." And then he was gone.

I pushed away from the door and walked over to the touchpad. I pulled my phone out of the back pocket of my jeans and unlocked it. I had no signal, as usual, but I still tried calling Gallan and Shane multiple times before giving up.

I sniffed and turned on my phone's flashlight. I searched the wall around the touchpad in hopes of finding the code, but came up empty-handed. And when I pressed the numbers at random on the pad and nothing lit up, is when I realized that the entire system was indeed wired with electricity, and because Aubrey had switched off the main fuse, there was no way for the shutter to open until and unless someone powered up the main electricity board and entered the unlock code from the outside.

Sweat dripped into my eyes, making me hiss. I managed to turn around, even though my right leg was aching to the point where I wanted to throw up. I flashed my phone's light on the vent at the very top of the left-side wall, and then dragged myself around the room in search of a tool crate. Once I'd found it, I grabbed a screwdriver from it and hobbled over to the empty crate I'd used earlier as support. With a cry of pain, I knelt in front of it and began unscrewing the wheels from under it. I then threw the screwdriver, screws, and wheels to the side before slowly getting to my feet. With a huff, I lifted the crate and walked it over to the supply box right below the vent. It took me a while, but I finally placed the crate on the box exactly how I wanted it, and then, with a huge intake of breath, I placed my left foot on the supply box and grabbed the steel bars of the crate before lifting myself up.

"Fucking hell," I groaned when half my body weight fell on my right ankle, causing pain to almost blind me. White spots obscured my view, and when I shook my head to get rid of them, my glasses slipped off my face and fell on the floor with a sickening *crash*.

"Damn it." I sniffed and continued climbing upwards.

Once both my knees were on top of the crate, I brought my phone close to the vent and dialed Gallan's number. The call didn't go through. I closed my eyes as fresh tears fell on my cheeks. "Please…" I breathed. "Please, please, please…" I tried calling him again, but it didn't work. I couldn't even connect to 9-1-1, despite trying more than six times and practically shoving my phone against the vent in hopes of finding signal bars.

With my fingers slick with sweat, I sent Gallan a quick text, and prayed to every God out there that it would reach him.

My head swam all of a sudden. I turned off my flashlight and pocketed my phone. With fatigue tightening my shoulders, I slowly stepped down the crate, the box, and finally landed on the floor. My left foot connected with my broken glasses, destroying them beyond repair.

Out of the blue, my heart began beating rapidly. I trembled a little as I made my way towards the shutter. It felt as if someone had grabbed the nape of my neck in a vise grip, making it almost impossible for me to think straight. I fell on the floor and placed my back against the door. I hugged my knees to my chest and began rocking back and forth as I worked on slowing my breathing.

There was nothing I could do but wait.

There was nothing – *no one* – who could hear me right now.

Fear wouldn't gimme aid, and neither would the darkness.

I began counting numbers backwards. Maybe they could help me get out of this mess? Maybe they could show me the way?

One hundred…

Ninety-nine…

Ninety-eight…

It didn't hurt to try, did it?

Ninety-seven…

Ninety-six…

Ninety-five…

Was it working? I honestly couldn't tell.

Ninety-four…

…Ninety…ninety…

…Ninety…

What comes next? I asked myself, and the answer – it came only as darkness.

Cold, clammy, and suffocating darkness.

49.
gallan

October 4th, 2020

I quickly put on a pair of jeans, and then began ruffling through my spare t-shirts in Zaira's closet in search of something easy to put on. I pulled out a plain white tee, and hastily threw it over my head before grabbing my phone and wallet from her dressing table.

I should have taken her to the restaurant with me for the movie's wrap-up celebration.

I shouldn't have listened to her when she'd said she wanted to stay back and help the others on set.

Kenzie had decided to leave early because she had dinner plans with her family, so the last stroke of comfort I'd had of knowing that Zaira would be okay and with someone I knew and trusted – yeah, that'd been fucked.

It was 3:30a.m., and my level of concern was rising with each *tick* of the clock's hand. Her phone was out of coverage area, and even my texts weren't reaching her. Although I knew she was fully capable of looking after herself, my anxiety still kept raking its claws down the back of my mind.

I unlocked my phone and opened the group chat. Call it an intuition, or maybe just a fleeting thought, but I wanted to send a text out to the others just to get some notes of positivity for my otherwise anxious brain. I knew it was late, but at least I could try.

Me: *Zaira isn't home yet. I'm trying to call her but can't. Texts aren't going through either. I'm headed to set. I'm worried out of my mind.*

Almost immediately, my phone began buzzing with incoming messages.

Kenneth: *I'm on my way.*

Shane: *Be there in a few.*

Dylan: *Conner and I are coming. Don't stress. I'm sure she's fine.*

Kenzie: *I tried calling but it isn't connecting. I'm headed there now. Text me if she contacts anyone.*

I let go of a short breath as I typed in a reply.

Me: *You guys rock. Thanks.*

I'd only just crossed the living room when my phone *pinged* with another text. With a madly beating heart, I stopped and looked at it, and sighed in relief when Zaira's name flashed across the screen. But, as soon as I read the message she'd sent, my entire body went ice-cold, and my head began buzzing incessantly with the words on my screen.

Zaira: *Aubrey and her friends have locked me in the studio. There's hardly any network, and it's dark. Martin helped her. I'm hurt and scared, Gallan. Please come fast.*

My breaths came out frosty, and when I read the text a second time, I saw red.

I'm hurt and scared, Gallan.

I'm hurt...

I'm hurt...

I straightened and took a screenshot of the message before sending it on the group chat. I then also sent it to Ross, who got back to me surprisingly fast.

Ross: *I'll see you there.*

I didn't wait to see what the others had texted, and grabbed my car keys before marching out of Zaira's apartment. I locked the door and all but sprinted down the stairs. Once in my car, I placed my phone on its holder and backed out of the parking lot.

I was moving on autopilot, that much was obvious. My brain had thankfully decided not to shut down on me, but my body – it was openly betraying my act of wanting to stay levelheaded after reading Zaira's message.

I was sweating, trembling, fucking close to throwing up all over myself.

I was hardly breathing, hardly seeing straight, and my heart – it felt like it was in my mouth with the way it was beating against my chest.

My fingers kept slipping on the steering wheel because of the damned sweat, and as I tried to swallow the growing lump in my throat, a knot began tightening my stomach to the point of pain.

She was scared.

She was hurt.

I pushed my hair back and clenched my jaw.

My God, she was fucking *hurt*.

As I hit the road, I unlocked my phone with a shaky hand and made a very important call, and was relieved when he picked up on the second ring.

"What's up?"

"I need your help," I said. I took a right and drove as fast as I could.

"Shoot me the address and I'm there," Ronen Luan, my good friend and one of L.A.'s best lawyers, answered.

I rattled the studio's address to him, and he promised to be there as soon as possible.

Once the call ended, I hit the gas and sped through the empty streets with anger riding on my shoulder.

Aubrey didn't learn to stay in her lane the easy way, and now that she'd gone and done the unexpected – she'd pay for it with everything she had.

Of that, I would make abso-fucking-lutely sure.

50.
Zaira

October 4th, 2020

Something was touching my face, I couldn't tell what. The left side of my body felt numb, and so did my head. My lower back hurt like I'd been kicked, and my throat burned from the aftermath of all my screaming.

I moved back and sat up with a gasp when I felt something on my face again. I looked around me, and it took me a second to realize where I was.

I was in the dark studio, locked in by Aubrey and her batch of crows.

Somewhere between trying to not lose my shit and trying to stay calm, I must've dozed off. I had no recollection of lying on the floor, but maybe I'd fallen, or had done it unknowingly in my sleep.

I wiped my mouth with the back of my hand, and grabbed my phone from the pocket of my jeans before turning on its flashlight. I moved it around, but stopped when I saw a rat staring up at me with big black eyes. It was sitting in front of me with its head tilted to the side, and when I made a shooing gesture at it, it squeaked once before running to the other side of the room.

Tired – I was so damn tired. I could barely keep my eyes open, let alone stay seated without falling sideways.

I shifted and lied back down on the floor before closing my eyes. I hid a yawn behind a hand, and began questioning the reason for my situation. The motive behind it.

Why me?

Why was I being targeted?

Why was I being treated like this?

Why was I the source of mockery and bullying for people?

Why was I the one in the wrong?

What had I even done wrong?

Why had things in my life gone from basic to drastic? When and why did my normalcy flee from me?

As I curled into myself and hugged my phone to my chest, I realized that I already knew the answer to all of the above questions. I've known it even before the questions started echoing in my mind.

As I cried onto the rocky floor and let go of my frustration and pain and anger, I realized that despite knowing what the consequences of my decisions would be, I still went along with the change, and with everything else that came with it.

Despite knowing how much this would affect me, I still decided to fall, and fall hard and fast and deep.

For *him*.

For Gallan.

I changed everything for him.

I accepted the alterations – both good and bad – only so I could have him.

I molded myself into a version of myself that was so different from the one I've known my whole life.

I gave up on the basic aspects of my routine just so I could start practicing his.

And was it worth it?

Were the changes worth my comfort?

Was the overwhelming feeling of being the center of attraction and a bait to those who thought were better than me, worth even a smidge of my morals?

I squeezed my eyes shut and placed a fist over my mouth as I sobbed harder; as I answered my questions with a heavy heart but a resolute mind.

No, it wasn't.

As much as I loved Gallan, everything that'd happened in the past few weeks, including the situation I was in, wasn't worth it. It wasn't *deserved*.

I didn't deserve it.

My love for him would never fade, yes, but our paths – they couldn't stay parallel anymore. I'd reached the brink of my patience and willingness to ignore the negativity. I had no fight left in me. And as much as it broke and wounded me to admit it, I also couldn't deny that life before Gallan may have been boring, but at least it was safe and carefree. At least it wasn't restrictive and inundating.

And as I lay on the hard ground and wept my heart out, I realized that the chapter Gallan and I had started all those months ago in his trailer, had now come to an end, leaving behind traces of its once-beautiful echoes and memories.

If only there was another way…

But there never really is one, is there? a voice in my head said.

"No," I breathed between tears. "No, there isn't."

51.
gallan

October 4th, 2020

"The main fuse has been powered off," Ross said. His voice cut through the otherwise thick silence around the seven of us.

"How do you know that?" Shane asked.

Ross pointed at the touchpad next to the studio gate. "The lights on this aren't on." He turned and handed a pair of keys to Dylan. "Go open the meter box and pull up the orange fuse."

Both Conner and Dylan ran towards the back of the studio.

"Does Martin have a set of these keys?" Kenneth asked Ross.

"He does," Kenzie answered. "I've seen him with them before."

"She's right," Ross said. "Martin is one of the supervisors, so he does have a copy of each set of keys."

We'd all gathered outside the studio just a couple minutes ago, and even though anger and worry were on the forefront of my mind, there was also dread chilling my veins. The expression on everyone's faces matched the feeling in my gut: fear and shock. Fear because when we'd called out Zaira's name multiple times, she hadn't responded to us. Shock because it was so hard to come to terms with what Aubrey had done.

The roar of an engine turned our attention towards the studio's entry gates. A slick grey Lamborghini Aventador breezed in and stopped right next to my car. The door opened, and Ronen, dressed in a black dress shirt and pants, stepped outside before striding over to us with purpose. His vibrant green eyes scanned the area, and then landed on me as he stopped in front of me.

"Tell me everything," he said, and then folded his arms over his chest.

So, I did. And once I was done, only then did he introduce himself and shake hands with everyone.

I'd met Ronen through Shane. The former was my manager's best friend's son, which is why he'd come to be a solid advisor and help to me, especially after he'd started his own firm three years ago. Ronen wasn't one for small-talk or heart-to-heart, and it was his ruthless dedication towards his profession that had made him this successful at the age of thirty-four.

He worked differently, that guy. He liked to investigate things on-ground – all by himself – before signing on clients or agreeing to give his suggestion on something serious. He was a deadly combination of Arthur Kirkland and Sherlock Holmes, and even the men and women in uniform thought twice before trying to hold him back when he was in work-mode.

Ronen looked around once more, and then pointed at something above Shane's head. "I need a copy of the CCTV footage in my office by 10a.m.," he said, addressing his words to Ross, who nodded without hesitation.

He looked at me again. "Can I see the message Zaira sent you?"

"Yeah, of course." I gave him my phone.

Dylan and Conner rounded the corner and handed the keys to Ross.

"The fuse has been turned on," Dylan said.

Ronen whipped his head up. "The electricity wasn't up?" he asked Dylan.

"Nope. Aubrey had shut everything down," Conner answered.

Ronen looked at Ross. "Then the cameras must've been turned off, too."

Ross shook his head. "Not really. The ones here are battery-operated, so they're still on."

Ronen nodded. "Perfect." He stared at my phone for a while, and then looked at me. "Email me a screenshot of this, will you?" He handed my phone back to me.

"I will." I pocketed my phone. "Can we please open the door now? Zaira's in there," I said, and cleared my throat when my voice cracked a little.

With another nod, Ross walked over to the touchpad and quickly pressed in the code. The massive shutter began rolling up, and once there was enough space for me to pass through, I ran in without a second thought.

It felt like one minute I was breathing too fast, and the next, my chest contracted and refused to let me exhale.

Boom, pause, *boom*, pause.

Boom-boom, pause.

...Pause, *boom*.

I'd only just entered Stage 20, though, when my steps faltered upon seeing her on the ground. She was curled on the floor, with her hair a mess, her jeans and hoodie muddy, and her ankles crossed over each other. Under the white fluorescent lights, she looked so small, so tired.

So *broken*.

Her back was to me, and as I walked closer to her, I saw that a rat was standing next to her forehead. It rose on its hind legs and placed its hands on her head as if assessing her, and then sat back down before sniffing her nose.

"Zaira..." I breathed her name into the air, and then crouched behind her. "Zaira? Babe, it's me." I placed a hand on her shoulder and shook her a little.

She jerked at my touch, and screamed before moving away from me, her eyes wide and expression wild.

Her sudden movements scared the rat. It squeaked and ran away from us, just as Zaira shifted and scrubbed her hands over her tearstained cheeks.

My heart all but shrunk when I looked at her features. Her eyes were puffy; her chin had dirt on it. Strands of her hair were stuck on her temples, and her lips were chapped as they quivered.

"Baby–" I stopped when the others joined me.

Ronen began scanning the room, and Dylan walked over to Zaira before lifting her in his arms.

"Kenzie has called an ambulance," he said to me. "Let's get her outta here while Ronen goes through with his investigation."

Zaira wrapped her arms around his shoulders and buried her face into the crook of his neck. She was shaking and crying as she said, "My right leg hurts so bad, D."

Dylan's jaw hardened, and he blinked before holding her tighter. "I got you, babe. I got you."

I was still processing Zaira's words as I stood there before her like a dumb piece of log when I heard sirens blaring in the background. Red-and-blue lights flashed soon after, and as Dylan walked out with Zaira still in his arms, I just kept watching the latter. She wasn't looking at me for some reason, which confused me.

"Hey." Shane placed a hand on my back as he came to stand next to me. "You okay, kid?"

I looked at him. "Why won't she look at me?" I asked him. "Why won't Zaira look at me, Shane?"

He seemed a bit taken aback by my question. "She's been through a lot. Give her time, G; she'll come around."

I shook my head. "You don't understand." I sniffed and pushed my hair back. "She won't…she…" I shook my head again. "She wouldn't *look* at me, Shane. She didn't…"

"Hey, hey." A hand gripped my left bicep. Kenneth.

"Look at me," he said.

I did, and the pain in his ice-blue eyes almost undid me.

"I know what you're going through right now," he said between gritted teeth. "I know *exactly* what it feels like, because I've gone through a pain far similar to this. She has a lot on her mind right now, okay? Just let her breathe and get to terms with everything. She's going to be fine, but only if you take things slow."

Conner, who'd come up behind Kenneth, nodded at me. "He's right. That's all we could do when it came to Amara: wait; give her time."

"Although, I didn't leave her alone, despite what everyone said," Kenneth added, and jerked his head towards the ambulance. "Go, be with her. She may not show it now, but I'm sure she'll appreciate it."

"Thanks, guys." I walked away from them, but stopped and glanced at Ronen. "You gonna be okay here?"

He looked at me. "For now, yeah." He gestured at Ross next to him. "I have him to answer any questions. But you'll have to drop by my office later today for a quick Q&A."

"Definitely." I gave him a grateful smile and walked out of the studio.

By the time I made it to the exit, Zaira had already been loaded into the ambulance. I made to step in so that I could join her, but her raspy voice stopped me in my tracks.

"No…"

I looked at her, and she finally met my eyes. And what I saw swarming in her hazels – like a picture painted in ink – knocked the breath right out of me.

Rejection.

Her chin trembled a second before she started sobbing. "I can't…can't do this anymore," she choked out, and then shook her head at me. "I can't do this anymore." Her crumpled expression spoke volumes, and only added to the weight of her aching words.

I stepped back and stared at her. She couldn't do *what* anymore?

But even as I asked myself that question, I knew exactly what she meant. I could read her like an open book; I could *feel* everything she was trying to tell me.

She didn't want me anymore; she didn't want a relationship with me.

And the reason behind it? Aubrey and her cheap stunt.

Kenzie walked past me and joined Zaira in the ambulance. She looked at me and mouthed '*I'm sorry*', just as the doors closed and the ambulance sped away from me.

As I continued to watch its fading lights, I let my shoulders fall forward and a lone tear slip down my eye.

Was it really the end of our chapter? Was this really the full stop that would conclude it all?

Was our love not strong enough to pass the test? Was *I* not enough to come back to after facing the dark?

I didn't even have to turn around to know that the guys had seen the little interaction Zaira and I had had, which is why when Kenneth and Shane tried to pull me away from the road and into one of their cars, I didn't stop them. Not that I had an ounce of drive in me to do anything after Zaira had quite literally crushed my very soul into the palm of her hand.

Not when she'd decided to give up on me and stomped on my belief in us so easily.

And especially not when I had nothing to offer myself but doses of overpowering numbness and isolation.

If only I could just make her *see*.

But you can't, can you? said a voice inside my head.

No.

No, I can't.

52.
gallan

October 15th, 2020

With hands that had begun trembling the moment I'd stepped outta my car and into her apartment building, and a heart that wouldn't stop acting like a ticking time bomb, I moved forward and knocked on her door like a fucking teenager approaching his crush for the first time. I then pushed my hair away from my face, and scowled when it fell forward and covered my right temple again.

It'd been a little over eleven days since I'd seen, or heard from Zaira. When I'd reached the hospital last week after she'd refused to let me join her in the ambulance, Kenzie, along with Zaira's parents, had refused to let me see her. They were just as confused by her sudden shift of behavior towards me as I was, but they had no other option but to respect her wishes. I'd done that too – not only on that particular day but the next ten or so days as well. It wasn't like I had a choice. She didn't wanna see me after being discharged, and she's been continually ignoring each and every one of my calls and texts ever since. It's a different story that some of the messages I've sent her in the past week have been long-ass, whiney monologues of me asking her to talk to me, and also of me professing my undying love for her as if I were a Shakespeare-designed character. But in my defense, those monologues had only spilled outta me during nights where I was too drunk to tell the difference between Tom Hanks and Kevin Spacey.

Yeah, I was a weird ass bitch after a few glasses of scotch, what can I say.

I sighed and ran a hand over my face as I waited for Zaira to open the door, but when she didn't, I swallowed and knocked again.

Everything I've learnt about her health and general wellbeing since the...*incident*, has been through either her parents, or through Kenzie, Kenneth, Dylan, and Amara.

However, none of those traitors ever told me why Zaira didn't wish to see, or even talk to me anymore. I'm sure they must've asked, and I'm surer that she must've told them. But those four asshats kept refusing to answer me whenever I tried to get something out of them.

Kenzie, though, had told me that Zaira was seeing a therapist because she was facing occasional frights and nightmares. It had quite literally *maimed* me to know that she was going through something so drastic, and the idea of her facing those very frights and nightmares alone – yeah, that killed me a little on the inside.

I loved her so fucking much, and the fact that she's chosen to keep me away while she goes through such darkness – it's been biting away at my conscience and heart.

I wanna be there for her, but she won't even acknowledge me or my attempts of reaching out to her. How am I supposed to do anything unless she lets me in again?

Why did she push me away in the first place?

Aubrey has paid, and paid *well* for everything she's done. She was prosecuted for each and every despicable thing she's done to Zaira. Not only her, but her manager and friends have also been caught up in her mess. She's solely accountable for most of what she did, with only some minor help from her 'girlfriends'. But because it was her manager who'd filled her head with certain ideas that could successfully hurt Zaira and damage her reputation, that bastard, too, had had to pay.

Ronen, that goddamn heaven-sent motherfucker, made sure Aubrey paid back the contract money for *Waves That Hold Us* as part of her legal charge, along with a couple of her assets and a large amount of cash as a cherry on the fucking cake. She was pulled out of media appearances for the movie, and a few of the big-name magazines and fashion brands that had signed her on for one-time collaborations also stepped back when Ronen reached out to them.

Aubrey's parents had prevented the news of their precious daughter's massive fuck-up from reaching the media. The news that had instead gone out was one of the happy family enjoying a wonderful vacation in their holiday home in Miami after Aubrey's 'months of hard work' on *Waves That Hold Us*.

What a joke.

I'd been furious about the whole escape lie. Ronen couldn't do anything against it because his work ended when Aubrey took accountability for her wrongdoings and paid the legal charges. But for *me*, it wasn't enough. Not after all she's put Zaira through.

I wanted Aubrey's reality to be revealed to the media, and for her disgusting layers to be peeled before the world's eyes one by one, but there wasn't anything I could do but fume in my empty penthouse with two bottles of Johnnie Walker and a constant resting dick-face.

Dylan had offered to expose Aubrey to the media, but Shane had reminded us that in doing so, we would end up putting Zaira in the spotlight, too. She'd be just as much the talk of H-town and the tabloids as Aubrey, and that would serve no purpose but cause more distress and drama.

I've been getting uncountable DMs, tweets, and comments from fans asking about Zaira and I's absence on social media. We haven't shared anything at all in around two weeks, so for the fans – who are used to seeing multiple tweets and posts and stories from us on a daily basis – it is bound to be a little confusing.

On Shane's request, I did send out a neutral tweet the other day talking about getting some downtime in with Zaira before the press tour of *Waves That Hold Us* began. Call it bravery or stupidity, but I tagged her in my tweet, and was surprised when I didn't hear any objections from her. Well, I got no other response from her either, so there's that.

At least she didn't block me on all of social media, right?

Right.

Kenneth and I were to head to New York – the first stop in our dreadful press tour – in the next four hours. So, before I got busy with travelling and the whole promotion shebang, I wanted to meet Zaira one-on-one and see where she stood.

Where *we* stood.

I rose my left arm to knock on her door again, but stopped halfway when it flung open.

I sucked in a quick breath as her eyes met mine, and swallowed as I gave her a once-over.

Her hair was a mess above her head, with some long strands falling on the sides of her face. The glasses she had on were gold rimmed, and looked so damn beautiful on her. She was wearing dark shorts, and a too-fluffy peach hoodie with a black cat poking its head out from behind the wide pocket at the front bottom – one I'd gifted her last month, despite her protests.

With another swallow, I looked at her face again, at her surprised expression, and every inch of my body buzzed with electricity when she blinked at me.

God, did she not know what she did to me?

Did she not know how much she meant to me?

Because if she did, then she wouldn't have kept me away from her for so long.

"Hey…" I began awkwardly, and then glanced down at her right leg – at the cast wrapped around her ankle. "You okay? How's your leg n–"

"Why are you here?" she asked, cutting me off.

"Why are you doing this, Zaira?" I really fucking wanted to know, because the way she was looking at me, and the tone she was using – it was hurting me.

"*Why are you here, Gallan?*" she asked again, but this time with anger in her voice.

Seriously?

I gritted my teeth and stepped forward, which brought us closer. "I'm here because I wanna know what the hell is going on, Zaira," I said. "I'm here because I wanna know why you're ignoring me like this."

She trained her eyes on the wall behind me and refused to say anything.

I placed a forearm against her doorframe and leaned in a little. "Talk to me. *Please*."

She glanced at me, but then turned her gaze to the floor. "I think I made myself very clear that night when I told you I couldn't do this anymore."

The weight of her words hit me like a downpour of bricks.

"You're not really looking at me while you say that, just like you weren't really looking at me that night when you said those words in the ambulance."

She closed her eyes and shook her head. "Gallan…"

"Why don't you want me anymore?" I questioned. "Why don't you fucking want me anymore, huh, Zaira? What did I do? What did I…" I looked away from her and pushed my hair back. "I didn't do *anything* wrong…"

She whipped her head at me, and glared at me with a clenched jaw. "You're the reason why I was targeted, Gallan Underwood," she practically spat the words at me. "You're the reason why things have changed in my life to the point where nothing feels like it used to before. You're the reason why Aubrey did what she did to me, and you're the reason why I've gained unnecessary attention from the media and social creeps." She sniffed and adjusted her glasses. "You can't say you've done nothing wrong, because you *have*. By making us public, you ruined my normalcy for me. By promoting me and including me in your glamorous lifestyle, you made me vulnerable to those who worship you and detest everyone who gets to be *with* you." She swiped the sleeve of her hoodie under her nose. "I shouldn't have walked into your trailer all those months ago," she whispered. "I shouldn't have let you keep me there; I shouldn't have let you sing for me, get to know me, or even kiss me. But most of all, I shouldn't have approached you with a copy of my book. I shouldn't have let Kenzie talk me into doing it. I should've continued to stay on the sidelines; I shouldn't have let my heart guide me in this." Her chin trembled, and a moment later, she began crying. "I just...I can't..." She continued to cry before me.

I stepped away from her as if she'd gut-punched me. She might as well have, because everything she'd said was a fatal blow to *everything* I believed in.

I know a heart has no bones, but in that moment, after hearing every one of Zaira's words, and seeing the tears in her eyes, I realized that it was possible to brutally fracture it, if not break it completely.

I was angry, upset, shocked, fucking *devastated*. It felt as if every last one of my veins were being pinched with the way my body was aching; with the way I felt powerless and useless standing in front of her.

"So that's it, then, huh?" I managed to say. "This is it? This is the end?"

She didn't answer me, and kept looking at the floor. Her tears were a constant, and did nothing but cause me more pain.

"You just slapped every last one of my beliefs, Zaira," I began. My voice was thick, and it was so damn hard for me to speak with a lump in my throat. "Every moment we spent together. Every touch, kiss, and laughter we shared. You threw it all away, and why? Because of Aubrey? Because of her tricks to separate us?" I scoffed. "You did exactly what she wanted you to, and even though *she's* the one who paid the price for her actions, it is *us* who lost. *We* fell apart. *We* weren't strong enough to come out of the whole thing unharmed. And *you*, Zaira," I pointed a finger at her, "didn't think I was worth *shit*, because you gave up on me and my love for you like it meant nothing at all to you. You gave up on everything we were and everything we had. You just...*gave up*."

She looked at me with misty eyes, but still didn't say anything.

"I don't regret you," I said to her. "I was honored to have read your book; honored to have been a muse for it. You're so fucking talented, and I'm glad you gave me a copy of your book." I ran a hand over my jaw. "I don't regret *anything*. I don't regret lying to you about my phone's signal that night just so I could keep you in my trailer for longer. I don't regret singing for you. I don't regret kissing you, fucking you, calling you mine." I released air through my lips and blinked when my eyes burned with unshed tears. "And most of all, I don't regret falling in love with you. Because Zaira?"

She swallowed and continued to look at me.

I took half a step forward, and then three full steps back, making her flinch a little.

"You're the best damn thing to have *ever* happened to me," I told her in complete honesty. "You're the very air I breathe. You make me happy – *truly* happy. You complete me. And even though I'm a mistake to you, you will forever be the very essence that brought my soul to life." With a final glance at her tearstained face, I let the very last piece of my heart fall at her feet before turning around and walking away from her.

53.
Zaira

October 15th, 2020

Every syllable of every word he'd spoken had pierced me right in the chest. His questions, the looks of shock, hurt, disbelief, and anger on his face – they were all rightfully justified.

Nothing he'd said to me had been wrong, but my mind was practicing a defense mechanism of sorts, especially after the studio incident, so for me to fully grasp the importance of my decisions and their consequences was hard.

Next to impossible, in a way.

It wasn't an excuse, no, but whatever I'd told Gallan came with the territory of self-preservation, and in the mental state I was in, thinking about myself first had been my top priority. It had given me unimaginable pain, but I had to be selfish and do what was right for *me*.

It wasn't easy standing before him and telling him the things I'd said to him. It wasn't easy to ask myself to believe my words, because even as I spoke them, they tasted like vile venom in my mouth.

And most importantly, it wasn't easy seeing the look of betrayal and utter confusion on his face after I'd told him – albeit indirectly – that I wish him and I had never happened.

It were the 'what ifs' that had made things worse for me.

What if I couldn't heal fully after this incident?

What if I wasn't strong enough to heal in the first place?

What if people saw me differently now, and mocked me for being an easy target?

What if my family and friends started treating me or looking at me differently?

Even though Aubrey had been dealt with, there was still a chance that someone else might take her place and try to do the things she'd done to me. That right there was the biggest 'what if' I'd been stressing about. It was like a vise grip that wouldn't loosen itself. Hollywood was a crazy place, and so was everything else associated with it. I wasn't cut out for it, and it had taken me being bullied and harassed to realize that.

I closed my apartment door and pressed my forehead against it. I focused on the slow buzz of the air conditioner in my living room, and then, squeezing my eyes shut, I let the fallout of my decisions consume me.

Gallan had poured his emotions out to me, and what had I done? I'd stayed mute and wounded him with my silence. I knew for a fact that more than the things I'd told him, it was my silence that had hurt him. I knew it, and still, I did nothing about it.

And what did that say about me?

I really wish I knew.

Did I even deserve him?

I wish I knew the answer to that as well.

54.
Zaira

November 12th, 2020

"I'm okay," I said to the woman before me. I then looked down at my hands and began peeling off the excess polish from around my nails.

I'd painted them yesterday, and because I was lazy and moody, I'd fallen asleep without cleaning off the extra lacquer that was on my skin.

"Zaira?"

I glanced up. "Yeah?"

Dr. Stacey Hill, my therapist, slightly narrowed her brown eyes at me. "I'll ask again: *how are you today?*"

It was 9a.m., and our weekly session had just begun. When I'd taken a seat on the plush sofa a short distance away from her a couple minutes ago, she'd given me a beautiful smile and asked me how I was doing.

She was kind, my therapist. She made me feel at ease with the thoughts in my mind. She didn't have to push me to answer her questions; I just felt okay enough to answer them. She didn't ask me to share things beyond the importance of my comfort, but whenever I began telling her something, I found that I just couldn't stop. She had that aura about her, I guess. Her calm demeanor and understanding eyes made it easier for me to open up.

I enjoy the hour I get to spend with her, because there are sessions where we talk and laugh, and those where I sit and sketch comic ideas on my tablet while she responds to emails and attends calls.

"I told you I'm okay," I said to her. I was the opposite of it, actually, but I also wasn't in the mood to tell her why. Strange, I know, but my head felt too heavy to be comprehensive. I just wanted to sleep, but I also didn't want to miss my session with her.

Dr. Hill placed a hand under her chin. "I know when you're lying, Zaira."

"I'm not lying," I countered as I continued to peel the excess polish from my skin.

She sighed. "Okay." She leaned back in her leather chair. "And how have you been sleeping? Just as good as before?"

"Yup," I answered honestly. I had zero trouble sleeping, which, according to Dr. Hill, was a good sign.

"What about nightmares?" she asked next. "Have you had any since our last session?"

I swallowed and hugged myself. "I had one last night," I whispered as I blinked at her. The air conditioner in her room was always maxed out, so I had to wear baggy hoodies and jeans to keep myself from shivering. I couldn't ask her to change the temperature, because apparently, she liked it when her surroundings were chilly.

She nodded at me. "What did you see in your nightmare?"

I crossed my legs on the sofa.

My cast had been taken off, and even though I felt a slight pull on the back of my knee every time I walked, I could at least walk without *limping*.

"The usual," I told Dr. Hill in response to her question about my nightmare.

She raised a brow at me – a silent command for me to elaborate.

"You already know what it is," I said to her. "I've told you about it every time I've had it. Why do you keep asking me to say it out loud?"

"Because it's good for you," she stated matter-of-factly.

"Reliving my nightmare is a good thing for me?" I asked her.

She shook her head. "You're not reliving it; you're simply *voicing* it. That way, the power it has on your mind grows weaker every day. Have your nightmares not become more distant now that you've been telling me about them?"

I nodded.

When I'd started visiting her, our sessions would take place every single day. Then she began dating them to every two days. And, when I finally started telling her about my random frights and nightmares, she scheduled our sessions once every week.

She was right. Where my nightmares had kept waking me up every night at first, they were now only making an appearance once or twice a week. Talking about them had helped me, and I hadn't even realized that until she'd just told me about it.

But...

She wasn't the only one I'd been sharing this stuff with. I may have eventually started telling her about my nightmares, but there was someone else I'd been talking to about them from the very beginning.

I exhaled and hugged myself tighter. "I'm in a dark room. I'm running towards an exit but keep falling. And when I finally get to the end, the door vanishes. I scream, and scream, and..." I sniffed. "I keep screaming, and then I wake up."

Dr. Hill's gaze softened a little. "Is there anyone else who knows about this?"

Her question caught me a little off guard. She's never asked me that before, so I looked at her with slightly wide eyes, but then slowly relaxed and got more comfortable on the sofa.

"I've been sharing them with Dylan since day one," I admitted.

A small smile tugged at her lips as she placed her elbows on the glass table in front of her and leaned forward. "Anyone else?"

I shook my head. "Only him."

"And why him?" she inquired. "You have your parents; you have Kenzie. Then why Dylan?"

I lifted a shoulder. "I feel safe when I talk to him." I pushed a strand of hair behind my ear. "I love my parents and Kenzie, but the comfort I experience when I hear Dylan's voice or see him – that's different and more…"

"Dependable?" Dr. Hill suggested.

"Yeah," I said around a smile. "He's like a blanket of warmth, in a way. He knows exactly what to say to make me happy, and to make me laugh."

"And what about his husband, Conner?"

"He's great, but he's not Dylan," I said, which made Dr. Hill chuckle. "Dylan is a literal queen. He's the bestie every girl needs. But most importantly, he's the brother I'd always wanted."

Dr. Hill grinned. "I'm so happy you've found that, Zaira."

"Thank you." I shifted a little. "But, do you think dependability is a bad thing?"

She shook her head. "Not necessarily. If it helps you heal, then it's acceptable. Just don't let it consume you."

"I won't," I told her. "Dylan gives me space and asks me to do things on my own – like learning to close doors when I'm in a room alone, or trying to stay calm when someone closes the door to the room I'm in."

It was another issue I'd developed after the studio incident. I couldn't be in a locked room, or a room whose doors were closed. At first, I couldn't close any door on my own except for my apartment door, but with the help of my sessions with Dr. Hill, and with Dylan's constant help, I'd learned to slowly get back on track.

Dr. Hill seemed a little shocked by my confession. "You told him about that?"

"Yeah," I said. "He's one of the reasons why I've gotten better with doors."

Dylan and Dr. Hill were the only ones who knew, and even though it'd been hard to keep that part of me from the others, I'd managed to do it. Every time I'd try to tell them about it, my mind would shut down. I didn't know why, but I also wasn't mad about it. Talking about these things was stressful, to say the least. It took so much outta me that I felt exhausted after speaking of them.

"Have you heard from Gallan?" Dr. Hill suddenly asked.

My chest tightened at the mention of his name. Memories of our last encounter flooded my mind, making my eyes sting.

"No." I cleared my throat. "No, I haven't." He'd stopped calling and texting me after he'd walked away from me last month, and the only updates about him and his press tour that I'd been receiving, had come from Amara. Dylan was on tour with Kenneth, Shane, and Gallan, but he never spoke of the latter with me, or even mentioned his name during our video, text, or voice chats. I appreciated him for that, but somewhere deep down, my skin would prickle in anticipation every time Dylan and I spoke, quite possibly in the hopes of him slipping something about Gallan to me.

I knew I was punishing myself. It was *I* who had pushed him away, so I had zero rights to think about him, or even dream of getting updates about him.

I'd brought down the hammer on my own foot, and I didn't deserve to bandage my wounds now just because they hurt too much.

"And how does that make you feel?" Dr. Hill's voice cut through the silence.

"Huh?" I fidgeted with my glasses as I looked at her.

She got to her feet and stepped away from her table. I watched the way her black stilettos pressed against the white faux carpet on the floor as she walked over to me.

She sat down on my left and gave me a soft smile. "Do you miss him, Zaira?" A simple question, but it damn near knocked the breath right out of me anyway.

I closed my eyes and tried to focus on the clock behind me.

Tick, tick.

Tick, tick.

Tick–

"Zaira?"

I snapped my eyes open. "*What?*" I said loudly, but immediately regretted my tone. "I'm sorry," I said with a frown.

With a neutral expression on her delicate face, Dr. Hill placed a hand over my knee. "It's okay." She sighed. "Do you miss Gallan, Zaira?"

"Why do you wanna know?" I whispered as I scanned her face. "Just…why?"

"Do you think you've lost him?" she asked, ignoring my question.

I clenched my jaw when it tingled, and sucked in a breath when emotions numbed my skin.

I had lost Gallan, hadn't I? By pushing him away for my own selfish reasons, I'd lost the one human being who meant the entire fucking world to me. I'd hurt him, angered him, and driven him away from me. And now that he'd finally given me what I wanted, I couldn't live with it. I couldn't *accept* it.

Gallan's absence hollowed my rationales and clawed at my decision of self-preservation. It drowned me in a pool of loneliness and regret – regret of letting him walk away and not standing up for our love, our beliefs.

Our connection.

I was a fucking coward.

"Yes," I finally braved answering Dr. Hill. "Yes, I think I've lost him." I shook my head. "Actually, I *know* I've lost him." My vision blurred, and even before I knew it, I was crying.

I'd done what I had for *me*, and yet, I had only healed physically, not mentally.

Not *internally*.

Dr. Hill handed me a couple of tissues. "Has he severed all contact?" she asked slowly.

I nodded, and pushed my hair back before wiping my nose.

"You knew this would happen?"

I looked at her again. "Yes."

"And yet you stood your ground and decided to end things with him."

I dumped the soiled tissues in the bin behind the sofa. "I did."

"Why did you do it?"

"Because I thought that if I kept him away from me, then the things that have happened to me would not repeat themselves. I blamed him for everything. I…" I ran the back of my hand under my nose.

Dr. Hill let go of a long breath. "Do you regret your decision of letting him go?"

I sniffed and shrugged. "I don't know." I pulled my glasses off and wiped my eyes with the sleeve of my hoodie. "I wanna go home," I said shakily. "Can I please go home?"

"Will you be okay to drive?" Dr. Hill asked.

"Yeah, I'll be fine."

Will I be?

The pounding in my head would say otherwise.

Dr. Hill stood up, and so did I. "Take care of yourself, Zaira," she told me. "You're doing wonderful, and I'm very proud of you." She smiled openly. "I'll see you next week."

I returned her smile. "Thank you, Dr. Hill. I look forward to seeing you next Thursday." With another smile, I stepped back and walked out of her office.

I'd only just gotten in my car and put the key in when my phone *pinged* with a new message. I sighed and pulled it out of my hoodie pocket before looking at the screen.

Shane: *Hey, kid. I hope you're doing good. I know it's probably not the best time for this, but I wanted to confirm something with you. Should I, or should I not, make an official announcement about yours and Gallan's breakup? I'm in no rush to get your answer, of course, but please do get back to me about it when you can. It's getting harder for him to dodge press and tabloid questions about the two of you during the tour. They wanna know your plans for Christmas, and how your relationship is going in general, etc.*

Kenneth and Dylan can only jump in on limited basis, you know? Anyways. I'm sorry if I bothered you, and I really do hope you're doing well.

Breakup...

The term scraped against my mind like nails on a chalkboard. It made me nauseous, so I opened the driver-side window in order to get some air into my lungs.

I wanted to ask Shane why he wanted *my* permission to do anything in the matter, but instead, I closed his chat page and opened another one.

Me: *Are you home?*

She responded a minute later.

Amara: *It's 10:30 in the morning. Where else would I be?*

Me: *I don't know?*

Amara: *Lol. You okay?*

I had to laugh at that question. Humorlessly, of course.

Me: *You really wanna know the answer to that?*

Amara: *Oh dear :/ That bad?*

I ran my fingers through my hair as I sighed.

Me: *Yup.*

Me: *Can I come over?*

Amara: *You don't even have to ask :–**

I smiled.

Me: *Thanks, Ams.*

Amara: *Don't mention it! I'll put the leftover pizza from last night in the microwave. Come quick.*

Me: *On my way :–)*

55.
Zaira

November 12th, 2020

"Imagine what would happen if a drop of wine fell into Isaac's mouth right now," Sloane said to Amara, who'd just finished drinking her wine and had placed the glass next to her phone on the table to her right. "I've never seen a drunk baby, so it'll be fun to watch yours act wise and tell us how good of a mother you are to him."

Amara looked down at Isaac sleeping soundly on her lap, and then up at Sloane before giving her a deadly scowl. "I can't believe you just said that. He's *one*, Sloane. *ONE.*" She clicked her tongue. "The only word he's spoken so far is 'goo-goo'. I don't know what in heaven's tits does that mean, but Kenneth seems very happy with it. Says it's *good progress.*"

Kenzie cackled and took a sip of her wine. "Oh, the joy of parenthood."

Sloane agreed in the form of a grunt, whereas Amara nodded with a crooked smile on her face.

The drive to hers and Kenneth's penthouse had been a blur, because my brain was too busy trying to clear the fog that Shane's question from earlier had caused. And when Amara had opened her door to let me in around an hour ago, I'd almost stumbled into her house and thrown myself on her large living-room couch.

It felt like I had zero strength; like a massive weight had been placed right on the center of my chest.

It wasn't easy dealing with the heavy stuff in life, especially when you were constantly bouncing back-and-forth between pain and confusion.

Amara had called Sloane and Kenzie over to make it a small pity party for me. I'd consumed more pizza and wine in the past hour than I have in the last six months. It didn't hurt that the company was comforting and highly welcomed.

Amara looked at me, and her expression quickly softened. "You okay?" she asked.

I hugged Coco, her two-year-old bunny, closer to my chest and buried my face farther in his soft and comforting golden fur. "No, I'm not," I mumbled. I closed my eyes and nuzzled against his neck, to which he let out a tiny huff and began licking my jaw.

"You should talk to Gallan, Zaira," Sloane suggested. "Things didn't exactly go smoothly the last time you two interacted. Maybe reach out and see where he's at right now."

"But why would she do that?" Kenzie jumped in. "He walked away from her all those weeks ago. It's *him* who should reach out to her. Not only that, but he should also apologize to Zaira for his behavior."

"But Zaira wasn't exactly welcoming to him then, and neither did she give him much to go by," Amara said. When I rose my head and looked at her, she raised a brow and pointed a finger at me. "It's true and you know it. You blamed him for something that wasn't even his fault. You didn't reason with him; you didn't tell him how you really felt in that moment. You pushed him away just because he was *there* and was an easy target for you. You had so much on your mind at the time that you found the nearest outlet and poured all of your pain and anger and accusations on it – on *him*." She frowned a little. "Instead of opening up to Gallan and seeking calm and safety in him – *with* him – you made him the villain. You let go of the one lifeline that could've pulled you out of the ocean and onto solid ground way better and quicker."

I felt a pinch in my heart at her words. She wasn't wrong, was she? And I knew that her giving me a dose of tough love was her way of telling me what an idiot I was.

Coco wiggled in my arms. With a kiss on his nose, I gently put him down, and watched as he ran over to his litterbox before jumping in.

"Motherhood has turned you into a badass bitch," Sloane said to Amara, who rolled her eyes at her best friend.

"I'm legit scared of you now. Not even going to think about messing with you," Kenzie added, and chuckled when Amara flipped her off.

I sighed and lied down on the plush couch with my head on the armrest. "You know why I did what I did, Ams," I told Amara. "It was a defense mechanism for me, and I'm still not sure I wanna let it go." I rubbed both hands over my face. "God, I'm so done with everything."

Isaac made a noise in his sleep, so I shifted on my side in order to look at him.

He was beautiful, with a head of dark hair and eyes so blue they'd grip you on the spot. He was also the cutest, chubbiest, and the happiest baby I'd seen. He was always smiling, whether it be while drinking milk, playing, or peeing and pooping in his diaper.

I wish I could go back in time and be a baby again. No stress about the real world, or the hassle of dealing with its ups and downs.

"Do you want kids, Zaira?" Amara asked.

Our eyes met, and when I gave her a little shrug, she huffed and rolled her eyes.

"You're being impossibly annoying right now," she said, which made me laugh.

"Sorry," I told her.

"It's not Amara who needs your apology," Sloane stated. "It's Gallan who does."

I glanced at her. "You're supposed to be on *my* side."

"There are no sides here, babe. You're wrong, and you know that."

"How is she wrong?" Kenzie came to my rescue. "Her decision was for her state of mind, and we should respect that. We know Gallan does. He's giving her the space she needs to heal and get better. There's nothing right or wrong in this. This situation just *is*. It exists, and that's all there is to it."

"Oh, but there *is* more to it," Amara said, and then gazed firmly at me. "Shane wants you to make a decision – one that'll lock things in. One that is *permanent*. I think it's about damn time you woke up and did something about it." She pulled her long hair up in a bun. "Look, healing will take time, but if you do it alone, then the mental scars you have may never heal. I made the mistake of wounding myself over and over again when it came to Kenneth, but when he finally stood his ground and proved himself to me, proved his *love* for me, I let him in. And the result?" She pointed at her son on her lap with a warm smile on her face. "With Kenneth, I actually *healed*, Zaira. With him by my side, I learned to be stronger and confident. I know the media, and people like Aubrey scare you, but if you really want Gallan at all – even a few months from now – then you'll have to brave that side of things because it's a part of his world. It's a part of who he *is*. And if you wanna be in his world, then facing the press, tabloids, and a few crazy exes is a small price you'll *have* to pay."

"I tried once and failed," I whispered.

Kenzie shook her head. "You didn't. You are so strong, Zaira. And even now, you're sacrificing something important to get back to where you were. I respect that."

"Yeah, but I don't know for how long I'll have to keep this going. I also don't think it's right by Gallan. He deserves better than this version of me. He deserves the old me."

"Then give him that," Sloane said brightly. "Or at least tell him that there's hope for things to go back to how they were."

"But what if he doesn't want that?" Amara asked. "What if he's ready to accept the change and move on with things? What if he's ready for the current version of you? Did you ask him about that?"

"No." I shook my head.

She clicked her tongue. "You really should talk to him, Zaira. Give him a chance to express himself better. You do realize that the incident must have affected him in some way too, right? I'm sure he has stuff that's nagging at his conscience as well, so why not sit down and hear each other out instead of going different ways without clarity and full understanding?"

I shifted on my back again. "I don't know…" I sighed. "I just…I don't know." I groaned when my head started pounding harder than earlier. "Fuck." I tightened my fingers in my hair and closed my eyes.

Was I hurting Gallan by pushing him away, or was it right to let him go?

Was I damaged property now and couldn't give him what he wanted?

What if I agreed to let him in, and he later decided that he wanted nothing to do with this new side of me?

Wouldn't I be a fool to put myself on the pedestal, only to fall when its foundation went slack?

"I'll make you some coffee," Amara said to me. She handed a still-sleeping Isaac to Sloane, and then gave me a small smile before heading out of the living room.

She'd just left, though, when Isaac began crying in Sloane's arms.

"You *always* do this to me," she said to him, which made him cry harder.

I chuckled, despite the pain in my head. "Check his diaper, maybe?"

Sloane shook her head. "He's fine. He just hates the smell of my perfume. It's probably too feminine for him. He's totally his father's son."

Kenzie laughed. "Maybe get him some fresh air. It'll help."

Sloane nodded and took Isaac to the wide balcony in the living room.

Kenzie walked over to me before kneeling by my side. "You okay?" She frowned when our eyes met. "You look a little pale."

"I'm fine," I told her. "Just a little headache."

Her frown deepened. "You can't lie for shit and you know that."

I gave her a smile. "I'm good, Ken; don't worry."

She leaned in and pressed a kiss on my forehead. "I know that me and the others have different opinions and reactions towards what's happened, but the one thing we have in common is our concern for you. I want you to hear what we have to say, but act only on what *you* think is right – for both yourself and your health." She straightened my glasses. "Your well-being is our #1 priority, and whatever decision you do end up making will be one I'll stand behind. I got you, even if things are about to shift. I love you and I want you to keep yourself first." She squeezed my hand before standing up. "I'm headed to the bathroom. All the pizza I had is protesting real hard in here." She patted her flat stomach.

"You okay?" I asked.

"I'm great. Just gotta clear up my system is all." She stuck her tongue out at me when I scowled at her, and then, with a wink, she turned around and walked out of the living room.

I sniffed and stretched my legs on the couch. Shane's voice – his *question*, in particular – continued to buzz in my ear.

With a sigh, I pulled my phone out of my pocket before opening our chat page.

My fingers hovered over the keyboard as I stared at the screen. My throat tightened, my stomach clenched, and thick tears dripped down my temples as I typed in a response to his message.

I'm doing this for ME, I convinced myself. But even then, I wasn't sure I believed my own damn statement.

Me: *Do it. Make an official announcement.*

Every second that went by after I hit send was like a knife in my chest. I kept looking at my words like they'd poisoned me. They might as well have, because I could hardly see straight, let alone breathe.

Shane: *You sure?*

I swallowed as I typed in a reply.

Me: *Yes.*

Shane: *He'll be devastated, Zaira. He'll break completely.*

I muffled a cry behind the sleeve of my hoodie so Sloane wouldn't hear it.

Me: *Just do it, Shane. Please.*

Shane: *You don't have to get back to me yet. I said you could take your time.*

Me: *I did take my time, and this is my decision. You wanted to know, and I've told you.*

Shane: *And what about you, huh?*

Me: *What about me?*

Shane: *Will you be okay seeing him move on?*

I knew what he was talking about. If I let Gallan go, he would end up finding someone who'd take up his world like he had mine.

Like I had his.

My jaw hurt with how hard I was trying to hold myself in. Everything hurt. So *fucking* much.

Me: *I'll be fine.*

Would I really?

Shane: *Okay.*

Me: *Okay.*

I quickly wiped my tears away in case someone came back, but the message Shane sent next – it brought fresh ones to the surface and almost blinded me with their force.

Shane: *It'll be done, then. Thanks for getting back to me about it. And even though I really wish things didn't have to be this way, I also understand that you must've made the decision with certain factors in mind. Take care, kid, and God bless.*

And with that, the only piece left of my battered heart disintegrated like it was nothing but an empty case of misplaced emotions.

56.
gallan

November 20th, 2020

When I was four, I'd once fallen off my bicycle and into a small construction hole near the edge of my street. The moment my skin had forcibly met the hard ground, I'd seen stars. Quite literally. And don't even get me started on the pain. The pain I'd experienced that day had been *excruciating*, and by the time my neighbor had found me, I'd slipped into a zone where nothing else but the constant throb and burn and ache in my heavily bruised body existed.

I've never felt agony so strong in my life, not since that time.

Not until *now*...

Not until a few minutes ago when we'd landed in Manchester, England, and Shane had told me something that had unknowingly brought back the wounded four-year-old me. Something that had left me just as injured as that day all those years ago.

Just as fucking damaged and numb.

It felt like my skin was being ripped open. Like my lungs had stopped working. Like my brain was on an unstoppable rollercoaster or something.

"Hey." Kenneth placed a comforting hand on my left shoulder and handed a glass full of Macallan to me.

"Thanks," I said a little gruffly, and then took the glass from him before looking at Dylan. "She didn't talk to you about this *at all*?" I asked. "You're the only one she really speaks to these days." I didn't wanna sound jealous or pissed off, but I knew for a fact that I *did*.

We were in my hotel suite, and as I sat there in my bed with a tumbler of scotch in hand, a voice in my head kept crashing against the sound of ongoing traffic outside.

She'd ended it.

She'd put a full stop on us.

She'd given up on everything we had.

Dylan sighed and leaned back in his chair. "I swear she didn't tell me. We haven't spoken a lot in the last few days. She hardly responds to my texts, and when I call, she either doesn't pick up, or gives me two-word answers when she does."

I looked at Shane next. "Why the fuck did you ask her to make a decision like this? Couldn't you have discussed things with me before texting her?" I took a drink from my glass. "You also kept her answer from me for the last *nine days*. Who the hell gave you that right?"

Zaira had asked Shane to make an official announcement in regards to her and I's breakup. If it wasn't for the damn press tour, I would've been standing outside her apartment banging on her door so I could give her a piece of my mind for her lack of willingness when it came to *us*.

How the fuck did she give up so easily? How and why in God's screwed up Earth did she think it was a good idea to begin with? Did she give no fucks about me or my feelings?

I was so livid I wanted to hit something. *Hard*.

Shane, who was sitting next to Dylan, scowled at me. "I'm your *manager*, in case you forgot. I did what I thought was right for you. I couldn't have the tabloids printing random, untrue stories about your current relationship status. You and Zaira have posted nothing on your social media accounts, and seeing your lack of activity there is giving everyone an itch to keep bugging you with questions about your love life during this press tour. I simply told Zaira all of this, and gave her time to think about what she wanted me to do. When she responded within the next few hours, I, too, was shocked. But she made her choice, G, and I gotta respect that. So do you."

I tightened my grip on my glass. "Why keep all of this from me, then?" I asked between gritted teeth. "Why didn't you tell me everything as soon as you got the response text from her?"

He ran a hand over his clean-shaven head. "Because you had huge junkets in Boston, Miami, and Chicago, and we then had to fly here. It was hectic enough that I didn't want to stress you out even more. You have a personal day-off today, so I thought I'd finally tell you."

I scoffed. "Wow, Shane; how *thoughtful* of you."

"Careful," Kenneth said to me. "Show some respect, alright? He's doing his job, at the same time making sure you don't feel the strain of everything too harshly. I understand that you're hurt, but taking it out on Shane won't fix anything."

I clenched my jaw as I glared at the carpet under my boots. "I'm sorry," I muttered, and then finished my glass before putting it out to Kenneth. "More."

He grabbed the bottle off the bar behind him and refilled my glass with a slight shake of his head.

"You're gonna drop dead on the floor if drinking is all you do for the rest of the day," Dylan told me.

I shrugged. "Don't care."

"Stop being foolish," added Shane. "Talk to her about this. I'm not putting anything out there immediately, so there's time."

I whipped my head up. "There's nothing to *put out there*, Shane," I said. "*Nothing*. You're not making any fucking announcements, alright?"

Like hell I'd let her get rid of me that easily. I loved her, even though she didn't seem to care about that anymore.

I'd given her space because I knew she needed it, but if that very same space was resulting in her to make insane decisions, then I had to at least try to get through to her one more time.

"Why didn't Amara tell you anything?" Dylan asked Kenneth. "You told us that she'd texted you about Zaira's visit to your house last week. Wouldn't they have discussed anything about her decision? Or did she visit *before* Shane's message?"

Kenneth glanced sideways at me before taking a seat next to the bar. "Ams did tell me about Zaira getting Shane's text," he began, and when I glared at him, he put a hand up in surrender. "She *only* told me about that, and nothing else. Zaira was at our house, yeah, but she didn't tell Amara or anyone about her decision. If she had, then my wife would've told me about it.

Zaira hasn't been that interactive with Ams, Ken, or Sloane since then, just like she hasn't with Dylan. And I didn't tell you guys about the text because I didn't think Zaira's answer would be the one she ended up going with. Hell, I didn't even speak to Shane about him sending her the message. I thought the whole thing would just blow over, so I'm just as surprised by Zaira's choice as you all are. I made a mistake, I know, and for that, I apologize."

"I don't think Zaira told *anyone*," Shane said with a frown. "That is why she's being curt towards everyone's calls and messages. Maybe she needs to process things on her own? Maybe she'll want to talk about it in detail after she's feeling a little better?"

"Maybe," Kenneth said, just as Dylan shrugged and added, "Yeah, perhaps."

I tipped my head back and finished my scotch, and then set the empty glass on the coffee table before wiping my mouth with the back of my hand.

"I don't know whether I'm turned on by your sudden drinking fever, or concerned about you getting a permanent hangover with you chugging Macallan like its fucking water," Dylan said, which made Kenneth groan.

"You're incorrigible," he told Dylan.

"And *married*," Shane joined in.

Dylan rolled his eyes at the two. "Choke me and bury me in Heaton Park, why don't you," he grumbled.

"That's…a very specific request," Shane stated.

"He's broken, Shane; don't bother with him," Kenneth said.

"Can you guys just leave?" The words came outta my mouth before I could stop myself.

Three pairs of eyes fell on me, and then softened at something they saw on my face.

"Call me if you need anything," Shane said as he stood up. "And if you can, please try to get some rest. You deserve it, G." He gave me a faint smile and then walked out the door.

Dylan waved at me before following after him.

Kenneth got to his feet. "I'm really sorry I didn't tell you about Shane's text to Zaira," he said. "I feel stupid, man. If only I'd told you, you would've been able to get in touch with her sooner."

"It's fine." It wasn't, but it also wasn't like I could go back in time and revert shit or anything. It wasn't how life worked, unfortunately.

But what if her decision was one made with certainty? Wouldn't going back in time be unfair to her, then?

Maybe she really didn't want anything to do with me, or maybe she was just confused after everything she'd been through.

Christ, I wish I knew. I wish she'd tell me.

Kenneth sighed. "I know you've got a lot on your mind, and it's the only reason why I'm leaving you alone right now." He pointed a finger at me. "But you better hit me up if you wanna talk or hang out, alright?"

"I will," I said to him.

He ran a hand over his jaw. "We'll have to get back to being media clowns tomorrow, Gall, so I suggest you get some sleep. It'll help in more ways than one."

I smiled at him. "I will, *Mom*."

He snorted. "Fine, fine." He chuckled. "I'm going." He shook his head, sent a quick look of warning in my direction, and then stepped outside my suite before shutting the door behind him.

Once alone, I refilled my glass, finished it off, placed it on the counter, and sat back down on the bed. I pulled my phone out of my pocket and opened my contacts. My thumb hovered over her name for a few seconds as I thought about getting to talk to her after more than a month of staying out of touch with her.

But would she even pick up?

Roaming charges were a bitch, but I didn't give six shits about them as I tapped her name and hit the call button.

"You better pick up, Zaira," I prayed in a whisper. "You better fucking pick up."

57.
Zaira

November 20th, 2020

I groaned and shifted in bed before covering my ears with my hands in order to cut off the sound of my ringing phone. When it didn't work, I reached out, grabbed a spare pillow from next to me, and hid my face under it.

"Fucking *stop*," I mumbled, but when it didn't, I sneered and turned to my left. I tried opening my eyes, but my tears from a few hours ago had dried down, in turn making it hard for me to blink.

I felt around my nightstand before locating my phone. With a huff, I hastily accepted the call and put the torture device to my ear. "Hello?"

Wow, I sounded like a beat-down truck's horn.

"Zaira?"

His voice caused a symphonic shiver to run through my entire body. Any trace of sleep that I had fled away, leaving me wide awake and panting.

I sat up and pushed back against the headboard, and then swallowed as I listened to him breathing evenly on the other side.

It was dark in my room, with only a sliver of the moon's light piercing in through the small window to my right.

"Were you sleeping?" he asked when I didn't say anything.

I rubbed my eyes and glanced at my bedside clock. "Well, it's three in the morning, so yeah, I was sleeping."

"Wh–" He stopped. "Shit," he whispered. "Shit-shit-shit." Silence. "I'm so sorry, Zaira. I didn't think about the time zone difference."

Time zone?

"Where are you?" The question fell from my lips before I could stop it.

I fisted my free hand and bit my tongue as I fumed over my incompetence.

Stupid.

Naïve.

Fucking gullible.

That was me. All of it.

"I just landed in Manchester," Gallan said.

Why did my heart long to watch his face as he said those words? Why did my mouth beg for me to ask him how he was doing? Why did my stomach tighten in anticipation of hearing his laughter? And why, oh why, did my heart ache at the pain and sadness I heard in his voice?

"Oh..." I breathed the word like a damn fool.

"Yeah." Pause. "You know, there's this song that's been stuck in my head for the past couple of days," he said. "I can't stop humming it. Want me to sing it to you?"

I opened my mouth to say no, but when he began singing, I stiffened. His voice – that familiar rumble paired with husk – made my eyes sting with the memories of our past.

Yeah, I know I'm gonna say things that should never leave my mouth
When your world's flyin' off the handle, I'll try keep you on the ground
It won't always be roses, even though you deserve 'em
I wanna make sure you know that what we got is worth it
I don't wanna fight, I don't wanna let you go
Baby, I don't wanna know what it's like to lose you...
Oh, 'cause people break up, fall in and outta love
But giving this up somehow just won't do
And I don't wanna give you a reason to leave me
Watch you drive off in the night
I never wanna feel that freedom that people say they find
I don't wanna know, I don't wanna know
I don't wanna know what it's like to lose you...

I was breathing hard. I could barely see straight as I wiped my damp cheeks and pushed a wave of hair behind my ear.

The song he'd sung was *Lose You*, by Jordan Davis, and God was it making me feel *everything* he wanted to say to me.

"Gallan..." My lips tingled in pleasure as his name brushed against them.

"Why did you ask Shane to make our breakup official, Zaira?" he asked with a strain in his voice that matched the one in mine. "Why did you do this to me – to *us*? Why, baby?"

I swallowed again as I tried to keep fresh tears at bay. The way he called me baby was enough to leave me helpless, but I couldn't give in so easily, not after I'd tried so hard to convince myself that him and I's paths couldn't stay parallel anymore.

"I just gave Shane an answer to his question," I said simply.

"Fuck the question, Zaira," he growled. "Did you really think you could make a decision this big without involving *me* in it? Did you really think it was that easy?"

I clenched my jaw. "Whatever I did, I did for *myself*, Gallan. I did it because I'm broken and I need to fix myself. I did it because I'm terrified that I won't be able to heal if I keep putting myself through the same thing over and over again. I'm doing it because I wanna prove to myself that I have the power to get better without having a helping hand around."

He sighed. "But you're *perfect*," he said so matter-of-factly that it made me suck in a quick breath. "You don't need to fix yourself; you don't need to heal."

I exhaled as I stretched my legs before me and bumped my toes against each other. "Please don't say things like that..." I whispered, and then closed my eyes. "Please."

"But it's the truth," he said slowly. "I don't give a damn about anything but *you*. I don't want anything but *you*. I'll give you more space if you need it, and I'll even do everything else you want me to, but *please* don't let go of me, Zaira. Just...please."

"Gall—"

"I can't lose you," he cut me off. "I seriously fucking can't, baby. You're the very pulse beating under my skin. You're a purpose so necessary that it's hard to go through things on a daily knowing that you're not with me. You're my fucking hope and greed and desire. Hell, you're the reason I haven't gone batshit crazy yet." He chuckled, and the sound traveled all the way to my core. "I've been living off of photos and videos of us for the past few weeks. The only way I've been able to tackle all those interviews and photoshoots is by keeping your smile, and your voice, in my head. Do you even know how important you are to me, Zaira? Or have you forgotten?"

I've never felt a rush of emotions so strong as I did in that moment. Gallan has always been vocal about his affection for me, sure, but the words he'd just uttered – those were like a tidal wave with an inevitable motive.

Destruction.

He'd ruined me with his proclamations, and because I was too weak to hold my own against the force of his determination, I decided to stay quiet lest I betrayed myself and said something that would contradict my resolve.

"Why are you doing this?" he asked again. "Just tell me why and I promise I'll stop questioning you."

"I've already told you everything."

"No, you haven't," he challenged. "You're punishing the both of us, and for what? For keeping yourself safe from a future incident similar to the one you went through? To avoid unnecessary attacks from the media? For some inner debate on whether or not you can get better on your own? *Bullshit*."

"You don't know what I'm going through," I said between gritted teeth. "Don't try to bring yourself into this."

He scoffed. "How will I fucking know what you're going through when you don't even *share* anything with me?!" he all but yelled. "Come on, Zaira; tell me that I'm wrong."

"Stop this," I hissed. "I don't know what you're doing, or even *why* you're doing it, but I don't wanna talk about it. I don't want you to call or text at all, for that matter. I already told Shane to make an announcement. I don't know why he hasn't done it yet, but I was very clear about my decision."

The silence that followed after I'd finished told me that I'd hurt him.

I began clenching and unclenching my fist as I waited for him to say something. I was hoping to get a harsh comment as a comeback, but the words that met my ear a heartbeat later held more impact and damage than any of mine ever would have.

"Goodbye, Zaira," Gallan said, and then, the line went dead.

I pulled my phone away from my face and stared at it, and when nothing but cold darkness looked back at me, I hugged my knees to my chest, squeezed my eyes shut, and let go of the weight on my chest without restraint or tenacity.

With only the dark, silent night as my witness.

58.
Zaira

November 20th, 2020

I turned on the bedside lamp, tucked my blanket under my chin, and then received the incoming Instagram video call.

"Hey, ba–" Dylan stopped mid-greeting, and the smile on his face quickly turned into a deep frown when he looked at me.

"What happened, Z?" he asked hurriedly.

I wiped my nose with the hem of my blanket. "Gallan called."

Christ, why did his name taste so good on my tongue when his final words to me had almost ended me?

Dylan looked utterly surprised. "He did?"

I nodded, and then told him about Gallan and I's conversation from an hour ago.

After I'd cried myself to the point where I could barely stay awake, I'd DMed Dylan on Instagram and asked him to call me when he could. I knew that his voice was the only thing that'd help ground me, and even if he was busy, he would drop everything just so he could sit down and talk to me.

"I'm not going to ask how you're holding up, because I can see the answer on your face quite clearly," he said, and then sighed. "Gall didn't know that you'd been asked to make a choice. Shane told him about it today – right after we got off our flight."

I hadn't known that. No wonder he'd sounded so angry and hurt and…sad during our call earlier.

"Also, he asked Shane not to make any sort of announcement," Dylan added next.

I sucked in a breath as I stared at my phone.

I don't know why I was shocked. This was a very *'Gallan thing'* for Gallan to do. He was stubborn and determined; he didn't like giving up. And when it came to us, I knew that the level of his headstrongness would multiply itself by a hundred.

Maybe even a thousand.

"Why would he do that?" I asked Dylan despite already knowing the answer to my question.

He clicked his tongue. "Do you really have to ask that?"

I sighed. "Not really, no." I scratched my left cheek and shifted to my side. "So, how's Manchester?"

He grinned and shook his head at the sudden change of topic. "It's as beautiful as the last time I was here. I wish it was snowing, though, but I can't exactly hope for that in this city." He rolled his eyes.

I smiled. His presence, albeit a virtual one, was really helping me relax in my skin.

"Where are you? It's a beautiful view behind you," I said.

He moved his phone around to show me a lavish room, a busy street below, and then a gorgeous stone building opposite to where he was. "I'm in my hotel suite. Ross booked the best one this time because Gallan's with us. That old ass has a soft spot for your guy." He cursed immediately after saying the last two words. "I'm sorry. I–"

"It's okay," I cut him off, but it *wasn't* okay, not by a long shot.

"So…" Dylan started. "I'm planning on visiting Heaton Park today 'cause I have a day off."

"You a fan of the Holland family and their diverse history?" I asked.

He tilted his head a little. "Who the heck is Holland?"

I couldn't help the chuckle that left me at the confusion on his face. "The Holland family is who the Heaton Park originally belonged to," I told him. "I thought you must've planned a visit because you're a history enthusiast." I smirked a little. "Clearly, you're *not*."

His mouth formed an O. "*Rude*," he sassed.

I grinned. "Nope. *Honest*." I sighed. "So, what are you getting for me from Manchester?"

"My beautiful self – all safe and healthy?" he said with a gleam in his ice-blue eyes.

"Seriously?"

He grinned. "A hot model with twelve abs, shaved armpits, a slightly curved cock, and a permanent pout on his face?"

I laughed. "What, no! Jesus, D." I laughed more.

His grin broadened. "I'm going to get you lots and lots of Eccles cake and cookies from this *adorable* bakery just down the street. That sound good?"

"*So goooood*," I all but moaned.

He chuckled. "Thought you'd say that." He raised a brow. "So, you made any progress in that new comic idea you were working on?

I shrugged. "A little. I finished outlining the first scene, and made a rough draft of how I want the beginning of the story to go."

He was the only one who knew I was working on a new comic. It was a long road, but I knew I'd get to the finish line halfway through next year.

A lot went into writing, designing, and publishing a comic, let alone *any* other book. And now that I had a huge audience – thanks to the giveaway Gallan had done a while ago – I had to make sure I put quality stuff out there for all my readers. The pressure was strong, but I knew I could do it. I somehow didn't doubt myself this time, and inspiration was hitting me left and right whenever I sat down with my tablet and stylus in hand.

Dylan's smile was so beautifully infectious that I couldn't help but smile along with him. "I'm so proud of you, Z!" He chuckled. "Man, I'm getting emotional here."

"Thank you, D."

He gave me a wink. "You got it, babe."

I hid a yawn behind my blanket, to which Dylan pursed his lips.

"Sleepy?"

I nodded. "Yeah. I woke up at three, and it's almost five now. I gotta hit the hay and shit."

He laughed airily. "Alright, you go sleep. The Rolland family is calling my name from the depths of Heaton Park anyway, so I gotta go and indulge them."

Good Lord.

"It's *Holland*, not *Rolland*, Dylan," I said.

He lifted a shoulder. "Same difference."

I rolled my eyes. "You're a piece of work."

"Awww." He placed a hand over his heart. "For that wonderful compliment, I promise that you'll wake up to a bouquet of pretty roses and a box of handmade chocolates."

I started to shake my head, but he waved a hand in front of his face to stop me. "Shush. Take this as my away-from-home hug to you. Think of the flowers and chocolates as a way of me saying that I love you and am so fucking proud of you for starting a new comic!"

My eyes stung at his words. "I love you too, D."

His expression softened. "Don't cry. I love you too."

I sniffed and wiped my eyes with my blanket. "I'm not."

"Right…" He made a contorted expression that I couldn't help but snicker at. "There you go; there's my smiling sister."

"You rock," I told him.

"I know." He smirked. "Oh, and Z?"

"Yeah?" I said.

"Before you go back to bed, make sure you put up a picture of yourself on your IG feed. Shane and I's social media teams are navigating yours and Gallan's accounts, and people wanna know why you aren't posting anything. Maybe just a quick, cute little selfie to tell your readers that you're doing great and are busy working on a new book?"

"Uh…" My mouth went dry.

"Relax; it's just a photo, Zaira. Nothing you haven't done before."

"But is it really necessary?" I asked.

He sighed. "To make things easier for Gallan's upcoming interviews and press junkets in England – yes. And also to quiet down the whispering tabloids."

I rubbed a hand over my face. "Okay, I'll do it."

He gave me a thumbs up. "That's my girl." He looked ahead suddenly. "Ugh, someone's at the door. I gotta go, Z. Have a good sleep, and lemme know what you think of the chocolates! Bye!"

"I will. Bye, D." I ended the call and sat upright. With a huff, I fixed my hair and face with my hands, straightened my oversize t-shirt, and opened the camera app. I angled my phone in the way I usually did to take my regular selfies, let my hair fall forward just a bit, and pouted slightly before clicking on the shutter button. I glared at the photo for a good minute or two, and then, when I realized I was pretty close to changing my mind, I quickly opened Instagram, used a mild filter on my selfie, and began typing a caption for it.

Hope is my strength.

I followed that phrase with a bit of information about how I was and what I was up to. Once happy with everything – or as happy as I would be – I hit post, and was about to close the app when a like and comment notification popped up on it.

I clicked the heart icon, and licked my chapped lips when I saw Gallan's name at the very top of my notifications list.

therealgallan *liked your photo.*

therealgallan *commented: God, you're breathtaking, baby. I love you, and I'm so d*mn ready to show off your new book to the world! Proud boyfriend here :–)*

I locked my phone and pressed it to my chest before closing my eyes.

Why did he keep doing this to me?

And how, in the name of everything sane in this world, did he keep succeeding at getting past my freshly cemented walls?

Fucking *how...*

59.
gallan

December 14th, 2020

I stretched my neck side-to-side as I unlocked my car and opened its back door. I threw the design sheets, contract files, my suit jacket, and my laptop on the backseat, and then closed the door before walking over to the driver's side.

I was so damn tired. To say that every fiber of my body ached would be an understatement. I was low on sleep, and even though I'd had around eleven cups of coffee throughout the day, it hadn't done shit to fix me up. Not that I needed it now. It was almost 9p.m., and I was *so* ready to head home and fall face-first on my bed and not wake up unless I either peed or pooped my pants, or the apes suddenly decided to take over the world.

A good shut-eye was an immediate priority of mine, what can I say.

I'd gotten back to L.A. two weeks ago, and ever since then, I've been hard at work with Natanya Barnes, Kenneth's elder sister, in planning and designing a new and diverse clothing line for *Under the Woods*.

Kenneth had suggested that I reach out to her for the idea I had in my mind, because Natanya and her brand, *NB Couture*, were well-known for their fierce and unique styles.

I wasn't even surprised when her thought tangents had matched mine perfectly during our first sit-down meeting two weeks ago, because not only was she a strategic businesswoman, but Natanya was also willing to try out things she knew would bring joy and excitement to the people who love our brands.

Her and I's teams had given us a few initial designs to choose today, which is why Natanya and I had been at my HQ going through sketch after sketch, and digital presentation after presentation since eight in the morning.

She'd left only an hour ago after scheduling another meeting for tomorrow, and as ecstatic as I was to pick the final designs and come up with a name for our collaboration line, I was also ready for this stage of the process to be over. Once the actual making of the apparels began, Natanya and I would only be needed to approve the samples and/or give minor instructions if changes were to be made in the quality, color, or layout of the designs.

I groaned and flexed my back and shoulders. Christ, I was stiff from sitting in a chair and staring at papers and a projector screen all day. I needed a drink and some sleep. *Stat*.

I was about to open the driver-side door when my phone began ringing. I clicked my tongue and pulled it out of my pocket, but it almost slipped from my hand when I looked at the screen – at the name flashing on it.

Zaira.

It felt like my thumb was made of butter with the way it kept slipping past the accept button every time I swiped the screen.

"Get it together, asshole," I mumbled, and then sighed when the call started. I placed the phone to my ear and set my elbow on the hood of my car. "Hello?"

"Gaaaallannn…"

Jesus on a surfboard.

"Gaaaallannn… Where are you, Gaaaallannn?"

"Zaira, are you drunk?" I asked.

Someone please give me a Nobel Prize for asking the stupidest, the most baseless of questions known to humanity.

I shook my head. "Of course you're drunk," I muttered with a huff. The first time she contacts me in *weeks*, and she's drunk off her pretty ass.

She giggled. "I had – *hic* – four glasses of…" She giggled again. "Four – *hic* – glasses of champagne, that's all." More giggling.

If I wasn't terrified for her safety, I would've teased her and told her that she was too fucking adorable when she was drunk, but I didn't even know why she was drinking, or with *whom* she was drinking.

"Where are you?" I asked. There was loud music playing in the background, but I otherwise couldn't hear anything else.

"In my – *hic* – apartmenttttt with my new – *hic* – sexy as fuck neighbor." She burped. "Oops…" She laughed.

What the hell?

"Your *who*?"

She made a noise. "My neighbor, Gaaaallannn. NEIGHBHOR."

"Jeez." I pulled my phone away a little when she screamed the last word and almost damaged my eardrum.

"You know…" she started, and then burped again. "He has just as many abs – *hic* – as you. I even counted them to make sure." She sighed. "He's a fitness trainer." She giggled. "You know what he – *hic* – told me?"

I was scared to ask, but did anyway. "What?"

"He said that he wanted to kiss me." She snickered like a little girl.

What the actual fuck?

My hands were shaking in white-hot anger as I got in my car and banged the door shut hard enough to hear something snap. "Where the fu–" I stopped myself and cleared my throat. "Where is your sexy neighbor now? Is he with you?"

"No. He's in the – *hic* – in the washroom."

God, make that fucker slip to his death before he makes the mistake of putting his hands on my Zaira.

"Right." I started my car. "If I ask you for something, will you do it for me, baby?"

"Baby…" she slurred, and then laughed. "Okay – *hic* – I will."

Thank fuck.

"Will you grab a bottle of water from your refrigerator and start drinking from it? Drink *only* that, and nothing else."

"Okay," she said softly.

I sighed in relief. With my phone in one hand, and the steering wheel in the other, I began driving to her apartment.

"Can you also not kiss your sexy neighbor? Please?" I said.

"But you asked me to do one thing. *Hic.* This is two things. No, wait…" She went quiet. "What comes after two anyway?" She giggled.

Fuck me with a bottle gourd.

"Zaira?"

"Gaaaallannn…"

I couldn't help but chuckle. "I'm coming over to your place in a few, okay? Can you promise not to kiss your neighbor until then?"

"Can I count his abs instead?"

I took a right and started driving a little faster. "Yeah, sure; count his abs. And once you're done, count them again. Keep counting them until I get there, okay?"

"Can I count yours when you're here?" she asked.

I chuckled again. "Of course. You can count mine as many times as you want, but just don't kiss your neighbor."

She hiccupped. "Okay, deal."

"Alright, I'll see you in a few."

"Byeeeee, Gaaaallannn…"

I shook my head around a grin as I changed blocks to take a shortcut to her apartment. "Bye, Zaira."

God, that woman was going to be the literal death of me someday.

60.
gallan

December 14th, 2020

The color red isn't one I'm particularly a fan of. I usually don't associate myself with it, and I hardly even wear clothes that are made of that damn color.

But...

Red – fucking *red* was all I saw the moment I opened Zaira's apartment door and rushed inside.

Red-hot rage. So red I could scan human beings at the airport customs for a living.

Mr. I'll-chop-his-balls Neighbor was sitting on the couch with my Zaira. His body was angled towards hers, and his face was merely inches away from hers. She was holding a half-empty bottle of water in one hand, and grinned when *Mr. Asshole Neighbor* said something to her.

He was an average guy, I guess. Tall, lean, blonde hair, pale skin. Maybe a case of rashes too, because he was squirming and shifting on the couch way too much, which looked both uncomfortable and irritating.

But his probable skin disease was not what had made me see red, no. It was his increasing proximity to Zaira that was making me all kinds of angry and…murdery. Not sure if that's a word, but it's exactly how and what I was feeling.

He kept closing in, and in, and in, but stopped suddenly and jerked back when I kicked an empty pizza box to the side before marching over to him.

"Get up," I spat. "Get the fuck up!"

He stared at me with wide eyes. "Wh–what?"

"Are you deaf?" I stepped into his personal space and bent so we were face-to-face. "Get. The fuck. *Up.*"

"Why?" the asshole dared to ask. He was sweating and shaking, but somehow continued to make eye-contact with me.

"Because I'm telling you to," I told him.

"Gaaaallannn…" Zaira sang. "You're hereeee!"

I looked at her, and my chest tightened when she looked back at me with a beautiful smile on her full lips.

I scanned her face to make sure she was okay, and once satisfied, I turned back to Asshole before saying, "Do you want me to book AC/DC in your honor? Do you want a musical exit or something?"

He swallowed. "I don't know who you are, so I'm not going to leave her alone with you."

That was it; I was done waiting.

I bunched the collars of his sweatshirt and pulled him to his feet. When he tried to grab my wrists, I pushed against his shoulders and shoved him towards the apartment door. "Leave!"

With a look of comical horror on his face, he began fumbling with the doorknob, but stopped and looked at me. "Wait, how did you even get in? The door was locked."

I gritted my teeth. "I have a set of spare keys, you dipshit. I'm her *boyfriend*. So, if you want your ass to walk outta here unharmed, I'm going to suggest that you leave quickly and quietly. *Right now.*"

"Gall…"

I pivoted on my feet and faced Zaira. She gazed up at me with an expression I couldn't put my finger on.

"Hey." I knelt in front of her. "What's wrong?"

"I don't feel so good," she whispered.

Fuck.

I took the bottle of water from her hand and placed it on the ground. "Stay here. I'll get to you in a second." I looked behind me, and saw that the pale idiot was still standing next to the door.

"Are you crazy?" I got to my feet and walked over to him. "Didn't I just ask you to leave?"

He wiped a hand over his sweaty face. "I was about to, but she said she isn't feeling well and I–"

"I got this," I told him. "I'm sure you weren't half as concerned when you got her drunk as you are now."

He shook his head. "I didn't, I swear. I just brought some pizza and champagne over and–"

"Just go, man," I said. "Just leave already."

He frowned. "Okay." He tried to look above my shoulders, but I blocked his view.

"Don't test my patience," I warned.

He raised his hands in surrender, and then, with a loud sigh, opened the door before walking away.

I clicked the locks in place, took my shoes and socks off at the entrance, turned off the music, and then turned around, only to curse and run over to Zaira. She'd puked on herself, and was looking at her chest like she didn't know what exactly had happened.

I grabbed a small towel from the kitchen counter, wet it, and rushed back to her. "It's okay, hmm?" I said when she kept glancing back-and-forth between me and her chest.

I bent, took her glasses off and placed them on the coffee table, wiped her mouth clean, and then tried to get as much puke off of her t-shirt as I could. Folding the now soiled towel, I set it on the floor. "Lift your arms," I told her.

"You didn't let me count Seth's abs one more time," she mumbled, and then lifted her arms.

I pressed my lips together and shook my head as I slowly pulled her t-shirt over her head. I walked back to the kitchen, threw both the t-shirt and the towel in the bin, and then returned to Zaira.

"Stand up, come on." I helped her to her feet, and when one of her bra-covered breasts brushed against my forearm, I swallowed and tried not to get worked up about it.

It's okay, Gallan, I told myself. *It was just a slight touch; calm the fuck down. Don't get your dick and hopes up like that. You're a grown man. Act like it.*

"Can I… Can I ask you a question, Galllll?" Zaira slurred.

I wrapped an arm around her waist and started walking us to her bedroom. "Yeah, of course."

She smiled. "What starts with an 'f' and ends with 'u-c-k'?" She beamed like she'd asked the most intellectual of questions.

"Uh…" I placed my phone, car keys, and wallet on her dressing table before stirring us away from her bed. "I don't know what–" I stopped and barked 'Fuck!' when Zaira threw up all over my blue dress shirt.

"Firetruck – the answer is *firetruck*," she said, and then puked on me some more.

I inhaled sharply to prevent my nausea from growing, and then pushed her bathroom door open before turning on the lights.

Zaira leaned against the faucet, gargled, and then started brushing her teeth as I began unbuttoning my dirty shirt.

"You okay?" I asked her.

She kept her eyes on her reflection in the mirror as she nodded.

"You wanna puke again?"

She shook her head.

"Good." I bunched my shirt. "Stay here. I'll be right back." I headed back to the kitchen, dumped my shirt in the bin, washed my hands in the sink, and filled a glass of water before taking it with me to the bathroom.

Zaira was sitting on the toilet lid and picking at a thread on her shorts, but looked up when I walked in.

"You thirsty?"

She nodded.

I opened the cabinet next to the bathroom mirror and pulled out a couple of anti-inflammatory tablets from a bottle, and a Tylenol from the other. "Here." I handed the meds and glass of water to her.

She quickly downed them both, and then placed the glass on the marble counter.

"Let's go get a shower," I told her.

She got to her feet. I stripped her out of her bra and shorts, and then took off my pants and underwear. I threw our clothes in the washer before switching it on.

Zaira's lips spread into a funny smile. "Abs..." She began running her hands up and down my stomach, which made my dick harden shamelessly.

I chuckled and wrapped my fingers around her wrists. "Not now." I pulled her into the shower with me.

She blinked. "Do you think envelopes moan when we lick them?" she asked.

My brows creased on their own. "What?" I turned on the faucet and grabbed her shampoo bottle from behind her.

"What?" She tilted her head to the left as she stepped under the showerhead. Her eyes were clearer than a few minutes ago, which was progress.

I watched, with a slightly unsteady breathing, as water cascaded down the swell of her breasts, her dark nipples, and then onto the rest of her body. I wanted to follow its path with my fingers and watch Zaira's reactions to it, but I knew I couldn't touch her like that.

Frustrated with my situation, I pushed my hair back with a wet hand and shook my head. "Nothing," I answered her question. "Turn around."

She did. "Gallan?"

"Yup."

"How drunk is too drunk?" she asked.

I put my tongue to my cheek. "Too drunk is too drunk."

"Do you think I would survive against a horde of zombies?" she asked next.

I was *speechless* at the utter randomness of her questions.

"Uh…"

"Actually, don't answer that." She chuckled. "I have the survival skills of a bunny on cocaine, so there's no chance I'd make it."

I laughed. "God, you're the best."

She remained silent as I washed her hair and body, and when I asked her to turn around again, she smiled and dragged a lazy finger down my throat. "You're so…" She licked her lips. "So…tempty-tempty."

My lips twitched. "You mean tempting?"

She clicked her tongue and grinned at me. "Nooooo. *Tempty*."

I laughed once more. Unable to reign myself in, I then wrapped my arms around her waist. Under the lights in her bathroom, with no makeup on her face and a carefree expression illuminating her soft features, Zaira looked like the most stunning thing I'd ever seen.

She was like a complex and eye-catching mosaic of emotions. With every shift, every action, and every word, she showed her dimensions and singularity to me. And God, was I crazy about every inch of her personality.

"Look at my nails." She brought one of her hands in front of my face. "They broke when I was doing dishes the other day. They're so short now that I've had to file them." She sighed and moved her hand back before staring at it. "I don't know why I painted them navy. They look like short and round blue potatoes." She glanced at me. "Have you ever thought of nails as potatoes, Gallan?"

That woman wasn't a human being, that much was clear. She was some other species entirely – one unknown to man.

"Gallan?"

I looked at her. "Hmm?"

"Can I wash your hair?"

I grinned. "Of course you can."

After a sloppy shower, we walked out of the bathroom and into Zaira's bedroom. When I opened her closet, I was surprised to find all of my spare clothes still inside. A few of my t-shirts seemed ruffled – like they'd been pulled out and then thrown back in. I grabbed an underwear from the closet and put it on, and then handed Zaira one of her long Gwenpool hoodies.

She quickly pulled it over her head, and with a sigh, she then got into bed with her back to me and wrapped her blanket around herself.

Halfway through the shower, she'd gone quiet and serious. I had no idea why, but I decided to blame her change of behavior on the meds and the champagne.

Probably even the extra cheese pizza.

Maybe she had finally realized that I was in her house with her, and maybe she didn't like that. Maybe she didn't want me there, but was scared or unsure of telling me that.

Whatever the reason, though, I wasn't going to leave her side until and unless I was sure she was okay.

I followed suit after her and lied behind her, and almost choked on a groan when my neck and shoulders started aching.

I was already sore from the day I'd had, and with the alcohol-and-puke-infused events from a few minutes ago working as the icing on the cake, I couldn't keep my eyes open the moment I placed my head on the pillow. My body didn't do well with painkillers, so I couldn't even pop in a couple of ibuprofens to dull the muscle pain.

I didn't dare get any closer to Zaira as I got comfortable in her bed, and as I drifted off to sleep, my mind kept counting the water droplets that dripped down her wet hair and onto her coral bedsheet.

Drip-three.

Drip-four.

Drip-five.

Drip-six.

Drip-seven.

Drip…

Drip…

…Drip.

61.
Zaira

December 15th, 2020

I opened my eyes and stretched my arms in front of me. I yawned, and then licked my dry lips before running my fingers through my hair.

There was a muffled throbbing in my head, but other than that, I didn't feel any of the other aftereffects of drinking too much.

God, last night had been *crazy*. My new neighbor, Seth, had come over with champagne and pizza to introduce himself. I'd thought it was a sweet gesture, but then he'd gone on and told me that he'd been seeing me in the hallway ever since he'd moved in and wanted to talk to me, which made it seem like he'd been planning on coming over for a while. I wasn't one to drink, but when he'd offered me a glass, I couldn't say no.

After around glass #3 of my champagne, he'd asked if I was single, to which I'd told him about Gallan – with a snotty nose and a slurry voice, of course.

Seth had later said that he wanted to take me out on a date so he could earn the right to kiss me, and my brain – over-brimmed with bubbly alcohol – had decided to call Gallan to ask for his permission on it.

But wait…

Was that before or after Seth had told me that he was from Ohio and had decided to come to L.A. to pursue modelling, and I'd asked if I could count his abs?

Jesus on a roller-coaster, I can't believe I'd counted a stranger's *abs* in my drunken stupor. Not only that, but I'd also called Gallan and told him all about it.

Fucking *great*.

I felt a slight shift behind me, and memories of Gallan asking Seth to leave, of him cleaning me up, of me throwing up on him, and of us showering together flooded my mind and made my pulse race.

He'd come for me; he was in bed with me.

Gallan had taken care of me when I'd stupidly gotten myself drunk.

Halfway through our shower yesterday, I'd realized what exactly was happening, and like the coward I was, I'd decided to shut down and go to sleep like it would erase my foolish acts as a mature human being.

I swallowed and turned around – *very* slowly – only to come face-to-face with the most beautiful sight I knew I would ever witness.

I've seen him during the mornings so many times, but it never ceases to amaze and weaken me that Gallan with a bedhead, sleepy eyes, and a lazy smile on his face is the most angelic view in my world. He was effortlessly handsome, especially with his all-consuming gaze and dark stubble.

"Morning," he said groggily. "You feeling okay?"

I blinked as I continued to shamelessly ogle him. My eyes travelled from his strong neck to his broad shoulders. From the smattering of dark hair on his chest to his muscled stomach. From his forearms to his large hands. From the thin line of treasure trail below his abs to the sharp V of his hips.

"Zaira?"

I looked at his face, and let go of a shaky breath when he leaned in and stared at me with an intensity so potent that my toes curled under my blanket.

"Won't you talk to me?" he asked in a whisper.

I was about to say 'I don't know', but gasped instead when he subtracted the little space between us by pressing his warm lips to mine.

I trembled as the first bout of his heady taste buzzed against my senses, and when he traced his tongue over my bottom lip, I opened my mouth and took it in. His stubble grazed against my skin, making it burn with impulsive pleasure. I wanted to claw at him, consume him. I wanted to take everything from him and hope he still had more to give.

I *knew* he'd always have more for me.

Gallan groaned, and with a pressure both sudden and strong, he moved forward so that my back was on the mattress and he was on top of me. He straddled me, and when I sucked on his tongue, he brought his hands under my head, laced his fingers through my hair, and then bunched them into tight fists as he continued to fuck my mouth with his.

I should stop this, right? I shouldn't let this get too far.

I had no right on him, and he had none on me.

After all, I'd frozen his beliefs under the weight of my shortcomings, and had shattered what was left of it by asking Shane to announce the end of us.

"Gall–" I tried to speak, but he cut me off.

"The only reason you'll open your mouth now is to either moan or scream my name as I fuck you the way I want to, you hear me, Zaira?"

I was breathing so hard it should be concerning. "Gallan, we…" I stopped when he bent and began trailing sound kisses on my jaw, neck, and my throat. "Gallan…"

"Mm…" He bit down on the skin below my ear. "I'm so fucking hard right now," he growled.

"Gallan…"

He pulled his hands away from my hair and moved back. He then got off the bed, took off his underwear, and gave me a once-over before saying, "Spread your legs wide so that I can see just how wet and eager you are for me, Zaira."

I inhaled sharply at his command, and then parted my legs for him. The cold air from my bedroom air conditioner hit my pussy, making me part my lips in a silent cry.

Don't do it, a voice in my head said. *Don't give into temptation so easily.*

But it was so hard not to do what Gallan asked me to. My compliancy towards him was one of the reasons why it was so hard for me to pull back from him.

He gripped at me with a hold so vise-like that I would splinter to pieces if I were to pull away.

But wasn't I already broken from having pushed him away after the incident?

If only things weren't so damn complicated in my head.

Gallan's eyes all but gleamed against the sunlight pouring in through the window in my room. "Lift your hoodie and pinch your nipples."

I quickly reached for the hem of my pink hoodie, and pulled it up enough to reveal my breasts. With my eyes on Gallan, I dragged my fingers over my peaked nipples and pinched them. "Fuck!" My hips arched, and goosebumps erupted throughout my body at the temporary pain.

Gallan smirked, fisted his cock, and started working it in long strokes. "Put your hand on your cunt and give yourself a taste." With his free hand, he cupped and pulled at his balls.

My cheeks heated at his use of the word cunt. He'd never said it before, and something about the way it fell from his lips felt madly arousing to me.

The beads of precum on his crown made me lick my lips, and as he continued to stroke his cock, I brought a hand between my legs and rubbed two fingers over my wetness before bringing them to my mouth and sucking on them.

Gallan hissed. He let go of his cock and climbed on the bed. "Hands over your head, come on." He settled between my thighs and hovered over me.

I lifted my arms, and cried out when he took my left nipple in his mouth.

He grinned and gave me a chaste kiss. "You're mine, baby," he whispered. He grabbed himself and rubbed his crown over my clit. "You know you're mine." His hips moved forward, and he pushed into me in a single thrust.

I moaned and wrapped my legs around his waist. He linked his hands with mine, and with a heat in his eyes that almost undid me, he began fucking me in short and rough thrusts.

My eyelids turned heavy as the feel of him stretching me intensified. I accepted the initial burn, and took him in as much as I could.

My breaths hitched each time he pushed into me, and as the sound of our skin slapping paired itself with his occasional grunts and my constant moans, I honestly forgot where I finished and he began.

"You hear your pulse dancing under your skin, Zaira?" he asked as he pulled, and then thrust back into me. "That's *mine*." He tugged my bottom lip between his teeth and placed his forehead against mine. "Your breaths and your blinks – those are mine. Every inch of your skin, every thought in your head – they are mine, too." He kissed me so hard that my vision turned spotty. "Your lips are mine to taste, to maul. Your moans are mine to give. Your pussy is mine to fuck, to claim. Your dreams are mine to mold. And Zaira?"

I swallowed as I stared into his eyes. "What?"

His thrusts turned deep and slow, which drove me insane. "Every single chamber of your wildly beating heart is mine to have, mine to own," he said, and God was that enough to make me come undone.

I squeezed Gallan's hands, threw my head back, and screamed his name as I came all over his cock.

He groaned, and took my mouth in a burning kiss as he released inside me.

"Fuck, that was perfect." He let go of my hands and settled his face into the crook of my neck.

As I finally came down from the impossible high he'd taken me to, I realized what I'd done.

What I'd *let* myself do.

Weeks of practicing the same mantra; weeks of convincing myself that the new version of me was one I'd have to stick with. Weeks of crying into my hands; weeks of feeling conditioned to move on in order to try and forget about the past. *Everything* I'd worked so fucking hard at establishing – it all came tumbling down like a pile of unburnt ashes.

With my hands trembling in anger, I pushed at Gallan's chest hard enough that he stumbled back and slumped at the edge of the bed.

"What the fuck?" He stared at me in utter shock.

I sat up, pushed my hoodie down, and moved away from him. "Leave," I said.

His brows creased as he continued to look at me. "*What?*"

"Leave, Gallan. Can't you fucking understand simple English?!" I barked.

"Are you being serious right now?"

"Does it look like I'm lying or fooling around?"

He ran a hand over his jaw. "Well, you weren't asking me to leave two minutes ago when I was balls-deep inside you, so forgive me for being confused over your sudden change of behavior," he sneered.

"It was a mistake," I spat. "It was a big fucking mistake, okay? We shouldn't have done this; it was wrong."

He jerked his head back in shock. "Wow, Zaira…" He shook his head slowly. "Fucking *wow*." His throat bobbed as he got off the bed with his jaw bunched tight. He grabbed his underwear from the floor, put it on, walked over to my closet, and pulled out a pair of his spare jeans and t-shirt before putting them on, too. He pushed his hair back and pocketed his wallet, phone, and car keys. He marched towards my bedroom door, but stopped right in front of it before turning around and facing me. "I thought I could change your mind," he said, and then sniffed. "But man, was I wrong." He chuckled darkly, and the sound sliced at my chest. "You're so fucking stubborn, Zaira, that you can't even see how wrong you are in this. You're so blinded by your own thoughts and plans of doing things your own way that you don't even *want* to see the other side of the coin." He moved as if to step forward, but stopped and shook his head. "I tried, but I'm only a man, and now I'm *tired*. I'm tired of trying to make you see, of hoping that you'll realize how baseless your rules are. I'm tired of trying to make you love me again, and I'm so damn sick of waiting around like a stray – in hopes that you'll pick me again. That you'll *choose* me, put me above whatever beliefs you've developed during the course of these past few weeks." He opened my bedroom door. "But I'm done now, and unlike you, my thoughts are one-tracked and logical. I'm *done*. And this," he pointed between us, "is over. You won; you got what you wanted. *Bravo*."

Silver lined his expressive eyes as he looked at me with so much pain that something inside me just...snapped.

"Gall–"

"Don't," he warned. "Just don't, Zaira. I don't wanna hear it. I'm done. Good-fucking-bye." And with that, he turned around and walked away from me.

I placed a hand over my mouth as a broken sob left me, and as Gallan crossed the living room and reached for the apartment door, I got to my feet and ran after him.

"Gallan!" I called, but he didn't stop. Didn't so much as falter as he crossed the hallway. "Gallan, *please*," I begged from my doorway. "Gallan, stop."

He didn't. He just took a right and disappeared from sight.

I closed my eyes and fell on my knees before bowing my head.

Stupid – I was a living joke in the face of commonsense. I'd spent days and nights since the incident blaming Gallan for everything, when he'd spent those very same days and nights trying to convince me of how wrong I was. Where I'd decided to give up, he'd continued to hold on to the strings that bound us, until they at last broke under the weight of my absurdity.

Maybe I was too proud to admit that I'd thrown him under the bus just to find an easy solution to my fears, or maybe I was just flat-out dumb.

And why had it taken me so long to see through my mistakes? Why had it taken Gallan walking out on me for me to come to terms with the reality of my decisions?

It was the way he'd looked at me right before turning his back on me that had shown me the mirror. It was the pain and defeat and frustration on his face right before he'd said goodbye that had woken me up from my unneeded sleep.

And, as I opened my eyes and stared at the cold floor in front of me, I realized that it was the finality in his voice as he'd said he was done that had pierced right through my self-imposed walls and turned them to rubbles.

"I love you," I breathed as I cried into the early-morning silence. "I love you and I want you... I *need* you."

But did I even deserve him after everything I'd put him through?

Would he even want to reason with me after everything I'd told him?

And most of all, would he even want to look at me after how I'd treated him right after we'd had sex a few minutes ago?

I guess I wouldn't know until I did something about it, now would I?

62.
Zaira

December 15th, 2020

"You know how ridiculously broody he can get, right?" Sage said to me. "He literally stomped out of the elevator and into his cabin three hours ago."

I pursed my lips. "You recorded it?"

Her mouth quirked up as she leaned back in her chair. "Of course I did. I'm not a dimwit, thank you very much."

"Email it to me later."

She chuckled. "Will do." Her expression dulled all of a sudden. "He's hurt, Zaira," she told me. "I've been working for him since the beginning, and I've never really seen him this upset and angry. He refused to have lunch when I called him and asked him about it, and hasn't come out of his cabin once. Whatever meeting he's conducting inside can't possibly be so important. He's keeping himself busy with work because he's hurting, and you and I both know that when something gets to him, it gets to him real hard."

As if on cue, a chorus of voices started sounding from inside the cabin.

I was standing in front of Sage's desk, waiting for Gallan's meeting to be over.

"Who is he with anyway?" I asked.

She shrugged. "I don't know. I was out on my break, so I've got no idea. He did tell me last night that he had a meeting today, but successfully forgot to mention *who* it would be with."

"But you're his *assistant*…"

She rolled her eyes. "An assistant he doesn't always tell everything to," she stated, which made me click my tongue.

It had taken an hour after Gallan had walked out of my apartment for me to woman-up and tell myself that I'd been an O-grade bitch to him ever since the incident. It had taken me even lesser than that to call Sage and ask her if he was at the HQ. And, it had taken me all but a heartbeat to decide that I was going to go to him and tell him that I'd finally woken up from my self-induced sleep and was ready to let go of all the excuses I'd been worshipping in hopes of feeling better again.

In hopes that they'd turn things back to how they used to be before Aubrey decided to taint them for me. Before she broke a major part of me.

Because the truth was that I hadn't felt even a sliver of peace or relief or *anything* after distancing myself from Gallan. All I *had* felt while I'd stayed in bed these past few weeks waiting for everything to magically go back to its rightful place was hurt, numbness, and restlessness.

Sage cleared her throat, which made me look at her. "You know very well that it's next to impossible to get through to him sometimes," she said, and then smoothed out her neatly tied blonde hair. "And after everything you've said to him and how you've treated him, despite his constant efforts, I think it'll be a task to get him to really *listen*, or to even make him understand why you did what you did to him."

"You're just salty you had to stay here and continue to work for him instead of retiring like you had initially planned," I mused.

Her mouth opened in shock as she stared at me, which made my lips twitch.

"Relax," I told her. "It was a joke, not a dick. Don't take it so hard."

Her eyes widened. "Good Lord, woman. You kiss your mother with that mouth?"

I chuckled. "I'm just trying to keep things light. I'm already freaking out on the inside thinking of all the ways Gallan will murder me the moment he sees me. Death by stationary products or chairs is *not* the way I wanna go."

Sage laughed. "You really are one of a kind, aren't you? No wonder he loves you so much."

My chest tightened at her words. "Not sure about that anymore."

"Pssh." She waved a hand in front of her face. "He's just upset. If you play your cards right, you may even walk out of here alive. But..." she pointed a finger at me, "...if you don't, then I get to have your glasses. I think they are super cute and chic and would go perfectly with my facial structure."

I glared at her. "Wow, Sage; thanks for the vote of confidence. I appreciate it."

She winked at me. "I've got you." She gestured her head towards Gallan's cabin. "So, you gonna go in now, or are you going to continue to stall?"

I crossed my arms and shifted on my feet. "I'm not stalling."

She smirked at me. "That so? Then why aren't you going in?" she challenged.

"He's in a meeting, remember?"

She shook her head. "You're definitely stalling."

"Am not!"

"Are too!"

I huffed. "Fine." I stepped away from her desk, straightened my black pencil skirt and coral wrap top, and with a determination as strong as that of a fart after a Chipotle meal, I cleared my throat and walked towards Gallan's cabin.

Fingers crossed I don't get pencils stabbed in my throat by the end of this...

63.
Zaira

December 15th, 2020

I looked at Sage – who gave me a huge grin and a thumbs up – and then at the door in front of me. With a deep inhale and a long exhale, I wrapped my fingers around the cold handle, knocked on the door twice, and then opened it slowly.

Gallan stopped in the middle of saying something to the people in front of him, and when his eyes landed on me, they narrowed a little as a look of surprise took over his face.

He looked absolutely gorgeous in a grey dress shirt whose sleeves were rolled up to his forearms, black pants, and his signature messy, wavy hair falling over the right side of his forehead.

"Hey," I said to no one in particular as I strode further inside the room.

Gallan's companions turned, and the one on the left gave me a huge smile.

"Hey, Zaira," Kenneth greeted.

"Hey." I waved at him, and then glanced at the woman on his right. "Hello, Lady-who-looks-like-Kenneth."

Gallan made a sound but didn't say anything, whereas Kenneth just laughed. "She's my elder sister, Natanya," he introduced.

Natanya smiled at me. "It's so good to finally meet you. Gallan talks about you all the time." She offered me a hand.

"Fucking perfect," Gallan mumbled, to which Kenneth chuckled.

I shook Natanya's hand as I looked between her and Gallan. "He does, doesn't he?"

"Oh, he *does*." She smirked. "And why wouldn't he? You're a sight for sore eyes. I was so sick and tired of seeing these two idiots' faces for the past hour. I needed my beauty fill."

I grinned at her. "Why do I get the feeling that we're going to be the best of friends?"

She chuckled. "Because you're smart. I've got the exact same feeling."

Kenneth cleared his throat. "So…I think, uh, Natanya and I should…leave?"

Natanya's brows furrowed as she looked at her brother. "What? Why? We were just getting to the design patterns…" She trailed when Kenneth raised his brows and gave her a *look*. "Oh…I see." She closed and grabbed a few files from the table before getting to her feet. "We can go over the final picks tomorrow. What do you say, Gall?"

Gallan's jaw ticked as he nodded at her. "Sure, no problem."

"Perfect!" She clutched her purse in one hand and smiled at him.

Kenneth stood. "I'll see ya later," he said to Gallan, and then faced me. "Bye, Zaira."

I smiled. "Bye."

As he stepped out of the cabin, Natanya stopped and looked over her shoulder at me. "*Good luck*," she mouthed, and then gave me a subtle wink before closing the door behind her.

I wrung my hands together as silence filled the air. "Hi…"

Gallan glared at me from his chair.

"Uh…" I wiped my upper lip with the back of my hand. "I love you…" The words suddenly spilled out of me. Not that I didn't mean them. I don't think I've ever spoken a truth truer than the one I'd just blurted in my haze of sheer nervousness.

Gallan's expression remained stoic. "Stop this, please. I'm not interested."

"But it's true; I love you." I stepped closer to his table.

He scoffed. "You love me, and that's why you pushed me away and said you didn't want me anymore? Is that how love works for you?"

I blinked when my eyes stung. "I fucked up, okay?" I said honestly. "I fucked up, and I'm not ashamed to admit it. I thought I was doing the right thing, but I realize now that I was wrong." I pushed my glasses up a little. "Everyone kept telling me that I'd need you to heal and to get better, but I wanted to do it all on my own. I was so confident that I could go back to being the old me if I focused and did things my way, but..." I shrugged.

Gallan placed his elbows on the table in front of him. "And what about me? Didn't *I* tell you I was ready to be there for you? Did you not trust me? Did you think I was lying?"

I shook my head as I swallowed my tears. "No, it's just..." I sniffed. "I thought you wouldn't want the new me. I thought you would bolt the moment you saw me wake up after a nightmare – all frantic and crazy. I thought you wouldn't understand why I screamed out of the blue for absolutely no reason whatsoever, and..." I fisted my hands when they started shaking a little. "I thought you'd think I've gone nuts or something. Until a few weeks ago, I couldn't even be in a room whose door was closed. I had a hard time touching or shutting doors, too. I was a literal mess, Gallan, and I didn't want you to see me like that because I blamed you for everything. I kept telling myself over and over again that you were the one who caused these things. That you were the reason why I'd gotten so screwed up."

He looked a bit taken aback by my words. "I didn't know about the door thing," he said slowly. It meant that he knew about my nightmares and frights.

"I didn't tell anyone but Dylan and Dr. Hill about it."

"Dr. Hill?"

"My therapist," I clarified.

Gallan frowned. "You still see them?"

"Yeah, I meet up with her once a week."

He pushed his hair back and stared at his table. "I feel so out-of-loop," he began. "I don't even know what exactly you're going through, and what all you've already faced. I kept asking you to let me in, or even talk to me for a bit, but you were convinced that I was the villain, and decided to punish me for it." He looked at me. "I would have given you anything and everything you needed to get better; space, no space – *anything*. I just wanted to be *involved*. I just wanted to hold you and kiss you and tell you that I love you, but you didn't even give me that. You dove headfirst into Aubrey's trap and hurt me. You said you regretted me – *us*. You said I was a mistake." He pushed away from the table and rotated his chair so he was looking away from me. "God, Zaira. You *really* fucking hurt me…"

"Gallan…"

"I felt nothing for the first few days after the incident," he said with his back to me. "I was functioning on autopilot and didn't speak with anyone." He scratched his stubble. "Every time you didn't respond to one of my messages or receive my calls, I shattered. It happened little by little, but the day I came to your apartment and you told me to my face that you blamed me for everything and didn't want me anymore – I broke completely. I genuinely felt like I'd been punched, and it took weeks before I even came to terms with the fact that you didn't want anything to do with me." He cleared his throat and continued to avoid eye contact with me.

"Gall…" I breathed between a sob as I walked around the table and knelt before him. "I'm so sorry. Please… I'm sorry." I placed my hands on his thighs. "I don't regret you or us. I never could. You can never be a mistake to me when you're a literal part of me, just as my heart is." I sniffed. "I was upset and frustrated and confused. I kept asking myself: why me? but didn't exactly get an answer, which frustrated me even more."

He faced me. "You weren't the only one suffering, Zaira," he said a little shakily. "Not knowing what you were doing or how you were feeling – it tortured me. Not being able to touch you or see you in person – it drove me insane. I couldn't stop thinking about that night; couldn't stop thinking about what you must've gone through and how you must've felt in those moments. You must have a hard time trying not to think about them or reliving them in your head on a daily basis. That's one of the reasons why I wanted to be there for you – so that I could share your fears and sadness and pain with you."

I rose on my knees. "My idiocy was a major milestone keeping me from you. I can't tell you the number of times I've questioned myself over these past few months. I wished to be close to you, yet I feared what that would mean for my intentions of healing. I'm so sorry." I looked into his eyes. "I'm sorry I hurt you. I'm sorry I pushed you away. I messed up, but I'm ready to fix it. I promise I'll be better from now on. I promise I'll–"

Gallan shook his head. "I don't want that, Zaira," he said.

My throat clogged; my chest tightened.

He must've seen the shock on my face because he shook his head again. "That's not what I meant." He slid his chair back and got to his feet. "Stand up." He offered me a hand.

I took it and stood, and as I gazed up at him, he stepped closer to me and wrapped his arms around my waist.

"What I meant was: I don't want you to try to be something you're not. You don't have to get better for me. *Never*. I know you're still healing, and the last thing I want you to do is act as if everything is okay." He smiled at me, which made my heart race. "I want you as you are, Zaira. I always have. I want the nasty, the anger, the sorrow, the smiles. The fear, the tears, the mood swings, the jokes and blood-boiling questions. I want *everything*. Not just the good but also the bad. Give it all to me, because baby…" He leaned in and touched his nose to mine. "I love you, and I don't want you to hide. I don't want you to try to get better just because you think I need that from you. Because I don't, Zaira, trust me. I'm happy with what you give me. Don't you know that I'm selfish for you? Every drop of you is my oasis, and I'll cherish you for the rest of my life, I promise."

I placed a hand over his chest. "I love you too, and I'm sorry I was a bitch to you."

He shrugged. "You didn't call the psychiatric ward on me for the long-ass love-monologues I sent you during the first few weeks, so I think we're even." When I chuckled, he gazed intently at me. "But in all seriousness, *I'm* sorry if I pushed your boundaries or hurt you; if I said something that I shouldn't have.

I'm sorry if I was an asshole to you. I'm not perfect; I suck. But with you I feel like I'm actually living, and I don't wanna let go of that essence ever again."

I slapped his jaw playfully. "You don't suck, you corny weirdo. You never have and never will."

His eyes gleamed as he grinned beautifully at me. "God, I missed you." He bent and pressed his lips to mine.

I smiled as I kissed him back, and when he grabbed my ass and pulled me against his hardness, I moaned and tangled my hands in his hair.

"You know, I thought you were going to murder me with a stapler or something the moment you saw me," I said against his lips.

Gallan moved back and looked at me with confusion on his face. "*What?*"

I bit my bottom lip. "I was telling Sage how death by stationaries was not my mojo."

"I'm so confused right now," he said, and when I laughed, he tickled my sides before wrapping me tighter in his arms. "You're crazy, woman."

"I know." I pressed a kiss on his chin. "But you like it."

"I *love* it, actually," he said.

Soft afternoon light hit his floor-to-ceiling windows and painted us with its warm embrace. "Do you promise not to walk away from me again?" I asked Gallan.

He touched his forehead to mine. "Only if you promise to never push me away again," he answered.

I grinned. "Deal."

He peppered soft kisses on my lips. "Perfect."

And indeed, it was perfect; everything was fine. From the many trials and errors, I'd learned that if something was truly meant to be, then it would come to be, no matter the milestones and full stops. If someone was truly meant to be in your life, then they'd end up being in your damn life, no matter the misunderstandings. If you were meant to find happiness, then you bet your sweet ass you'd find it, no matter what others said or believed.

And I – I'd found it all in my rat-chasing, dirty-talking, baboon-nicknamed, and too-sexy-for-his-shirt boyfriend.

Gallan.

My Gallan.

Never doubt your worth; never tell yourself that you can't do it. Because you *can*. You can move fucking mountains with a heart as fierce as a knight, and a determination as strong as a diamond. No one is born great, but they learn to be it when life gives them the chance.

So, stand up, own who you are, and stay standing as you rock the world with your blinding light. Nothing is impossible, so why not give it a shot, right?

Right ;–)

EPILOGUE
gallan

March 7th, 2021

"Zaira! Hey, come on; it's about to go live!" I called out from my home office. I was sitting in a chair in front of my laptop, and every few seconds, I'd unintentionally bounce my legs and tap my fingers against the mahogany table out of anxiousness and anticipation.

Zaira walked into the room and placed her hands on her hips as she scowled at me. "I'm not deaf, Gall. Why are you screaming like a 13-year-old Shawn Mendes fan?"

"Because I'm excited?" I said.

She rolled her eyes. "Try again."

I lifted a shoulder. "Because I wanna share the moment with you?"

She pushed her glasses up. "Close. Go again."

I put my tongue to my cheek. "Because I'm a starving bastard when it comes to you and I can't bear not having you by my side at all times…?"

She smiled victoriously. "There you go; there's the truth. Wasn't so hard to admit, now was it?"

I rolled my eyes. "Come here."

She shook her head. "Answer my question first."

Oh God.

I groaned. "Do I have to?"

She gave me a wink. "Yeah. That's your Privilege Pass, after all."

"Seriously?" I raised a brow at her.

"Seriously." She crossed her arms in front of her chest. "So, do pigs smell like bacon when they fart?"

Jesus H. Christ.

"Do they even fart in the first place?" I asked her.

She clicked her tongue. "Yeah... *I think*."

I chuckled. "Just come here, you."

She grinned and skipped over to me, and with a look that tugged at the strings of my soul, she sat on my lap and wrapped an arm around my neck.

"*Heyyy*," she sang.

I placed a hand on her bare knee. "Hey."

The soft skin of her thighs rubbed against my jeans, and her orange t-shirt dress lifted just enough when she pushed back against me and brought herself closer. "Do I feel heavier than usual to you?" she asked.

I glared at her. "No, you don't. Why would you even ask that?"

She shrugged. "Because I'm trying to gain a few pounds. The more I weigh, the lesser the chances are that one of your clothing-world rivals will kidnap me to get back to you. Smart tactic, huh?"

I gave her a scowl. "Not funny, Zaira."

"This is what you get for peeling apples so brutally," she said. "I was staring at them while unboxing my clothes and felt strong sympathy towards them. Not only did you peel their skin, but you also peeled away the actual...fruit." She frowned. "The pulp? The beef? The...thing that is the actual apple? I don't know. You get what I mean though, right?"

I nodded, because what other choice did I have?

"I peeled them because I wanted to make a pie for you," I told her.

"You murdered them, Gall; you murdered the apples. You fucking *killed* them – skin by skin; piece by piece."

I opened my mouth to answer her, but stopped when my phone *pinged*.

I grabbed it off the table and read the text.

Shane: *12 seconds! It's time! So happy for you, kid.*

I smiled and showed Zaira the text.

"So am I," she said with a grin.

I placed the phone back on the table and woke up my laptop. Zaira and I both looked at the screen – at the countdown in progress on the official *Under the Woods* website – and as the timer went 0:00:00, I felt my heart soar as my newest fashion line in collaboration with Natanya went live.

GALLAN UNDERWOOD
Natanya Barnes

EXPRESS

AN 'UNDER THE WOODS' & 'NB COUTURE' PRODUCTION.
© UNDER THE WOOD, NB COUTURE
® 2020

EXPRESS has been something I've wanted to bring to life ever since I started dating Zaira. Her personality, her dressing sense, her talents – they've all contributed to this line.

EXPRESS is all about being unique and fierce and *true*. It's about making a statement when out and about, whilst also sticking to one's roots and signature dressing style. It's a women-only, plus-size line, and is dedicated to every Zaira out there who wants her voice to be heard; her boldness to be seen.

When I'd told Kenneth about the idea during our press tour, he'd suggested I discuss it with his sister.

Natanya Barnes didn't shy away from diversity, and when her and I joined forces, *EXPRESS* took form. And God, was I proud of what we'd achieved together.

"Oh-my-God! Things are selling out already, babe!" Zaira said as she scrolled through the various outfits in the *EXPRESS* range.

I looked at the screen, and sure enough, a lot of the casualwear was rapidly selling out.

"There goes another one." She giggled. "This is so fun!"

I laughed. "It's all thanks to the endless promotion we've been doing for weeks."

"And also your face-magic," she added. "*Under the Woods* is *your* brand, and you've got a crazy ton of female fans. Of course they wanna buy all your new stuff. I'm sure they're thinking more about taking selfies in these clothes and tagging you in them than actually wearing good-quality apparels."

I smirked. "Jealous?"

She rolled her eyes. "Not a chance. I'm way past that amateur bullshit."

I chuckled and pressed a kiss on her cheek. "You rock, babe," I told her.

She batted her lashes at me. "Oh, I know."

Ping.

I shook my head at Zaira before opening the message.

Kenneth: *Dude, Amara and Zaira are rocking the EXPRESS collection outfits. No wonder your web designer didn't want us to see the page until the release. I'm feeling a lot of things right now as I continue to stare at my wife in all these clothes, G – things that can quite possibly give Isaac a sibling.*

I laughed.

Because *EXPRESS* is dedicated to the plus-size female audience, I'd asked Amara and Zaira to be the product models for every item in the range. We have casuals, formals, sportswear, nightwear, occasional, seasonal, lingerie – *everything*. The clothes are available in a variety of designs and colors to match the vibrant personalities out there, which is an added bonus.

Zaira and Amara had been hesitant in modelling for a couple of things, but with little motivation from me and the others, they'd rocked the cameras and their respective shoots with natural confidence and grace.

I typed a response to Kenneth.

Me: *TMI, man.*

Kenneth: *Don't act like you're not feeling the same about Zaira's photos.*

I glanced at my girl, and found her eyes glued to the laptop screen.

Me: *Asshole.*

Kenneth: *I'm an asshole because I'm right?*

Me: *You're an asshole because you're an asshole.*

Kenneth: *Message received. I'll leave you be, but promise me that you'll let me throw you a success party. I'm not taking no for an answer, so you don't exactly have a choice but to say yes.*

I smiled.

Me: *I don't think I could reason with you anyway. You're incorrigible.*

Kenneth: *Always the giver. It's your day, man. You're the one who should be getting all the compliments, not me.*

I laughed again.

Me: *Screw you.*

Kenneth: *Same to you ;–)*

Kenneth: *Gotta go. Ttyl.*

Me: *Sure.*

I quickly sent out another text message.

Me: *Congratulations! WE DID IT! I honestly couldn't have done this without you. Thank you for believing in me and my vision. I hope we make a difference.*

Her response was immediate.

Natanya: *Yes!!! Congratulations to you too, partner. Your concept was too good to not be a part of. I'm just glad I could help you as much as I did. EXPRESS calls to the true values of NB Couture, and I can't wait to expand it further with you and your brand.*

Pride was all I felt after reading her message.

Me: *Thank you, Nat.*

Natanya: *Of course! You're welcome.*

With a grin, I set my phone down and pointed at the laptop screen to one of the gowns Zaira had modelled in. "You look so beautiful in this," I told her. "The beige complements your skin really well, and the full sleeves bring out a sophisticated vibe." I turned to look at her, and saw that her misty eyes were trained on me, and not the screen.

"I'm so proud of you," she said, and then kissed me. "You're doing so good, and I'm honored that you invested in, and dedicated an entire clothing range to women like me and Ams. You're a great guy, Gall, and I love you so fucking much." She ran her fingers through the back of my head. "Your vision and ideas are inspirational, and your determination is one everyone should have. What you and Natanya have done today will make history, in a way, and I'm so happy to be a part of it with you."

I buried my face against the side of her breast and took a deep inhale of her perfume. "*You* are the inspirational one, not me." I moved back and looked at her. "If it wasn't for you, I wouldn't even have thought of creating EXPRESS. If it wasn't for you, I would have never understood the real meaning and power behind love and sacrifice. So *you*, my gorgeous girlfriend, need to take just as much credit for this as Natanya and I."

A few tears slipped down her eyes as she cupped the side of my face. "Presuming you was the best thing I've done in my life so far," she said. "I'm so glad I misjudged you after our first meeting; so glad that I was upset enough about it that it showed me how strongly your opinions mattered to me. I'm glad I decided to stay with you in your trailer that night, and I'm so fucking glad for every moment we've spent since then knowing and loving each other." She let out a short laugh as she shook her head. "Who knew that a tiny little *rat* would bring two people together in a way only fate did?"

"Maybe he was our road to this – to the moment we're sharing right now," I told her. "Maybe he was the catalyst that set our relationship in motion."

She smiled and gave me a quick kiss. "Cheesy baboon."

I grinned. "Ay." I ran a hand up and down her smooth thigh. "We got lucky with each other, though, didn't we?" I said. "I don't think anyone else would want us anyway. We're crazy and opinionated, and that's a deadly match. We'd blow up homes and tear down parking lots. We're better off together."

Zaira laughed and placed her forehead against mine. "Lord, Underwood. Don't you ever freaking change, you hear me? I love you and your random weirdness so much." She ran the back of her fingers over my jaw. "And yeah, I'm lucky I have you, just as you're lucky you have me. No one would tolerate you like I do. You're annoyingly sexy and really bad with your comedic timing. But hey, that's what makes you, *you*, and that's all that matters to me."

"I can't tell if you just complimented or insulted me."

"A little of both." She brushed her nose against mine. "Promise me that you'll love me forever, no matter how impossible I get. Promise me that you'll make me *see*; that you'll continue to read me like you do."

I smiled as I held her tighter. "I wouldn't know what else to do," I told her honestly. "I'll make all of those promises to you, only if you promise to never hide any of your layers from me. Only if you promise that you'll never try to be a version of yourself that you think will make me happy. Because baby, I like everything about you, and the only reason I signed up for this is because I knew – and still do – that I want it *all* with you. Be yourself and show me everything, and know that I'm gonna continue to love you inside out, no matter what. It's you and I – always." I leaned in and gave her a chaste kiss.

Zaira blushed, and when I pushed her hair behind her ear, she grabbed my wrist and pressed my palm to her cheek. "An always sounds perfect, especially because it'll be one I'll get to spend with *you*," she said.

I hummed around a smile. "So, we've got ourselves a deal, then?" I asked her.

She chuckled as she nodded. "We do. I'm not giving you up again. Been there, done that. I'm never going to put myself through that pain again."

I grinned. "Good, because I'm not ready to give you up either – at least not in this and a dozen other lifetimes. You're mine, Zaira Khan, and you'll forever be mine, no matter what happens."

As she leaned in and kissed me again, I pulled her flush against my chest and just…savored her. Her taste, her smell, her moans – I let them all seep into my very bones.

We'd fought the odds and learnt from our fuck-ups. We'd gotten stronger after standing up against those who'd tried to bring down our empire on us. We'd fallen and bruised ourselves quite a few times in the process, sure, but did we ever fully give up?

No. No, we didn't.

Because giving up was for those who didn't believe in themselves. It was for the liars, cheaters, and the fakes. And fighting? It was for the gutsy and slightly reckless souls, and Christ were Zaira and I the craziest in the category. It would be fun to see where the future took us, and whatever came next in the action-packed movie that is our lives, I was ready to experience it all from the front-row seat with my girl by my side.

Along with a few buckets of cheesy popcorn and glasses brimming with coke, of course.

Ciao!

THE END

ACKNOWLEDGEMENTS

A massive thank you to my ah-mazing and patient beta readers. You know who you are. I love you all so damn much. Thank you for sticking by my side and believing in Gallan and Zaira's story. You made a difference; please know that.

My family – without whom I would still only be dreaming of writing books, of telling stories. Thank you, Mom, Dad, Qadir, and my lovely aunts.

A cuddly thank you to my bunnies: Coco, Moon, Snow (I miss you), and Velvet. You four are my babies, and I'm beyond happy to be your momma. Thank you for the endless cuddles, kisses, and sniffs. Those got me through some of the hard times.

My lovely readers, I love you so much. You've stood by me from the beginning, have given my stories a chance, and for that, I'll forever be in your debt. Thank you – from the very bottom of my dramatic heart.